To Mum, Dad & Charlie,

My Light in Every Storm.

-x-

The Life I Never Knew

Independently Published

ISBN: 9798322365747

Dear Reader,

Thank you for choosing to read 'The Life I Never Knew'. This book is a historical romance which is purely fictional. However, although I have not written this novel with the intent to upset, there are a few matters within it that some may find triggering. As an author, I believe it is my duty to inform you of these. So, with that in mind, I must advise that this book contains the following:

- Brief mention of suicidal thoughts
- Verbal abuse
- Emotional abuse
- Ableism (for story purposes only)

Thank you for your support and I hope you enjoy reading this book as much as I have writing it.

Tina.R.Abbott

THE
LIFE
I NEVER
KNEW

Chapter One

Wren

"I take it they've gone out again, Miss Wren," Mrs Cornish huffed, pressing her flour-dusted hands into the perfectly round mound of dough on the kitchen table. Soft grey strands of hair fell in front of her kindly face as they freed themselves from her loosely gathered bun atop her head. They swayed subtly, back and forth, dancing with the rhythm of her body as she kneaded the unbaked bread, her knuckles pressing into it, as though it were her greatest enemy. The determination on her crimsoning face told me she was just getting started on giving it exactly what she thought it deserved.

"They have, Mrs Cornish. Some social gathering at Lord Abbott's, I believe," I replied, watching the muscle in her jaw twitch in a controlled spasm as she ground her teeth together.

"Makes my blood boil when they leave a beauty such as you home here while they gallivant about like you don't exist, it does," she huffed, pushing the full weight of the anger she'd stored in her upper body through her arms and into her hands, her knuckles tearing at the dough as they dug much deeper into its elasticity. "It ain't right, Wren."

"You know why they won't take me, Mrs Cornish." I replied, fighting the invisible fingers that were spitefully pinching my throat. "Mama says people won't want to socialise with someone like me, and the mere sight of me will only ruin Primrose and Gladys's chance at marriage."

I ran my finger slowly over the wooden table, following the lines of the woodgrain with perfect precision, in the hope such a menial task would detract Mrs Cornish from the usual telltale signs of my emotions whilst simultaneously offering my mind something else to concentrate on, a distraction, as it were, from what I could not allow myself to dwell on. I'd expected that by such an age one would have perfected the art of hiding such displays, but I had to wonder that if that were indeed a plausible expectation, then why could I not quite master such matters? Either way, I was clearly quite terrible at it, for the tightening of my chest was pressing fervently against my bruised heart, pinching me, hindering my usual steady breaths. My eyes watered, as an uncomfortable sensation pricked the back of my eyes. The heat was gradually rising behind them, calling forth the tears I did not want to spill.

"What poppycock!" Mrs Cornish snapped. Her grey eyes glittered with indignation and the usual hurt she always portrayed on my behalf. "So, you've got a little curve in your spine. What does that matter? That ain't so much as a blemish on your fine looks and big heart. What your mother does is plain cruel, Miss Wren," she seethed. A tear had formed in a glistening drop in the corner of her eye. To see her suffer unnecessarily on my behalf generated a guilt that swirled in my gut as I watched her, the sadness finally slipping free in a droplet of water and trailing slowly over her soft skin.

To see her upset, snuffed out the last traces of any anguish I may have felt. My concern for my friend was much greater than that for myself. It erased any thoughts I had once been fearful of exposing.

Leaning forward across the table, I reached for her hand, allowing our eyes to meet in understanding. "Shh, Mrs Cornish. If someone hears you, they may tell Mama. She will dismiss you just to spite me, and then who will I have here on my side?" I chided her gently, careful not to offend her.

Mrs Cornish raised her arm and ran the back of her wrist over the glittering path of her tears, attempting to wipe the evidence away. "It pains me to see them do this to you, Wren. It ain't right," she sniffed, offering me a kind, sympathetic smile.

"Don't you worry about me, Mrs Cornish. As long as I have you and my books, I shall be just fine. We will be fine." I swallowed the ache in my throat, stubbornly stuck there as it clenched with a deep sense of longing and hurt at my family's willingness to cast me aside. I despised weakening to their unkindness, but there would be no escaping the undeniable truth that I was the daughter they never had, according to the world outside the door. I was their best-kept secret, destined to be confined within four walls for the rest of my days.

The raucous clamour and tittering of my family as they returned from their evening at Lord Abbott's rushed up the stairs, washing away the silence of my bedchamber. Even on the topmost floor in my small room of a rather dismal design, one was privy to the chatter of my family's everyday life.

The single candle on my bedside flickered in the gloom, casting an amber hue over the beige and brown bedspread. The copper tones made the drab old thing look less dreary and rather more regal than what the light of day revealed it to be. Sadly, my life proved to be just as dreary, and with all the excitement evident in the distant voices, I knew when the morning came, it would be made to feel even more lacklustre, for there was no doubt Primrose would divulge all the events of the evening in a rather romantic and scintillating story, involving herself as the main character, the ton as the scenic background, and my other sister and my mother as the side characters. However, I was quite aware that all the while she would speak of such things, oblivious as to how her reliving every moment aloud made me feel, I would listen intently, feigning utter glee for my family's joy, when deep inside another part of me would crack open with sorrow for being born into a world where I did not seem to belong.

Releasing the pins from my hair, I let the chestnut waves tumble down my back. They slipped silently over the gentle curve of my spine in a cloak of glossy tresses, hiding what apparently, according to Mama, would pain the eyes of society.

Apart from the raised shoulder, when one looked in the looking glass, there were no differences to behold. There was just a young lady staring back at me. Her eyes were beseeching; an undeliberate pleading swirled within them, filled with a silent desire to be seen, to feel the sweet embrace of acceptance, and to be loved. The purple shadows beneath my eyes were the only sign I was withering with every day that passed. Gazing back at my reflection, my body turned to face me head-on, I wished that particular image was all anyone could see when they looked at me. I did not dare to turn and see the profile of my body. Reality lay in that image, but the woman in it, the one I did not want to confront, the one who was laced with memories of wicked words of shame so freely offered by others, did not represent who I was nor who I am. I am the woman who lives in every other, in my mother, in my sisters, in every daughter, and in every wife or lover, yet I was not allowed to exist beyond the walls of my home.

The throb of my aching heart nestled deeper beneath my ribcage. It balled into a fist, pressing passionately against the ache of my constricted throat, and burned, once again, in the prickling of tears at the backs of my eyes. Slipping my night gown over my head, I inhaled, and as the cool cotton slid over the pale skin of my tired body, I released my pain in an extended, defeated breath. There was no use for my tears. I'd told myself the same thing time and time again. Their only use was to wet my pillow, which was utterly pointless, for they would simply vanish, unseen, and uncared for. Sleep was the only thing that had ever offered me release from the heavy shackles of my life, even if it was just for a few hours at a time. It is the only place where I can forget, I reminded myself as I snuffed out the flame dancing on the wick of the candle. It was a cruel dance that kept me imprisoned in the light—friend and foe all at once.

As I lay down upon the mattress, pulling the blanket up over my shoulders, I allowed the sweet caress of slumber to wash over me; so very thankful, as it pulled me into a world where nothing mattered at all.

"Wrenny, wake up." Primrose's glittering blonde ringlets bounced as she dropped down and perched on the edge of my bed.

"Good morning, Prim," I mumbled, smiling sleepily. I was unaware of what time it was, yet I halfheartedly braced myself for what I knew was about to come. The inevitable, compulsory broadcast of their wondrous evening, along with a rundown of gossip and summaries of potential husbands, was ready to spill from my youngest sister's lips in a crushing, unapologetic tidal wave of reality—the one I had just spent several blissful hours oblivious to.

My sister was the embodiment of the gossip column of a London newspaper. As terrible as the feeling that sometimes accompanied her rush of the latest news could be, I was fully aware that her words were never spoken with any malice. Primrose had just turned seventeen, and it was the year of her very first season in London. In preparation, Mama had insisted that she, Primrose, and my other sister attend as many prestigious events as was possible. Unlike my mother's wishes for me, she was thoroughly emphatic that her two perfectly beautiful daughters must be seen amongst the ton.

Primrose's face was flushed with petal pink against the powder blue of her eyes. The twinkle in them mimicked the dimples in her cheeks as she tried to refrain from the excitement, gripping her within its dazzling fingers.

"How was last night?" I asked.

Asking for the inevitable news before it was spoken seemed to soften the blow to my heart. It was almost as though, in the few seconds in which the words filled the air, I had managed to create a temporary barrier. One simple question was all the encouragement Primrose required, if any was indeed needed, to gush profusely about the splendour of Lord Abbott's soiree. She spoke of so very much, I could barely keep up.

"Oh, Wrenny, I do wish you could have been there. I think it's awfully sad that you couldn't come with us," she trilled kindly. "You would have thought his home was greater than that of Queen Victoria's. Why, if the lady had seen it, I would think she would claim it for herself," she beamed.

"You know, Prim, I could have come with you,"

I breathed. "But you know Mama won't allow it." I had not meant to, but I found myself resting an intense gaze on my sister. We had had this conversation many times, and yet, every time I relayed the truth of why I never attended any soiree being solely because of Mama's shame and Papa's weakness, I was always met with the same practiced line.

"Well, yes, I know, Wrenny, but that is because Mama is trying to do what is best for you."

'Best for me?' I scoffed silently, and rather bitterly, to myself. A pang of guilt nipped at my conscience with its sharp teeth. To feel such a way toward my youngest sister was not warranted, for she was the kindest of them all. However, that is not to say that I felt any such guilt when applying said anger toward my mother. I felt very much like scoffing in her face at the lie they constantly repeated. Mama only knew to do that which was best for her, Primrose, and Gladys. My well-being was not even an afterthought.

Instead of voicing my honest and somewhat scathing opinion, I merely nodded in agreement. "Quite right, Prim. Now, speaking of what is best for everyone, you must leave me so I may get dressed and ready for breakfast. I am in a dreadful state, and I fear that if you stay here a second longer, Mama will be terribly angry with us both." I gently squeezed her hand, my lips pursing in a tight, strained smile as I tried to refrain from revealing just how distressed I really was. "I am quite used to Mama's tongue, but I fear you are not," I sighed cheerfully, forcing out a light chuckle in the hope of easing the uncomfortable truth of my words.

To confront any further deep conversation of my predicament was not something I desired to partake in, for the hurt had begun to pierce my chest in tiny blades. I knew the continuation of the discussion about my lack of attendance would only result in an onslaught of tears. *My tears.* My body was already at war with the insistent tremble in my limbs as every fragment of emotion surged within, rumbling through my veins at full speed. I did not want Primrose nor anyone else to witness my despair, for although it scraped further scars across my heart, my pain was my own and not to be laid out on display for all to see.

Primrose chuckled in response. She leaned forward and placed a kiss on my forehead. I wondered then whether she had any idea how I felt. "I will see you downstairs for breakfast, sister."

With an excited smile and the bobbing of golden curls, my sister hurried from my bedchamber, leaving me alone with a much heavier heart struggling to maintain its steady beat.

"There you are, Wren. What on earth could have taken you so very long that you feel you are able to waltz in here casually as though you do not owe the rest of us an apology? Breakfast is at eight o'clock sharp." My mother pursed her cherry-red lips scornfully. "As a result of your usual tardiness, there is only bread and butter remaining, so you may eat that and be grateful." Mama's sharp eyes followed my every movement as I walked toward the vast walnut table. The heat of her assessing stare burned my skin beneath the fabric of my clothes as her eyes wandered up and down the length of my body. Her critical gaze finally settled on my skirts as she peered down her nose, sneering at the gentle limp in my walk. The woman's face was stern against the thunderous black of her hair piled loosely upon her head. It was only when her expression wrinkled with distaste did her hardened features alter.

"I apologise, Mama. My corset is difficult to fasten by myself, especially with my back being the way it is."

She was quite aware of this already, for it was the same every morning. Nothing differed in the sequence of events nor the sparse, strained conversation at the table.

Lowering my body carefully into the seat, I cast my eyes towards the meagre remains of food that had been pushed aside, like the crumbs on their own plates, solely for my breakfast. The bread had been ripped in half, pieces splayed across the porcelain, and discarded as an afterthought, much like the scraping of butter at the edge of the dish. Without stalling, which would have given them tremendous satisfaction at my assumed reaction to their attempts to aggrieve me, I happily helped myself. I was used to bread and butter and quite content to feast upon that alone, despite the seductive scent of cooked bacon lingering in the air. The plate was devoid of any meat, but as the salty, sumptuous fragrance drifted eagerly towards me, teasing my senses, I reminded myself that Mrs Cornish would, undoubtedly, have saved me a rasher or two. It was something she always did in secret, out of the way of prying eyes. I smiled in the knowledge that I knew something my mother did not.

"Yes, well, we do not have the money to afford a lady's maid for you, Wren. It would be an unnecessary expense. You do not go out anywhere, so your attire is of no concern nor importance. Here, in this house, no one cares what you wear. It is not as if you are going to meet anyone, is it? Heavens, perish the thought." Mama's laughter pierced the air as she openly trilled her amusement at her own words.

Gladys tittered, her black ringlets bouncing as she elbowed Primrose. Primrose, however, grew pink with shame as she shot me an embarrassed and apologetic look across the table.

"Yes, Mama, you are quite right," I replied, helping myself to the last broken slice of bread. I didn't bother amusing them further by trying to scrape the remainder of the butter onto the butter knife, for there was not enough there to even spread across a quarter of the bread.

"I know I am, Wren. You may think me harsh, but it is for your own good, not to mention your sisters'. Gladys and Primrose will be cast out of society and classified as unsuitable for marriage if people know about you. They will think the bloodline is tainted with imperfection." My mother's severe emerald eyes flickered with what I hoped was a fraction of guilt, yet it was a foolhardy hope, for I knew it was merely her reaction to how much of an inconvenience I was. My very existence pestered her to the point of seething, putting the definitive twitch into her usual steady gaze. "You know, I often wonder if someone knew about you last season," she sneered, her eyes averted. "What other possible reason could there be for Gladys being so unsuccessful? I don't know what we will do if someone knows of you this season. It will be an utter disaster."

"Mama, that is unkind," Primrose whispered in disgust. "Wren is lovely. She is far prettier than some of the frightful young ladies who were at Lord Abbott's last night. You should have seen them, Wren. Some of them looked like the turkey, already stuffed for Christmas day."

"That is enough, Primrose!" Mama spat.

Primrose's gleeful giggle at the memory of the overzealous-fashioned young ladies faded in a gulp, her face paling as she hung her head down. "Sorry, Mama."

"If truth is unkind, then I am indeed unkind," Mama began. "However, I believe hiding Wren from polite society is in fact a kindness. Gentlemen do not want to look upon someone with such flaws as Wren when they are trying to find a wife. It would be like trying to look through a window that is smeared with dirt."

I stifled the disbelieving gasp that mirrored my youngest sister's. My mother was spiteful, but those words were the worst to date. I kept my head down, my mouth devoid of moisture from the shock. Waiting for her to continue her churlish attack, my fingers lazily picked apart the remainder of the crumbling slice of bread.

"As for a kindness to Wren," she continued, addressing Primrose. "I believe that the fact we allow her to be here, to eat our food, live under our roof, and receive one of the finest educations," she practically growled, turning her head towards me. "Paid for by your father, I might add. Why he bothered, I am not sure," she added, turning back to my sisters. "All adds up to kindness, does it not?" Her eyes locked on Primrose, daring her to deny it. "No, this is the best thing for all of us."

Mama's body grew taut in her elaborate grey gown, her spine rigid with power, daring any of us to disagree.

"Of course you are right, Mama," Gladys piped up. Her crimson lips pinched spitefully as they were known to have a habit of doing when she was about to say something wicked. "You know, Wren, some young ladies like yourself end up in terrible places. Mama could have put you in an orphanage or an *asylum*." Gladys took great pleasure in dragging the syllables of the word to emphasise the scandal and terror of such a place. "You could have been abandoned, left to fend for yourself. Although, thinking about it, perhaps you could have been *famous*." Her eyes danced deviously. "You know, Wren, I quite fancy knowing someone famous," she continued. "But perhaps not someone such as yourself who would only be notable for an obvious peculiarity and sought after to appear in one of those shows for strange people. You know the ones I'm talking about, don't you? Oh, silly me, I seem to have a terrible memory, for I forget what they call them now."

Gladys dabbed the napkin at the corners of her

mouth to hide the pleasure curling her thin lips. "Oh, perhaps you could help me, Wren. I believe it begins with F and ends in 'reak show'." Gladys shot me a malicious grin as her eyes darkened several shades of green. She was nothing like Primrose in manners nor in looks. It was as though she was every inch our mother and Prim was every inch our father. As for me, I was simply Wren Jennifer Davenport, moulded from life's lessons. I wondered who I would have resembled if I had been born like them. In hindsight, it is difficult to say, although I do hope I would have been more like Primrose, but perhaps, as much as it pains me to say it, I would have wished to have inherited the strength of my mother. However, I would hope that if I had been blessed with her strength, I would have used it for good and have had the courage to speak up for those who needed defending. Alas, it really is quite irrelevant to even contemplate such a thing when life clearly had rather a different plan for me.

"That is quite enough, Gladys." Mama patted the napkin against her lips, shooting my spiteful sister with an equally spiteful glare of her own. "Wren should be quite aware of what life would have been like if we hadn't been so generous. I would imagine she feels quite indebted to us."

"I am not sure why you are all bickering." My hurt had bypassed the need for tears, flowing into a pool of bitter anger. I had had enough of them speaking about me as though I were not even there. "I have never asked to attend any such events with you, nor have I ever asked to leave the house. I have never, not once, been ungrateful, nor even implied that I am." My chest rose and fell as I tried to cool the blood rushing through my veins at how callous my mother and sister were. "I am quite content with my life. Now if you will excuse me, I have matters to attend to."

With the finality of my words, I rose from my seat, the muscles in my jaw twitching as my teeth ground against each other.

Chapter Two

Wren

"What's the matter, duck?" Mrs Cornish asked as I claimed my regular place at the kitchen table.

"The usual," I sighed, raising my hands to my face to cover as much of my anguish as was possible. My breath was hot beneath the press of my warm palms. I did not want to be seen, nor did I want to see the faces of those who bore witness to the effect my mother had on me. A draught from the window tickled my skin. Its touch at the side of my face was a welcoming sensation, cooling the heat of my frustration as it rose in my cheeks. All I could focus on was one breath at a time, my lungs burning as I inhaled, the air dragging against the scream I wanted to release.

"Let me get you a cup of tea, love," Mrs Cornish crooned. "I think I can guess what it is that has you all upset like this. I reckon it's that bloody ol' witch again."

"Oh, Mrs Cornish, you would think at three and twenty I would be used to this."

"Used to it?" she spluttered. "How on earth can someone get used to that kind of treatment? You shouldn't even have to get used to it," she raved, incensed at seeing me hurt again. "If I had money like your mother and father, I would have taken you away years ago and raised you as me own. You would have been treated like the princess you are. Not like what they do to you. Bloody Lady Muck. And as for your father, I ain't ever known a man so blooming weak. What kind of father sits back and says nothing?" Mrs Cornish was seething as she clunked the kitchen utensils and crockery about the kitchen with frustration.

"Primrose isn't so bad," I interjected, feeling a little sad that my youngest sister was included in such a bad opinion. I understood how the others were part of it; in fact, they were the entire reason for it, but Primrose was the youngest. She really didn't get to voice her opinion and have it respected.

"Primrose is still a young girl, a child even at seventeen, but there is no excuse for Gladys and your mother, nor even your father," Mrs Cornish replied, her hands shaking as she poured the tea into my favourite cup with a tiny chip just above the trim. She slid the tea across the table until it sat in front of me, the steam curling and caressing the air.

I couldn't argue with my friend's words, although sometimes the stark truth bit into my flesh, deepening the wounds that never seemed to be given enough time to heal. The healing of a broken heart thrives off the very act of reasoning, the pacification of pain, quelling the ache with lies so that one may breathe between the heavy rhythmic beats within one's chest, but to hear the truth did none of that; it only served to add to my torment.

"I'm sorry, duck. Me moaning like this ain't helping, is it? I'm just making it worse." Her words had indeed stung, but the poor woman looked thoroughly remorseful, as though it were she who had made my life hell all those years. After knowing her for so long, I wondered whether she knew how she had always been my light in every storm.

"Not at all, Mrs Cornish," I lied, simply to save her feelings, for I was more than aware her intentions were kind. "You are not voicing anything I do not know already. I'm just frustrated that my life will always be like this. I will always be an inconvenience within these four walls and invisible beyond them."

"Get that down you, duck, and I'll get the bacon I saved for you," Mrs Cornish smiled, turning away. Her voice was pinched with emotion as she continued to speak, all the while placing fresh bacon into the pan. "You busy today?" she asked, changing the subject as she kept her back to me.

"No more than usual," I replied. I lifted the teacup to my lips, glad for the change in topic.

"If you ain't got much to do, do you fancy 'elping me in the kitchen? I think your mother is off out again with your sisters. Dressmakers or something fancy like that." Mrs Cornish tipped her head back a fraction and tsked loudly. Even without standing in front of her, I knew what she was doing. She was performing her usual exaggerated roll of the eyes followed by a quick mockery of Mama, believing no one knew what she was up to, but I was quite aware, and it never failed to amuse me.

"Oh, yes, of course," I said, smiling secretly at witnessing her little performance. "They are preparing for the season. How could one forget such a momentous occasion?" I groaned. "But yes, Mrs Cornish, I would be delighted to help you. Perhaps I can make some of those sweetbreads we like so we can have them with tea later? Save one for Primrose too."

Mrs Cornish turned to face me once again, a cheery smile gently crumpling her features. Her eyes were rimmed with pink. It appeared she had not just been mocking Mama, but she had also been shedding an abundance of tears. She was everything to me that my mother failed to be. "That sounds perfect, Miss Wren," she sniffed, dabbing under her eyes with the lace trim of her apron.

"You know there are some perks to a season, Mrs Cornish," I continued, steering the conversation onto a more positive path. "For it is the time of year they send me to our cottage in Somerset," I smiled, reminiscing at the wonderful memories. "I was there last year when Gladys had her first season. Of course, I know it is for their benefit, as I will be out of the way in case gentlemen call, but I do so love it there. If I could, I would live there all the time."

Closing my eyes, I painted the picturesque scenery of the open land across the canvas of my mind. My memory conjured the soothing heat of the sun, its warmth caressing the side of my face as I tilted it toward the blue skies. Scattered clouds of broken white drifted overhead as though they had all the time in the world. Small birds twittered happily amongst the rustle of leaves, their melody only audible to my ears as the memory of the clean air filled my lungs.

"D'you prefer it to London, Miss Wren?" Mrs Cornish asked, tactfully breaking me free from my reverie and immersing me back into the grey stone-floored room with its white walls and copper pans.

"Very much so. Well, what I have seen of London anyway. It is not as though I can truly tell what London has to offer from my bedchamber window." My nose wrinkled as I pictured the only part of London I had ever seen. "It peers out onto the back streets, so there really is very little to see. And as you know, I am not allowed near the windows at the front either, so that very much puts a spoke in the wheel, but in Somerset, Mrs Cornish, I have freedom. Sometimes more freedom than I know what to do with," I smiled. "There are vast open fields, and it is just so terribly beautiful. One should imagine that it very much resembles a patch of heaven if one were to pluck it from the skies and place it here on earth. When I returned to London after last season, I felt quite lost and utterly imprisoned. It was as though I had left my soul at the cottage."

"It sounds marvellous, duck, but I can't say I am not sorry to see you go when you do, Miss Wren. It was awful quiet here when you left last time." Mrs Cornish wiped her hands on her apron and sat across the table from me. "Maybe one day I'll come and visit you while you're out there. I will get to see what you talk about." The corners of her eyes creased as a smile tugged at her lips. "It's been a long while since my Alfred passed, so it's about time I started living a bit."

"Oh, that would be so wonderful, Mrs Cornish. I feel it would be a far better experience if you came with me. What fun we would have." The thought of company was not something I had considered before.

As Mrs Cornish served me the long-awaited bacon, the prospect of her joining me on my travels to Somerset formulated into a rather genius plan in my brain. The very idea that I would not be alone but accompanied by someone so dear delighted me so much that I could not simply cast it aside. However, if I were to voice my idea aloud to Mrs Cornish, I feared I may end up disappointing her. Indeed, if my plan was to be successful, privacy was of the utmost importance as a requisite when speaking to Papa. What I had in mind certainly wasn't something I could mention to Mama nor in front of her. The woman would undoubtedly quash any hope I had within seconds, simply out of spite. This one was for my father's ears only. There were no two ways about it.

"And who, pray tell, will replace Mrs Cornish while you are both away, Wren?" Papa sat on the opposite side of the large oak desk as he regarded me. His anxious eyes were a pale blue beneath his silver-grey hair as he steepled his fingers in front of his lips in deep consideration.

"Betty can do it, Papa," I offered eagerly. "She has been working side by side with Mrs Cornish for years now. I should imagine she would love to be in charge of the kitchen and all its staff for a few months."

"A few months? It is hardly a few months, Wren. It is over half a year." Papa exhaled, his eyes searching the air, his thoughts troubled.

"Well, yes, and surely that makes it even more of a reason for me to have someone who I care for with me. I am all alone out there, Papa," I added, deviously desperate to ignite the wick on the candle of guilt I knew he possessed. "Surely, you would not begrudge me some company, would you? I was terribly lonely last time; there is no one for miles around at the cottage."

My father looked torn. His frown fluctuated between concern and consideration. "Hmm," he began. "If I agree to this, Wren, then you must keep it between us and Mrs Cornish. Your mother and sisters are not to know until after you and she are well on your way to Somerset." Papa rose to his feet and began to pace, slightly agitated.

"Of course, Papa," I promised.

"Yes, I am quite sure that should work," he mumbled to himself.

His shoes hissed on the carpet as he turned swiftly to catch my eye, his pace slowing yet still very much active. "Wren, for this to work without interference, it is paramount that you will be well on your way to The Aviary before your mother even suspects that Mrs Cornish is no longer in the house. If we can manage that, then by the time she realises Mrs Cornish is no longer here at her beck and call, there will be nothing she can say or do to stop it."

My father's feet ceased wearing a moat into the carpet as he stopped to stand in front of me. "You must not breathe a word of it to anyone, Wren. Your mother is a woman whose wrath is of no small measure, and if she should get wind of our deception prior to your escape, as it were, there is no limit to the nagging I will receive from her. Dear Lord, I cannot be doing with all of that, especially with all the other nonsense of the upcoming season."

Papa's greyish blue eyes flickered with sadness as he swallowed; his posture, softening as his shoulders slumped a little. He looked exhausted, defeated, and filled with remorse. It was disheartening to see.

"What is it, Papa?" I whispered.

Papa placed his warm hands at the top of my arms. "You know, Wren, if your mother was more amenable, I would be seeing to it that you had your season too. Heavens, you would be married by now."

"It's okay, Papa," I offered, scoffing slightly at the unimaginable possibility of someone wanting to marry me. I did not want to be unkind, for deep down in the hidden depths of my father's feelings,

I knew he had always wanted me to be amongst society like my sisters were. Although I was slightly bitter at his weakness where Mama was concerned, I could not deny the truth of how my mother would have conjured the depths of hell for my father to reside in for eternity if he had so much as suggested that I were to enter society or even be mentioned as their daughter outside the four walls of our home. "You know," I added. "I rather prefer spending the season in Somerset. It is my favourite place."

Papa's eyes twinkled. "You are a good girl, Wren. I will make sure Mrs Cornish will be with you this time, but not a word. Promise?"

"I promise, Papa."

A roar of chatter and tittering about the sudden downpour of autumn rain burst through the entrance of our home, shattering the calm, as Mama, Primrose, and Gladys returned early from their shopping trip. A little drop of rain saw to it that the weather was the only subject of the afternoon as they took tea in the parlour. I wondered how one seemed to find so many ways to discuss the weather, but, as they continued with full tenacity where the subject was concerned, I realised I could not take much more of the racket resounding in my ears. You see, when one has spent a great deal, if not all, of their life amongst few, an uproar, even that of three familiar voices, can be somewhat overwhelming. Picking up my book, I excused myself and began to proceed gingerly to my bedchamber, afraid I would be demanded back into the room just for torment's sake.

"Before you leave," Mama trilled.

I froze on the spot, holding my breath.

"Gladys needed some new corsets today." Her tone was clipped and resentful toward me as she continued. "So, of course, I have bought her some.

"Now, if you are wondering why I would inform you of such matters, it is merely because Gladys has been quite charitable and insists that you may have her old ones."

Gladys snorted. "I would have preferred they were given to a monkey rather than her," she remarked bitterly.

Mama smirked. "There is little difference, Gladys. Now, do be quiet and allow me to continue, darling. The girl is giving me a migraine just by being here, so the sooner I say what needs to be said, the sooner she can scurry off to her bedchamber."

"Sorry, Mama," Gladys drawled in a sickly-sweet voice, satisfied at the degradation directed at me.

"As I was saying, Wren," Mama sighed. "They

are old and tatty, but they will do for the likes of you.

"But know this, Wren Davenport, they are corsets that fasten at the front, which means, of course, the ease of them will prevent you from being late for breakfast next time; therefore, I will not tolerate any more excuses."

"Thank you, Mama. That is most kind," I replied.

Turning my back to her, my hand curled around the smooth, cold brass handle of the parlour door. In truth, I'd wanted to rip it from its fittings as the invisible knuckles of my mother's unkindness pressed into my breastbone.

"My thoughts precisely, Wren. It is as Gladys said, I could so easily have put you in an asylum, especially now that you are no longer a child." The hiss in her voice announced her pleasure at the taste of the venom trickling from her lips. "You know there are many like you there. Perhaps you would prefer it," she added.

I feigned ignorance to the malicious threat laced in her words. Refusing to give her the satisfaction of seeing the hurt upon my face, I simply exhaled slowly, turned the doorknob, and proceeded from the room.

Up in my bedchamber, I sat at the window and listened. The heavy drops of rain drummed against the glass as though they were begging to be let in. Why they would want to live amongst such vile people was incomprehensible, I thought, amused at the very idea of it. Large, bulbous tears from the sky mocked me as they coursed through the thick residue of smog smeared on the pane. It was like watching the remnants of misery trail down a woman's heavily painted face. The stormy clouds outside dimmed the light, darkening the brown walls of my one and only refuge in the house until it was almost black.

A whisper of cold air blew silently through the cracks of the weathered, wooden window frame. It tickled my skin, sending an unwanted shiver shuddering down my spine. Wrapping the woollen shawl Mrs Cornish had made me last Christmas around my shoulders, I warded off the chill, willing the goose bumps to smoothen and the gentle tremor in my body to subside. My eyes wandered beyond the glass barrier, observing the disappointing view as I curled up, letting the solidity of the wall take the weight of my body as I leaned heavily against it.

Outside, there was nothing more than a simple, small yard and a maze of empty alleyways, leading to the backs of houses and out onto cobbled roads that I could only imagine. The lightly padded seat beneath me had been deliberately positioned so low that it was quite impossible to attract the attention of passersby, yet I couldn't help but watch for that one curiosity-satisfying glimpse of a stranger or even just a little of what lay beyond the world I knew. I wrapped my arms around my knees, pulling them towards my chest, and waited.

Eventually, when there appeared to be nothing for me to see, I rose with my book in hand and made my way towards the comfort of my bed, relenting reluctantly in my foolish endeavour. As I pulled my gaze away from the life I never knew, I turned my eyes and mind to the magnificent pages spread open upon my lap, the ones that were filled with the love I longed for, friends I would never meet, and worlds I would never see. I lived my days swept away in such awe, every fibre of my soul immersed in the characters I became. There, and only there, I found peace.

Chapter Three

Wren

"Good morning, Mrs Cornish," I beamed, stepping into the kitchen.

Warmth flowed from the oven whilst water bubbled and boiled atop the stove, sending billows of steam curling up into the air. I watched them gather in white plumes, creating a damp fog that kissed one's skin. A fresh pot of tea sat lonely, stewing on the table, slowly turning cold.

Betty was in an utter panic as she worked her way around the chaotic kitchen. It was her first day in charge of it all, and it was obvious the poor woman's nerves were getting the better of her. The sink was piled high with pots and pans, ladles, bowls, and an array of used, unwashed utensils. Betty's confusion and turmoil on the inside spread beyond her body as it was mirrored on every countertop. The tension of her distress was palpable, slowly sucking any hope of an orderly calm out of the air as her face turned crimson, the hue growing deeper and deeper with every second.

"Oh, Mrs Cornish," she wailed in panic. "I ain't as good as you. The mistress is going to be right un'appy with me, she is."

"Breathe, Betty," Mrs Cornish soothed. "You've done this many times before, and you've never had any issues. Truth be told, young lady, you outshine me every time. Believe me when I say that you will be just fine, duck. You're just panicking, that's all."

Betty took a deep breath, her hands wrapped tightly around Mrs Cornish's, as though she would be swept away in the chaos if she so much as dared to let go.

"Betty, how about we help you get this kitchen organised before we go? I offered. The guilt of stealing Mrs Cornish away to Somerset, so I would not be alone, was gnawing at my insides. I'd never thought it would put so much pressure on the young woman crumbling before me. However, none of us were ignorant of what my mother would say or do if she caught Betty struggling with it all. Mama, although she had never once applied her nimble, soft fingers to a day's work in her entire life, regarded the work of servants as menial and easy—a trifle in the grand scheme of things. She believed that to be a lady upholding all that was expected of her, was far more taxing on one's nerves and body.

"All that has happened here is an unnecessary

bout of nerves," I continued, kindly. "If we help you get ship-shape before we leave, then you will have one less thing to worry about."

"Oh, Miss Davenport," she bobbed. "What must you think of me?" The poor woman's face had drained significantly in colour. Although, I must confess, it was rather a vast improvement to the red, which had me a tad concerned she would swoon.

"Come sit down, Betty." I pulled out a chair whilst Mrs Cornish guided her towards it. "Do not concern yourself with me. All I am thinking is that I have put you in the most awkward position. I can only apologise profusely for taking Mrs Cornish away with me."

"I'm just being daft, miss. It's like Mrs Cornish says, I have done it all before, but for some reason today, I just can't get me 'ead straight." Betty waved her hand in front of her. Strands of straight brown hair fell about her face, sticking to her clammy skin. "I'll be right as rain in a minute," she said, smiling weakly.

"Before this tea goes cold, why don't you have a cup, duck?" Mrs Cornish offered, passing a teacup to Betty. "It might make you feel a bit better."

As Betty leaned against the back of her chair, slowly sipping the tea, Mrs Cornish and I restored some order to the kitchen, sincerely hoping that an organised kitchen would mean an organised mind for the poor young woman.

"There, that's better," I grinned, hands on my hips. With the last clean pot returned to its rightful place, I was thoroughly pleased with the much tidier kitchen. "There you go, Betty. Mama will never know now, will she?"

"Oh, Miss Davenport, Mrs Cornish, thank you. You two will be missed around 'ere, I can tell you," she beamed.

"You may miss us, duck, but you will be fine," Mrs Cornish assured her. "You know what you're doing, so you've got to stop doubting yourself, you 'ear me?"

"Yes, Mrs Cornish. I promise I will do you proud." Betty wrapped her arms around our friend. "You'll be missed," she sniffled.

"Oh, go on with you," Mrs Cornish chuckled. "You have luncheon and dinner to prepare. You best get on with it."

Betty inhaled deeply, then smiled confidently, plunging back into her work like nothing had ever happened.

I felt the cool creep into my muscles, my shoulders slowly relaxing as I simply stood still. A deeply desired gulp of air filled and emptied my lungs in a steady pattern, seemingly decreasing in velocity as the minutes progressed. My heart was thumping beneath my ribcage, adrenalin coursing through my body, and despite the kitchen no longer being a mess, my insides were not relenting. As my breathing deepened, a wave of the most tantalising aroma of freshly baked apple pie greeted me. It appeared that in all the fluster of a few minutes prior, my senses had completely ignored it, but as I took note of everything, it was all I could smell.

"That smells incredible," I commented, following the delicious fragrance like a hound hot on a criminal's trail, the scent drawing me closer towards a filled basket on the table. "Is that apple pie?" I asked a little too eagerly.

"Just a little something for us for the journey, Wren," Mrs Cornish whispered, patting the very basket I had my eye on. "Plenty of grub to see us through, I reckon."

"I knew it was a good idea for you to come with me, Mrs Cornish," I smiled, inhaling deeper until my nostrils quivered in delight at the glorious scent of sweet cinnamon. Proof of my pleasure was enforced quite dramatically as my stomach replied with a rather pleased grumble.

The day had finally arrived for me to make my retreat to the one place where my restraints were not. I could not wait to be miles away from the shackles of London and my mother. Primrose and my father would be missed, but the constant reminders of who they wished I was, were a burden I needed much respite from. I like to think of myself as resilient after so much practice under the scrutiny and criticism of those who I hoped, yet very much doubted, loved me, but even I, Miss Wren Jennifer Davenport, had my limits. What I needed was the vast open land, flowers, quiet, and the extremely welcome companionship of Mrs Cornish.

Papa and I had managed to keep the vital informational snippet of Mrs Cornish's departure conveniently away from my mother and sisters' ears. I very much doubted Primrose would have willingly given the information away, but under Mama's influence and steady manipulation, it was highly unlikely Prim would be able to keep it from her, nor would it have been fair to have requested such a feat from my youngest sister, so, as Papa had quite fervently requested, she too was kept in the dark about the plans that had been made.

"Do you have everything you need, Mrs Cornish?" I asked, barely able to contain my excitement at our pending departure.

"Ooh, I think so, duck. I got all me lady's things, a few dresses. Nothing fancy, like, but it'll do me. They're all ready and waiting to be loaded onto the carriage, Miss Wren."

"Fabulous, Mrs Cornish. This is going to be so much fun. Let me just say farewell to my father and Prim, and I will be back."

"Shall I get in the carriage now in case they see

us leave together?" Mrs Cornish asked. Her voice spoke of her concerns as her eyes flitted left and right, as though she were waiting for someone to jump out of nowhere and spoil everything with one loud chastisement. Apprehension had gripped her as tightly as the clasp of her hands, which she held in front of her.

"Yes, that would be very wise. But, Mrs Cornish, please know that everything will be just fine. Mama is far too busy with my sisters to even concern herself."

The woman smiled, picked up the heavy basket, and hurriedly headed out of the servants' door to where the carriage awaited us.

Tapping my knuckles on the door of the study, I called out to my father, "Papa, may I come in?"

The door opened as my father stood tall in front of me. His dark jacket emphasised the silver of his hair as his slight frame towered over me. "Is it that time already, Wren?"

"It is, Papa. Mrs Cornish is waiting outside for me. I thought I would say goodbye to you and Primrose before I leave." I pulled my gloves tighter over my fingers. They did not need adjusting, yet I found the busy nature of my hands a welcome distraction from the tension building up inside of me. I was afraid my father would rescind his promise, and I couldn't have borne it if he had.

My father's eyes bore gently into mine. "What about your mother, Wren?"

"She will not care if I have left, Papa. You know she won't. She does not even care when I am actually here." I broke the connection between our eyes that he willed me to sustain. My mother was not a subject I enjoyed discussing. It made me feel childlike, even guilty. What for? I cannot tell you. I only know that it did. It was as though I owed her something—a loyalty truly undeserved.

"She loves you in her own way, Wren. You must see that. Perhaps a quick farewell for me?"

The plea in my father's eyes caused me to relent. "For you, Papa. Only for you."

"You're a good girl, Wren. If only Gladys and your mother had an ounce of your kindness." Papa looked wistful as the words tumbled thoughtfully from his lips.

"Don't let them hear you say that, Papa. Heaven forbid they should be anything like me," I jested.

My father smiled sadly at me, for even I could hear the slip of sorrow in my voice as I said it.

Without a word, my father wrapped his arms around me, placing a kiss on top of my head. "Be careful in Somerset, darling. If you have any worries, then you must send word, and I will come to you."

"Oh, that would please Mama," I softly chuckled. "If you disappear in the middle of the season as Primrose and Gladys seek a match, then who will give permission for their betrothal?"

"They will manage, Wren." My father's expression had become taut with the gravity of his words. "You are also my daughter. I have three daughters, not two."

My heart swelled in my chest, pushing aga-inst my ribcage, to hear my father speak so fiercely of my importance to him. If I could have, I would have bottled the feeling and carried it everywhere, but instead I had to make do with the memory. Gathering up his words and pocketing them in the far corners of my mind, I made my way to my mother's chambers to bid her my father's requested farewell.

"Come in," Mama called from beyond the door. She sounded chirpy, no doubt expecting the arrival of a maid so she could try on one of the many elaborate and regal dresses she had purchased only that morning.

"It is only I, Mama. I have come to inform you of my departure. I shall be leaving to travel to Somerset now."

The expression on my mother's face plunged

from the happy one she held for the expected maid to the dark and fierce alternative she reserved only for me. "And you felt the need to bother me with this?" she asked incredulously, her tone clipped and malicious.

Mama's hair sat primly upon her head; waves of black hung in ripples, softly framing the sharp edges of her face. Her lips pinched and her eyes squinted as she stared into the looking glass. She was sitting at the perfect angle, imprisoning me in her sights as she continued to scowl at me through the reflection. I tried to step out of her view, but my efforts were in vain, for no matter where I stood, her eyes sought me out to burn me with their gaze.

"Yes, Mama. Papa said you would want to see me before I left." In hindsight, I wish with all my heart that I had stood my ground and faced her with pride, head high, and locked eyes, but alas, my eyes simply fell upon the tips of my carriage boots beneath the many layers of petticoats and skirts.

"Your papa is a ridiculous, soft-hearted fool. You have wasted your time, Wren. Now run along; I am busy."

All the heat drained from my body as I remained fixed to the spot. I had expected a stiff, impolite goodbye, undoubtedly laced with fierce restraint, but I did not expect a farewell, or lack thereof, so vicious as the cruel blow she had just inflicted upon me.

"Why are you still here, Wren?" she spat as she turned to face me. Accusation and horror stretched the features of her powdered white face as though the presence of her eldest daughter in her bedchamber was an utterly scandalous event. "Are you too stupid to realise the season has begun, girl? Eligible men and young women will be arriving in London looking for their match as we speak. You need to remove yourself from polite society before they see you. The sight of you will bring nothing but the heavy weight of shame upon us. Now run along, and make sure to close the door behind you."

Speechless, I took my leave, closing the door as requested. Only the air remained between my face and the flat wooden panels as I froze momentarily in disbelief. As I turned, my father and Primrose stood before me. Their faces were ashen, revealing just how much they had heard of my mother's tirade. They had indeed heard every single syllable.

"Wren," Primrose began, her arm reaching out tentatively towards me. There were tears in her eyes as she searched mine.

"Please don't, Prim. I was a fool to even try." My eyes met my father's, but they did not scold him. How could I bear anger towards him when all he had done was hold a flicker of hope for me and our family?

Papa's hand was on my face, his thumb brushing away a tear that was involuntarily sliding over my pallid skin. "I'm so sorry, Wren. I thought,"

Before he could continue, I flung my arms around him, burying my face briefly in his chest. Then, as I released him, I ran along the corridor, down the stairs, and towards the kitchen.

The crisp air soared into my lungs as I threw back the door to the servants' entrance, stepping into the discreet arms of London life, my existence hidden from its people. I wondered what it would have been like to have taken my leave via the main entrance, but, in all honesty, it did not matter then, for freedom was the only thing I craved.

The stroke of my father's thumb over my face was the first I knew of the tear I had shed. I had assumed it was just a little overflow of emotion and nothing more than a single drop, but as the air rushed towards me, it was apparent I had released far more than one. My face was wet with remnants of the pain my mother had caused me. *Was it humiliation?* I pondered. *Or perhaps it was merely grief for the mother I longed for?*

Straightening my posture, I rummaged in my reticule, setting my hand upon my embroidered handkerchief. I refused to let Mrs Cornish see my tears yet again. The poor woman had known enough of them, even when she had not even seen them fall.

"Come on, duck." Just like that, Mrs Cornish was there again. She had stepped down from the carriage to be by my side. There was nothing I could hide from her. "Let's get going and leave this lot behind, shall we?" Her face was solemn and sympathetic as she held out her hand towards me, encouraging me to move.

"Indeed, I believe that is the best idea I have heard in a very long time, Mrs Cornish," I sniffed. Her presence was a balm as a smile curled my lips. Several months away from Mama were most definitely needed.

Letting out a breath I hadn't realised I'd been holding, I stepped up into the carriage and closed the door.

Chapter Four

Wren

The gentle curve of my spine lay hidden, disguised beneath the thick fabric of my velvet cloak as it draped over my shoulders and glided down my back in a rich, indigo waterfall. The hood of the garment curled up over my head in a curtain to cover my hair, the remainder spilling down the sides of my face and neck, draping softly in rumpled fabric upon my shoulders. The small concealment of my face behind the thick velvet was indeed a comfort, as I avoided gazing upon the faces of those who may have deemed it necessary to inspect me the way my mother did. I was exhausted and knew any hint of unkindness from strangers would most likely send me into a temporary state of self-loathing and melancholy.

The prior year, my travels to the cottage had been somewhat smooth, albeit a little daunting, so I had decided to return once again via the same route, resting overnight at the familiar inns. Planning had been meticulous, for I was all too aware I would have company, and I was determined to ensure Rose was as comfortable as one could possibly be on such a long journey.

We arrived at every inn under the cover of darkness, silently slipping through the crowds in a deliberate attempt to shield me from onlookers. Why I had kept to that particular rule the second time around could quite simply have been because Mama had drummed it into me as though my very life depended upon it, yet I had an irritating suspicion that the safety of my life did not concern her, nor did it depend upon the rule at all. However, I highly suspected that it was more the case that it was *her* life, or, should one say, *her reputation,* which depended upon it instead. When one looks at it from that perspective, one would suspect that to adhere to the rule as though it were a religion may have been more out of habit for me, or perhaps it had become a deep-rooted fear, buried like a splinter beneath my skin, painful and difficult to remove. It was the very reason I, apologetically, sent poor Mrs Cornish once more into the fray at the very last inn. Guilt wedged itself alongside that painful splinter as I watched her battle her way through the throng of raucous men and women to speak with the innkeeper about our lodgings. It was perhaps cowardly of me, I thought, asking her to protect me in such a manner, but my nerves were in tatters, and I just couldn't muster the last morsel of courage. I was not ready to disturb the calm waters of my freedom, and Mrs Cornish insisted she did not mind.

Despite having travelled solely via the aid of a carriage as well as making several stops along the way to freshen up and rest, we were thrilled to reach Somerset in good time.

Mrs Cornish dozed in the seat opposite me, her head juddering in time with the carriage wheels as they rattled over the uneven ground. It was the second time slumber had taken a hold of her on the same day, yet, although it was extremely obvious, the woman was not willing to admit she had been sleeping. "I weren't sleeping, Wren," she insisted when I subtly tried to check on her to see if she was okay. "Just forty winks, like I told you before. Resting me eyes, that's all, duck."

"Of course," I replied. "One would never suggest such a thing, Mrs Cornish." An insistent grin tugged at the corners of my mouth. *Who knew one could snore quite so loudly when they were still awake?* I mused to myself.

Mrs Cornish had partaken in many a display of what she referred to as *forty-winks* throughout our journey from London to Somerset. The carriage ride kept on lulling her into what appeared to be several much-needed sleeps. It was quite endearing, really, and I did not have the heart to wake her on any occasion. She worked so hard and looked so peaceful when lost in her dreams that it felt harsh to disturb her.

The carriage rolled up to The Aviary. The elegant Somerset cottage, and our home for the foreseeable future, was positioned most prettily amongst an abundance of glorious open land. I wondered whether my mother knew that she had inadvertently gifted me something so wonderful. If there was a silver lining to the malevolent and stormy grey cloud my mother was, then The Aviary was it. Its picturesque scenery stretched out before me, and I realised I was thankful to her, for without her desire to place me so far from the eyes of strangers, I would not have been blessed with the joy of being there.

The cottage was fairly large, yet cosy in comparison to the exuberant affair that was our London home. Mama had requested the property be purchased not long after the birth of Primrose. A sudden urge to take matters, *meaning me*, into her own hands swiftly fell upon her as realisation of the implications of my existence dawned rather drastically. The aristocratic well-bred lady had two perfect daughters who required the eldest, perfectly-not-perfect daughter, to disappear for a time when they reached the age of their 'coming out'. Although one might say her timing was a tad premature, one could not deny that my mother was nothing if not thorough.

"Cor blimey!" Mrs Cornish exclaimed as the driver helped her down from the carriage. "It's like something out of one of those fairy tales." Mrs Cornish's face glowed with awe as her eyes feasted upon the view in front of us.

"It is, isn't it?" I replied excitedly. There was no denying the beauty of The Aviary. If there was any benefit to what life had thrown at me, we were standing in front of it. It may have taken years for me to receive the selfishly thought-out gift, but now that I had, I found myself longing for it whenever I was back in London. "You wait until the spring, Mrs Cornish," I beamed, inhaling the clean air. "These rustic hues will be replaced with the most vibrant shades of green, and the grey skies with the clearest of blue. It will be like you have stepped into the most vivid painting. You won't believe your eyes."

Autumn had set in across the landscape, with oranges, reds, and golds aflame upon the ground. Fallen, crisp leaves decorated the earth, whilst others remained steadfast, scattered on twigs poking out from the plump hedgerows and clinging to the branches of trees. The green of the fields cowered in comparison to their magnificence.

The thatched roof was dark with the kiss of

rain; the compact surface, thoroughly drenched in the wake of the dark clouds that had previously passed overhead. Ivy crept up the walls towards it, desperate to take a closer look.

The Aviary required a thorough clean, I noted, setting down my valise at my side. There had been no visitors and no gentle hands to tend to it. The last sign of life it had seen must have been me.

"Let us go in, shall we, Mrs Cornish?"

"Oh, yes, duck, let's." Mrs Cornish led the way as the driver followed, his strong arms carrying our luggage with such ease that the weight of them appeared meagre.

Neither of us had packed a great deal in our cases. There was certainly not an abundance of clothing in my luggage, not that I had that much anyway. I had packed only the mere essentials. However, I must confess that I had dedicated one valise entirely to books, as well as a few pencils and a sketchpad, just in case the mood to dabble with drawing ever decided to take me again.

I liked drawing, but I rarely found inspiration, for the chances of finding anything creatively inspiring within the boundaries of my home were practically non-existent. I'd hoped Somerset would ignite my artistic desire once again with its authentic beauty. However, I must sadly admit that, although I would very much like to tell you that I was—and am—a budding artist, art wasn't—

and isn't—my real love. That privilege belongs to reading, for books have the ability to whisk me away when my soul desires such escape, and they are as faithful as the dearest of friends, forever there to keep me company when I feel quite alone.

I had spent many days curled up in front of the lit hearth with a good book at The Aviary. Primarily, those were the days when the rain would pelt down from the skies, or when the snow would blanket the earth in the most purest of whites, whilst frosting the windows with its icy fingers which left a shattered-sugar-like glaze in its wake. But there were also the days when I would take my book outside with me on a walk just so I may sit and read by the river, or whilst laying in the open fields, hidden amongst the tall blades of grass. The promise of just one more page, more often than not, rolled into just one more chapter until I could no longer see the words, for the evening had consumed the last drop of daylight and I would be forced to make my way home.

The driver eventually abandoned us to the quiet of the property, leaving all of our luggage neatly in the hallway for us to do with it as we wished. Before she could object, I quickly carried Mrs Cornish's luggage to her bedchamber, then carried mine to my own.

"Where are the servants' quarters, duck?" Mrs Cornish asked, following me up the hallway as she peered in every open door, her eyes perusing the cottage with obvious curiosity.

"There aren't any, Mrs Cornish. You are not a servant here. You are here as my guest. Whatever work needs tending to, we shall do it together."

Mrs Cornish's expression faltered, her mouth rounding into a perfect O. "I won't know what to do with m'self," she breathed. Her gentle grey eyes were sparkling with an excited glimmer of gratitude.

I chuckled happily as understanding dawned brightly upon her features, echoing her surprise that she was very much a free woman at The Aviary.

"You did not think I had invited you here to wait on me, did you, Mrs Cornish?"

"I didn't really think at all, Miss Wren. I was just happy to come 'ere with you. I certainly didn't think I would become a lady of leisure though."

"And do you object?" I asked tentatively, praying that she did not.

Mrs Cornish straightened, her expression thoughtful and filled with determination. "I won't, but only on one condition," she began.

"What may that be, Mrs Cornish?" I asked, amused. I should have known she would not conform so willingly to the unexpected change, nor quite so easily.

"I clear up all the pans and dishes after breakfast, luncheons, and dinners," she said firmly, hands on her hips, like she was not willing to accept anything other than my full cooperation on the matter.

"I will agree to that, Mrs Cornish. This is going to-" I began.

"And I make most of the meals," she added. This time, her eyebrows were raised authoritatively, daring me to disagree.

"Well, that is two things, Mrs Cornish, but if it will make you feel better, then okay, I agree," I smiled. "This is going to-"

"Last thing," she smiled.

I let out an amused sigh of exasperation from my lips. The strands of hair hanging loosely over my face flailed briefly with the force of the air.

Mrs Cornish practically glowed with satisfaction and mischief.

"Okay, one more thing, Mrs Cornish, because I feel as though I am being tricked into letting you do exactly what you would normally do back in London, when I have expressly said that is not what I want for you."

"Just this last thing, Wren," she pleaded.

"Okay, go on," I offered.

"You call me Rose. All this Mrs Cornish business, when we have known each other since you were a baby, ain't right. Will you call me Rose, Miss Wren?"

There was a genuine plea in her eyes as she requested that I call her by her first name. It was the last barrier to be broken between us. The one that separated us from the stifling formality of servant and mistress to what we truly were, which was friends, "I would be honoured to call you Rose, Rose. Thank you."

Rose's eyes glittered as a smile lit up her face. "Come on, then," she remarked. "Let's get settled."

Chapter Five

Wren

Over the weeks that followed, Rose and I settled into a comfortable routine. The memories of my mother's words faded into the background, packed away into an empty valise, as I gave my mind permission to bathe in the tranquillity of our new gloriously rustic surroundings. I was determined not to dwell on what was, for fear of spoiling the many months we had ahead of us. While we were there, I knew I did not have to suffer the audible verbal lashings of Mama, and so I was adamant that nor should I subject myself to the ones stored in my mind either.

True to her word, Rose had insisted on cooking most of the meals; however, I did not allow her to deprive me of the privilege and joy of preparing the food alongside her.

"When one has a rather sweet tooth, it is paramount that one is allowed to partake in the preparation of food. To deny such pleasures is surely a sin, Rose," I gasped playfully. "I simply have to have the sugary decadence of cakes, sweetbreads, biscuits, and pies," I insisted, grinning at the ease of conversation between us.

In truth, I revelled in the education provided by such simple tasks, immensely grateful to Rose for the opportunity to bake by her side where there was so much to learn. The intricacies of it all were indeed an art, I realised, much like painting, I thought, although Rose laughed when I told her so. But as I cut a simple leaf and flower from the remainder of the pastry dough to embellish the top of our apple pie, she grinned, impressed.

"See, Rose, what did I tell you? That is art in its greatest form, for you cannot eat a canvas, but we can eat this," I giggled happily, lifting it from the table and carrying it to the oven.

"I think you're right, Wren. Never did I see a pie so artistic. If I could, I would frame it."

"Rather messy for the walls, Rose, but I get your point."

With the oven lit and its door closed, Rose filled the kettle and set it to boil on the stove whilst I began preparing the teacups, milk, and sugar for the table. Our work in the kitchen was done, and we were more than ready for a well-deserved cup of tea and a break, but as the sound of knuckles rapped on the front door, the heavy beat of someone's arrival cut through the familiar peace, and I did all I could to prevent the crockery from clattering to the floor.

I held my breath.

“Shouldn’t we get that, Wren?” Rose asked, frowning at me.

There was a tremble in my hands as I reached the table, lowering the prepared tea tray with only a single drop of milk spilled from its jug. “No one ever visits here,” I wheezed as I released my breath.

"Well, it looks like it’s time for a change then, don’t it?” Rose stood with determination, dusting down her gown.

Releasing the ribbons at her back, she cast her apron aside and began to walk towards the kitchen door. Without thinking, I reached out to her, my fingers wrapped gently around her arm, squeezing it softly to stay her. “We mustn’t, Rose. What will they say when they see me?”

Mrs Cornish’s eyebrows rose with an expression of disbelief. “They’ll probably say hello like most folk would, Wren. What else could you possibly think they would say?”

“Mama says-”

“Your wretched mother says a lot of things, Wren, but when have you actually heard someone else say what she insists they will?”

The knock sounded again.

“One minute!” Rose bellowed, then turned back to me. “Now you listen ‘ere, Wren. I don’t want you to worry. Yes, you do have a bad back, but what you have is barely noticeable. It's nothing like those poor loves who get whipped up and thrown into those disgusting shows for the entertainment of ignorant fools, nor is it like those poor folks who get discarded in an asylum. Not that they've got anything to be ashamed of either. You must make the most of what God has given you, Wren. Don't shy away from the world." With that, Mrs Cornish turned on her heel and headed to the door.

I barely had time to register her words when the sound of a male voice danced down the hallway and into the kitchen, soon to be followed by the steady tread of shoes upon the stone floor.

"I hope you do not mind my visiting. I am new here and at a bit of a loss." The man's voice was low and gentle. There was something about his tone—I cannot quite put my finger on it—that suggested he was the same age, or thereabouts, as Rose.

"Not at all, vicar," Rose replied. "Do come in. We were just about to have tea. There will be some apple pie too. However, I'm afraid it is in the oven at the moment, but if you are happy to wait with us, you are most welcome to join us if you would like."

"Oh," the vicar replied, his voice lifting in pleasant surprise. "That would be lovely. Thank you."

Rose and the vicar entered the kitchen as I stood against the wall to keep my back hidden from our new guest. The man was not much taller than Rose, and, as he removed his hat, his silver hair flopped in a soft, dishevelled mop upon his head. His suit was ink-black, albeit the stark white collar, and pressed to perfection, completely at war with the wayward strands of his hair.

"Vicar," Rose offered a gentle smile as she looked at him, ready to make the introductions.

"Please call me Charles. All this vicar or sir nonsense is far too formal," the vicar said, returning a kind smile of his own as he briefly interrupted.

"Right you are, Charles." Rose's cheeks brightened into the shade of a sweet pink as she repeated his name, then quickly cleared her throat and continued. "Charles, this is Miss Wren Davenport."

Charles's kind gaze turned to me as my breath stilled in my lungs. An awkward blush crept over my face, knowing I must have looked like a scared, meek, little animal as he looked upon me. If I did not look terrified, then I can assure you I certainly felt it, but as joy broke across his kindly features, the fear that had tightened into a ball at the centre of my chest unravelled, releasing a sigh of relief that allowed me to return his smile with one filled with gratitude.

"It is a pleasure to meet you, Miss Davenport," he said, the curve of his lips still genuinely creasing his face as it reached his eyes. "I was saying to your friend..."

"Rose," she offered. Her eyes were intent on us both as she observed our interaction closely.

"Yes, Rose, of course. I apologise. I was saying to Rose, Miss Davenport, that I hope you do not mind me calling. I am new in the village, and people are rather few and far between."

"Not at all, Vicar." I swallowed the lump of anxiety wedged in my throat. "Admittedly, I am not used to meeting new people, and I was perhaps a little apprehensive, but now that you are here, I feel a little ridiculous to have been concerned at all."

Rose beamed with satisfaction, an expression of '*I told you so*' plastered across her face. I conceded to acknowledge she had been right as I returned her look of affection, further deepening my already quite vibrant pink blush.

As I served up the warm apple pie, the vicar did not mention my curved spine nor my raised shoulder. I wondered whether he had noticed what my insecurities would not let me forget but had been too considerate of a gentleman to have mentioned it. The heat burning deep into the knotted muscles of my upper torso buried itself even deeper as my mind turned over every thought. The discomfort and pain were simple reminders of the curve's presence, deliberately making me feel uncomfortable in my own skin. I was never allowed to feel beautiful, nor to even feel somewhat *normal*, for lack of other words.

Even though there were times when pain sat back in silence, they were very few indeed. The window of reprieve was confusing, for on one hand, I was indeed grateful for it; I basked in it, forgetting who I was; I became the woman who lives inside my head, the real Wren. But then, on the other hand, when fatigue set in and the fire raged once more, that window slammed in my face, abandoning me outside in the cold reality of my life.

It was only when we were deep into conversation and on our second slice of pie and cup of tea that he unknowingly sat upon the fence of my life, peering in on the peculiar plant that was me. I know with all my heart he had not meant to pry, yet I wondered whether there was anything that may have triggered his curiosity. However, when he spoke, there was no malice laced within his words. "When I first arrived, you said that you are not used to meeting new people. If you don't mind me asking, is there any particular reason, or is it because the countryside is just so unbelievably quiet?"

Rose gave me a beseeching look, one that encouraged me to be truthful. I found myself chewing the inside of my cheek as I considered my next words. The man hadn't commented on my appearance, and he certainly hadn't run from the cottage screaming for his life because he thought me a monster. I had come so far, it seemed pointless to undo all of that by lying to him. "I am here to escape the season in London, Charles," I began.

He looked puzzled.

"You see... Well, I don't know whether you may have noticed, but I have a bad back. My spine is a little curved. It is what gives me the limp when I walk and the raised shoulder here," I continued, tapping my left shoulder.

Charles nodded. "I hope you don't mind me saying, Miss Davenport,"

"Wren, please," I interjected.

"Wren," he smiled. "But I did notice, for I have seen it before in another, but I have to confess it wasn't right away. However, I still don't understand why you would be out here when there is so much fun to be had for a young lady like yourself in London at this time."

My face and chest heated with an embarrassed

vulnerability. Somehow, to speak of my spine so openly left me feeling like an exhibit. I was startled by a sense of shame that burned in my chest. There were no amount of layers of fabric that could have ever covered me enough to relieve me of how utterly exposed I felt.

My throat ached as I inhaled, reminding myself that he seemed unfazed by my condition. It may not seem much to many in the way of comfort nor in compensation at my predicament, but, for me, his acceptance was a lifeline in a turbulent storm of panic, for I knew I had just opened the Pandora's Box version of my life and I would have to explain how my mother did not want for me to be amongst society; *how she did not want me.* I took a deep breath and continued. "My mother insists that my attendance amongst the ton would harm the chances of both of my sisters in the quest for them to marry." My cheeks burned brighter as I laid my stark vulnerability on the table for all to see.

Rose placed her soft, papery fingers over my hand, a supportive smile perched on her heartbroken face.

The vicar looked utterly confused. "You have scoliosis, am I correct?" he asked.

"I believe so," I replied. "I have only ever seen one doctor when I was a small child. He confirmed it as such, but after that, I'm afraid my life has been confined to our home in London. It is only the past two seasons that I have been able to escape to spend the months here."

Charles looked thoroughly shocked. "Scoliosis is not as uncommon as you may think, Miss Davenport. Sorry... Wren. Science is progressing, and did you know it was first discovered in ancient Greek times?"

Rose's mouth fell open.

"No, I did not," I replied, taken aback by the new information.

"Oh, yes, indeed it was, Wren." Charles sipped his tea thoughtfully. "They've been using bracing, or what some may call corsets," he coughed, blushing as he continued, "as a form of correction for centuries. Sadly, the world does not appear to have caught up, for if your family had, they would also have known there are exercise treatments for such a condition. However, I do not think you would need such drastic treatments, as it appears rather mild. I believe I only noticed because I am familiar with the condition."

I nodded at his words. Mrs Cornish had been trying to convince me of how discreet my curve was for as long as I had known her. For some reason, I had been hesitant to believe it, but hearing it from a person who was practically a stranger felt more convincing when they had neither the need nor desire to pacify me. It was not because I had never wanted to believe Rose. Good lord, I truly wanted to, but with my mother's constant reminders of my inadequacies, I just assumed Rose was being kind and trying to make me feel better.

With the vicar's words tumbling about in my head, a part of me I had been unaware of seemed to unlock, and I cannot say I did not like it.

"What a lovely man," Mrs Cornish commented as she closed the door behind him.

"Yes, quite, Rose. It makes one wonder if there are more like him here in Somerset," I mused.

Rose picked up the empty crockery from the table and carried it to the sink. It was practically overflowing with dishes, and I refused to permit her to tend to it all alone. I picked up a tea towel in one hand and held the palm of the other up to let her know I would brook no argument. "I will dry the dishes, Rose. There are far too many things here, so I insist."

Without a word, we set to work, both quiet in contemplation of the hours that had passed.

As the sun began to descend amongst the trees, Rose and I set off for an evening stroll. The air was warm and mild as the foliage crackled beneath our feet.

"Do you think you would consider visiting a nearby village now that you have witnessed how friendly the vicar was with you?" Rose asked tentatively.

Her question caught me a little off-guard, for her words reiterated one of the many questions I had been asking myself since Charles had taken his leave. "I'm not sure," I replied thoughtfully. "I mean to say, I would like to, but I have so many doubts."

"They ain't doubts, duck; they're her words buried in 'ere," she said, pointing to her head as if it were my own.

I did not need her to elaborate as to who she referred to when she mentioned 'her', for my mother was very much a permanent presence in my everyday life, whether I wanted her to be or not. "I fear emotional scars are much deeper than those that are physical, Rose," I commented, trying to conjure the correct words to explain all I was feeling. "One can forget a scar on one's body if one covers it with clothing, but I am afraid, even though the scars my mother and sister have left me with from their words are hidden from the eye, they are painful and prominent in both heart and mind, so sadly, dismissing them is not quite so easy."

"May God forgive that woman," Rose seethed

under her breath.

"You mustn't fret so, Rose. There is nothing that can be done to remedy the past, and anger will only affect you, I'm afraid. My mother doesn't give one fig of the effect she has on you or I, nor anyone else for that matter. I believe she only cares for the pleasure our pain could and would bring her if we were to reveal it. Please don't allow her to upset you. I couldn't bear it if she hurt you like she has me."

Rose grew quiet in contemplation, her thoughts etching an array of ever-changing expressions on her pretty face. "Does it hurt you terribly, Wren?" Rose kept her eyes averted from me as we walked side by side. Her hands were clasped at her front, carrying a heavy-laden picnic basket.

The residual warmth of autumn had been gradually fading over the last few days, so, despite it not being the perfect summer weather that the ideal picnic requires, we had decided to make the most of what we did have by taking a slow walk down to the lake to have our evening meal there.

"When I was a child, her words were as sharp as a knife," I began to explain. "I believed that her detachment from me was my fault." A sharp pinch twisted in the middle of my breastbone as I gathered the courage to continue. "The only love I had to cling to was that of my father's, but then he was hardly there."

"Hmm," Rose muttered sharply in an aggravated agreement.

"Now, though, I understand that he had responsibilities, but back then I felt as though he had abandoned me and that perhaps he thought as ill of me as my mother did, or should I say, does. There were times when I did not want to live anymore. I mean, what was the point when no one wanted me around?"

Rose turned her head away from me to hide the misery my words were causing her.

"You are upset, Rose. I have said too much. I am sorry," I offered.

"No, please," she smiled, turning back to me.

The tip of her nose was as pink as her lips and as bright as the rims of her eyes. I felt guilty that my self-pity had brought her to such obvious tears.

"Continue," she encouraged.

"I will not go into much more detail than that, other than to say that it was only when I had the opportunity to know you better that I finally found a reason to want to be here, Rose. You showed me a kindness I had never known, nor dared to believe, was possible for someone like me."

"Someone like you?" Rose scoffed. "Do you know who you are, Wren?"

"What do you mean, Rose?" I asked, a little taken aback by the disbelief in her voice.

"You, my dear girl, are one of the sweetest, if not the sweetest, souls I have ever met. You are more virtuous than that vicar we met this morning, and to top it all, you have the biggest heart," she continued, making me coy under the intensity of such compliments.

"I very much doubt I am more virtuous than the vicar, Rose," I jested, in order to lighten the intense atmosphere reigning over our conversation.

"Well, if not more than, then equally as virtuous. You know what I think of your mother. I may work for her, but that don't mean I have to like the ol' bi-"

I coughed loudly before she had a chance to finish her sentence. It wasn't because I would be offended that she would speak of my mother that way, but because I knew the pain it caused Rose. She had been more of a mother to me than my own, and I could never afford to repay her for her devotion to me. I hoped that the little things, such as steering her away from matters that only caused her distress, would go some way towards giving a little back.

"Well, you know what I mean," Rose finished as we reached the edge of the lake.

"I do, Rose. I understand you more than you know."

The conversation that achieved nothing but to rehash the painful emotions I'd hoped to leave in London was soon forgotten as we settled the blankets upon the damp grass. The rippling water of the lake soothed away the remaining remnants of tension as we sat in companionable silence. Nothing in the world could interrupt the passing of time or the way nature insisted upon the continuation of all that it was in every subtle sound or movement it made around us as though we were not even there.

"Do you see how beautiful it is, Rose?" I asked, tilting my face to soak up the last remaining golden rays as they flowed through the bare branches of a tall, proud oak tree. "I could stay here forever, if life permitted."

"Can't say I blame you, Wren. It is a far cry from 'ome. Only a fool wouldn't want this kind of thing every day."

"Let us eat, my dear friend," I prompted.

As the sun continued its descent, and whilst our tastebuds indulged in the pleasure of the food and drink at our fingertips, our souls feasted upon the stunning scenery before our eyes as it dwindled the looming shadows of London to nothing more than an afterthought.

Chapter Six
Wren

Winter sharpened the senses as it descended rapidly upon the countryside. The crisp scent of snow hung in the air as the last remnants of autumn vanished without a trace. Rain fell briskly, like tiny needles pummelling one's skin. The unforgiveable sting of its touch was carried across the open land by fierce, bitter winds as they blew at considerable speed. Air weaved through the spindly branches on trees, raging at the outer walls of the cottage as autumn fought in vain for one last moment of glory before the freezing temperatures of December ripped the sky open and painted the world white.

Rose and I spent most of our afternoons huddled by the roaring fire, beating back the chill of frost against the windows.

"I wonder if we should invite Charles to dinner?" I mused aloud one afternoon as Rose continued her knitting. "We haven't seen him for a while with all the work he has been doing at the church."

“I should imagine he could do with a decent meal in his stomach, Wren. You know what some men can be like when they’re on their own,” she replied, shaking her head. “Never known a man to cook himself a proper meal with all the trimmings when it’s just him he’s doing it for.” Rose wound the wool around the knitting needles and placed them back into her embroidered bag.

“Yes. It would be nice to catch up with him too, to see how the church is coming along,” I remarked. “I will take a walk down there in a little while and extend the invitation.”

Rose nodded. “While you’re out, I'll make a start. We have a lovely bit of beef for today. I’ll make us a proper Sunday roast. What say you, Wren?”

“That sounds perfect, Rose,” I replied. “That is exactly what we need in this weather. Something to warm us up from the inside.”

As Rose set to work in the kitchen, I dressed in my warm coat, bonnet, scarf, boots, and gloves and set out towards the church. My breath fogged the air against the pale pink of my lips as the sharp fangs of frost bit my cheeks until they were a not so dissimilar hue. Although the warmth of The Aviary was sorely missed, the winter-white scenery was a sight to behold. No longer did my feet tread upon grass alone, for there was a blanket of alabaster snow, concealing every blade as though the greenery of the previous seasons had been a mere figment of my imagination. Snowflakes had settled over every branch of the deciduous trees in a layer as delicate as powdered sugar. Winter had run its fingers over every inch of the land, creating lace-like patterns on spiderwebs and evergreen leaves. It had left no part untouched. The world was a canvas of brilliant white beneath a thick brush of powder blue, stretching in a sweeping sash of colour over my head, one simple ribbon of colour separating land from sky.

The doors to the church were locked by the time I arrived. Disappointed, I wrapped my coat tighter around my shivering body and headed towards the vicarage. He must surely be there, I thought, for he could not have travelled far in such terrible weather.

"Wren," Charles beamed. "To what do I owe this pleasure?"

"Good afternoon, Charles. I was just about to knock at the vicarage. I did try the church, but the door is locked," I explained. My bones were throbbing as the cold penetrated my flesh. The surface layer of snow beneath my feet had melted; its freezing liquid, invading the insides of my boots and seeping into the thin fabric of my stockings. It was hardly a surprise, for the boots were another of Gladys's cast-offs, worn and torn at the soles. I had been perfectly happy to wear them until then, when I realised that they were not much of a defence as far as winter was concerned.

"My apologies, Wren. I have been working outside today. I thought perhaps I could clear some of the snow from the headstones in the cemetery. I also created the path," he added, pointing back to the way from which he came.

My teeth began to chatter. "W-w-"

"Let's head to the vicarage, and I'll make you a cup of tea, Wren. You look utterly frozen. You will catch a chill like that."

Charles did not wait for an answer, for he simply offered me his arm and continued to walk in the direction of the vicarage.

"I'm so sorry, Charles," I offered as I walked beside him, my arm linked with his.

"Whatever for, Wren?"

"I am pulling on you like this," I replied, gesturing to my arm in his. With the up-and-down motion of my walk, I felt as though, with each step, I kept pulling him down abruptly.

"Like this?" he questioned.

"The way I walk, Charles... It cannot be comfortable to walk with me when I keep pulling on your arm with each step." At that moment, I was glad of the pink hue the winter had bestowed upon me, for it hid the embarrassment heating my face.

"There is absolutely nothing wrong with the way you walk, Wren. It is a pleasure to walk arm in arm with you. You make me feel like a young man again." Charles smiled broadly at me, his eyes glittering in the way Rose's always did.

"You know, Wren, we could all spend our lives apologising to one another for our differences, but I do not see why you should apologise for being you," he began. "Do you believe in God, Wren?"

"Yes, Charles, I do."

The vicar nodded as he took in my answer. "I am glad," he replied. "It is rare that someone such as yourself, who has been dealt hardship in their life, still possesses their faith. It always concerns me when it fades for some, for I think to know that someone," he said, pointing upward, referencing to God, "will always hear you when you need to talk or be there when you feel alone, is extremely important. One doesn't need proof of God's existence because faith is exactly what it says. It is the belief and trust in something or someone that you cannot necessarily see."

I nodded, listening to every word he said. His words were soothing, a reinforcement of my own beliefs.

"Tell me this then, Wren," he smiled. "Do you think God would want you to apologise for the young lady he intended you to be?"

"No, Charles," I rasped. Words failed me. It was

not something I had ever considered before.

Charles placed his key in the front door of the vicarage and pushed it open. "I will just light the fire and get you something warm to drink. Please make yourself at home."

As the vicar busied himself, his question about God played repetitively in my head. My thoughts had trapped me inside of my own mind as I remained silent.

"Is everything okay, Wren?" Charles asked as he brought the tea into the drawing room. "You are awfully quiet."

"Pardon? ... Oh, yes. Apologies, Charles, your words caught me a little off-guard. I had never thought of it like that before. I mean the part about one apologising for the way they are, the way that God has made them... has made me."

"And what do you think, Wren?" The vicar leaned back into his armchair, his teacup and saucer perched in his hands.

"Well, it has certainly caused me to review my own attitude towards myself, and it is something I would like to live by, most definitely."

"But?"

"Well, it's not really a *but*. It's more of an if *only*."

I took a sip of my tea. The hot liquid slipped over my tongue and down my throat, the delicious heat warming me on the inside.

"Go on," Charles encouraged.

"I don't know how I can forget what my mother has taught me." Saying my worries aloud felt strange, too real, as though I was expecting a magical solution to make it all better, one with instantaneous results that I knew did not exist.

"That is something I wish I could fix for you. I have not been on the receiving end of such cruelty and can only imagine the damage it has caused, but perhaps from this moment forward it could be something you can strive to remedy by always reminding yourself that you are God's work of art, and by criticising yourself, you are criticising God."

Charles's words were beautiful. There was a pang of guilt at the thought that God would be disappointed, but I wondered whether this new way of thinking would be something I could really take on board and follow in my everyday life. I hoped God would understand when he knew all too well what my mother was like. "I shall try, Charles," I promised.

"That is all any of us can do, my dear. Now would you like something to eat?"

"Oh, heavens!" I gasped. "I am so sorry, Charles. I came all this way to ask you if you would like to join us for one of Rose's splendid roast dinners with all the trimmings, and I had completely forgotten. We would love for you to join us, Charles. It is roast beef, if that pleases you."

Charles laughed. "Well, why didn't you say so,

Wren?" The vicar stood and walked towards the coat stand to fetch our coats and hats. "Roast beef is my favourite. I would be honoured to join you."

"I was going to send out a search party," Rose called from the kitchen as Charles, and I stepped into the hallway. "The roast is almost ready, duck. Is the vicar with you?"

"I'm here, Rose," Charles called in reply. "I couldn't resist the offer of roast beef with all the trimmings."

Rose stepped out of the kitchen to greet us, wiping her hands on the tea towel. Some of her hair had fallen loose from her chignon, framing her kindly face. Her cheeks were flushed with the heat of the kitchen.

"Is there anything I can do, Rose? To help you, I mean?" I asked.

"Not a thing, duck. Everything is already cooked. All you two 'ave to do is wash your hands, sit down, and eat it."

The aroma of rich beef gravy lingered like a leash as it pulled both the vicar and I towards the awaiting feast. And a feast it most certainly was.

"Oh, Rose, this looks splendid. You have outdone yourself!" Charles beamed.

"Sit yourselves down, both of you," she encouraged. "I want all of this eaten," she added with a wink. “It’ll put ‘airs on your chest.”

I thought I saw Rose blush profusely at her last remark, and I wondered then whether she was growing romantically fond of Charles. I had never witnessed Rose turn pink in the presence of a gentleman, but now that I had my suspicions, I vowed to keep a close eye on them both just in case they needed a little nudge in the right direction.

“Oh, don’t you worry, Rose,” Charles grinned, unaware of my thoughts as I observed the pair. “I shall not waste a morsel.”

And as the smile lit up Rose’s face, I knew I was not mistaken.

“Charles has become quite a lovely addition to our little family here, don’t you think, Rose?” I asked nonchalantly one morning a few weeks later. Rose's blushes had increased tenfold and were accompanied by the odd secret glance in the vicar’s direction.

“Do you think so, duck?” she replied. “I can’t say I don’t enjoy his company, I must say.”

“Oh, you must, must you, Rose?” I teased, pinching my lips together to avoid my amusement spilling into the room. “Well, if you must say that about Charles, then I think Charles must say the same about you.”

"What are you on about, Wren? Get that cheeky smile off your face. I know what you think, and it's nothing like that. I ain't into all that at my age, and even if I was, he wouldn't want an old scruff like me," she chided gently.

"You are not an old scruff, Rose Cornish. You are a beautiful woman with a big heart," I reminded her.

"Now you are using my words against me," she sighed, slipping her apron off over her head.

"Perhaps it is because your words made me think, Rose, and perhaps it is because we are similar and we both deserve to be confident and happy in ourselves," I offered as we retired to the front room.

Rose sighed as she lowered herself into the floral armchair, pulling a blanket over her legs. "Be that as it may, it hardly matters because vicars don't think like that. They ain't like other men."

"If you say so, Rose, but," I continued, holding my forefinger up to stop her interrupting, "where Charles Berrycloth is concerned, do not be so sure."

Turning my back to her, I threw another log onto the fire.

"He don't, does he?" I heard her mumble quietly to herself.

"I think perhaps he does, Rose," I whispered back.

Chapter Seven
Wren

In the several weeks that followed, Rose and I continued to spend our days pottering about at The Aviary. The vicar's visits had become a daily occurrence, which I very much suspect had little to do with me and everything to do with the prospect of seeing Rose. Charles blended well amongst us, as though he had always been there, quickly becoming very much part of our mismatched family.

With the festive period fast approaching and with the comfort and ease of Charles's presence, we extended an invitation to him to spend Christmas with us at the cottage. The church congregation was never very many on a Sunday, but with the harsh weather wrapped around the land, roads, and properties, people were reluctant to venture out away from the warmth of their homes, thus the few parishioners had depleted to nothing more than a desolate church.

Although Rose outwardly expressed her

sympathies for Charles's disappointment because of the number of parishioners declining, she failed remarkably at hiding how thrilled she was at the promise of his company. Where I had been suspicious of Charles's increasing affection for Rose, I was just as suspicious of Rose's increasing affection for Charles. Their friendship was slowly shifting before my eyes to something more, something wonderful, a blossoming, requited love.

The couple would often take long walks together, returning with festive foliage such as crimson berries, holly, pinecones, and even mistletoe to elaborately decorate the shelves and walls of our home. Always invited, I would make my excuses to give them the time and space to enjoy one another's company. The solitude of The Aviary was all I required. Well, that, and the opportunity to submerge myself in a romance of my own, written so poetically upon pages within my favourite books.

By the time Christmas morning arrived, the cottage was lavishly decorated with luscious greens and vibrant reds. Clusters of scarlet berries adorned the shelves and every mantlepiece above the fireplaces, garlands of green framed arched doorways, and mistletoe dangled overhead, where I would often catch Rose and Charles lingering, young again and utterly smitten. For me, the only decorations that were missing were beautiful Poinsettias, the ones like those I knew my family would be surrounded by in London as they celebrated the day without me. Sadly, we did not have the means nor the access to such suppliers to purchase my favourite decoration of the season, and so I forfeited their garnet leaves that have the ability to bring any home to life.

The vivid colours inside The Aviary tormented the winter sky. Grey clouds hung gloomily over the landscape, threatening to burst and cover the fields and trees in yet another layer of snow. The view beyond the window of my bedchamber was glorious despite the grey, I thought, whilst sitting in my rocking chair. It made everything feel more cosy as I wrapped a blanket around my body, preventing the cold from seeping through the thin cotton of my shift. I had woken quite early as the chill had slipped under the sheets and blankets, sending a shiver over my skin, which pulled me from my restful state. Unable to sleep, I'd tended to the hearth as it beckoned to feel the warm lick of flames, then simply settled back into my chair to watch the world outside gradually brighten into day.

Rose gently rapped her knuckles on the door. "You awake, duck?"

"Please come in. I've been awake for quite some time," I called out, not willing to depart from the warmth of the woollen cocoon I'd created with the blanket.

The door creaked open to reveal Mrs Cornish. She had obviously been awake for quite a while, for she was already dressed in her best clothes in preparation for the day. Her dress was a simple woollen one. A lace trim of a floral design caressed the neckline and cuffs; its colour, a soft cloud-grey that matched her eyes. It was extremely pretty, especially on Rose. She looked so content, which was no surprise, for The Aviary could do that to a person.

"Morning, duck," Rose smiled. "Happy Christmas. I wanted to give you this before I get started in the kitchen." Rose held out a small brown parcel, neatly tied with string. "It ain't much, I'm afraid, but I hope you'll like it, love."

"Oh, thank you, Rose. That is very kind, but hold on, just one minute, for I have something for you too."

Keeping my blanket around me, I uncurled my legs and made my way over to my bed. The cold stone floor penetrated through the soles of my feet and into my bones, sending a shooting pain through my limbs. I ignored it as I lowered to my knees to retrieve the gift I had prepared lovingly for her.

As I took the parcel from Rose's hands, I passed her the gift I had for her. It was just a simple handkerchief, but I had embroidered tiny roses in the corner with her name.

"Oh, Wren. You didn't have to worry about me, duck," she crooned, her voice catching with emotion.

"Of course I do, Rose. I hope you like it," I offered, encouraging her to open it.

As she pulled back the paper, she gasped, her eyes glistening with even more emotion as she ran her fingers over the satin stitches. "This must have taken you quite a while, Wren. It's beautiful. I shall treasure it forever," she beamed, holding it close to her chest. "Open yours," she prompted.

Careful so as not to release the blanket from my shoulders, I sat down on the bed and pulled the string until the knot loosened. The paper and bow unravelled to reveal a beautiful apron with a small bird embroidered on a pocket below the waist.

"It's a Wren, like your name," she offered sheepishly.

"Oh, Rose, it is utterly beautiful. Thank you so much." Her gift showed a great deal of thought and a level of love I had never known before. My throat tightened around my quest to thank her, rendering me capable of nothing more than an awkward squeak, so instead I placed a kiss on her cheek, hoping she would understand the words I could not manage.

"You are very welcome, duck. It seems we have

both been busy with the embroidery this winter," she grinned, holding up her new handkerchief. "And both with our names on them too. You make an old woman feel very special, Wren. You really do," she sniffed.

"That is because you are special, Rose," I began, finding my voice again, albeit still a little shaky. "When you tell me that you wish you could have taken me away and raised me as your own, I hope you know I wish that too."

"Oh, don't, duck. You'll set me off crying," she chuckled between sniffles.

"I certainly don't want to make you cry, Rose. That is the last thing I want to do, but I do need you to know that I love you as a daughter should love a mother."

That was all it took for the tears to stream silently down her face. I observed how she tried to hold it all in, but as her throat bobbed and her lips quivered, she couldn't contain them any longer.

"And I love you, duck, as I would love my own had I been blessed with the chance," she croaked.

I wrapped my arms around her, and as the blanket followed, we chuckled at the awkwardness of it all.

"I think I should get myself dressed, Rose, and then we can begin the day. What say you?"

"Yes, duck, that sounds like a great idea."

"Is there anything else we need?" I asked Rose as I gazed across the display of prepared vegetables, freshly baked bread, and a bottle of wine. The aroma of roast turkey wafted from the oven as my stomach rumbled in glee at the promise of such a sumptuous meal.

"I think that's all, duck. There's cake, biscuits, and tea as well. I have a feeling we will have plenty left over too," Rose replied thoughtfully, with a satisfied smile.

"You have done a marvellous job, Rose. Thank you."

"Don't thank me, duck. It was both of us. I think we did a marvellous job-"

A loud thrum of knuckles rattled the wood of the front door, startling us. The rapid beats were filled with desperation and panic. A flash of fear swept across Rose's eyes as she looked from me to the door. Charles had never knocked like that, not ever.

As the knocking thundered again, I hurried towards it. All thoughts of whether the person beyond would recoil at the sight of me had been forgotten, replaced by the unsaid concern of such a knock.

"Just a moment," I called, my feet picking up the pace as I limped closer. The winter air blasted my skin as I pulled back the door to reveal Charles standing there, another gentleman slumped heavily at his side. There was blood on both men's shirts, while fresh blood trickled down the side of the stranger's head.

"Come in quickly, please," I rasped against the cold air flowing into my lungs. The snow was falling fast, and both of our visitors were visibly cold. The unknown gentleman appeared to have a blue tinge to his lips, as well as other areas of his skin, as Charles hoisted him up the step and into the hallway.

Rose was ready, waiting in the drawing room as she threw more coal onto the fire to keep it burning, willing the temperature to warm the strange gentleman, whom we feared was in the most dangerous of health.

"What happened?" I asked as the vicar lowered the man into the chair. My hands moved quickly as I wrapped a blanket around the dark-haired stranger and began rubbing them up and down his biceps and shoulders without a care for any sense of propriety. Propriety did not matter a drop in such cases as the one before me.

The stranger did not speak, but his eyes followed my every movement as he continued to shiver beneath my fingers.

"It appears there was an accident," Charles replied, as Rose guided him to the chair opposite the young man, placing a cup of tea in his hands and gesturing for him to drink.

"It'll warm you up, duck," she encouraged.

"Thank you, Rose," he whispered affectionately. "I didn't know what to do with him, but I knew you would help him. I found him on the side of the road, the carriage tipped on its side. Driver and horses were gone."

Charles looked disgusted that whoever had been driving the carriage had simply gathered themselves up and left the man there.

"That's terrible. You poor thing," Rose crooned, eyeing the gentleman who was trying in earnest not to drift off.

"Yes, quite," I remarked as I passed the man his tea. "Try to drink this if you can," I encouraged gently. "There may be a little extra sugar than you are used to, but it is supposed to help in situations such as these."

Relief filled me as I noticed the blue tinge of his lips and skin was fading into a healthy pink as he shakily reached for the cup. It was a hopeful sign that he would recover, I mused, as I helped him raise the cup towards his mouth. His piercing blue eyes continued to watch me carefully as he took a small sip of the hot liquid.

"Thank you," he offered. His voice was gruff but kind, putting me at ease.

"You are very welcome, sir," I replied. "I will just get something to see to that nasty wound on your head. I shan't be long."

Without another word, I diligently removed the teacup from his hands, worried he would scold himself in my absence. And, as if to prove my point, as I exited the room, the stranger drifted off to sleep.

Chapter Eight

William

I cursed nothing and everything at the same time as I sat back in the seat of the carriage. My journey to Somerset was spontaneous, yet not quite as unplanned as one may assume, for I had every intention of travelling in completely the opposite direction of where my father would be.

Desperate to escape all that life held for me back in London, I bore no guilt for my rebellion but could not shake the anger that clung to me despite very much wanting to leave it behind. Another Christmas with my argumentative siblings and my forceful, arrogantly opinionated father was something I was not willing to entertain for the twenty-fifth year in a row. If it weren't lectures on how art would never be the making of me, it would be the constant ear-battering of how I had a duty to marry some young and foolish aristocratic lady of his choice, inherit her worth, and simply be a 'gentleman'. Marriage was never about love but predominantly, if not all, about money and image for men like my father.

My father had many beliefs as far as my life was concerned. However, there was one in particular that probably irked me the most, for he believed that for one to follow their love and adoration of art was irresponsibly fanciful and wasteful, utterly unfit for purpose, unless, of course, the appreciation only extended as far as to view it from a distance or hang it upon the wall where it remained to fade over the years. His idea of time well spent would have been for me to have followed in his footsteps and to have lived my life as a replica of his own, one he deemed to be far more respectable and prosperous than that of an artist, no matter how talented.

My obstinate, pompous boar of a father could never quite bring himself to understand, nor try to understand, that I wasn't like him nor any of the other gentlemen we were acquainted with in London. His failure to respect my own views and wishes was beyond vexing and completely suffocating.

As for the season that he expected me to wholly immerse myself in, it was nothing but the most terrible headache and inconvenience. Thankfully, I had avoided the initial frippery of all the events and invitations, making my escape when no more excuses for my intended absence sprang to mind.

I loathed the unwanted attention that the season brought with it. The young ladies that my father appeared to be rather obsessed with were frightful. Young harpies with concern only for such matters as my financial worth and the latest fashion. If I had to marry, I wanted it to be with a woman of substance, beauty, and intellect. And, as romantic and foolish as it may sound, I wanted to marry for love.

Sadly, my father's idea of the perfect match for me never once adhered to one of the above requirements, and the ladies certainly never showed any sign, not even an iota, of substance, and, quite shockingly, the majority never possessed even the slightest smatter of intellect.

Ever so quietly, the carriage wheels scored deep, unforgiving grooves into the carpet of ice and snow rolled out on the earth beneath them. The temperature of the brick at my feet had long since depleted to one that was borderline freezing, rendering it absolutely null and void in my quest to find warmth. The only heat provided was that of the blanket draped over my legs, which I tucked tighter beneath my thighs, praying it would rid me of the shiver vibrating within my rigid, aching muscles. Plumes of white painted the air in front of my face in time with every breath emanating from my lips.

In hindsight, I berated myself for not thinking it all through a little better. Perhaps if I had, I would have had the sense to have opted to travel by train, for all the magnificence of its speed and rather splendid comfort were considerably more appealing than the rickety carriage my body was currently being jostled about in.

I yearned, like a lovesick fool, for a warm meal and comfortable lodgings with a roaring fire at a cosy inn. My stomach rumbled at the thought of hot food, whilst my body ached for a soft bed to rest upon, making the carriage ride far more irritating than it necessarily was. I found myself praying for the blasted inconvenience to be over sooner rather than later.

Pessimism at the chances of a vacant room at such short notice poked my already rather rattled rambling of thoughts, darkening my mood even further. Perhaps I had been slightly rash by leaving it all to the last minute. It was Christmas day after all, which left the rather unfortunate question as to whether I would be so lucky as to find somewhere to stay, dangling precariously over my foolish head.

Spontaneity may be exciting any other time of the year, but perhaps not so much on a day as demanding as the 25th of December.

In my hurry to escape, I had not considered the possibility that all the effort I was making would be in vain. The very idea that I would have to return home with my tail between my legs made me wince, for it did not bode well for me in the slightest. The prospect of such a hideous outcome only caused the grumble in my stomach to twist painfully into nausea, fearful that I may have to suffer my father's dratted company after all.

Somerset was deprived of life as I gazed, thoroughly bored and impatient, out of the window. Its vast open land appeared to be a rather limitless blanket of white ambling by as I sat, statuesque, and agitated upon the thinly padded seat. The earthy-brown and slender trunks of trees marked the edges of roads, guiding us as their dark shades peeked through the snow, revealing the brittle skin of nature. Although the deep hue of the rough wood was obvious to the thankful eye, it appeared coy, hidden beneath the umbrella of branches, deepening its shade to almost black.

The only wildlife was that of a single robin perched upon a frosted branch, his feathers puffed out around him, trapping the winter air beneath them. I had read in one of my father's many books that it is something they do to warm their little bodies, and I was suddenly not quite so ungrateful for the blanket nor the few minutes of warmth from the brick. How much easier life was for mankind, I mused. I wondered whether the little bird would fly away to somewhere warmer, for I could not imagine being out there with nothing but my clothes to keep me warm.

As I continued to watch the world pass me by, lost in my own muddled thoughts, the sudden lurch of the carriage triggered my senses into a state of high alert. My heart quickened at the unexpected, abrupt interruption of what had so far been a somewhat smooth journey, albeit the occasionally wonky moment that appeared to occur from a little inebriation on the driver's part. I failed to see the point of mentioning it to the man, consoling myself with the reassurance that it had been merely a blip and was very unlikely to happen again.

Adjusting my position, I pushed my spine against the back of the seat and attempted to calm the thudding in my chest, but, as soon as I was comfortable again, I was thrown violently forward, only saved by my hands as I reached out and grabbed at the meagre fabric of the curtains. The carriage began to tip, possessions tumbling rapidly as everything descended into chaos.

The driver had lost every ounce of control over the vehicle, causing the carriage to creak loudly as it rocked on its wheels. Blood drained from my knuckles as I tried desperately to keep hold of the stiff, embroidered damask, determinedly keeping my eyes on the door. The world seemed to slow as I watched the back-and-forth motion shift the door up and down within its frame, until finally the latch eased free from its component and the world sped up once again.

Control involuntarily relinquished, my body was hurled against the now-unlocked barrier, the impact of my shoulder forcing it wide open and propelling me out onto the uneven, icy road.

The illusion of soft, powdered snow was sharply dispelled when a protruding, hard object cracked loudly as it painfully kissed my head.

Or perhaps it was my head that cracked.

The pain penetrated the flesh and bone on one side of my face in a sharp, piercing agony, stealing my breath. Shock froze my features as comprehension threaded amongst the resounding throb, vibrating through the entirety of my skull. The awful sensation felt far too deep to be considered merely pain, for there was a bone-shattering ache swimming amongst something I wasn't familiar with.

Nausea filled my insides as dizziness lapped in waves over my body, intensifying as I witnessed the carriage finally give in, tipping precariously and leaning further towards the ground. A final creak tore through the air, as if the vehicle let out a sigh of defeat, punctuated by an almighty crash. The sound forced its way through the rapid beat of my heart, thudding loudly in my ears.

Finally, as the vehicle lay completely on its side,

looking as useless as I had felt, the frosted world faded around me.

"Are you hurt?"

My lungs released a staggered groan as I ventured to open my eyes. My vision was blurred, a soft haze cupping the scene, hindering my focus on the friendly face peering down at me. The deep voice and large, blurred definition of the person's outline informed me of the masculinity of my rescuer. Another groan emerged from the back of my throat, stronger this time. I couldn't seem to help it. It was all I could do as the pain pulsated over my scalp in an excruciating, lingering torture.

"It's okay," the man muttered. "I am going to help you."

Placing his arm under my back, he gently eased me into somewhat of a sitting position. My body protested weakly as he proceeded to help me to my feet, guiding my arm up over his shoulders.

Left ankle roaring in protest, my left knee buckled. The violent stab of pain in my skull mirrored the agony they projected as I had tried to place the weight of my body upon the ground.

"If you lean on me, sir, I shall take you somewhere you can get warm so we may see to your injuries," the man offered kindly. "It is not too far from here."

The crisp scent of winter filled my lungs as I breathed against my body's protests. The man next to me could not carry me by himself. Drowsy with shock, cold, and a sense of failing consciousness, I allowed him to walk me a little further, bearing what small amount of weight I could. Thoughts of where the driver had disappeared to kept me vaguely alert. I could not ascertain what had happened to him.

"Your driver appears to have taken the horse and fled," the man offered, as though he had read my mind.

The news made me seeth at the driver's callousness, although it didn't surprise me, for I had been subjected to the odour of Christmas festivities on his breath prior to climbing up into the carriage. Indeed, it had been reckless of me to trust someone who was clearly a little inebriated, I thought, scrambling to remain vertical at my rescuer's side. Hindsight was a gloating, smug little bastard, but I only had myself to blame, for I had let my desire for solitude overrule any iota of sense I possessed.

"The driver was corned," I rasped. It was all I could manage, hoping the man would understand.

"Corned?"

"Too much of the old..." Painfully, I mimicked

bringing a tumbler to my lips, then let my arm hang limp at my side, cold air sawing through the clench of my teeth.

"Ah, I see," he nodded. "Started on Christmas early, I assume. No doubt he made haste, fearing he would get into trouble. He must have lost control of the carriage, and after seeing you, well," he grumbled. "The man is a scoundrel, sir; that is what he is. If I hadn't come along, you could have frozen to death."

The way my head and ankle were taking turns to remind me of their presence, I wasn't entirely convinced that being frozen to death was such a bad idea.

"Come in quickly, please." A feminine voice filtered through the air. The velvety tone flowed from the lips of a young lady standing in the doorway of a cottage. Her extraordinary blue eyes were wild with concern as she glanced at the man at my side and then at me. I do not know whether it was the relief to have finally arrived at the man's intended destination or whether it was because I was bitter to the bone with cold and exhaustion, but another wave of weakness washed over my body, practically begging the man to carry me as I was hauled up the step, down a hallway, and into a small room.

The heat of a roaring fire stung my skin, but as my body acclimatised, the warmth melted into a welcome caress upon my hands and face. Questions and explanations filled the air as I was lowered diligently into an extremely comfortable armchair. It was glorious beneath my folded body, the pain in my ankle dulling rapidly, free from the pressure the walk had applied to it.

The young lady had wrapped a thick, woollen blanket around my shoulders, her hands caressing the tops of my arms as she tried to encourage the heat between her palms and my body to warm me. Enraptured, I couldn't take my eyes off her. The desire she displayed to help a stranger, me, was as natural as breathing, her body brimming with genuine, unadulterated concern. Perhaps her concern for me did not warm me on the outside, but it most definitely heated me on the inside. To be that important to someone I had never met before moved me. I do not believe anyone has ever touched my heart the way she did in that moment.

As her hands continued to glide up and down my biceps, her chestnut hair bounced about the sides of her face. The amber flecks within each strand glittered to life as the light from the fire poured its molten glow over her angelic face.

"You poor thing."

I had hoped the words had come from her soft pink lips, but sadly, they did not. The voice was more mature, belonging to another, much older lady in the room. When the young lady agreed with her friend's sentiment, a slither of warm satisfaction rippled under my ribcage.

She intrigued me. Even after only a few minutes in her presence, I could see she was not like the other women I had been subjected to. It begged the question as to why my father had not introduced a lady as pleasantly different as she was to me. If he had, I wonder whether I would have left London at all.

'Why on earth are you thinking about marriage now of all times, William?' I silently berated myself. *'The impact of my head against the rock must have been far greater than I have given it credit for,'* I added, trying to give my unexpected thoughts a valid reason.

Inwardly, I sighed, for injury or no injury, she was extremely beautiful, and for the first time in my life, I was hopeful to have met a woman whose appearance mirrored her heart.

Oh, good lord, I was staring, I knew I was. My eyes wandered over the length of her delicate hands as she placed a cup of tea in my much broader ones. Her skin was like silk as her fingers slipped over my suddenly sensitive knuckles, encouraging me to drink as she raised the cup within my hand to my lips.

Even as I took a sip and her cheeks flushed

champagne pink, I couldn't divert my eyes from hers. Apparently, I had left my manners at the side of the road where I fell, or perhaps it was merely a matter of the spell she had unknowingly cast over me.

The sudden intrusion of strangely wonderful feelings was peculiar indeed, much too much for me to consider with the depth of thought those feelings required after such a traumatic experience. The last memory I had before my body relented to its weakness was the sweet, reassuring melody of her voice as she exited the room.

Chapter Nine

Wren

"He's nodded off, duck," Rose whispered as I returned to where they were gathered by the hearth.

The fire was a steady roar as it welcomed me back into the room, my eyes lingering on the sleeping stranger propped in the chair where I had left him. His chest rose and fell in deep breaths, his eyelids closed, lashes resting against his cheeks as he slept soundly.

"We thought it best if we left him there, as his injuries need seeing to," Rose offered, concerned.

"He must be exhausted," I sighed, perching on the edge of the seat beside him. "I shall see to the cuts on his head and bandage his ankle. After I am done here, we will probably need to wake him, so we may help him to the bed in the guest chamber."

I squeezed the excess water from the dampe-ned cloth and raised it to the sleeping man's head, dabbing the moistened fabric gently upon his skin. He groaned softly as the cotton grazed over the raised and reddened area on his forehead, inciting a pang of guilt in my chest.

"Charles, Rose, would you mind awfully if I asked you to prepare the bed in there and clear the room for him? It hasn't been used before, other than for storage, and I fear it may be rather cluttered. The last thing we need is for him to have another accident and cause himself further injury."

"Would be my pleasure," the vicar beamed. "What say you, Rose?"

"Not a problem, duck. If you need anything or if he wakes up and gets a bit too friendly," she said, her voice darkening with a sense of warning. "You give us a shout, and we'll come running."

Rose appeared torn by the suggestion of leavi-ng me alone with the stranger, but the depth of the new guest's slumber told me he would not be waking any time soon.

Continuing to delicately pat the cloth to the wound on his forehead, I observed the dirt and blood trickle slowly amongst the trails of excess water down the side of his face and hairline. The earth, blood, and water oozed from the fabric grasped in my fingers, and as the water cleared, the extent of the wound revealed itself.

I was pleasantly amazed that, after all had been washed away, the injury was no more than a scuff to the skin. However, the bruise surrounding the broken flesh was already discolouring—a ring in multiple shades of blue, plum, red, and even threatening to turn into a rather vengeful black.

Eventually, content that it was clean, and the bleeding had ceased, I dabbed a little alcohol on it for extra measure. The man whistled as he inhaled sharply, drawing the air abruptly between his suddenly clenched teeth. The pitch and shock of his reaction caused me to pause before continuing with what was indeed necessary. I loathed to hurt him, but it could not be helped if he was to get better.

Lowering onto my knees, I began to carefully slip his brown boots from his feet. The swelling in his left angle pushed against the leather, highlighting the obvious injury. I had been aware of some damage to his ankle, for I had noticed the difficulty he'd had when walking, but I was not expecting it to be quite as vicious as it was.

Our dark-haired visitor winced from the pain as I attentively tugged at the boot. The guilt, although no fault of my own, was slowly expanding within me. Every time he groaned, winced, or whistled, it startled me. Every pain he endured became my own, not physically, of course, but more emotionally.

One had to wonder how he did not wake from the agony I was unintentionally inflicting upon him, although the sounds he was making would appear that perhaps he was indeed conscious yet simply chose not to open his eyes. His eyelids were glued tightly shut with an adhesive conjured solely from pain, whilst his breaths emanated from his lips in a succession of fraught sighs. However, as they quickly reverted to the peaceful sounds of a man captured by his dreams, I knew he was lost to us for the time being.

"Sorry," I muttered, a lonely whisper lost to the air. It felt utterly indecent and rude to not offer an apology. It mattered not whether he was awake, for there was no denying that I had hurt him, unintentionally or otherwise. If there was even a minute chance he could hear me, I was adamant that he should know I hadn't meant to. My conscience did not prick me, for instead it poked and prodded unfairly, knowing I had hurt this handsome stranger when he really did not need to be hurt any more.

As I'd suspected, his left ankle matched the colour of the forever-expanding bruise on his head, but where the bruise below his hairline adhered to the contours of his skull, this particular injury seemed to magnify the size of his foot and erase any definite shape his ankle may have once had.

"I think you are going to need to stay here a little longer than I thought," I breathed quietly.

His body flinched as though he thoroughly

disagreed.

"I know, I know. You probably do not want to be around someone like me, but what choice do we really have, sir?" I muttered, as though we were deep in conversation.

The disappointment that washed over me in a sudden wave of emotion surprised me.

'If you have been expecting anything other than what you have been taught, then you are being foolish, Wren Davenport!' I berated myself fiercely. The young man was aristocracy. It was obvious from the neatly pressed suit, silk waistcoat, and matching cravat. He was very much part of the world my family had hidden me from. But despite all of that, I would not see him out in the cold. If he wanted to treat me as my mother and Gladys had, then so be it. It was not as though I had not endured such treatment before. In fact, I should have been quite prepared for it. But, somewhere deep in my heart, I dearly hoped that the blue-eyed young man with ink-black hair and broad shoulders would be nothing like them at all.

"Well, that was an unexpected delivery for Christmas," Rose chuckled, changing the conversation as we were sitting at the table.

"Yes, indeed," Charles replied, quickly popping the last potato into his mouth. The man closed his eyes in ecstasy as he savoured the flavour of the roasted vegetable as though it were the last bite of food he would ever enjoy.

We had managed to move our new guest from the drawing room to his temporary bedchamber, where we hoped he would be more comfortable to begin his much-needed journey to recovery. Sleep was indeed rather paramount.

One would expect the impromptu arrival of a stranger to mar the festivities, however, it did no such thing; it only added to the flow of bubbling conversation over the mid-afternoon meal, lacing every word with a heavy dose of intrigue.

"I wonder where he travelled from?" I pondered. "Although my suspicions rather pain me, for I believe he may be very much part of the aristocratic circle." My stomach flipped as I hinted at my concerns for all to hear.

"You mustn't fear the aristocracy, Wren," Charles offered kindly. "Some of them may believe they are better than others, but truly they are not. Be proud, my girl," he added, beaming.

How could I have explained what would have appeared to be an irrational fear? A deep-rooted one that the stranger in the cottage would consider me as my mother did. The overwhelming concern had grown precariously like the ever-creeping spores of mould over a damp surface, tainting my mood in a great effort to ruin it completely since I had tended to him.

I found myself desiring words of reassurance to push my fear back down so I could breathe better, for the trickle of panic had begun to tighten my chest.

"Looks can be deceiving, duck. He might not be an aristocrat at all," Rose assured me. She knew me far too well, and I could tell she had already guessed what I had been thinking. "Besides, they ain't all like her." She sniffed at the memory of my mother and pursed her lips.

Charles's eyes flicked back and forth between Rose and I as he gathered the said and unsaid information. As the pieces fell into place, he patted the napkin against his lips, diligently placed it back on the table next to his plate, then cleared his throat.

"If that young man is cruel in any way to you, Wren, I shall remove him myself," he huffed, as though the evil deed had already been done and he was about to fling our new guest out into the cold.

Rose reached out, tentatively patting his hand in a grateful but silent thank you. Their blossoming fondness and respect for one another was heartwarming to witness.

I smiled. "Thank you. However, the main thing now is that we see to helping him recover."

"You have a wonderfully big heart, Wren," Rose breathed. "Why on earth you've had to deal with what you've had to in your life, I'll never know. Too good for this world, my gal. Far too good."

I squeezed her hand across the table. "As are you, Rose," I replied.

"Shall I take him some food?" Rose asked, changing the subject slightly. Her eyebrows rose with an additional question, one she respectfully refused to voice for all to hear. I realised she was testing me to see whether I was courageous enough to undertake the daunting task myself. She wanted to know whether I would shy away from the stranger in my own home.

Determinedly, I swept my napkin off my lap and placed it on the table. "It's alright, Rose, I shall do it," I replied, getting to my feet.

There was not a chance I would allow anyone to make me feel unwelcome in the cottage. It was the one place in this entire world where I felt safe, and I would not let anyone, not even one as handsome as he, take that from me.

Inhaling deeply, I pulled back my shoulders. My long, dark blue gown hung heavy over my hips, dropping suddenly as I stood. The rapid descent of the fabric matched the descent of my innards as my stomach swam with a terrible whirlpool of nerves. I deliberately tightened the muscles of my abdomen around the sensation as I collected a plate and turned to the array of food.

With clean crockery in hand, I scanned the

table and readily plated up a meal for the blue-eyed stranger. A considerably large part of me wished I didn't have to approach him yet again, alone. Had he been able, I would have much preferred that he had joined us at the table. Perhaps then it would have been far less nerve-wracking for me, as I would have been protected by the reliable and steady support of Charles and Rose. The easy flow of their chatter would have dispersed the awkward silence, and I would not have had to walk in front of our guest, displaying my raised shoulder and uneven gait. But alas, with the severity of his injuries, it was not to be.

"Alright then, duck, but if you need us, just call out, won't you?"

The contents of the floral porcelain plate were piping hot as I began my short journey towards the guest bedchamber, carrying an inviting meal for one. My hands gently pinched a tea towel at the edges to avoid being scolded as I stared down the corridor, afraid, as though a monster lurked at the end, blocking my path. The walls appeared to bend and loom in front of me, panic distorting my vision, making me believe the cottage was deliberately stretching at the most peculiar angles simply to prolong the agony of my apprehension. I desperately scrabbled to find an even keel that would cease the sway rocking my body.

'That's quite enough, Miss Davenport," I chastised myself. *"This is your home, and he is a guest. There is nothing to be afraid of."*

No sooner had I dismissed one aspect of my concerns, another barged to the forefront of my mind as I cursed it and the ground I walked upon. Quite literally, I might add, for it was inconsiderately announcing every inelegant and uneven thump of my steps in the most terrible rhythm. The noise met my ears at such a volume, I knew there was not a single hope in the entire world that he would not, nor could not, hear me.

My skin burned with heated anger.

'Curse my differences! ...No curse my mother and sister for making me curse my differences.'

Puffing out a breath of defeat and exasperation, I took the last remnant of hope I had been grasping onto, praying he would not think me as hideous as I had been led to believe, and gently pushed the door open with my hip.

The soft exhalation and inhalation of his breath caressed my ears as I placed the plate on the dressing table beside him, careful to avoid the silver cutlery clattering with the impact. I pinched my lips tightly around my own shallow-pulsing breath, the volume of it swiftly amplifying with the trepidation, trembling through every fibre of my body whilst I studied him, searching for a sign that he was aware of just how close I was.

Realising that the dark-haired stranger was blissfully unaware of my intrusion, his consciousness swallowed up in the illusions of his dreams, the rise and fall of my chest slowed until it found a steady pace, synchronising with that of the man in the bed. The tremor in my legs faded, the muscles strengthened, and I felt secure on my feet once again.

Lowering, I bent at the waist and folded my body into the vacant chair at the side of his bed. He looked so peaceful laying there. Not only were his features handsome, but they also possessed a kindness, I mused, leaning forward. My fingers found their way to his face, where they caressed his skin, curling over and cupping his cheek. The urge to touch this stranger, to know how this man would feel, was overwhelmingly insistent.

Quickly, I pulled my hand away.

I had no right to touch him. What was I thinking of to be so forward?

My audacity shocked me.

The sensation of rough skin on his chiselled jawline remained in a lingering tingle at the tips of my fingers. With one brief touch, I'd allowed my fingertips to cast a leisurely caress upwards, following and exploring his perfect bone structure, stopping only when my fingers almost touched the tragus of his ear.

Excuses were all I had as I tried to fathom why I had done such a thing. Although I convinced myself it was merely because I'd wanted to check for fever, the feeble attempt at consolation remained at the farthest end of the truth, dangling precariously close to the edge of propriety.

Everything about him made me believe we were of similar age. Maybe that was why he intrigued me so much? The only men I'd met prior to him were my father, the family doctor, and Charles, so to see one so young could only be described as compelling. I curled my hands into fists and placed them under my thighs. The desire to touch his face crept enthusiastically down my arms once more and settled impatiently in my hands, but I refused to relent. I already knew his skin was cool and dry. There were no signs of fever whatsoever, which relieved me immensely.

'That is all you need to know, Wren,' I admonished myself inwardly. 'Keep your hands to yourself.'

Knowing we were miles from the main village, I could only hope he would remain without a fever. If he required the attention of a medical professional out in the solitude of Somerset, I'm afraid I was quite ill-advised on the matter, for I did not even know if there was one. My parents hadn't advised me on such matters. Not that I had expected them to. Their desire to be rid of me far outweighed their concern for my well-being. That concern was buried much further down, if at all, on the list, well beneath my mother's desire for my sisters to become the most sought-after young ladies of the season.

'Perhaps Charles may know,' I thought, hopefully. If anyone may have been privy to such information, then I had no doubt it would have been him. His and Rose's presence at The Aviary was a true comfort, more than I can explain. I hate to imagine what I would, or even could, have done for the stranger had I been all alone. There was no doubt that I would have been completely at a loss with it all.

Feeling the sudden urge to remain at the young man's side for a little longer than was perhaps necessary, I walked over to the hearth and threw some more coal in to invigorate the slowly fading flames. A well-worn copy of 'Wuthering Heights' by Emily Bronte enticed me towards the bookcase, where I quickly slid it from its designated slot. Then, grabbing the unused blanket at the foot of his bed, I returned to the comfort of the chair.

Despite the heat of the room, the untouched food grew cold. I had not had the heart to wake him when he looked so content, and I suspected the cold light of the waking world would disturb all of that with the pain it would bring. My voice drifted quietly into the air as I read my book in a voice barely above a whisper, all the while imagining the stranger was listening to every word.

Perhaps he did not like 'Wuthering Heights', I pondered. I would not have found that prospect confusing, for I knew there were some parts that were somewhat dark and dramatic, but nevertheless, I continued as the romantic scenes within the pages were intoxicating to me.

As the world around us disappeared, I drifted into the story spread out upon the pages open in my hands. The eyes of the man I once imagined to be Heathcliff brightened to the most glittering blue; his hair was no longer just black, it was the glistening hue of raven feathers, and where the light skimmed its surface, a subtle hint of the darkest blue made itself known.

The moors rose up around me, I could almost feel the wind sweep through the blades of grass, rising up and rushing through my hair as I stared at the new version of Heathcliff I had unwittingly created.

I shook my head as though I could rattle the image free from my mind.

How had the stranger taken Heathcliff's place?

Good heavens, what was wrong with me?

Embarrassment rushed to the surface of my

skin as though the new version of Heathcliff had been tattooed on my body for all to see. I picked my way through excuses, finally settling on the least weakest one of all, assuring myself that Heathcliff only resembled the stranger because of the concern I had for the man beside me. I was adamant that once he had recovered and was back on the road to continue with his own life, back to the young woman I very much suspected would be waiting for him, I had no doubt he would forget all about us at The Aviary, and the Heathcliff Miss Bronte intended me to know would once again return. It was merely my mind playing silly tricks on me.

"Psst, Wren!"

Shadows stretched across the guest chamber as my eyes adjusted to the gloom. I had apparently lost myself as well as all sense of time, lulling my body into a rather pleasant sleep.

"Rose, is that you?"

"Yes, duck. Charles is just about to leave."

Mortified that I had not spent much time with them, I gathered up everything on my lap and tiptoed as quickly as I could past the bed and out into the corridor. "Oh, goodness, Rose. I am so sorry. You and Charles must think me very rude. I hadn't intended to fall asleep; I merely wanted to keep an eye on him and must have drifted off," I whispered apologetically.

"You were tired, love. Charles understands."

"It's dark out there, Rose; should we not offer Charles a room for a night or even for the Christmas period? It seems awfully cruel to send him back to the empty vicarage, not to mention he will probably catch a chill at this hour if he ventures out there."

"Do you think so, duck? I didn't want to ask what with this place being yours, and I wasn't sure if it was proper."

"Rose, first of all, this is our home, not just mine, and I do not think propriety needs to be considered with a vicar, especially with one as lovely as Charles, nor when we already have a gentleman here whom we have never seen before today," I assured her. "In truth, I would imagine it would be the most sensible for all those considered, just in case we do require Charles's assistance."

"I didn't think of that," Rose muttered. "I'll ask him, shall I?"

"Yes, Rose. I will go and make up a bed in the other guest chamber for him now," I replied, hoping Charles would agree to stay.

There were six bedchambers at The Aviary, which was turning out to be quite convenient. The ridiculousness that my parents had purchased a cottage quite so large was not lost on me, but as I made my way towards what would be Charles's chamber, I was feeling extremely grateful.

Mama had sent me away to The Aviary twice on the understanding I would be completely alone. *Was that merely a coincidence, or was it part of her horrid plan?* Knowing my mother, it would have been a cruel, humourless joke.

A smug smile of satisfaction broke across my face at the realisation of just how wrong she had been. *'If she only knew,'* I sighed triumphantly, for there was not just one person at The Aviary, not even two; there were four. I could only imagine her reaction if she ever found out.

Chapter Ten

William

Christmas entered my temporary bedchamber in a mouthwatering and tantalising aroma of roast turkey, roast potatoes, and all the trimmings. The promise of a delicious meal tickled my senses, but with exhaustion gripping me so tightly, I could not find it within me to simply open my eyes, let alone raise my body from the bed and eat.

Soft footsteps announced her entrance, each one a tentative tap upon the floorboards like a thief in the night. The young woman picked her way across the wooden surface with diligent consideration, careful not to arouse me from my assumed sleep.

Porcelain clattered against the wood as she placed the plate and its contents upon the dressing table, but still, I did not move.

My head throbbed, and the world spun despite my eyes being closed. Perhaps it was the inside of my head that turned on its axis, but either way I dared not look beyond my eyelids, for it was enough just to press my body into the soft mattress, a reassuring touch, acknowledging that I wasn't really falling. The bed was my only guarantee that gravity could not have its wicked way with me; the frame and mattress, a pleasant and solid barrier between us.

The cool, silken touch of a kind hand glided over my face. I swallowed a breathy sigh as the feminine fingertips tickled my skin, awakening my flesh with a pleasant shiver. Such a simple touch had me yearning to lean into it, to press my cheek against the palm of her hand.

Who was so brave as to place their skin so tenderly against mine?

Despite the feelings she had awoken in me, there was nothing improper in what she was doing, for her touch was one of fondness. There was an undeclared mutual curiosity that burned between us. It slipped under my skin and travelled to my chest, where it glowed warmly within. It had been a long time since I had felt a touch so comforting. Men rarely felt such tenderness, for we were expected to carry the load and be quiet, or at least that is what my father had taught me.

The young woman sharply withdrew her hand, as though the contact between us had seared her skin. Perhaps it had, for the retraction of her touch stole away the warmth, leaving me cold—much colder than before. There was an unfathomable sense of loneliness and longing in the chilling and dreadful absence of her contact. I realised then that I would have happily laid there with her hands resting upon me.

The need to reconnect with her rose in a mild, odd flutter of panic. I wanted to reach out to her, to pull her back, yet I knew I could not force her hand upon me, nor would I, despite the unrecognisable desire curling in the centre of my chest.

She was so quiet. To simply listen to her was insufficient. My eyes itched to gaze upon her, but I had no idea as to how I was to do such a simple thing without startling her or chasing her from the room. Everything about her approach cried uncertainty, and I did not want her to leave me there on my own.

Whilst I maintained the ruse of a deep slumber, I prised open my eyes just the merest of fractions, creating a curtain of lashes so I could see her face. Familiar sparkling, blue-grey eyes framed with long, defined, dark lashes studied me. Just as I had suspected and indeed hoped, the person was the same young woman who had tended to me when I had first arrived.

The young woman leaned over me, the pale pink of her bottom lip deepening as she repetitively grazed her teeth over it. Her perfectly sculpted brows lowered with concern, creating a V directly between them where her skin pinched together. She was just as beautiful, if not more so, than when I had first arrived, I thought, for as I simply lay there, I was afforded the luxury of drinking the sight of her in.

My eyes remained secretly fixed on her for several more minutes. I did not want to look away for fear of her vanishing or, worse still, discovering my deception.

How was I to explain spying on her as I had been?

I would have to confess the truth, and the truth was that she was thoroughly bewitching. It had become rather apparent to me that I found it exceedingly difficult to focus on anything else when she was in the vicinity. To be so forward would only inspire her to think me inappropriate, especially as we did not even know one another. For the time being, I was forced to conceal how mesmerising she was to me.

Her love of literature spilled out into the room as she settled down on the seat by the bed and began to read. She smiled and swooned so prettily amongst the different scenes that it took a great deal of effort not to return her smile as her imagination lit up her delicate features. Her voice was a seductive melody as she raised the words from the pages as though she were an actress upon the stage, bringing them so elegantly to life that there were times she sent goosepimples cascading over my skin.

Although I already knew the story of Wuthering Heights, a ridiculous pang of jealousy pinched my insides as the young lady storyteller seemed to embody Cathy with her words of love and adoration for Heathcliff. What was so special about Heathcliff? I'd bitterly thought. He was already a scoundrel to me within the first few chapters; I did not need to wait for the rest of the story to confirm it. I berated myself for such a juvenile reaction. The young lady was merely reading a story, but that wayward, fanciful glimmer in her eyes made me suddenly long for her to be thinking of me.

Sleep snuck up on me as she drew us both into another world. The tones of her voice lulled me into a heady bliss and a much-needed rest. It wasn't the words she spoke, but the very comfort of her presence beside me. My need for her to be there was strange and downright ridiculous. *Good lord, a man did not need to be assured. I was not a child.*

By morning, the seat by the bed sat cold and empty. An undesirable, yet unmistakable, void I could not ignore. Embarrassed by the overwhelming hunger for her presence the night before, I had resolved to try to forget it and put it all entirely down to a moment of madness brought on by the very obvious head injury still making itself very much known. Thankfully, the throbbing in my skull had dulled greatly to a simple ache, but my ankle, on the other hand—or should I say foot—was practically screaming in outrage at what the inebriated wastrel of a driver had inflicted upon it.

The pain seemed to reverberate through my body as I attempted to pull myself further up the bed into a sitting position. Any immediate plan to place my foot on the floor could not have been any further from my mind than it was. The moment I'd opened my eyes, I knew I would not be attempting such foolery so soon, for phantom daggers, piercing through the flesh and bone, soon put me in my place.

Any colour I may have possessed drained rapidly from my face in a cold plunge of reality, only to be replaced by a rising tsunami of nausea that sent tiny, cold, dry spatters over my skin like icy raindrops. It was no good, I warned myself, lowering my body back into a horizontal position. I would have to accept that my limbs and torso were far too heavy and out of sorts.

Lazily, the world shifted beneath me. It swayed like the deck of a ship on turbulent seas as I inhaled deeply, trying to reinsert myself into the reality my mind was so eager to drift out of. The creak of the bedchamber door filled the silent void where I had become suspended, trapped in a body that could do very little other than be quiet and listen.

As if offering a lifeline, a loud squeal of resista-nt hinges pulled me rapidly from the suffocating loss of equilibrium.

Footsteps followed; calming, familiar, and welcome footsteps, as the young woman walked quietly around the bed. My eyes willed her to look my way, yet the calm vulnerability she maintained demanded she keep her eyes averted. The new and obvious demeanour she had withered and curled into revealed her insecurities, for the woman I spied on through my lashes the night before was not the same version before me.

"Good morning," I offered. My words were cautious, and some might say they were a little stern. I had not meant for them to hit the air with such ferocity. It was a habit of mine, inherited from my father. A blasted nuisance of a trait, I thought, when I did not want to seem unkind or rude. It was an involuntary mannerism I found protective, like armour, in front of strangers. There was no denying that she was a stranger, but that was not the only reason. I was also tremendously embarrassed that I had been discovered in such a state and dragged back to her home, only for her to feel the unnecessary burden of the obligation to care for me. I would much rather have met her in better circumstances.

Her blue eyes peered at me through her lashes as the low winter sun streamed through the window, kissing the side of her face. Copper flecks sparkled, trailing over the smooth, elegant, gentle kinks in her hair.

"Good morning, sir." Her gaze rapidly dropped to the tray in her hands, as though looking at me hurt her eyes. "How are you feeling?"

"A little on the sore side," I replied. The smile I offered was wasted, even though I had managed to soften my tone to one that was amiable, for she refused to look at me. "Thank you for taking me in. You didn't need to, but I am extremely grateful to you and your family."

"Oh, they are not my family," she smiled, finally meeting my eyes. "Well, what I mean to say is that they are very much like family to me, but sadly, they are not actually my family.

"I see, or at least I think I do."

She grinned, her humour twinkling like tiny stars in her almond eyes. There was another world beyond the stars glittering amongst the blue, I mused, a lifetime crammed into no more than four and twenty years.

I cursed myself, for I must have looked at her a little too long. Getting lost in my own musings without uttering a word had made her question why I looked at her so. She shifted uncomfortably on her feet.

"I have a bad back. It's nothing really," she offered nervously.

Instantly, my stomach clenched with an overwhelming desire for the ground to open up and swallow me in its entirety. With the deepening hue of pink on her cheeks, I knew I had embarrassed her. I hadn't meant to stare, but by doing so, I had made her believe I was thinking the very worst one could possibly think. If only she had known that I failed to have any opinion whatsoever of her shoulder, for I believe I was far too busy admiring all of her. What did I care whether one shoulder was slightly higher or not? Even in the minute amount of time I had known her, it was as obvious as the nose on one's face that she exuded something that outshone any imperfection she feared she may have.

Good grief, I was doing it again, going all starry-eyed over the stranger before me.

"I think I better leave. I will get Rose to see to you," she blurted, turning on her heel.

The young lady was hurrying to the door, desperate to escape the assumption she'd made as to why I couldn't take my eyes off her. Not only was I being an absolute fool, but I was also scaring her.

"Please don't leave," I called.

Reaching out as though I could touch her from

where I was sitting, my fingertips merely brushed the air. She was already on the other side of the room, her hand fixed tightly around the handle of the rustic door. Her eagerness to be as far away from me as possible was visible in every line on her face, and I couldn't blame her.

"I didn't mean to make you feel uncomfortable," I breathed, begging her to stay as I pleaded with my eyes. "I believe the knock to my head has left me rather off-kilter, as I seem to be staring into oblivion every five minutes." To prove my point, I did it again, but this time it was her hand my eyes honed in upon. It was all an act. I was caught between not wanting to confess to her how she made me feel and not wanting her to believe there was something about her beauty that offended my eyes. "Please forgive me. I wish you to stay. Will you?"

The young lady nodded as the tension in the room melted away, leaving only silence.

"My name is Wren, like the bird," she offered after a few moments, cutting through the silence. "The lady and gentleman you may remember are Rose and Charles. Charles is the vicar here, and Rose, well, she is a very dear friend to me. They both are."

Her cheeks flushed pink with fondness. Goodness, there were neither pursed lips nor a tilted chin, no narrowed eyes, nor starchy formalities. The young lady embodied the purity and heart of a saint. It was a breath of fresh air from the sanctimonious superiority that usually came with the young ladies of London. She didn't even know how lovely she was. It was unrehearsed, unfiltered, and completely natural. I couldn't help but return her smile.

"My name is William. William Darlington. It is a pleasure to meet you, Miss..."

"Davenport, but there is no need for formalities here, Mr Darlington, especially as I am currently considering how best I should inspect your injured ankle." Miss Davenport grimaced apologetically. "It was rather swollen last night, and I am afraid it may be even worse today. You are quite welcome to call me Wren so that we may cut through any awkwardness there may be."

Pulling back the blanket, I revealed what looked very much like a purple and black misshapen ball, placed strategically at the end of my leg. I was happy to see the five perfectly shaped, albeit very disgruntled, toes making an appearance at the end for the sake of rebellion against the rest of my foot and ankle. "Does that make it easier?" I winced.

"Very much, thank you," she replied as the rosy hue of her face began to fade.

"But before I allow you to examine such finery," I interrupted, grinning, "you must agree that if I am to call you Wren, you must call me William."

"Agreed, William."

Wren inched forward, a stunning smile pressing dimples into her pretty face.

As her skirts brushed the side of the mattress, her array of perfectly white teeth and glittering eyes dimmed rapidly. A darker expression replaced them, one of thorough concentration. She was biting her bottom lip as her eyes warily scrutinised my ankle, setting my nerves on edge. Her sudden change in expression did not fill me with much hope that the damage may merely be a simple scratch.

"I think we will need to get a doctor to see that," she whispered. "The bruising appears rather angry indeed. Does it hurt very much?"

"Not really," I lied. The beads of perspiration trickling down the sides of my temples revealed my untruth. It was downright agony, and I hadn't even tried to stand on it yet.

Miss Davenport was staring at me. An unmistakable accusation of my obvious lie was expressed in the height of her eyebrows and by the positioning of her arms as they folded across her chest. I always knew I was a terrible liar in the most awkward situations such as these, but I had only feigned wellness in front of friends, and in an instant, she had taught me that I was just as unconvincing in front of those who hardly knew me.

"I'll ask Charles to fetch the doctor."

Chapter Eleven

Wren

He made his excuses as to why his eyes travelled the length of my body. I wasn't sure whether it was to pacify me or whether it was the truth, but the memory of the uncomfortable heat in my chest as panic had risen within me was almost impossible to shake off.

I wanted to believe him.

I longed to believe him.

To think he merely lost himself in thought was a much more pleasant reason than the assumptions my mother had already buried deep in my brain. They had scarred every inch of my mind long before I had been given the opportunity to stumble upon those who weren't members of the Davenport family.

Conjuring the memory of his face, I wanted to analyse every detail of his expression as he had gazed upon me, yet every time I believed I had captured him, his image would morph with the memory of my mother's scowl of distaste. Deciphering between the two had become impossible until my confusion as to whether he found me strange or not was a tangled mess of insecurities.

Perhaps I shouldn't have allowed him to persuade me to stay, but there was something about him that drew me in. I found myself eager to learn more about who he was and what his life was like out there in the vast, undiscovered world.

One could easily lose themselves in William's eyes. Never before had I seen a blue quite as captivating. It was as though his mother had plucked the blue from a summer's sky and put it there so that one, once in his sights, could never just simply look away.

He had made no mention of Wuthering Heig-hts, for which I was glad. I fear I may have gotten quite carried away as I had read it to him. Mortification would be an understatement if he had confessed to hearing the fanciful, girlish way in which I had brought Cathy and Heathcliff to life. He would have thought me terribly naïve, but he could not know how books were a wonderful key to the world for me. I imagined his life had been full of adventure, what with his sunkissed skin and rakish good looks, for they were certain to have opened many a door. There was no need for him to rummage in the depths of his imagination to find somewhere, or even someone, to escape to. He possessed more freedom than I ever dared to dream of.

"You alright, duck? You look lost in a world of your own." Rose studied me as I entered the kitchen, her hands placed firmly on her hips, tea towel bunched in her fist.

"Yes, quite alright, Rose, thank you. However, it is not quite the case for our guest," I stated.

"Oh?" Rose inquired.

"I think we will need to get a doctor to look at his ankle. I'm afraid it is rather swollen and particularly angry at being disturbed by the accident yesterday." I didn't feel it was necessary to divulge any more than was important. His ankle served as a rather convenient distraction from any other thoughts bustling through my brain. How was I to lay my concerns out on the table for everyone to rummage through when I couldn't even decipher where one began and the other ended?

I turned to Charles. "Charles, I was wondering if you were privy to such information. As terrible as it sounds, I have never thought of inquiring as to the closest doctor, nor have I ever needed one, for that matter. It seems in this case my luck has quite run out." My cheeks heated, ashamed that I was not as organised as I had liked to think I was.

"I do as it happens," Charles beamed. "Don't you go worrying. I will pay a visit to Cox Farm and ask Bernard if he can send word. He's a good man;

I doubt he will have a problem helping us."

The winter winds rushed into The Aviary, nearly knocking Charles off his feet as he pulled his thick wool coat tighter around his torso. The ends of his scarf whipped about his face as he buried his chin amongst the folds of knitted fabric bunched loosely in a loop around his neck. "Hopefully, I won't be too long," he called back. "After I've seen Bernie, I'll walk to the vicarage and get a few things. I'll head back here straight after.

"All being well, the doctor will be here this afternoon, and we can see what's going on with your guest."

Rose lovingly tucked the ends of the vicar's scarf over his chest beneath his coat. "Just be safe out there, love. I'll have a nice cup of tea and some of those biscuits you like ready for when you get back," she smiled. She pulled her shawl tighter around her shoulders, her body trembling as the cold air beat against the thin fabric of her blouse.

With a tender kiss placed upon Rose's head, Charles battled through the flurry of snow and out into the cold. Guilt riddled me that he had to walk so far just to ask another to fetch a physician for William, but there really was no other way. I made a mental note to beg my father to purchase a carriage and horse for such an occasion. I just had to make sure that Mama would not hear about such a request. If she had the slightest inkling that I had asked for anything at all, then I may just as well have saved my breath.

“How’s he doing, other than the ankle, duck?” Rose asked as she readied breakfast for William. “Was he awake when you went in earlier?”

“He is wide awake and probably magnificently bored from being in bed, but other than the obvious damage, he seems in good spirits,” I replied.

“That’s good, love. I bet he was glad to have your company for a bit.”

“I don’t know about that, Rose. He has such an intense gaze.” I concentrated on my finger as I ran the tip of it over the lip of the teacup, unwilling to allow every space in my head to be filled with criticism and self-loathing. “Of course, he was polite. He made some excuse that his mind kept drifting, but I think he was trying to make me feel better after I caught him staring.” I lifted my left shoulder, pointing out the obvious—a simple indication of what I meant—so I wouldn’t have to go into detail and rehash my biggest insecurity across the kitchen.

“If he says his mind keeps drifting, then believe him, duck. He wasn’t rude to you, was he?”

I shook my head.

"Scowl at you?" Rose squinted her eyes and pinched her lips in a mock scowl, then grinned.

"No, Rose, he certainly did not pull that face," I chuckled.

"What about this?" Rose tilted her chin as she stuck her nose up in the air, then scrunched one side of her face whilst peering down the line of her nose in an exaggerated mockery of what looked very much like my mother.

My face ached with the involuntary smile, bunching the muscles in my cheeks. "Oh, good heavens, Rose, if he did that, I would have thought our time here at The Aviary had all been a lovely dream and I was back in London with Mama. What an absolute nightmare! So, no, he did not do that either."

"Well then, my dearest Wren, I believe the young man must have been telling you the truth. Even if he hadn't, just because he looked at you, it don't mean he don't like what he sees. You are a lovely young woman, Wren. You do not see what others do."

"Not all others, Rose," I reminded her.

"Decent folk, Wren. I ain't referring to the likes of your mother and Gladys. They're a rule unto themselves. You know, I wouldn't be surprised if they just used the excuse of your back as a cover-up for their jealousy of you. A stunner like you...

Blimey! They'd never want that sort of competition to be seen or heard. No fella would look at them because they'd be looking at you instead."

Discomfort settled in my chest, despite her words being kind. To the ear, they sounded genuine, but they could not reach beyond the high barrier of my low self-esteem.

"I know you don't believe me, duck, and I wish there was some way I could make you see yourself through my eyes, but believe me, you are not the monster they make you believe yourself to be. From head to toe and inside and out, my sweet Wren, you are perfect."

The tea pot clattered against the sugar bowl as Rose misjudged the size of the tray. "Well, that ain't going to fit on there any time soon. I'll have to leave the teapot here and take the tea in once it's been poured into the cup. Let's just hope it don't get cold."

The poor woman looked flustered as she kept busy, whilst mumbling to herself. "Where on earth has he gotten to?" she breathed as she lifted the teapot into the air and watched the steaming, hot, amber liquid trickle loudly into the teacups.

I had lost count of the cups of tea consumed since Charles had set out, but I was sure we had reached double digits at the very least by the time the hands of the clock finally settled on twelve. "Don't forget, he said he was going to get some things from the vicarage before he came back here," I reassured her.

Rose's hands were trembling as she wiped them on her apron.

"If he isn't back in half an hour, I will walk down the lane to see if there is any sign of him, but I am sure he will be back soon, Rose. Please try not to worry," I offered kindly.

"Alright, duck," Rose conceded. "But make sure William has everything he needs before hand, and I will walk with you, love. You mustn't go out there alone."

"I hope I didn't disturb you?" I asked, sliding a single teacup and a plate of biscuits onto the dresser. Poor Rose had grown so flustered trying to fit everything onto the small tray that, in the end, we discarded the tray entirely, simply agreeing I would carry the two items separately instead.

William was watching me from where he lay beneath the warm blankets, but this time he seemed only to be studying my face. "No, not at all," William replied drowsily.

The dishevelled mess of his raven hair and the crimson hue on his cheeks disputed his answer, making it all too obvious that he had been in quite a deep sleep. "I was just resting my eyes." His mouth formed a handsome, lopsided grin.

My lips pinched together, straining to hide the doubt-fuelled humour bubbling up in my throat. The man was a beautiful, sleepy mess of politeness, causing the corners of my mouth to twitch as I ached to smile at his perfection.

I inhaled.

"Well, if that is the case, then I am glad, for I would hate to disturb you, William."

William pushed himself up the bed as I rearranged the soft white pillows behind him.

"Charles has gone to fetch the doctor so he may look at your ankle. He should be back soon, all being well," I added.

"Thank you. You are, once again, very kind. I'm afraid I do not have many other words to show you how grateful I am to you. I despise being such a burden."

"I assure you, you are not a burden, William. It is no bother to have another in the cottage. As you can see, there is plenty of room."

"Nevertheless, once I am able to, I will contact my father and be out of your way. I am hoping it will be sooner rather than later."

The words fell from his lips in a barrage of curt sounds. The surprising rapid attack of pinches at the centre of my chest wiped the smile from my face.

Pressing my knuckles over the uncomfortable spot, I tried, in vain, to push the sensation away. I realised then how much I wanted him to stay. My insecurities rose like a predator as I wondered whether he would have said the same if another young lady had been standing in front of him. Someone who didn't look like me. It hurt to think that way, but I simply couldn't help myself.

"You know you are very welcome to stay here as long as you like. There is no need to make your father come all this way, especially with the weather being so frightful," I offered, my voice barely a whisper.

My insecurities were swelling, forcing themselves between every organ and into every crevice of my body, making me feel as though I was about to burst into the disgusting creature, I'd always been made to believe I was. I felt:

Exposed.
Naked.
Different.
Unattractive.

The emotions barrelled inside me until I found myself standing on the edge of a cliff, my heart racing, sure that William's words would somehow measure my worth.

What exactly was I waiting to hear from him?

Why was I so desperate for this stranger to stay?

In all honesty, I am not entirely sure, but whatever the reasons, they seemed quite necessary to lift the sudden weight off my chest.

Chapter Twelve

William

"You know you are very welcome to stay here as long as you like," Wren offered. "There is no need to make your father come all this way, especially with the weather being so frightful."

She looked like the world had disappeared from beneath her feet the moment I'd announced my plan to write to my father so I may return home. Perhaps it had been the way in which I had addressed her, for my words were as clipped as they had been when I had first spoken to her. I felt terrible, yet I was quite aware that it was necessary.

Gradually growing fond of her terrified me, and so, even though she was nothing but kind, I had decided to build an invisible barrier between us. There was no point in pursuing my confusing feelings, for I wouldn't be able to stay much longer. I believed they were fresh, reversible, and unreciprocated. Acquaintances were all I could hope for.

"That is indeed very kind of you," I began,

taking the ice out of my tone, afraid to hurt her further. "But I fear my presence is an imposition upon your festivities. If my father is displeased, it will only be with me, I can assure you, Miss Davenport. One must keep up one's role as the disappointment in the family. Traditions and all that." I laughed briefly, snatching the sharp edge of my words away before they could be heard.

The young lady frowned at the confession of unease between my father and I. "Be that as it may," she continued, dragging her words across the air between us. An essence of sadness twinkled in her pretty blue eyes. There were so many unspoken questions behind them, I wondered how she managed to keep them all locked away like that.

There was a pause of deliberation, one I assumed was filled with curiosity about my father. I prayed she would not question me about that man, for the thought of even having to think too deeply about the tumultuous relationship my father and I had was not something I was particularly fond of.

Wren sighed heavily, revealing the slightest quiver in her bottom lip as she walked further away towards the other side of the room, her hands busily scrunching the fabric of her skirt as she continued to speak. "Please know that you are most definitely not imposing, and this room is yours for as long as you need it, William, or at least until you are fully recovered."

I nodded stiffly.

The way my name fell from her lips did something to me that I could not quite understand. A knot loosened and unravelled from somewhere inside of me as my fingers slackened around the sense of control, I'd prided myself on, and I wasn't so sure if I was comfortable with it.

Complete control of my life had kept me confident. It created a steel rod of assurity in my world, each and every day. It was probably the very reason I had never conceded to my father's obstinate ways, but there she was, this graceful, delectable stranger, so fierce in her charming individuality, happily denting something I thought could never be marred.

The security I had taken for granted had begun to crumble.

The thick fabric of Wren's skirts rustled as she moved to the window and pulled the ivory drapes wide open, stopping briefly to peer out, then returning to take the seat beside me. "There, that's better. We can see each other now," she smiled, nervously passing me my tea. "I hope it isn't cold. We had a little trouble fitting the teapot on the tray. I have to confess Rose was rather put out with the teapot and gave up trying, hence no tray at all."

"It is perfect, thank you," I replied. There was a

silence growing thicker between us as we searched for something to talk about. It was the worst kind of silence—the kind that seems to suck the oxygen out of the air.

"Is it always just the three of you here, Wren?" I asked.

As deep as my voice may be, it had all that was required to pierce the suffocating bubble of self-consciousness. The freedom from the unmentioned tension of silence melted over us.

"Oh no, I am only here for the season." Wren looked thoughtful. "I suppose I must live here longer than I do in London, if one considers how many months that is, but truth be told, William, it is never a chore to be here, for I much prefer it."

"Of what I have seen, I have to agree. I imagine it would be splendid in the warmer months. But I wonder, Wren, why a young lady such as yourself would be all the way out here when there is a season to be enjoyed?"

Curiosity had loosened my tongue and erased the barrier I had tried to place between us. I could not understand how a woman as lovely as she was not married. Perhaps she and I were not so dissimilar, desiring love in a marriage rather than what our parents demanded of us.

Surely that was not so rare?

A knock on the door thwarted her chance to answer, leaving me disappointed, yet when Wren let out a breath, she gave the distinct impression she was almost relieved not to answer. "Come in," she called.

"Charles and the doctor are back," Rose announced.

Quickly, Wren stood. "Here we are, William." Her eyes confirmed she was thankful for the intrusion, for it had saved her from revealing something she obviously wasn't willing, or perhaps ready, to reveal. "The doctor will be able to have a look at your injuries, then hopefully we can get you better."

Before Wren stepped out of the room, she turned quickly, her eyes soft and questioning. "Think about what I have said, William. You do not have to leave so quickly." With that, she turned back, leaving the doctor and I alone.

"I am afraid, Mr Darlington, you will not be fit to travel for at least another six weeks. You must remain here."

The doctor's skin was purpling with frustration as I pestered him profusely to offer another solution. The thought of being idle for six weeks irritated me, not to mention how much of a nuisance I would be to my new hosts when I had arrived uninvited. "Surely a carriage ride and a train ride would not be an issue, doctor? What damage am I likely to do with just those?"

The doctor raised a single eyebrow and stared down his long nose at me. "Tell me, Mr Darlington, how did you say you received these injuries again?"

He smiled smugly as his point hit right between my eyes. He already knew how my severely sprained ankle came to be and was simply rubbing salt into the very nasty wound.

"Point taken, doctor. I concede to your advice," I snarled. "However, I am not sure it will be pleasant news to the people out there." I nodded at the door.

"Oh, never fear on that score, Mr Darlington. Miss Davenport has already expressed that you are most welcome to stay, which I have no doubt you are already aware of. So, I will hear no more arguments or excuses. You must recover. If you do not, then it may result in a need for surgery. Or worse still, sir, amputation." The doctor smiled wickedly as he taunted my bad mood. "I only jest, sir, about the amputation, but you really must rest."

I flomped back on the pillow as the doctor closed the door behind him. I'd spent so much time believing that if I told myself the hideous swelling was nothing much whilst making definite plans so I could leave my poor hosts in peace, then that would be exactly what would happen, yet the doctor had spoken, and I had suddenly found my stubbornness sparring with my rationality. It was only when Wren returned, followed by Rose and the vicar, did I realise that rationality appeared to have an army.

"That settles it, duck," Rose quipped. "You are to stay here until that ankle of yours is all better. That's right, ain't it, Wren?"

Wren stood behind her. There was a twinkle in her eyes as she absentmindedly twiddled with a loose strand of hair. "Yes, William, that is correct. Of course, you are not a prisoner here, but you heard what the doctor said, and I have already told you that you are welcome here."

The older lady glanced sideways at Wren. "We'll leave you to it, duck. Come on, Charles, I'll make that cup of tea, and we have some freshly baked biscuits, too, like I promised." Rose's voice faded as she walked away, chattering to the vicar.

"It seems that you have won on this occasion, Miss Davenport," I smiled.

"Surely it is not so bad to stay here at The Aviary?" she asked, running her hands over the bookshelf.

"Of course not, Wren. I am just one of those who dislikes being a burden, that is all."

"Please be assured that you are not a burden, not to any of us here. It is a pleasure to meet new people and spend time with them. Although one does not need to throw oneself under a carriage to be introduced." Her shoulders bobbed up and down as she began to chuckle lightly, then let out the most endearing soft snort at the end. "Oh, heavens. I do apologise; I did not mean to make that sound. Oh, how embarrassing."

I had no control over the grin that spread across my face. Her laughter and pleasing ways had erased any tension from my predicament. "Please do not be embarrassed. I think it's rather endearing."

She clamped her lips together as she suppressed a coy smile. "Piglets snort, William, not young ladies," she grinned, brushing down the front of her indigo gown.

"Well, that is a shame because I quite like it."

A flush of crimson peeked out from under the lace trim of her neckline as she swiftly diverted the conversation to that of my injuries. "You know, I can't say I am not relieved that you are staying, William. We may not know each other very well, but the thought of you having another accident out there and we know nothing of it... well, it doesn't bear thinking about. You never know, William, we may become firm friends, and I would like that very much. That is, of course, if it is agreeable with you?"

"I think I would like that, Wren. Yes, I would like that very much."

Chapter Thirteen

Wren

Leaving William alone in his bedchamber and I dangerously alone with my thoughts, insecurities flooded my body in a wave of shame. They grabbed me by the throat as I was bombarded by a million questions until my time with our dark-haired and blue-eyed guest became distorted in my mind. A taunting finger of doubt criticised everything—the things I had said, the way I moved, the expressions on my face—until I found myself wanting to go back to him and ask whether everything I had been thinking was true.

Knowing that for me to return to his bedchamber so that he may offer me words to appease my insecurities would indeed seem quite unhinged, I ceased walking, my feet frozen beneath me, fixed to the spot. Inhaling, I uncurled the tightly knotted fists my hands had become. My palms stung where my fingernails had pressed into the soft pads. Acutely aware of the pinch, I held on to the lifeline it offered me as it reminded me to stay within the present and distance myself from the past. I was desperately aware of the power the past, and all that it contained, had over me. It was controlling and relentless, always marring the present. Deciphering between the two is difficult, to say the least. It is like separating sand from salt. Salt being the present, the one substance that is said to ward off evil yet can also be lost quite easily in the shedding of a tear.

As my breathing slowed, so too did my mind. The memories that had scattered like pieces of a puzzle slowly found their way to where they belonged, and I could finally remember the undistorted truth.

My body cooled as the built-up heat of shame dissipated. *William did not think I was strange, nor did I say anything that would alter that.* I did not know where my confidence had come from, enabling me to speak with him as easily as I had, but it was... *How can I possibly put into words how it felt?* It was *different, freeing,* and bordering upon the word *glorious.* To be around William put me at ease, even with the strange flutter of happiness in my chest that I could not tame. He made me feel important and appreciated.

The ease of his delightful company had apparently unlocked something in me that I never knew existed. Had I always been so forthright, or had I been waiting for the right moment for the courageous part of my soul to be uncaged? My future did not have to be as dismal as I had come to believe. There was the tantalising taste of a new future on the tip of my tongue, and I must confess I enjoyed it.

William and I grew more and more comfortable in each other's company with each passing day, and by the fifth day, I found myself looking forward to spending the evening by his side.

"I'll take it to William," I offered, sliding the tray from Rose's fingers a little too eagerly.

"I thought you might," she chuckled.

I grinned, ignoring the natural rouge her words had planted on my cheeks. "He is good company, that is all, Rose," I insisted. "Besides, whilst I am in there," I continued, pointing down the corridor. "You and Charles have some time to yourselves without me playing the odd one out."

"If you say so, duck," she teased, her eyes glittering with mischief.

"I do," I replied, the corners of my mouth twitching as I turned away. I knew she didn't believe a word I had said, for that woman was quite open about her suspicions. Sometimes a little too open, but, thankfully, she knew when to curb her vocal teasing when William was close enough to hear. The prospect of convincing her of my detachment from William had long since passed, for if I didn't even believe the words I'd told myself, how was I to make others believe them?

"Ah, here she is, my very own personal nurse," William grinned mischievously.

"I would have to say I may be more of a maid, William, rather than a nurse," I scolded playfully. "Of course, if you would prefer it, I can leave your supper in the kitchen so you may fetch it yourself." I gave him my best pointed glare, as though I were thoroughly offended at the suggestion of being his personal nurse, which of course I was not.

"No need for drastic measures, Miss Davenport, but please accept my apologies, for I meant no offence." William reached over and patted the seat next to him. "Won't you sit and keep this poor accident-prone fool company?"

Without uttering a word, I ventured around the edge of the room to where his large hand and broad fingers splayed on top of the bed. His other hand rested on his leg, pressing the blanket down, unintentionally revealing the contours of his muscular thigh. I tried to act nonchalant as he watched me manoeuvre, but the subtle scent of sandalwood, seducing my senses, was growing considerably in intensity with every step closer towards him.

Since William had arrived, the very fragrance had become his signature scent. How was I to hide the flip of excitement my heart made as I breathed it in? It was uncontrollable, and I was positive that it was blatantly obvious to onlookers, even from within my chest—an obvious clue as to what the simple act of being in his company did to me.

"Will it be cards, reading, or just my glittering personality tonight, Wren?" he asked with a wicked glint of pleasure in his eyes. "I do so love when you read, although Heathcliff is a bit of a scoundrel, and I can't say I approve of him, if I am being entirely honest."

"Oh, good heavens, you did hear. I am mortified!" I gasped. My hands flattened over the skirts of my dress awkwardly.

"Whatever for? You read it so beautifully. I simply tease you, Miss Davenport." His delicious smirk sent my heart into a foolish gallop.

"You must think me rather fanciful and dramatic, for I get rather carried away when I read alone. I did not think you could hear me."

I was surprised to see William blush. "Perhaps I heard a little," he offered.

"Why did you not stop me or at least let me know you were listening?"

"If I had let you know I was listening, would you have continued to read, Wren?" The man before me was quickly showing an understanding of me that I did not think possible. I had been so convinced that any emotions I may have had were always neatly tucked away beneath the permanent mask I wore, yet, with William questioning what I would have done if I'd known he could hear me read, I realised I must wear some of them like a vivid sash for all to see.

To be so discernible in such a short time caught me off guard, leaving only a half-hearted truth for an answer. "Perhaps, perhaps not," I mumbled, lowering myself into the chair.

"I believe you would have stopped and replaced it with some awkward small talk."

His words startled me. "Is that what I do, awkward small talk, I mean?" I was horrified to think that was how he viewed our conversations.

"Not now, no. Of course not, but doesn't everybody suffer the awful awkward bout of small talk when they meet people for the first time, or is it just me? ... Oh, heavens, it is just me," he mocked, clutching his chest. "I must be broken."

"You are not broken, silly," I sighed, grinning. "I only asked because I was not blessed with an abundance of confidence, I'm afraid. I wasn't given the chance."

William's smile faded, replaced with a look of sadness. I had opened my mouth and obliterated the light chatter with a thunderbolt of unnecessary truth.

"Anyway, I want to hear more about your life, William. It sounds terribly exciting," I encouraged. I was perspiring with the embedded shame of just being me.

"I think we should talk about you tonight, Wren. You know enough about me, and I know so little about you."

"You do not want to hear about me, William. I am quite boring, in all fairness."

"I very much doubt that, Miss Davenport."

There was something thrilling when he reverted back to my formal name. It always added a demanding tone to his voice that was difficult to deny. "Oh, do not doubt it, Mr Darlington, for I really do not have much to tell."

"I know you live in London, but you never speak of your family. They must miss you very much."

When my response came as a short burst of laughter from my lips, it caught me off-guard. I hadn't intended to reveal some of the resentment I had for my family, yet just that one reasonable statement had forced it out. I owed him an explanation. "I'm afraid it is quite the opposite, William. It is their pleasure to see the back of me."

I don't know when he had moved to place his hand on mine, but as I looked down at it, trying to avoid the intensity of his questioning gaze, there it was: thick, masculine fingers wrapped around my rather thin, feminine ones. I stared at the differences between our hands, marvelling at how they were different yet fit perfectly. His skin was rough, sending trails of goosebumps up my arm.

William didn't say anything as he continued to hold onto me, his fingers lacing through mine, lifting our hands up together to examine how one curled around the other in an embrace. My breath caught in my throat. The pattern of movements was broken suddenly as a single tear fell from my eye. I hadn't known it had existed until it splashed against the back of my hand. "Oh, good grief," I muttered, snatching my hand away. "I have something in my eye," I lied. "There are no ends to what one can get in one's eye in the countryside."

William's silence plagued my ears. What he was thinking, I had no idea, but it worried me, believing I had made an utter fool of myself.

Finally, he spoke, "I think I would miss you very much, Wren."

My throat constricted at his words. They had pushed me towards the precipice of a waterfall of tears. I tried in vain to cool the tidal wave of grief for the family I never had, yet it broke through every defence and poured in two parallel streams from my eyes.

"Please come here, Wren," William pleaded. "I cannot comfort you while you remain in the chair."

"I will be okay, I promise," I sniffed. "I am just a little fragile today, that is all."

"Nevertheless, Wren, please come closer."

Ashamed and fractured, I rose from the seat and sat closer at his side, the mattress softening beneath me.

And, as he wrapped his strong arms around me, twenty-three years of rejection finally broke me in two.

Chapter Fourteen

William

Lavender and chamomile, a fragrance as soothing as the young woman's company, tickled my sense of smell as I held her in my arms. Two fragrances combined to make one delicate scent, a fair representation of the feminine curves my hands wished to explore.

As I pulled her close against my chest in what I hoped was a soothing embrace, her shoulders bobbed up and down, her muscles bunching and relaxing with every sob. I was staggered by the obvious torment she had been subjected to, for I had never seen a woman cry as she did. My heart ached for her, this young woman so beaten by the world, yet no matter what she had endured, she had never thought twice about caring for me in my hour of need. How anyone could possibly want to hurt someone so obviously precious exceeded far beyond the boundaries of bewilderment.

Wren settled against my body, her tears soaking deep within the fabric of my shirt as the rapid rise and fall of her chest settled into a calm and steady pace. I cannot say how long she remained there, but eventually she shifted her body, and I reluctantly released her to the sounds of her issuing unnecessary, embarrassed apologies.

"I am so sorry, William. I am supposed to be looking after you, not unburdening my emotions upon you," she muttered.

Her lips were swollen into a delicate pout, and her eyes were rimmed with the same pink that kissed the tip of her nose. Seeing her so fragile made me want to pull her back into my arms. "You have no need to apologise, Wren. In fact, I am honoured that you were able to let yourself be vulnerable in my company. If anything, it makes me feel useful again."

A curious smile made her eyes twinkle as she tilted her head to one side.

"It is true. I have done nothing but lay in bed for days on end. You have saved me from throwing myself out of the window in despair at how useless I felt."

Wren's gaze lowered to her hands neatly positioned in her lap as her chestnut hair tumbled down the sides of her face. The silken tresses had freed themselves from several pins, falling in an exquisite curtain, attempting to cover her face, but alas, they could not hide the broad, beautiful smile that had broken across her equally beautiful features. She was beguiling and radiant, sitting only inches from me, making my arms feel terribly empty and cold.

"Thank you," she whispered. "I do not believe I have ever cried quite so passionately before. I'm afraid it appears I am one of those who hold onto their emotions until they burst out on poor, unsuspecting victims," she laughed, wiping the last tear away.

"Friends are never victims when the other needs them, Wren. I hope you consider me a friend."

The word 'friend', although not unpleasant, felt strange on my tongue as I spoke it aloud. I had friends, plenty of them in fact, but I had never looked at them in the way I found myself looking at her, nor did my heart pound in their presence the way it did in hers.

"Yes, I would like to think we are," she replied kindly.

Was I imagining the hint of disappointment in the tone of her voice?

I nodded my head in an awkward agreement, unable to speak against the discomfort of forcing my true, yet confusing, emotions into a tiny box. Labelling it as something as trivial as a friendship was inadequate, leaving a bitter taste in my mouth, but to confess that I viewed her as so much more so soon, would only cause damage to what I hoped would be the beginning of something special. Wren had very little regard for herself, and if I waded in singing her praises all at once, there was no doubt in my mind that I would only end up pushing her further away. She was a once-in-a-lifetime blessing, and I would not risk losing her.

After what felt like hours, Wren finally spoke again. "I still feel extremely embarrassed to have cried in front of you, and by the looks of your shirt, all over you too," she grimaced, staring at the tear stains slowly drying on the cotton.

I waved my hand in the air as if to say it was nothing. "There is no need. If it makes you feel better, it is an old shirt, so please put it far from your mind."

"But that's just it, William, I can't forget it because it is my life." Wren stood and began to pace the floor. She fiddled with her fingers in an agitated fashion, deliberation set in her features, contemplating whether to expand on a matter that was obviously very serious to her.

I waited patiently, for fear of swaying her decision.

"You commented that my family must miss me while I am here, which of course is an understandable assumption," she began. "One would expect that to be the case, after all." The muscles around her jaw tightened as she clenched her teeth together, adamant to continue with what she needed to get off her chest. "But I can categorically say that they do not."

My heart lurched at the conviction of her words. "Not any of them?" I asked. The tone of my voice had elevated by the appalled disbelief I couldn't hide from her.

"Well, if there is anyone who might miss me a little, then it would be my youngest sister, Primrose, but she will be so busy with the season, I very much doubt she would give me a second thought." Wren took a deep breath. It staggered as it travelled into her lungs, then she closed her eyes.

The reaction trembling through her body emphasised the obvious pain that coincided with her thoughts. They chipped away at the strength she portrayed, a strength I had never seen in any young lady before.

She was far greater than courageous, but it only made my heart ache for her even more. I wanted to protect her, to ease the inevitable pain and burden of everything she'd had to endure.

How long had she suffered before she'd learned how to master the art of masking what must have cut her to the core?

I wanted to ask her again why she was not participating in the season, but I feared a question so direct would only have silenced her again.

As if she had read my mind, she continued, "You asked me why I did not participate in the season, but as I usually do, I avoided answering the question, only to be saved shortly after by the arrival of the doctor.

"It wasn't because I did not want to tell you, but more to the point, I was not sure if I could find the words to say it. But seeing as I have blubbered all over you in the most unladylike fashion, I feel it is only fair that I answer you. You see, I have never been offered the opportunity of a season."

Wren held up her hand to pause any questions I may have had. "I apologise, William. I do not mean to appear rude, but I fear that if I do not tell you without interruption, I will never be able to tell you at all.

"You see, William, the possibility of finding me a match in the matter of matrimony has never, and will never, be put on the table for me to accept. My mother forbids it, and my father is too weak to argue with her."

My mouth was agape in obvious shock at her family's cruelty. My expression appeared to amuse her, for when she looked at me, she chuckled.

"Why are you laughing, Wren?" I asked, astounded. "There is nothing funny about the way your family treats you. It's disgusting!" I was outraged, flabbergasted that these strangers that I had never met—nor ever wanted to meet—were so vile towards her.

"One must learn to make light of it, William. If I

don't, then they have won, and I will not let them win." A glimmer of anger flashed across her eyes. Pride swelled in my chest to witness the feisty outrage of the hidden warrior within her.

"You and Charles are the first people I have ever met outside of my immediate family and the household staff," she continued. "I am not allowed to leave the house in London other than to journey here, and when I do, I must take the servants' entrance, so I am not seen.

"To society, there is no Miss Wren Davenport. I simply do not exist."

Resentment raised her voice as she spoke. The actions of those who were supposed to have loved her had twisted and broken her heart, but she had risen up into the strong, formidable woman before me. However, like every other human, I knew she needed to feel cared for, to feel like she mattered.

Blast the doctor, I fumed, inching myself towards the edge of the bed. I would not sit idle while she stared at the wall, struggling with something I had never thought could exist. I wanted to go to her, and go to her, I damn well would.

Using the furniture for support, I lifted my body off the mattress and stood, following the line of neatly placed furniture and shelves around the room until my chest was only a few inches from her back.

Before I had the chance to offer words of comfort, Wren turned to face me. There was no surprise on her face to find me standing there. It was as though she had already sensed how close I was.

My breath brushed her cheek. It was the first time we had stood in front of one another. She was smaller than me, but by very little, I thought, as my eyes lowered to her lips.

"You should be in bed, William," she croaked. The air crackled in the few inches between us.

I did not reply, but simply looped my arm around her tiny waist and drew her in against me. "And you should never have been treated that way," I whispered. As I planted the kiss, I'd so desperately wanted to press against her lips, on the top of her head. It was then, I realised I never wanted to let her go.

Chapter Fifteen

Wren

My mind was a thief, for it robbed me of sleep until the early hours of the morning. My body ached to feel the warmth of William's embrace. My soul's unexpected longing had been like gunpowder inside my head, sending thoughts scattering in every direction until I could make neither hide nor hair of them. The unexpected, yet evident, craving to be near him, to be locked within his arms, left me cold and aching. Try as I might to conquer what seemed somewhat of an irrational reaction, my mind would not detach from the way his arms had felt around me, the memory taunting me for weeks on end. The seductive fragrance of sandalwood never left me, nor did I want it to, and when my mind could take no more, it finally relented to the persistent tug of sleep, submerging me into my dreams where they were filled with him.

The dreams were certainly not those I could divulge to Rose, for they were personal and went far beyond the bounds of propriety. Simply to remember them in private would make me blush, but to speak them aloud? Well, they were dreadfully scandalous indeed. In my own company, despite the natural rouge upon my cheeks, I did not have to hide the thoroughly wicked smile that would curl my lips. Perhaps I should not have confessed as much, but it is the truth.

William had unlocked something rather thrilling inside of me that, without being informed of such, I was subconsciously aware a lady must keep secret. The sensation of his body against mine, every contour of his chest revealed beneath the thin layer of his cotton shirt, sent tingles over every inch of my flesh and a delicious molten warmth deep into the centre of my core. Yet it wasn't merely those feelings that gratified me, for as he listened, absorbing my fears and frustrations so I wouldn't have to bear them alone, he had willingly offered me a sense of security I had not known before. I had never been held with such a gentle, unbreakable strength. I wondered whether it was elation that had tickled beneath my breastbone, for the emotions he returned were protective. I could have curled against his body and stayed there. His arms were the only place I had ever felt safe.

As bizarre as it may sound, the longer I remained outside of his arms, the stranger and more alone I felt. However, I do not mean I was lonely; it was rather more the case that something, or should I say someone, was missing. I craved the closeness of him as a plant craves water and sunlight, taking whatever I could get as we spent every day in each other's company.

At night, I would lay awake with a deep hunger for the touch of the man I knew I couldn't have. The closeness of his body had been intoxicating. It made me feel loved beyond words, but every time I dared to light a single candle of hope that a man like he could love someone like me, Mama's voice rang out in my head, dampening the air and snuffing it out, rendering me a slave to the belief that he would never see me the way I wished to be seen by him. Nobody could convince me that a man as wonderful as William could have eyes for me. Those piercing blue eyes were reserved for those who were perfect in body, those who were deemed eligible for the London season. He was my friend; he had told me as much. I would just have to accept that and make the most of the situation. He would be gone in a few weeks, and I very much doubted I would see him again.

The thought of his absence burned and twisted into the most frightful of stings that took my breath away.

"You're very quiet this morning, duck," Rose crooned, wrapping a woollen shawl around her shoulders. "You're not coming down with something, are you? You look rather peaky." Rose placed the back of her hand on my forehead. "You don't have a fever. Perhaps some sunshine will do you good."

"You needn't worry, Rose. I think I am just dreading the return to London, that's all. The time is going rather fast, and before we know it, I will be back in that carriage to return home and be locked up with my family again."

Although it was an excuse for why I was so quiet and deep in thought, the truth of it crashed into my stomach with the force of a boulder, only to intensify the lingering dread of never seeing William again. The very mention of home only brought forth what I was trying so hard to forget. I felt utterly nauseous from it all.

"You got the spring to get through yet, love," she smiled gently. "You said it was your favourite time of year at The Aviary. Why don't you see if William will take a walk with you?"

"Already planned," I replied, returning the smile.

William's name danced across the air without a single shadow marring its brilliance, reminding me of where I was and who I was with. The reassurance of his presence made me feel lighter and more at ease as I berated myself inwardly for being so pessimistic.

"The poor man is going crazy just pottering

around the cottage. As long as we are careful, his ankle should be okay," I continued. It was a beautiful day, and I longed to step outside to make the most of it.

"Do you want me to organise a picnic hamper for you both?" she asked kindly. "You should take a blanket and sit by the lake. The weather looks set to be pleasant for the entire day. It's perfect picnic weather."

"That's a wonderful idea, Rose. Thank you. I can prepare the food, though. You concentrate on your day and get yourself off to meet with Charles. William and I will be just fine." I waggled my eyebrows at her, teasing her about her date with Charles, hoping to lighten the mood. I was also desperately trying to avoid her usual attempts at deflecting the conversation from her and Charles, and then, no doubt, her proceeding with her rather indiscreet and quite regular method of matchmaking between William and I. To contemplate something more than friendship with the man my heart responded to with such fervour was dangerous to me. I needed to quash the silly notion of William and I as more than what I already knew, for I knew my heart would crumble at the hands of rejection, even if it was only ever unspoken.

"Did someone mention my name?" William grinned, his good nature announcing his presence.

My heart did a little somersault as his deep voice rumbled from the doorway. His broad shoulders filled the frame as his lips settled in a lopsided smile, oblivious to the funny little flutter of butterflies curling in my stomach; they only ever seemed to take flight whenever he was near.

As my eyes involuntarily, and quite leisurely, roved over his torso, my body practically swooning at the image of him in just his shirtsleeves and perfectly fitting breeches, I reprimanded myself for being so unnecessarily reactive every time I looked at him. On the final detour of my wayward eyes, they met with his. The twinkle at the centre of his piercing blue irises, beneath his usual endearingly dishevelled mop of black hair, was mischievous and wanton, sending a wave of heat from my stomach, crashing over my chest, and up my neck until finally it sat as two separate beacons on my pale cheeks for all who cared to look. I was practically on fire with something sinful. Shame quashed it quickly as it threaded through my thoughts, reminding me I was being ridiculous, for it was a girlish fantasy for him to ever look at me with reciprocated desire.

"Well, I'll be off then, shall I?" Rose chuckled, returning a waggling set of eyebrows of her own. She had seen everything, and if anyone had the privilege to know my thoughts without me uttering a single word, it was her.

"Enjoy your day, Rose. Hopefully we will see you and Charles at supper." My voice trembled, as did my hands.

Rose stepped forward and wrapped her steady, warm fingers around mine. "You will, duck." She leaned in to give me a peck on the cheek, simultaneously taking the opportunity to whisper in my ear. "Remember just how perfect you are, Wren. I'll say it until my dying breath if that is what it takes for you to believe me because it is the truth."

I inhaled, as though her words were a remedy to cure all the self-doubt vibrating in my bones. "I'll try. I promise," I replied.

"That's my girl." Rose said one last goodbye to both William and I, then headed out for the day.

"Is this the beginning of a picnic, I spy?" William walked around the table; his footsteps uneven, careful not to place too much pressure on his ankle.

"It is. It's a lovely day, and I think we both deserve some time away from the cottage." I turned to the basket I'd placed on the table and began gathering up several items of food to put in it. I wasn't quite ready to look at him after the shameless display of desire I had involuntarily revealed only moments before.

"Oh, Miss Davenport, what about propriety?" William teased, feigning shock and horror. "What will the neighbours say?"

A bubble of joy pushed up from my centre, greeting the air in my rather embarrassing snort of amusement as it was expelled from the back of my throat and nose. The unseen, devilishly handsome smile I knew he was wearing across his equally handsome face was contagious and most definitely the trigger for such an outburst.

I'd always despised being teased, but I had come to realise in such a short amount of time that it really all depended upon who it was that was doing the teasing. With William, it was as sweet and golden as honey, like that of affection, but with my sister, Gladys, it always dripped with the bitter venom of spite.

"What neighbours might that be, William?" I asked, stifling a smile of my own as I kept my head down and carried on packing the basket.

"The ones that hide in the bushes, Miss Davenport. Please do not tell me you have not seen them."

"I don't believe I have, Mr Darlington. How frightfully nosey they are." My lips gave in to the insistent twitch of amusement, tugging at the corners. Keeping a subdued expression was a pure waste of my time when I thoroughly enjoyed those moments with him. "And as for propriety, Mr Darlington," I continued, meeting his gaze, "one cannot be expected to adhere to such trivial matters when one has not been taught such things, can they?" I grinned.

Of course, I was well aware of what was required of a young lady, but even though I had never put any of the rules and regulations into practice for lack of outside socialisation, I knew I did not give a fig for it. I had been couped up for far too long, and there was not a chance in the entire world that I was going to stop myself from spending some time with such a dear companion.

"That is an extremely fair and reasonable point, Miss Davenport. How can one possibly argue with it?"

"I do not believe they can, Mr Darlington," I replied, tilting my chin as I feigned haughty obstinance.

My skin tingled as William's hand guided my own through the crook of his elbow. His eyes were alive with glee as his glorious lips sat crooked in a devilish and mischievous smirk upon his face.

"Let us be on our way then, Miss Davenport," he beamed. "We must be gone before propriety police catch up with us and lock us up for life."

"Yes, let's."

Outside, the sun dazzled the earth with its glittering golden hue. William and I walked side by side, arms no longer entangled in a companionable link as they had once been, for as pleasant as it was, the joining of our arms ceased to be comfortable as we ambled over the uneven earth. With William leaning considerably on his temporary cane and the subtle limp in my own steps, it was neither wise nor viable. Instead, unconsciously, our bodies remained close, keeping contact with the brush of our arms, the tap of our hips, and the intermittent touch of our fingertips.

William's ankle was taking longer to heal than we had expected, and the doctor was quite adamant that William remained with us at The Aviary. A little exercise was permitted, but he was urged to refrain from doing anything rash that may hinder the process of recovery or damage his ankle further.

As selfish as it was, I could not help my relief when the doctor had informed us that William was to remain at The Aviary. The guilt of excitement, and excitement itself, had burgeoned within my chest when I had heard the news, for it meant we would have more time together.

Clouds draped across the sky in stretched white lace. The countryside was alive with a myriad of lavenders, blues, yellows, reds, and greens.

"My favourite season," I whispered, tilting my face towards the sky. "This, the glorious weather, the peace, and the undeniable beauty laid out before us, makes me very glad to be excluded from the season. You would never see such a magnificent scene in London."

"I certainly cannot argue with that, Wren. It is indeed a beautiful sight to behold. What I would give to have the talent to paint such splendour, but I fear I simply would not do it justice." William looked thoughtful as he appeared to bask in the scenery as I had been.

As the sun stroked a finger over his hair, a blue as deep as the midnight sky caressed the curve of a lock, positioned neatly to one side on top of his head. I had never seen black hair with such a splendid colour, a hue secretly woven into the strands only to ever be revealed by the light. There was no denying that William was intriguing—a book filled with wonders that I so desperately wanted to read.

"I didn't know you were an artist, William. That must be wonderful," I offered.

"I don't speak of it much. My father disapproves wholeheartedly. One would say I am a bit of a secret artist," he smirked.

"Secret?" I questioned. Sadness crept over me to think that one would have to hide such a talent when it really should be celebrated like those of the greats.

Perhaps William was one of the greats, I thought, but he had not been fortunate enough to have been given the opportunity to be discovered. That thought alone was enough to make one weep.

"Please do not misunderstand me, Wren, for if I could, I would shout it from the rooftops and let everyone know how much I love it, much like I would shout about what we-" William stiffened, clearing his throat as though he had said something he shouldn't have.

His awkwardness bled into my own body as I searched his face, willing him to finish what he had wanted to say about us.

I had foolishly waited in vain, for he responded with no more than the pink peeking over the edge of his collar as he reverted back to the subject of his art. "Forgive me, I was getting carried away. What I meant to say is that I have become tired of the looks of disapproval from my father and the lectures that usually accompany any announcement of what, or should I say who, I really am."

"Well, I think being an artist must be sublime. I believe it is something that should be celebrated rather than scorned. Perhaps we can get some supplies for you while you are here?" I suggested. I despised seeing him so discouraged as he appeared, and all as a result of the opinion of one man. One terribly ignorant man.

"Perhaps, but I do not know how much longer I am able to stay." William exhaled a troubled sigh. "Believe me when I say I have grown quite comfortable here with you, and I am reluctant to leave. Sadly, however, I am aware of my duty to my father, and I shall have to write to him soon. If I do not, he will track me down eventually, and I would imagine his temper will not be something you would wish to witness.

"When I do write to him—and I will need to eventually—he will undoubtedly demand I return to London."

My heart began a slow descent into my stomach at his words. I knew his return to London was inevitable, but to hear him say it made it somehow painfully real. Having William at The Aviary was like a wonderful dream, and I did not want to wake from it yet.

"You won't leave until your ankle is better, will you?" I could feel my throat constrict with sadness as I squeezed my voice through my airway to form the necessary syllables and sounds upon my tongue.

William slipped his hand reassuringly into mine. The brush of his skin upon my fingers sent delicate crackles of electricity up my arm until they settled as a pleasant glow in my chest. "If you permit it, Wren, I shall return here to visit you."

"You know I would permit it, William, but I too have to return home. I will be leaving here in June."

"I shall visit you there too."

"I don't exist there, William. Even if you called

on me, Mama would deny knowing anything of a lady called Wren Davenport."

A glimmer of anger at my mother's denial of me flashed across his face. I had seen it before, when my mother was mentioned. I recognised it for the solidarity that it was. "Can you not stay here? At least at The Aviary, you will not have to deal with the likes of your mother. Here you are able to live as you wish."

I stared down at our hands. They fitted together perfectly, as if our palms and fingers were always meant to be entwined. Sighing, I turned my gaze to his searching eyes. I wondered whether there was more I could do to save what we had. I could no longer deny what was so undeniably obvious. I was not so delirious as to imagine the way he held my hand or the look of admiration and fondness he bestowed upon me. "I have wished for nothing else since the moment I returned to London last year, William," I replied. "Sadly, I have never been courageous enough to broach the subject, but that does not mean it has not plagued me every day. Perhaps when I do return, I will ask Papa. I will risk it, even if it is simply to see you again. However, I must tread carefully, William, for I fear sending my request in writing will only alert my mother, and if that happens, then my dream will be over before it even starts."

Chapter Sixteen

William

"Sadly, I have never been courageous enough to broach the subject, but that does not mean it has not plagued me every day. Perhaps when I do return, I will ask Papa. I will risk it, even if it is simply to see you again. However, I must tread carefully, William, for I fear sending my request in writing will only alert my mother, and if that happens, then my dream will be over before it even starts."

Wren's eyes glittered with unshed tears as she spoke of the barriers and obstacles that always seemed to hinder her in life. It pained me to see her so trapped when the world needed people like her to brighten it, and, from the way she practically glowed with joy in the light of the spring season, she clearly needed the world.

"Perhaps I can hand deliver the letter for you?" I offered. I was eager to make sure that the letter reached her father without interruption or interference.

"You would do that for me?"

I couldn't understand how she could look so surprised by my offer. *Did she not realise how deeply I felt for her? Were the stolen touches and embraces not enough to make her see that I was falling in love with her?*

"I would do anything for you, Wren," I announced, far more boldly than I believed I could.

Placing my fingers gently on her elbow, I guided her to slowly turn and face me. Words were one way to convince her of my truth, but I knew I needed her to see it in my eyes. She had spent so long believing she was all that her family had told her, I couldn't let her go on believing such cruel nonsense.

Despite the awkward walking support, I remained steady in front of her. "I think a lot of you, Wren Davenport, "I began. My heart pounded in my chest as I nervously took my first step towards voicing only the mere surface of my feelings that had blossomed over the past few weeks. Words left unsaid would not convince her of just how precious she was. She needed to hear it; that much was obvious. "Probably more than I have a right to," I continued.

I knew my words had reached Wren in the way I'd hoped they would when she blushed profusely beneath the freckles I hadn't noticed before. The sun had teased them to the surface in the most mystical and alluring way. “You are so beautiful, yet it confuses me how you do not know this.”

Wren stood still, her body taut with only a gentle sway as I trailed my finger along her petite jawline, tilting her face as I lowered my own towards her. Silence, only hindered by a soft, staggered feminine breath, bridged the gap between us. Her eyes searched mine, faces merely an inch apart. “Do you understand, Wren, that it is hard for me to just be your friend?”

The delicate young woman gasped, stepping back as though I had burned her, but before she could leave me completely, I looped my free arm around her waist, preventing her from walking away. “I do not mean it in the way you assume,” I soothed, pulling her close. “You misunderstand me, for what I was trying to tell you is that I cannot be just your friend, Wren, because I believe—no, forgive me, I do not just believe; I know I am falling in love with you.”

“Me?” she breathed. “You are falling in love with me?”

“Yes. Is that so hard to believe?”

Wren studied my face, confused yet hopeful all at once. My heart was teetering on the edge of a void, overlooking a chasm of despair, and I was praying she would not let it fall into that dreadful darkness.

“It is not something I dared to contemplate,” she

whispered, as though she were talking only to herself. "Do you really feel that way about me?" she asked, still not daring to believe me.

"Good grief, woman, of course I do. How could I not? You are kind, caring, funny, and, not to mention, utterly beautiful. No man in their right mind would be able to resist you."

"I hardly dared hope," she whispered. She brightened as though a candle had been lit behind her powder blue eyes. The light seemed to pour out of her as she kept her attention on me. It brightened every line of her features as a smile curled her lips. "I know that I feel the same way about you," Wren continued, her voice growing stronger. "But I have not allowed myself to ever imagine it would be reciprocated."

"Believe me, Wren, when I say it is reciprocated right here." I clasped her hand in mine and placed her palm over where my heart beat proudly.

She simply stared at the centre of my chest as though it were the first time she had noticed it, her expression altering from one of wonder to one of pure defeat. "It will never be accepted, William. We will never be accepted."

Nothing seemed to convince her for long. Not even the sincerity of my words. Every hope she had was soon washed away, drowned out by the tidal waves of her past. Her mother's words were much louder than my own. They were deeply ingrained in her. Any fool could see that she would need time, if not forever, to erase them. It didn't matter how long it would take me to make her see, for I would never let her live with a lie.

"Let us walk, Wren. I think I need to tell you more about my life and who I am. Maybe then you can decide whether other people's opinions really matter to me."

We walked in silence most of the way, never releasing one another as our fingers intertwined as though the other would disappear if we dared to release them. In the silence of her company, with nothing but the harmony of nature, I had decided that perhaps the letter to my father could wait for a few more days. I couldn't bear the possibility of him barging in on what we had, only to obliterate it with his ridiculous demands.

What I had with Wren was too dear to me to risk. I could only imagine what plans he had drawn up with regards to my future in my absence, which begged the question as to where did he think I had been all these weeks? Surely, he could not have been as gullible as to truly believe that I had continued my residency in Kent.

"It is not far now," Wren smiled nervously.

Dear Lord, I wanted to shake the audacity of her mother and sister from their very bones for stealing the confidence she should be bathing in. I wanted to bury my fist in her father's face for being so pathetic and weak as to not stand his ground and protect his daughter the way a father should. It shocked me to feel so much venom, as I have never been a violent man, but the mere thought of her family drew out more hatred from me than I ever knew I was capable of.

"I shan't write to my father straight away. I think perhaps it is better to leave it a few days, if that is agreeable with you?" The awkward silence that hung between us was killing me. I couldn't bear to leave her in Somerset with doubts as to whether she would see me again. I didn't want her to rebuild the walls and protective barriers, I had fought so hard to break down. For all I could tell, she may have wanted to forget me, so she did not have to risk her heart. If only I could convince her that I wasn't a risk and that I would spend my life trying to make her happy, if only she would let me.

Wren nodded. "That is up to you, William. I do not expect anything from you."

She seemed a little cold as I watched her place the first brick of the wall between us back in its place.

"Please don't do that, Wren," I pleaded.

"Do what?" she asked innocently.

"You are pulling away from me."

"You have my hand, William," she laughed, her smile failing to reach her eyes. "I am not going anywhere."

"That is not what I meant, Wren. We have spent every day together for weeks, and I would like to believe that you would not put a barrier between us now. I would also like to believe that you trust me with what I have told you of my feelings."

Wren placed the picnic hamper on the ground, then spread the large blanket across the slightly damp grass.

Dropping my walking aid to the floor beside the woven fabric, I lowered myself awkwardly to the ground. "Sit with me, please," I begged.

Wren lowered herself at my side, her dress billowing briefly in a cloud as she sat. "You know, I do not mean to create a barrier between us, William, for I would love to never have doubts of what you say. It is not that I do not believe you; it is to think a man as handsome and incredibly wonderful as you could consider someone like me as more than what I am, which is unbelievable, if that makes sense?"

"Someone like you?" I knew what she had meant by the way she had accentuated the words, 'someone like me'. I would not allow her to doubt her worth. "Heavens, how can you say or think so low of yourself? If you could only see the woman I see before me, you would never question it."

My heart ached as it seemed to reach out for

her, tugging at the centre of my chest as though my heart no longer belonged to me. It wanted to be with her, as did I. "I wish you knew how many young ladies my father has tried to push me into marriage with. Each one of them, terribly shallow beneath their pretty exteriors.

"Dresses and polite conversation leave a man cold. I have never considered one of those ladies, even though my father has bellowed and threatened on every occasion.

"I want love, Wren. I do not care for riches nor social standing. I do not care about any of that. So, believe me when I tell you, I do not consider you to be more than who you are. I consider you to be every inch of the beautiful, incredibly wonderful lady who I have been given the honour and privilege to know. I consider you to be exactly who you are, and I am indeed very fond of that woman."

My fingers played over her hands, softly trailing her fair skin in tentative caresses. She was struggling to absorb anything beyond the cage she had been placed in from such a young age. "I can see that is hard for you to believe," I continued. "I would imagine that any person who has had to endure such relentless abuse as you have throughout their life would be very much in the same frame of mind, but if I promise you that I will endeavour to convince and remind you every day of your true worth, Miss Davenport, would you please give me a chance to prove it to you by allowing me to court you?"

"Oh, heavens, William, you will have me a blubbering fool. My eyes are already leaking," she chuckled softly.

I grazed my thumb over her velvety skin as I wiped away a tear rolling down her cheek. "Will you do me the honour of allowing me to court you, Wren? Please do not break this man's heart. I do not think I can bear it."

"Yes, William," Wren croaked.

"Can you repeat that, please?" I smiled. I wanted to hear her repeat the words I had been hoping for.

"Yes, William, I give you permission to court me."

Before she could change her mind, I weaved my arm around her waist and pulled her closer, pressing my lips against hers. All the tension in her body vanished as she melted against me. She tasted of hope, happiness, and more than that, she felt like home. It is the only way I can describe the way she affected me in that moment. She was everything I'd longed for all at once, and I knew that one day she would be my wife.

Chapter Seventeen

Wren

Elation, nerves, excitement, and fear. They were just a few of the emotions exploding within me as William's declaration hung in the air, teasing my ears with their beauteous melody, penetrating my body, and nestling at the very heart of me. I never believed for one moment that I would be living in my own romantic novel. That was what it was to me, for there was an overwhelming apprehension that the page would be turned to one with a cruel twist, or someone would slam the book shut and I would be locked out of my own life, my dream, forever.

William's revelation encouraged me to hope, daring me to believe in him, and in doing so, I felt as though I was walking over exceedingly thin ice, praying it would not shatter beneath my feet.

I should imagine that were another young lady told that they possessed William's dearest affections, they would not question one bit of it, but I was not, nor am I, that hypothetical young lady. I had lived my life as the subject of mockery, forever aware of my imperfections. One cannot expect someone to simply dismiss all that has scarred them so deeply. You see, the worst scars one can have are those that cannot be seen. No one can truly understand how deep they are buried within the flesh, for they can never be revealed other than in an explanation, and even then, one has to know the right words to say in order to portray just how painfully ugly they are.

When I was a little girl, I'd watch myself in the mirror. I would smile when Mama was not watching and bounce up and down, innocently fascinated by my ringlets as they'd stretch and curl in time with every movement. I never knew then that there were those who only focused on my spine to determine whether I was pretty or not, nor did I realise that even the dearest in my life were also some of those people.

That all changed quite dramatically the day my parents decided to take a family outing without me. As a child, it was a natural assumption that it was to be the first family trip for all of us, delayed only by the apprehension that Gladys had previously been too young to behave under their strict instructions. I had always been an obedient child and had been very excited to spend the day with Mama and Papa. The very idea of walking proudly beside my parents through the park on a

Sunday afternoon thrilled me, but when they'd left without me, I was devastated. I thought I had done something wrong, that I was a naughty child, for I couldn't understand why they would take Gladys and not me. On that day, my world veered onto the path I was destined to take alone. It was the day I stared in the mirror for the last time. I was no longer beautiful with pretty curls; I had become the girl that would be laughed at, disliked, and mocked because that is what Mama had told me. *That* is what she made me believe.

One does not forget such words. They become the truth if they are repeated enough. To believe them was as simple as breathing.

The river rippled with life from within its depths as William continued to gaze at me. The trickling harmony whispered in the cool breeze as he waited for me to absorb his words, desperate for me to believe him when he said that everything I had been taught was nothing more than a lie.

Tension laced amongst my thoughts, pinched every muscle in my face as the gates to my mind flung wide open. New, exciting possibilities were charging in, trying to dispel the past, yet they were merely being tainted with the impurities of self-loathing as my mother screamed to be heard. My back and shoulders ached from the stress and confusion. No matter how warm and soothing the sun was above us, it was not enough to loosen my limbs.

William lifted his hand to cup my face, brushing his thumb over a tear snaking down my cheek. His touch was warm and kind. Now that it was meant only for me, I didn't want to live without it. "Yes, William." The words bled from my lips so easily. My heart had begged me to let go of apprehension, willing me to take a leap of faith on the man before me.

"Can you repeat that, please?" His eyes creased in the corners as a smile lit up his face. I couldn't believe this man wanted me, but there he was, like the sunshine, bright and beautiful.

"Yes, William, I give you permission to court me." My lips curled happily on my face, only to be loosened by an involuntary gasp as he scooped me in towards him and covered my lips with his own.

As his perfect mouth moved against mine with some considerable expertise, a scintillating, delicious heat crawled over my body, melting me into a puddle within his arms. Our breaths mingled together as my body pressed greedily against his. All sense of propriety was dismissed from consideration as the most intoxicating, overwhelming desire engulfed me.

A low guttural growl emanated from William's throat as he broke away from the kiss, his lips brushing over my cheek and trailing along my jawline. The vibration of the perfect sound scattered goose pimples down my neck and beneath the fabric of my clothes. A little embarrassed, I was thankful that the cotton hid the newly discovered and thoroughly exciting reaction—one I never knew my body was capable of.

"I think we should eat, Miss Davenport, before I ruin you." His breath tickled my ear with the low rumble of his chuckle as he lowered his face, burying it into the arch of my neck, where he placed one last kiss.

Speechless as my body trembled, I merely sat, my mind reeling from his touch, wanting so much more.

The morning passed in a glorious dream-like blur of easy conversation as we sat by the river. And, when the chatter failed to flow, it was not because we did not have plenty to say, for we simply chose to speak in the unspoken words of stolen and tender kisses.

The safety of his arms was an impenetrable barrier, warding off my insecurities, for I could not deny the solidity of them curled around my body. Terrified I would wake up at any moment, I nestled closer. Touch was all that tied me to the truth. I had hoped that the more time we spent together, the surer I would be that a man like he could eventually love me as I wished to be loved, but no matter how hard I tried, I could not shake the dark grey shadow of doubt that always seemed to linger at my shoulder.

"You are questioning everything again, aren't you?" William took my hand in his. It seemed I could not hide anything from him.

"It is not that I doubt you, William. I cannot explain how thoroughly etched my past is within me. I would love to see myself as you see me, to forget my imperfections."

"You do not possess any imperfections, Wren."

I placed my head on his shoulder as we both stared across to the other side of the river. The sun was lower, glittering between the gaps in the trees as though it were spying on us.

A breath puffed from my lips with humour at the irony of it all. "Where were you when I was a little girl, William? I would have loved to have you by my side, assuring me my mother was wrong. Perhaps then I would have no hardship in believing you now."

William wrapped his arm around my waist as I snuggled even closer still. "I wish I was there too," he soothed. "But because I was not, I hope in time I may convince you enough so you may never doubt yourself again."

"As do I, William," I sighed as he guided me down onto the blanket beneath him. His lips brushed gently over mine in a delicate kiss. "Are you trying to distract me, Mr Darlington?"

"No, my darling. I am merely trying to prove my point."

"Psst, there's grass in your hair, missy," Rose whispered as she walked past me in the hallway. "I take it you had a good time?"

My face ached with a grin that nothing could dampen. Every time I thought of William, an overpowering sense of joy rushed from the ends of my toes, up my legs, through my torso, and into my chest, where it spread like the rapids of a river to the tips of my fingers until I thought it would burst me open and spill across the room in the most amazing rush of pure light. "We did, Rose," I blushed happily. "Did you and Charles have a lovely time?"

"We did, but I don't think we had as much fun as you." Rose winked sneakily at me, so Charles couldn't see the secret understanding between us. "Is William resting?"

"Yes. We thought it best after walking on his ankle."

"Quite right, duck. Let's have a cup of tea, and you can fill me in on what's been happening whilst we've been out."

"Are you staying for a cup of tea, Charles?" I asked, watching him loiter at the doorway.

"I'm afraid I will have to get back to the vicarage. I have some letters to write and some church matters to attend to. But I will see you soon," he assured me.

"Of course. You know you are welcome here anytime, Charles. I shall leave you two to it." I turned away and headed to the kitchen to give them some time alone. It looked very much like Rose had some news of her own.

The amber sun kissed the interior of the kitchen in a deep orange hue as it bled through the windows, touching every surface. Evening was drawing in, and my body ached for my bed, whether I would manage to sleep or not. I filled the kettle, placed it on the hob, then arranged the teacups on the table with a plate of biscuits. If I needed to drag every fine detail from Rose, those biscuits I had made were paramount, for I would need to ply her quite liberally with them to loosen her tongue. They would also come in extremely useful when one was avoiding answering any rather awkward and embarrassing questions she may have had for me.

"Ah, lovely, I am parched, Wren; I don't mind telling you," Rose beamed as she headed straight for the table and plonked herself down into her usual seat. "So, let's hear all about your day," she encouraged with a mischievous grin.

"Oh no, you don't, Mrs Cornish. I made the tea and biscuits; you do the talking." I smiled, satisfied with my answer, knowing she could not argue with me.

"Mrs Cornish, is it, missy?"

"Don't deflect, Rose. Tell me what you did today." I sipped my tea. The heat hit the back of my throat with a glorious burn, washing away the smoke from the lit hearth after it had been happily settling there in a cloying residue.

"What would you like to know exactly, duck?"

"Oh, I have to prise it out of you, do I? Okay, if that is the case, my first question is: Where did you go first?" I wanted to ease into the conversation gently, so she would let slip every single detail without missing a crumb.

"Well, we first walked to the vicarage. He has a lovely home. I never thought a man could keep his home looking so spotless. He says he don't have a maid, but I ain't sure I believe him," she laughed. There was an obvious twinkle, giving me hope.

"Did you meet Bernard? The farmer?"

"No, his wife said he was at the market, but I did meet a few of the parishioners. They're lovely folk, Wren. No airs and graces, just normal men and women like you and me. Maybe you could walk to church with me one Sunday?"

"Perhaps," I offered. "But I fear we are going off subject here, Rose. You wouldn't be doing that on purpose, would you?"

"Who me, love? Never." Rose placed her cup on the table, the smile dimming on her face. "There is something I need to talk to you about, duck."

"Go on," I encouraged, a little nervous. I wondered whether she had received some demand from London, ordering her home only to leave me here.

"Well... Oh, good 'eavens, I feel terrible for what I am about to say, but if you don't want me to, I won't; you know I won't."

"Do what, Rose? You have me quite concerned." And I was, I was petrified. My heart felt as though it was very well near ready to plummet into my stomach with the dread stirring up inside my gut.

"Charles has asked me to stay on here with him when you return to London."

My heart twisted briefly beneath my ribcage. It felt selfish to feel so upset that she would wish to remain here. Who wouldn't want to? I know I did. "That is splendid news, Rose. Does that mean you will be living with him as man and wife?"

"Yes, duck," she said, lowering her head to better see my eyes as my face was tilted slightly down towards my tea. "You know I won't leave you if you don't want me to, love."

Rose placed her hand over mine. Her papery skin was soft and cool as I turned my hand over and wrapped it around hers. "I want you to be happy, Rose. If marrying Charles is what makes you happy, then I am glad, very glad indeed," I smiled. "I will be back here again next season, no doubt, and even if Mother and Father refuse, now that I know that you will be here, I shall sneak away in the dead of night just to pay you a visit. They will be none the wiser until the morning, and by then it will be far too late. It is not as though Mama would willingly claim I am her daughter in public now, is it?" My mouth pinched into a smile as the image of my mother, in all her anger, flashed through my mind. I pushed it away. It was not a time to linger in my memories, for my dearest friend was getting married. "Anyway, let's not talk about her," I continued. "I believe congratulations are in order, which means we have a wedding to plan for."

"Good Lord, I do not think I will ever stop praying that you were mine, Wren. That woman doesn't deserve a daughter as lovely as you."

Chapter Eighteen

William

Dipping the quill into the inkpot, I thought about how I was going to word the letter I had no choice but to send to my father. I had no desire to return to London; in fact, the very thought of it conjured nothing but misery, but I knew if I were to remain in Somerset with Wren, then I would need to tie up any loose ends and make sure I could provide for us.

My art was all I possessed, the beginning of a profitable venture that could provide for us, yet I knew that, in order for me to be successful, I would need prominent contacts in the trade, or at least one. An art dealer was paramount, one who would be willing to peruse and promote my work to the galleries as well as the Lords and Ladies of stately homes. It would be a struggle to be certain; an artist's income always was, but even if I had to work the land in the interim between the present and reaching my goal, I knew I would do anything, work anywhere, to ensure my heart would stay where it belonged, with Wren.

My quill rushed over the parchment as I tried to focus, my mind often wandering to the joyful moments my love and I had spent together. It had been a few days since our picnic by the river. My fingers still tingled at the recollection of her body as I ran my hands over her tight bodice. The memory of the soft moan from her lips as I pulled her close and of her hands smoothing over the contours of my chest through the thin fabric of my shirt did things to a man... to this man. She had captured me in so many ways that, at times, I wondered whether I would be capable of breathing without her. I was on tenterhooks, always afraid she would change her mind, yet neither of us had rescinded our affections. That does not mean I did not have to remind Wren of my feelings for her and convince her of my adoration and love every time her confidence faltered. My words were like a musical instrument, the notes reaching her ears loud and clear, only for their soothing melody to fade, broken by a silence that allowed for every other thought to rush into her fragile mind and consume her. She fought the intrusion of her mother's words, but it was obvious she was lost without the harmony of mine.

I would often gaze into her eyes, the abundance of questions mingled amongst the pain so clearly visible. It wasn't about whether she believed me, I realised; it was about trying to hear me above the bitter words she had only ever been allowed to hear, but no matter how much and for how long it would take, I knew I would keep talking, keep assuring, until my words were ingrained in her very being.

I blew on the parchment to dry the ink. Each word was sculpted into a very brief, to-the-point letter of how I ended up in Somerset, the woman I had set my heart on, and a hint at my intention to return after I would see my father in London. I hoped it would be enough to forewarn him a smidge, lessening the blow for both he and I.

As I dripped the wax onto the folded letter, sealing it from prying eyes, I pressed the brass emblem into the glossy liquid as it began to solidify. After addressing it to my father in London, I put it aside to post at a later date. I was not ready to leave Wren. Just a few more days, and I would begin my travels as my letter began its own. I shuddered at the thought of sending it right away, for my father was somewhat rash and overbearing. I had no doubt he would make his way here without a care in the world for my request, simply so he could chastise me. The thought of my father blustering his way here before I had the chance to protect her from him and the vicious tongue, which I knew he had, was a leaden weight in my stomach. I only hoped I would time it impeccably, thus avoiding such an atrocity.

"There you are," Wren beamed. "I wondered where you had gotten to."

"Did you miss me?" I asked. I had casually walked towards her, reaching out and scooping her against my body. Her cheeks brightened to the sweetest pink beneath her twinkling blue eyes.

"Perhaps a little," she smiled coyly.

"Just a little?" I growled, playfully nibbling the lobe of her ear. "You, Miss Davenport, do not encourage a man's ego, for I have missed you a great deal." My lips captured hers as she laughed, pushing me away without the slightest conviction as her hands splayed greedily over my chest.

"That is better," I grinned, releasing her.

Her eyes had briefly glazed over, clearing as the red of her swollen lips faded. "Of course, I missed you, but I have also been busy."

Her fingers trailed along the joining of my shirt, gently lifting the fabric away from my skin as she teased each button, giving me a devilish hope that she was about to release them from their buttonholes. "Are you going to ask me what I was doing?" she asked.

"Would you like me to ask you, my love?" I teased.

"Of course. I like to share things with you."

I grabbed her hand gently but firmly, ceasing

her fingers from toying with the buttons. My blood was searing with desire, and if she were to actually undo one of them, I knew I would not have been entirely responsible for how my body would have reacted to her. "Okay, my darling, pray tell, what have you been up to today?"

Wren turned and walked towards the door, then began pacing the room. "Do you remember we talked about asking my father if I could live here at the cottage?"

"Yes, I do. I offered to take the letter to your father for you, so he was sure to read it for himself."

"That's correct. Well, I have been writing that letter. In fact, I have written it, and it is ready and waiting for you to take with you when you leave." Wren's eyes glistened with tears. "Although, I do wish that you would never have to leave," she added.

"As do I, my love. I promise I will return as soon as I can, but sadly, I cannot put it off for much longer. Truth be told, I have been writing a letter, too. There is one over there for my father."

I watched her eyes flick to the letter on the small table.

"I will post it soon," I smiled. "And when I do, I will also be leaving for London." I clasped her hands in mine.

"Please say you are not leaving today, William."

She swallowed, pushing back her emotions as her expression withered into one of sadness. She was searching my face, her mind aimlessly grasping onto some small morsel of unwavering certainty, but all I had were my words.

"Not today, Wren. I will wait a few days. I don't want to post it too soon, or he will turn up here guns-a-blazing like he usually does when I defy him. He's probably still seething over my absence over the Christmas period. I figured that if the letter leaves via post at the same time I am to leave via carriage, the letter and I will arrive with a safe amount of time between us. With the spare day or so in between, I will be sure to pay him a visit before he has the opportunity to leave London, no doubt fuelled by one of his famously renowned rash decisions. He would like nothing more than to seek out his disappointment of a son."

"I don't see how anyone could find you a disappointment," Wren soothed, wrapping her arms around my waist.

"Yes, well, I think you and I both know how some parents can be, my love." My jaw clenched at the implication of her parents, for my father would not be the only one I would be delivering the news of us to.

"Indeed," she mumbled. "When you return, if you still want to, we can leave all of that behind if we wish?”

Her glossy chestnut hair tickled my skin as my fingers trailed longingly through it. She was the most beautiful soul I had ever known. I wondered how I had gotten so lucky for fate to have brought us together. “There are no ifs, Miss Davenport. You have thoroughly bewitched me, so much so that my heart no longer gives me a choice, and quite frankly, I think my heart is quite a clever fellow.”

I didn’t give her a chance to argue as my lips brushed teasingly against hers. All words were lost in the moment as she ran her fingers through my hair.

“Marry me, Wren.” I groaned against her lips. My body was dangerously close to revealing a few secrets I was not entirely sure her innocence was aware of, for as she held her body flush against mine, it was waking up in areas a gentleman does not care to mention so freely.

“Yes, William.” A tiny squeal of excitement squeaked from the back of her throat as she blessed me with the most dazzling smile. I thought I had seen her at her most beautiful, but there she was in my arms, knowing I had asked her to marry me, looking the most radiant I had ever seen her.

“Yes, I will marry you,” she beamed.

Chapter Nineteen
Wren

"Would you like me to take these letters with me?" Rose called from the drawing room. "Charles and I can ask Bernard if he's going that way when we see him."

"Oh, yes, please, Rose. That would be splendid. There's a letter there for Primrose; I thought I would write to her as I haven't heard from her for a while."

Placing the last pin in my hair, I stared into the looking glass to see whether it looked as I had intended it to. 'That will do,' I thought, smoothing down the bodice of my pearl grey dress.

"You off out as well, duck?" Rose asked, now standing in the doorway of my bedchamber.

"Yes. William and I thought we would take a walk and explore a bit more of the countryside. I don't think we shall be gone very long, but I am looking forward to taking the air with him."

"I bet you are," Rose grinned. "It's a shame he will have to go home soon. You and he are quite close, ain't you?"

At the mention of William's impending departure, my insides grew heavy with despair. "Yes, Rose. So much so that he has asked me to marry him."

Even though he had made me the happiest woman alive, I knew there were loose ends needing to be tied up before I could be sure there wasn't anyone who could come between us. I hadn't mentioned William's proposal prior to that moment, for fear of everything crashing down around me. The fragility of what my future offered was both exciting and frightening. It was a strange medley that I wasn't entirely sure how I should handle.

"Oh, that's wonderful news, Wren. I knew there was something between you and him. The way he looks at you ain't the way a gentleman looks at a friend. Oh, I'm so happy for you both," she beamed, walking across the room to me.

Rose clasped my hands in hers. "You deserve this, Wren. Finally, someone who is showing you how much you deserve from this life. Makes a woman want to weep with joy, it does."

"Oh, you mustn't cry, Rose. Charles will think I've been mistreating you if he sees you with a puffy face and red eyes. Besides, we need my father's permission, and I assume his father's approval as well. In a few days, William will be returning to London to address everything, and then, provided he doesn't change his mind, he will return here to us."

"Why on earth would he change his mind, duck?"

"He may find another young lady much more attractive than I."

"Poppycock! That young man is well aware of his good fortune. You only have to look in the looking glass to see that."

I turned back to the glass in the hope I too could see what they did, but I guessed that was not for me to see, not yet anyway. "Perhaps," I offered, gazing at my own eyes. If anything, I could agree that they were quite pretty. How could I not when my youngest sister's were identical?

"No, perhaps about it, missy. William is one lucky man, and he will be back here before you know it."

"Thank you, Rose."

"No need to thank me. It's the truth, love." Rose cupped my face and kissed the top of my head. "I best be off now. I'll post these letters as I said I would, and you must try to relax and enjoy your day with your betrothed," she smiled warmly. "And whenever you have any doubts, remember what I've said. If you can't do that, then just have a proper look into that young man's eyes. I tell you, duck, all the answers are there if you look close enough."

"I will, Rose."

"That's my girl."

Rose took her leave as I took one last look at my reflection. Satisfied with my appearance, I set out to meet William.

William had left the cottage earlier to meet Charles, saying he had something he needed to do. I didn't pry, but by the twinkle in his eyes, I didn't believe it was anything I needed to concern myself with.

The day was working out perfectly, for as Rose greeted Charles, I spied William standing to one side, hands nestled deep in the pockets of his breeches as he rocked back and forth on the heels of his feet. He was smiling—a smile that could easily compete against the dazzling brilliance of a summer sun.

"You look rather happy," I greeted him. I wasn't sure if I had narrowed my eyes at how bright the sun was or because I was immensely intrigued by the glimmer of accomplishment in his gaze.

"I am, my darling. I am indeed." William scooped his arm around my waist, lifting me towards him as he brushed his lips over mine. "Would you like to know why I am so pleased with myself, my little bird?"

"Little bird?" I smiled at the new term of endearment.

"It suits you," he quipped. "Would you like to know why I am so pleased?" he repeated.

Despite my name, it was new to me to be referred to as such. To be honest, it thrilled me. "I would only like to know if you would like me to know," I offered. I was reluctant to pry, as prying always made me feel uneasy.

"Perhaps you ought to turn around." Hands on my hips, William turned me to face away from him. He smoothed his large hands over my bodice, sending a subtle warmth to my stomach as he pulled my back against his broad chest. "Look."

Just a few yards away, hidden from the view of the cottage, a gleaming red curricle and horse stood out from the scenery. "It's for you, my little bird." His deep voice rumbled against the nape of my neck as he wrapped his arms around me.

My skin shivered wantonly at the caress of his soft breath.

"Now you are no longer restricted to remain at The Aviary. This will allow you to venture further afield as and when you want to," he added cheerfully.

The shivers travelled down my spine in the most delightful way, weakening my legs to nothing more than blancmange. The strong, muscular arms around my waist were all that held me up. "You bought this for me?"

"I do not see any other little bird here," he laughed, kissing the side of my face as he pressed my back closer to him. "You must name the mare, though. She seems rather shy, but she is quite beautiful."

"Yes, she is," I breathed, astounded at William's generosity. "Where shall I take her, though? I don't know whether I am ready for the world to see me just yet."

"Why ever not, Wren?"

Realising I had brought unwanted attention to my biggest insecurity, I froze in his arms. I suppose it really didn't matter whether I had said it aloud, for I knew he would have picked up on my hesitation soon enough.

To feel something and to voice it aloud were two very separate things with very separate emotions. And so, when one bought them together in a malicious storm-grey cloud above one's head, they became a taunting and restrictive obstacle, lingering precariously. Then there is the awkward addition of having to pick it apart, attempting to explain something that you, yourself, have not quite grasped the meaning of in terms that another would understand. I was not so good at that.

Sensing my distress, William wrapped his arms further around my body and placed a kiss on top of my head. "The world needs beauty, Little Bird," he whispered adoringly. "Please do not deny it of that.

No matter what you may think of yourself and what others may wish you to think, you must know that all the venom they spit is a lie, especially when those such as myself and Rose have told you something quite different. I hope that you would trust us, my darling."

"Of course, I trust you, William. It is just such a huge step to take. In fact, it is something I did not believe I would ever have to face in this lifetime. I don't know whether I can face it alone."

"Then don't." William turned me back towards him. "Let me have the honour of facing it with you," he offered proudly.

"Do you want to face it with me, William?"

"I want us to face everything together, Little Bird. If this is where we start, then let it be today."

"Today?" I asked. My throat dried with panic.

"Do you think you will feel better prepared tomorrow? Or do you think you will be just as nervous, if not more, as you are now?"

I inhaled. I knew he was right. There was no perfect time when it would be easier. Perhaps an extra day, week, month, or even year would indeed make it more difficult for me to face it. "Okay, let us face this today...together."

"That's my Little Bird," William beamed as he lifted me off my feet. As he lowered me, my body slid down his chest until my lips slanted over his. He held me there as though I were as light as a feather, reciprocating every emotion until my eyes glazed over with pleasure. I pulled away breathless.

"If you do that again, Little Bird, I fear we won't be going anywhere," he chuckled, sneakily sliding his hand over my posterior, giving it a quick squeeze.

My feet eventually found the solidity of the earth as my lips tingled with pleasure from his tiny kisses. "Well, we shall stay here then," I teased, surprising myself.

"Oh no, you don't, Little Bird. This is important. I need to know you will be quite alright while I am away and that you will not be afraid to live a little." Taking my hand, William led me towards my new gift.

My body trembled with anticipation as the curricle took us away from the peace of the countryside, slowly submerging us into, and amongst, the life of the local village. There were men, women, and children of all ages busily going about their everyday lives. My arm had weaved itself into the crook of William's as I curled inward, closer to him. It was a futile effort to become invisible, for the evidence that I was indeed quite visible lingered in the eyes of strangers as they lifted them to meet mine.

I don't know what I had expected to see, but their eyes did not portray neither judgement nor unkindness towards me. The only expressions they held were those that were friendly, or far-away, lost-in-thought expressions that we have all been guilty of on occasion. I even managed to raise my hand in a wave to a young woman when she offered me the kindest of smiles.

"The people here, Little Bird, are good people. They do not judge others the way aristocratic society can and does," William commented, gently nudging me with his arm.

My chest pinched. "Do you see me like the others in London do?" I asked. Mentioning what I had escaped from made me feel suddenly exposed in front of him, naked with my curved spine on full display. My stomach flipped with a feeling of terrible discomfort, as though I were monstrous to behold.

"Of course I do not." William briefly looked offended. It was a flash of anger, nothing more, but it revealed the honesty of his words, provoking a wave of guilt within me for thinking so terribly of him. "You must never think that of me, Wren."

"I don't think badly of you, William. I'm so sorry; it's just that I am so very afraid," I replied apologetically. "You are so dear to me that I am petrified that I shall wake up at any moment, and all of this will have been a wonderful dream, nothing more. You are the only one who has ever made me feel as though I may be worthy enough to be loved by someone like you." My fingers fiddled nervously with the cotton of my dress. "I had foolishly assumed that when you mentioned it, it was because you could see it too. It scares me to the core that you may see the things they despise about me. I am sorry; I certainly did not mean to offend you."

"No, Little Bird, I am sorry. I should have been more careful with my words, but I promise you, with all my heart, I was only referring to what you have told me about your parents. To me, you are perfect. I never want you to forget that."

Placing my head on his shoulder, I kissed the top of his arm. "And you are perfect to me too, William."

Chapter Twenty

William

"Well, yes, I am rather a catch, aren't I?" I smirked, playfully nudging Wren as she nestled warmly against my side.

She smiled, her soft cheek brushing my arm as a chuckle emanated from her soft lips, the tension between our bodies subsiding. My conscience pricked at my terrible knack of even more terrible wording. It was obvious from her reaction that I had made her feel utterly exposed by mentioning the godforsaken vile attitudes of the aristocracy towards her. And, if that wasn't ghastly enough, by doing so, I had almost let her believe I viewed her in the same light as they did, which was as far from the truth as was possible. I adored her, and my heart would never let me forget it, nor did I want it to.

The day was supposed to be a special one, one I hoped Wren would remember for the rest of her life, but after my rather clumsy start to it, I found myself praying the next few hours would erase every word I had uttered that had made her feel sad and replace it with far more spectacular memories.

I pulled lightly on the ribbons, bringing the horse and curricle to a gentle stop. The village was pleasantly busy, a vast difference from the chaos that filled London, and as the people passed us by, either without a single glance or with a wide, welcoming smile, I felt Wren loosen her grasp on my arm.

"I thought we could partake in a little shopping, and then we can have tea at the lovely tearoom just over there," I suggested, tilting my head in the direction of a quaint tearoom on the other side from where we stood.

"I do not have any money with me, William, but I can certainly look," she smiled, her eyes wide with wonder as she scanned the shops.

It was a pretty little village with only a few stores, yet ample to satisfy one's needs and to keep one busy for a few hours as they perused at their leisure. "You do not need any money, Little Bird. Let me take care of everything today."

Wren gasped. "Oh, no, I couldn't, William. I am quite content to simply look."

The way she did not expect to indulge at my expense was refreshing, although I knew she had no choice, for I was adamant in my quest to spoil her. Wren was nothing like those my father had insisted on trying to match me with. The ones he handpicked were the type of young ladies who seem to come to life at the sound of coins jingling in one's pockets, yet there my Wren was, the most radiant young lady I had ever met, expecting nothing from me but my time and adoration. Even then, I knew she never expected but simply hoped for.

"The simple fact that you do not ask nor expect anything from me is why I want to do this for you, Little Bird. I insist that you let me take care of you."

Soft pink flushed profusely upon the apples of her cheeks as Wren curled the loose strand of her hair behind her ear. She nodded shyly. "Okay, if that is what pleases you, William," she relented. "But please do not spend too much, for you have already purchased the new curricle and that is indeed extremely generous."

"Just a little then," I suggested, afraid that if I pushed her, she would not enjoy the day for feeling awkward and embarrassed.

"Okay," she smiled.

"This is the last shop, I promise," I laughed, my eyes pleading as I took her hands and led her towards the door.

"William, this is a jeweller," she breathed. "We

simply cannot go in there. You have spent a fortune already."

We had visited the dressmakers, and after I had insisted that she choose at least three dresses, Wren had spent an hour with a modiste who welcomed her enthusiastically as though they were long-lost friends.

The modiste had introduced herself as Antonia Love in a rich Italian accent. I could not decipher whether the curves and lilts of her voice were genuine or otherwise, but it really did not matter in the grand scheme of things, for Wren seemed completely at ease in her company.

"You must call me Toni," Antonia offered kindly. "It is what all my friends call me."

The swish of the modiste's measuring tape hissed across the shop, sending my mind into a wayward spiral as images of a scantily clad Wren flashed across my mind. Good heavens, the woman was shamelessly loud in her task of measuring every inch of my love's tempting physical attributes. The memory of Wren's hourglass figure and tiny waist, which had teased my fingers, served only to heat the taunted blood beneath my flesh.

Bubbles of laughter amongst secretive chatter drifted across the shop, bringing me and my body back to our senses. My lips curled involuntarily with pleasure, for hearing how Toni seemed to make Wren forget all her inhibitions gratified me. Wren had not expected such kindness, yet there it was in front of her, and there was no denying it. The respect between the two women was palpable. However, I knew it was only the beginning of what I very much believed would be a difficult journey for Wren, in the hope that one day she would not feel the need for validation from others. I wondered then whether my leaving for London, no matter how temporary, could possibly spoil it all. The very thought that it would do such a terrible thing concerned me immensely. I didn't want her to ever doubt what we had.

In my mind, there was only one thing I wanted to do to remind Wren I would return, to remind her of what we were and what we would always be, and that was exactly what I was going to do.

The jewellery shop was to be the icing on the cake, so to speak. To be honest, to me, it was indeed the most important port of call. "Indulge me, please," I begged as she dragged her feet on the pavement, pulling me back with hesitance.

"Whatever for, William? You have already spoiled me more than I had ever dared to imagine. I do not need anything else. I swear, I do not."

"You cannot refuse this, for I want to buy you an engagement ring," I confessed. "However, I would like you to have one you will love, and I have been told I am extremely indecisive when it comes to matters that are as important as this, so, Little Bird, if I don't have your help, we may be here for hours."

Wren's features softened from panic to intrigue. Her eyes glittered, affection swimming in the mesmerising pools of blue that were her irises, as she allowed me to pull her through the door and into the darkened store. Gas lamps warmed the room with a deep honey glow. Bright flecks of refracted light sparkled off polished gems and gleamed over the smooth surfaces of gold bands and gilded edges. "Oh, heavens," Wren whispered. "Everything is so pretty. I fear I may be more indecisive than you claim to be."

The man behind the counter watched us curiously.

"Perhaps we can ask the expert what he suggests," I offered, simultaneously squeezing her delicately nimble fingers lovingly as she placed them within my proffered hand.

The jeweller portrayed his eagerness to serve as he stepped forward to offer his assistance. "Good afternoon, sir, ma'am. How may I be of assistance?" The jeweller stood proudly at the counter.

"We would like to purchase an engagement ring, sir," I began. "However, I would like something that matches the elegance and beauty of this fine young lady here."

The man's face was sombre as one side of his

mouth lifted into a practiced smile, never even attempting to meet his eyes. "Very good, sir," he drawled in a deep, resonating tone as he reached beneath the counter and produced several rings, then several more.

As I slipped each one on Wren's finger, it was proving more and more difficult to find the correct size for her dainty fingers.

"You are aware that I am able to alter the size of the ring, sir," the man sniffed, undoubtedly pestered because we were taking so long and could not make up our minds.

"Just one more, sir, please, and if that should not fit, then we will trouble you no longer, I promise."

The jeweller nodded as he continued to observe us.

The last remaining ring was no stranger to me. It had caught my eye briefly on entering the shop, but my indecisive nature had pleaded with me to ignore it, for fear of pushing the design on Wren when she may not have liked it as much as I did.

My stomach muscles tightened around the sudden somersault hidden within my abdomen. The ring was exquisite. Seeing it glide towards us incited the most dreadful bout of nerves and excitement that I wasn't sure I could possibly contain. The red of the garnets was so deep it was almost purple as it created sparkling petals around an equally sparkling centre of a lone, magnificent diamond. A gold band tapered outward from the sides of the gemstone flower, embracing Wren's delicate finger as though it had only ever been meant for her.

"It fits me," she breathed. Wren's eyes were round with wonder as she brought her hand up to take a closer look.

"What do you think, Little Bird?"

"It's stunning, William."

"Would you allow me to choose this one for you?" I asked. My ridiculous hands were trembling from the adrenaline coursing through my veins as I tried diligently to read her thoughts.

"Of course, I would allow it," she chuckled, warming my heart. "It would mean so much more to me if you did, William."

My heart somersaulted beneath my ribcage, wondering how I had been so lucky to find someone so utterly pure and incredible as Wren. I had no words for her. They had been choked into silence as my throat constricted with emotion.

Turning to the jeweller, I composed myself. "We'll take it," I rasped.

"Oh, duck, I'm glad you're back. You have a visitor." Rose greeted us as we entered the cottage; her face was grave with concern as she looked from Wren and I to the door of the drawing room.

It looked as though she and Charles had only just arrived back at The Aviary, for she was still wearing her cape.

"How can anyone be here for me when no one knows where I am?"

"Don't ask me, duck. All I can tell you is that he don't look 'appy. He's in the drawing room. I'm just making him some tea. You go in, and I'll see to it."

Nerves tightened my torso. There was only one person who could track me down without me ever telling them where I was, and that was my father.

"There you are, William." My father stood as I entered the room. His eyes darkened with the sharp blade of anger as he tried to disguise his displeasure at my actions. "You have had us all quite concerned."

"I apologise, father. I did not intend to be away from London for quite so long. I-"

"Yes, yes," he snapped, waving his hand dismissively in the air. "I know all about the accident. I've had my men carry out a thorough search for you, which means that many were spoken to, and we were quite enlightened as to your injuries."

William Darlington, Senior, ran his finger along the mantelpiece, then grimaced at the speck of dust on his finger. One, which I might add, no one else would have ever seen without the aid of a magnifying glass. “Dear, dear,” he tsked, his face wrinkling in spiteful mockery. “How the mighty have fallen. It won’t do, William. You shall pack your things, and we shall leave at once.”

“I beg your pardon, Father?” I had forgotten how the man could heat my blood with a frenzied rage. Had it not been for the years and years of practice at bridling such a detrimental response, my life would have steered me on a much different path. “I am five and twenty; I shall leave as and when I choose.”

My father’s lips pursed, causing his moustache to twitch as his skin reddened. “You cannot stay here with them!”

“I believe I can, Father. Therefore, I shall.”

“William,” he seethed.

“No, Father. There is no amount of blustering you can do to make me return... not yet anyway.”

The door creaked behind me to reveal Wren carrying a tray with a fresh pot of tea. She placed it slowly onto the table. “Your tea, Mr Darlington, William.” Wren moved to my side.

“You can go now, girl!” my father snapped unkindly.

Before I could react, Wren had grabbed my hands to still the shake in my limbs. I was sure I had soared past the point of ever withholding the rage. My father had gone too far by referring to her as though she were his servant. "Perhaps you should go with your father, William. I will be here when you come home, I promise," she soothed.

"What in damnation is all this?" My father was shouting, his face crimsoning as his fists clenched.

"Leave it with me, Little Bird," I whispered. My hands were trembling as I cupped her face and placed a kiss on her forehead. "I don't want you to have to deal with someone like my father. Please wait outside whilst I talk with him. If I must leave, I won't go anywhere without telling you first."

Wren nodded, ignoring my father, and left the room.

"You better have an explanation for all that!" my father fumed, waggling his finger towards the door that was now the one and only thing that stood between Wren and I. "Who is that creature? And why were you so intimate with her?"

My nails dug into the palms of my hands as I clenched my fists. "How dare you refer to my fiancée as a creature," I spat. My eyes were hot with anger as I leered over him. Sadly, for my father, I was the only one of the Darlington men who had inherited his grandfather's tall gene as well as the broad one too.

"Your *fiancée*? *That* is your fiancée?"

I stepped towards the man in front of me, the chord tying us together as father and son, fraying with every step as he shuffled backward away from me. My jaw muscles twitched as my teeth ground together. They were the only actions I could muster in order to keep my tongue and lips from forming the words I wanted to blare in his face. "*She* is my fiancée," I growled.

William Darlington, senior, sidestepped out of my shadow. "Oh, how the mighty have fallen," he taunted, turning his gaze upon me. There was a mocking glint in his eyes. "Have I not offered you finer specimens to be your wife? Yet you settle for someone like her. Her spine is crooked, and have you seen the way she walks? The girl is monstrous," he sneered.

I have no recollection of how I found myself being restrained by the local vicar as my father rose from the floor, wiping the blood from his lip, but the throb in my knuckles told me I was the one who had drawn the Darlington blood that dribbled down his face.

"You marry her, and you will get nothing from me, William. Not a penny. Do you hear me?" My father was goading me. He wanted to watch me crumble to my knees in front of him and beg forgiveness, but for what? I had nothing to apologise for. He assumed I was every bit the same as him, but I did not care about money. All I cared for was making a life with Wren.

"I do not want your money," I spat. "I want her.

That young woman is everything to me. If you cannot understand that, then I do not care what you have to say. And I certainly do not require your blessing to marry the woman I love."

Charles released my arms as my breathing steadied, the lingering ache in my chest refusing to vacate my heart, but it did not ache for my father; it ached for the woman I knew had heard everything from beyond the door.

"Are you alright, son?" Charles whispered as he squeezed my arm.

I nodded.

Chapter Twenty-One

Wren

I had heard every single word from the other side of the door. One might consider me nosey, but it was extremely difficult not to hear the feud in the drawing room. Rose's face was purple with indignation as she seethed over the way William's father had addressed me and the manner in which he had referred to me when speaking with his son.

William's anger bled beyond the gaps in the door and into the hallway. Even I was aware as to what it was that riled him so. My emotions were fragmented by an abundance of hurt at the proof of what my mother had warned me of, for William Darlington Senior's choice of words was exceedingly derogatory; most were a carbon copy of my mother's. And, as for my other emotions, they swirled around amongst my thoughts and fears for William's future, afraid of the man I loved being harmed, of being disowned by his father, and all because of me. Love curled up around the swirling mass of turmoil, rising up as fierce as a lion, seeming to roar when he defended me even though I was not in the room. His love for me showed no mercy, despite him being blissfully unaware that I could hear everything.

When the almighty clatter of the tea tray crashed upon the floor, Charles hurled himself through the door and grabbed William to restrain him. I managed to get a glimpse of his father with a bloody lip, crumpled on the floor, his face white with shock. However, his face didn't stay that way for long, for it soon pinched into a sneer as he rose once again, but I was not privy to any more visual evidence because Charles closed the door between us.

"You really believe you can support yourself and *that* on an artist's salary, don't you?" Mr Darlington scoffed warily beyond the door.

"It is none of your business how I will make my money. I will not leave Wren," William began, his voice lowering. His tone had become unwavering, and to those who knew him, you could not mistake the dangerous tone laced within it.

"Oh, that's the creature's name, is it? It's as ridiculous as she is, but not quite as ridiculous as the idea of you marrying her," Mr Darlington sneered bitterly.

"I think you better leave," William warned. His voice had deepened to a threatening rumble.

"Don't bother with all the theatrics, boy, for I am most certainly leaving this hovel. However, I will say this: if you should come to your senses within the next few weeks, I will forget all this nonsense and welcome you back into the bosom of our family, but if you do marry that, then we are done. As far as I am concerned, I do not have a son. Is that clear?"

"Don't hold your breath, *William*," William replied, returning the growl of his father's sneer. The way he emphasised the man's name showed the evident abandonment of their relationship without a moment of hesitation. "As far as I am concerned, my father died years ago."

Rose and I scurried backward as the door flung open to reveal a smaller, very disgruntled, and raging older version of William. His nose wrinkled as his eyes travelled the length of me in disgust.

"You will be the ruin of him," he spat. "Society will mock him."

"Why don't you sling your 'ook!" Rose bellowed, stepping in front of me. "You 'eard me, bugger off, you ol' windbag!"

Affronted, Mr Darlington's face turned more purple than the new bruise on his lip. I was sure he would say something, but instead, he turned on his heel and departed.

"Come 'ere, duck," Rose soothed, pulling me

into her arms.

My throat was dry as I tried to digest everything that had occurred since we'd arrived back at The Aviary. The drumming of my heart was fast and heavy, resounding against my breastbone.

"I need to speak to William," I rasped. "What must he think of me?"

On cue, William stepped out of the drawing room, his hand instantly wrapping around my own as he pulled me from Rose's embrace into his.

"How much did you hear, Little Bird?"

"Not very much," I lied, covering my face as I placed my forehead on his shoulder.

"The truth, please." William's hand stroked my hair at the nape of my neck as I breathed in his comforting fragrance.

Taking me by surprise, the sobs came thick and fast. My chest ached as Mr Darlington's words ripped through me, creating gouges in my heart.

"I see," William whispered into my hair. "I'm so sorry, Little Bird. My father is a cruel man. I hoped you would never have to endure him."

"He said I will be the ruin of you and that society will mock you, William," I sniffed, wrapping my arms tighter around his waist. I didn't want to let him go, terrified he would run far away from me and towards something—someone—much better. "I don't want to be the one who does that to you."

"The worst thing you could do to me, Wren, would be to leave me; to tell me that you no longer love me. You do still want to marry me, don't you?"

"Of course I do," I replied, lifting my face to see his. I must have looked frightful, but I had to see his eyes; to watch his expressions. I needed those to reveal the truth in his words. I did not want him to marry me out of pity. I only ever wanted to marry for love. Nothing more and nothing less.

"Then let us marry soon, Little Bird. My father does not matter, and society has never mattered, nor will it ever matter, to me, with or without you. You must know I want to be with you, and if society is too cruel and unkind to accept what we have together, then it is their loss, not ours." He kissed the top of my head. "I do not wish to spend my days with society, Little Bird. And as for the nights, I have to confess, I believe your company would be much more preferred," William teased, blessing me with his lopsided grin of mischief a moment before his lips slanted lovingly over mine.

"Do not worry, Little Bird," William smiled. "I will be back before you know it. Besides, you won't have time to worry because I have instructed Rose to take you to the dressmakers in the village.

Together with Miss Love and Rose, you will be able to create your perfect wedding gown. Of course, there are other wedding-related matters to tend to, taking up even more of your time, so when you decide to come up for air from all that is required of you, my soon-to-be wife, I will be standing in front of you again."

"It will be nice to see Toni again. She was ever so kind to me," I beamed, forcing myself to be more positive around William. "But I shall miss you, and quite frankly, my love, there really is nothing you can do about it."

"I should hope you would, Little Bird, or I have failed magnanimously to woo you in the manner in which a lady should be wooed," he grinned cheekily. "I just need to get all the loose ends tied up in London, and I shall be relieved to know that I shall never have to face the ton ever again."

"Just one moment." I held up my hand, then quickly trotted off to my bedchamber to retrieve the letter I had written to my father, returning with it to William's side post-haste and a little out of breath.

"Please don't forget to deliver this," I begged. "It is probably best that you do not mention my name, as I have said, for my mother will only deny I exist, and the letter will never reach Papa."

"Oh, what wonderful parents we have, Little Bird," he smiled sarcastically. "But never fear, for neither your mother nor any other member of that household will deny you to my face.

"Be careful, won't you?" I pleaded as I wrapped my arms around him once more. "I couldn't bear to lose you."

"Do not fret, Little Bird. What is it that Wordsworth said again? Ah, yes... '*Oh, sir, the good die first*' or something quite similar, and as my father has declared I am not good, it is quite clear that I shall be perfectly fine. Although," he drawled, the curve of his teasing smile nuzzling into my neck, "he never mentioned the terribly wicked!"

His breath was hot on my skin as his lips travelled to my ear. "Just wait until our wedding night, Little Bird, and I shall show you just how wicked I can be." William scraped his teeth softly over the lobe of my ear as his laughter rumbled against my sensitive flesh. My skin shuddered with ecstasy as, once again, my unfaithful legs discarded any need for their bones and turned swiftly into two rather needy sticks of blancmange. Heat spread throughout my body. I was bordering upon becoming a sinfully deliciously molten puddle, and I could not be Mrs Darlington soon enough.

"He'll soon be back, duck," Rose crooned as we watched the curricle fade into the distance. "If you ever doubt it, then you just look at that ring on your finger and remember that only a gentleman who thinks the world of you would give you something so beautiful."

I gazed down at the sparkling promise of our engagement, the sun glinting off the cut of the stones. "Yes, you are right, Rose, but I do hope he returns soon. I don't think my stomach will settle until I know he is home safe with us."

"Come on, love, best keep busy or it will drag like you wouldn't believe. There's a letter inside for you too," Rose announced. A frown of curiosity pinched her brows and twisted her lips. It was indeed strange that there was a letter for me. I could only hope it brought good news. "What with all the chaos of yesterday, I had completely forgotten all about it," she added, shrugging the curiosity off.

"A letter for me?" Nausea swirled in my stomach. The likelihood of good news was slim. "I don't suppose you recognised the handwriting, Rose?"

"I can't say for sure, but it looks like it could be Primrose's writing," she offered cautiously. "It would be nice for you to hear from her unless she has a message from that woman."

I prayed that the smile on my face covered the apprehension. "I don't think Mama would let Primrose relay a message. It would spoil her fun if someone else got to deliver the blow," I sighed. "I am utterly intrigued. I do so hope it is good news for her; Prim deserves to be happy."

"Primrose says she's getting married, Rose. Isn't that wonderful?" I beamed, holding the thin parchment in front of me.

I thoroughly meant it when I said my sister deserved to be happy. Although I had been ill-treated by my mother, so had she to a certain degree. It pained me to see the true nature of my youngest sister stifled by Mama's forceful and spiteful ways. Primrose was a wilting flower in the shadows, which my mother and sister had forced her beneath.

The letter was not a very long one, but filled with splendid, positive news with a pinch of Primrose's feisty side. "Although it does say that Mama doesn't approve, as the gentleman is not very wealthy and doesn't have a title. She says she doesn't give a fig for Mama's opinion as she has Papa's blessing anyway," I happily continued.

"What? You're telling me your father has stood up to your mother? Good lord, wonders will never cease!" Rose huffed. "He better stick up for you next time I see 'im, or I won't be responsible for what I will say to 'im."

"I very much doubt he will come here, Rose, so if you do want to have words with him, you and Charles had better visit us in London."

"I thought you were going to ask if you can stay, duck?" Rose looked saddened at the suggestion of me returning to London, but, although I wanted to be convinced of what I very much hoped would be my future in Somerset with William, to speak it and to lean wholeheartedly on that one path seemed dangerously risky.

"Oh, I have, but that does not mean he will agree. I only hope William does return as he promised," I said wistfully. "I don't know whether I can cope with the prospect of going back there again."

"I'll have none of that, missy. There is no if about it. You will not be going back to London ever again unless it is for a visit. Although I don't know why anyone would want to visit that lot, I'm sure," she grinned.

A breathy laugh burst from my lips as she joyfully pulled a face of disgust at the very idea.

"That's better," she continued, resting her hand on mine assuredly. "We'll have none of that sad, pessimistic nonsense. You need to trust that young man to do what he says he will.

"He adores you. It's as plain as the nose on his face. Big smiles, girlie, we have two weddings to plan now, mine and yours, so we best get cracking, for they ain't going to plan themselves."

Chapter Twenty-Two

William

"I'm sorry, sir, but these are not the sort of art this gallery is interested in. Your work is of a rather unique and unusual style, and our clientele prefers something far more refined, such as realism or rococo. Yours, sir, are simply none of those." The art dealer gave a haughty sniff as he clenched his fists around the lapels of his jacket. Red blotches spattered his skin as he stared, obviously offended by me and my art. His apparent disgruntlement at my *audacity* to inquire as to whether the gallery would consider my artwork was etched deep within every line on his sour face, in his beady eyes, and in the repetitive twitch of his peppered moustache. "I think it is best for you to seek an alternative art gallery, or perhaps an art dealer may advise you, sir," he huffed. "Here we take only the best, not *that sort of thing*."

"That sort of thing, sir? I am aware my work is indeed new, but it is not that new that you cannot recognise the impressionism and romanticism weaved into every brushstroke, surely?"

"It is *precisely that*, sir, which makes your art very new indeed. I do not believe society would appreciate your work as much as you appear to do.

"Now good day to you, sir."

I had inquired at every art gallery within London in the hope I could sell my art and prove my father wrong about the dream I'd had for so long. However, by the swift, hope-thwarting rejections that followed my inquiries, it appeared the earl was indeed correct, and I was doomed to be a failure.

Deflated and insecure in my own artistic conviction, I decided it would be best to take my sorrowful frown to the nearest tavern and wallow in the depths of a pint of ale and a plate of their finest food.

Smoke billowed around the table as I positioned the bundle of art and both canvases carefully on the chair beside me. A somewhat convenient place with a hidden message that I preferred to sit alone, for I couldn't bear the thought of having to share my table with anyone on the brink of inebriation. I was too full of despair, for I needed to give Wren's father every reason to believe I would be a good husband to his daughter and in a comfortable position to provide for her too. However, at the rate and direction in which my plans were going, I wondered if I would ever be able to make him such a promise.

"'Ere y'are, love, get this down ya. Looks like you're 'avin' a rough day of it," the barmaid commented as she placed a tankard of golden ale in front of me.

"Something like that," I sighed. "It appears my art is not required in London."

"Let's 'ave a look at it. I ain't no expert or nothin', but I 'ave eyes in me 'ead." The woman dragged her hands down the sides of her hips, wiping the spilled ale onto the deep brown and well-worn spill of skirts. "My 'usband says I've got an eye for art. Reckons I should've worked in one of those fancy galleries." She snorted at the memory of her husband's kind suggestion. "Fat chance," she laughed, discarding the idea as though it were ridiculous.

Slowly, I turned the largest canvas over to show her some of what I believed myself capable of. I didn't want to look, but since I had painstakingly worked on it for weeks, I made an effort to watch her face for any inkling of her thoughts. Although I was wary after being subjected to such derogatory opinions by the galleries, there was a large part of me who was eager to hear her opinion. The irritating doubt in my abilities had crept up on me in the preceding hours, confidence crumbling to mere hope, wondering whether I had been delusional, fanciful at best, all the time to ever have considered a creative career. I was ready to discard my dream if she agreed with the opinions of all those before, but I was surprised to see her face brighten as her eyes roved over the canvas, tired yet wide as she drank it all in. “Cor, that’s beautiful, that is,” she gushed. “Why on earth did they not like it?”

“Apparently, society only appreciates rococo and realism,” I laughed, exasperated at the memory.

“Well,” she huffed. “Each and every one of us is part of society, sir, and this member jus’ so ‘appens to think your art is incredible."

“Excuse me, sir, madam.” A gentleman stepped forward to join us. His pristine, unscathed suit set him apart from all the other men in the tavern. I did not know how I had not noticed him when he stuck out like a sore thumb amongst the patrons with evidence of hard labour smudged across their attire. “I do beg your pardon, but I happened to overhear that you are having difficulty getting your art pieces into the galleries. Is that correct?” he asked.

I nodded.

“Well, from what I can see of your incredible work, I believe I may be of service to you.

“My name is Albert Sterling, and although I do

not promote artists in London, I know of many other cities and towns that would love to see your art in their galleries. The world is much bigger and far more open-minded than the city beneath your feet, sir. It would astound you if you knew of the possibilities beyond the bounds of London."

Albert's eyes wandered over the woman in the painting as she sat oblivious to the scrutiny beneath a large oak tree. The familiarity of her features and her hair suddenly dawned on me, for she was the image of Wren. It was as though I had known her long before I had ever met her. My chest swelled at the thought of her and her adorable laugh.

"Do you really believe that to be true, Mr Sterling? I asked, not daring to believe such a wonderful prospect.

"I'll leave you both to it, love," the barmaid whispered as she patted my hand. "I look forward to hearing your name spoken amongst the great artists we already know," she winked, encouragingly.

"Thank you for your kind words," I offered as she made her leave.

"It's the truth, duck. You only have to ask Mr Sterling 'ere, and he will confirm it." The landlady bustled away, slowly swallowed by the crowd.

"May I?" Mr Sterling asked, gesturing to the chair opposite me.

"Oh, yes, of course. How rude of me. I apologise."

"Thank you, and as to your question, err..."

"William Darlington."

"Yes, as to your question, Mr Darlington, I certainly do believe the galleries, to which I have connections and exceedingly good relations, will indeed display your work. In fact, I am more than sure of it. There will also be those who will want it in their homes too. I believe you have all that is required of an artist to be most successful."

"I have more of my art here," I offered, passing Mr Sterling my sketchpad. "I particularly like this one." I turned the pages, hurrying past the many sketches I had of Wren. She was not to be perused and critiqued by the eyes of others. Oh, how I missed her already. I had only been away a couple of days, and it had felt like months.

I shook myself from my reverie, continuing with the matter at hand. Mr Sterling's eyes dimmed and shone according to the pieces I displayed before him. I was glad of the silent critique, for it would allow me to keep it in mind when I began another project.

The discussion bled into the early evening, by which time I was thoroughly exhausted, although relieved to have found an art dealer who deemed my work to be worthy of exhibitions. I had returned to London, assuming that it was the city for art. I had never once considered others across England, but after a lengthy discussion with Mr Sterling, he had assured me that by pinning all my hopes on London alone, I was merely dipping my toe into the ocean of possibilities available to me. The man even spoke of the possibility of Paris.

"Paris?" I breathed. My mind was alive with the wonders I had heard that the city held. Artists dreams were made there, and to even consider that my name may travel across the ocean to such a prestigious place astounded me.

"Yes, Mr Darlington, most definitely Paris. Paris more than any other city on earth," he beamed. "They are years ahead of us in their way of thinking. I am travelling there in the next few weeks, so I shall take some of your work with me.

"Of course, once I have secured your art a prominent and worthy place in a gallery, or perhaps several, I shall inform you via post sent to the address you have given me in Somerset. That is the correct one, isn't it?"

"Indeed, it is, Mr Sterling. I don't know how I can thank you," I breathed. What the man was about to do for my future was far more than what I had dared to dream of.

"Mr Darlington, please understand that it is only you who you need to thank. I am not an easy man to please. In fact, I have a reputation for being rather fussy with regards to who I agree to represent. Regrettably, however, this has only led me to have the additional reputation of being unfair in business matters. Please ignore that part of my poor reputation, for it is only those whom I reject who feel obliged to wield that bit of gossip. It is fuelled merely by resentment. I am no fool where art is concerned, and if it is anything to go by, I can assure you that as soon as I saw your art, I knew I had to represent you."

I held out my hand to the man as I battled a storm of nerves and excitement, flitting around my insides as though they didn't entirely know what to do with themselves. "Well, in that case, Mr Sterling, I very much look forward to working with you."

"And I, with you, Mr Darlington," he smiled, taking my hand in a firm handshake. "I will be in touch."

Watching him walk away with my prize pieces, albeit the sketchbook in my hands, I was feeling much lighter in my chest than I had only a few hours prior. I had never expected to find salvation staring into a pint of ale in a tavern, but it appeared that I did not need to seek out fate, for fate had indeed sought out me.

London had not been a single-minded trip. Truth be known, it was a web of errands that was slowly unravelling. So far, it had unravelled quite miraculously in the right direction, buoying me up for the remainder of the metaphorical knots that gripped my insides and stood perilously in my way.

There were two, to be precise, both of which were matters of a more personal nature that needed to be tended to. The first was confronting my father. After he had raged so vehemently at me, I was sure Wren had heard his cruel, derogatory words about her. Neither of us had repeated them to each other for confirmation, for I didn't want Wren to relive it, nor did I want to add words that perhaps she hadn't heard to the list. I was livid at the man. I did not care for the venom he spat at me, and less so now that I knew I was well on my way to proving him wrong. The ground beneath me felt solid for the first time in many days, a wonderful feeling borne from knowing I was in a position to support my wife-to-be, but there was still the grating truth that he had hurt the woman I love and simply did not care.

To make matters worse, I had the misfortune of running into an old family friend on my return to my lodgings. He assumed he knew more about my life than I did, as he repeated the gossip my father had obviously instigated on his return. According to the man, I had been held captive in my hour of need by a woman of fragile mind, and although I had escaped from her clutches, I had not yet returned to London because I had needed to convalesce after the *ordeal*.

"I can assure you, Richard, that I, most certainly, was not held captive, nor was the woman of fragile mind," I seethed. I clenched my hands into fists, channelling my anger from my chest into the rigid muscles of my arms as the blood drained from my knuckles.

Richard's face paled to a quite similar shade to that of his shirt as he stared silently in shock.

"And as for the need to convalesce, that is also an outright lie. I did not return to London with my father after my accident merely because the very thought of the journey with that pompous old fool would have given me every desire to wrap my hands around his neck and wring the life from him, as well he knew."

"Easy, ol' boy," Richard chuckled nervously. "I am only repeating what he said. I had no idea that you and he were on bad terms."

"Yes, well," I conceded. "Perhaps you may also spread the word that Miss Wren Davenport is not of fragile mind. In fact, she is one of the strongest people I know and is soon to be my wife. My father does not like this because he did not, and does not, get a say in my life any longer."

"I will, ol' chap. I assure you, now that I know the truth, should I hear of any misguided information, I will be sure to put them straight on the matter."

"Thank you, Richard. Forgive me for being so forthright with you, but the relationship between my father and I has always been strained, and more so recently, it is at a breaking point. I am only in London to tie up a few loose ends before I return to Miss Davenport in Somerset.

"Forgiven, William. I wish you the very best for the future with your bride-to-be. By what you say, you have been rather fortunate."

"Indeed, I have, Richard. Sometimes, I can't quite believe my luck."

As I walked away, the matter of misinformation resolved—which I could only imagine to be the first of many of my father's lies—I let out an irritated sigh, conceding that, once the night had passed, I would seize the day and face my father. Be sure, I was in no mood to discuss matters with the dreadful old fool that evening, for fear of keeping to my word and truly wringing his neck.

My mood darkened to almost black, competing with the night sky beyond the window. As I rested my head on the pillow, I tried in vain to push away my father's malicious words, which were playing repetitively in my mind. I wanted to erase them, but to hear he had spread vindictive rumours about Wren—not to mention the memory of the hurt swimming in her eyes that had thoroughly ingrained itself in a permanent scar in my mind—made it impossible. Everything was too raw to dismiss so flippantly. A fuse had been lit, constantly searing through my insides. A mere word against her from anyone, and I did not know, nor could I be blamed for, what I would be capable of.

I consoled myself with the comforting knowledge that none of it would matter soon enough, for it was to be the last time either of us returned.

Chapter Twenty-Three

William

Grey clouds loomed over all of London, mirroring my mood as I stepped out onto the street. The heels of my shoes clacked against the pavement as the muscles in my forehead and on the bridge of my nose scrunched against an excruciating pain. It burrowed deep within my flesh in a pounding throb, which felt very much like a hammer resounding against my skull. I was in no fit state to face my father so early in the morning and was more than willing to put a considerably decent measure of time between us. And so, my feet carried me in the opposite direction of my childhood home, towards where one could purchase a decent breakfast and plenty of strong coffee.

I had spent my entire life in London. Of course, we were privileged to be able to spend weeks away, residing on the country estate, but I had never noticed how thoroughly depressing the city was in comparison to Somerset. The rain clouds only forced the heavy weight of the grey further onto my shoulders, until I felt like I was confined to the insides of a slowly shrinking box, the walls closing me in in a tight, suffocating grip. There were hardly any bright colours other than those of the fabric of people's clothes and the odd sign on a shop. Nature had been torn away to make room for what most called progress, but for me, it was terribly dismal indeed.

I suppose one would argue the difference if they had only bothered to take note of the wealthier side of the city, but that was not all there was to London. You only had to view it from a different angle to see a new perspective. I had seen them all and could not ignore how different the lives of those in poverty were from the lives of those, such as myself, my siblings, and my father. It was all rather unfair, I thought, as I dropped some coins into a man's upturned cap whilst he sat huddled in the entrance of an alleyway. That could very well have been me if fate had not been so kind. The threat of rain for someone with no shelter concerned me. I had already been caught in a downpour a few days prior, but I had been lucky enough to have gone back to warm dwellings where I assumed he had none. I could not contemplate how terrible that could be for any person.

"Are you hungry, sir?" I asked.

The man looked up at me. His eyes were a deep brown, and his skin weathered from the kind of hardship one could only imagine. He nodded.

"Would you like to eat with me?" I suggested brightly. I spoke tactfully, not wanting to portray my concern in a condescending manner, for no man, whether fortunate or not, was a stranger to pride.

"I don't want to go in there, sir," he replied, his eyes flitting from me then towards the coffee house to which I was heading.

"Would you prefer if I brought something to you instead?"

Offering a smile of thanks, the man nodded once again.

"Okay, you wait here, and I will get you something to eat."

I made quick work of purchasing bread and butter, bacon, and cold beef, then carried the neatly packaged parcel out of the establishment to the unfortunate stranger, where I handed it to him.

"This should see you right for a while," I offered. I slipped my coat from my shoulders and laid it over his lap. "Keep it," I insisted. "The sky looks fit to burst, and this will keep you warm."

"But, sir," the man objected. "You will need it. As you said, it will rain soon, and not just a small shower either. Look at that sky."

The cold edge of the breeze slithered beneath the cuffs of my shirt. I simply ignored its icy fingers for fear of worrying the man in front of me. "I have another back at my lodgings, sir. I will go back and grab it, so don't concern yourself. I fear you will need it more than I."

"Thank you, sir," he rasped. His eyes sparkled with kindness as he reached out, clasping my hand in both of his and shaking them gratefully. "God bless you, son."

"And you too, sir."

The coffee house welcomed me once again; the intense, decadent aroma and warmth from inside the establishment curled around me pleasantly. The guilt of my wealth nestled in my chest as I observed the vagabond through the window. He had dragged himself from the cold stone, quickly gathering his belongings into his arms; his feet, and a sense of desperation, forcing him to venture out from beneath the simplistic shelter under which he had been sitting. The skies had ripped open angrily, the rain battering his clothes and the paths at his feet. It warmed my heart to have helped him, but I knew the food and a little change would not resolve all his problems. I only hoped he would have the sense to search the pocket of his new coat, where he would find the few guineas, I had purposefully left for him to find.

Raindrops chased one another down the windowpane, leaving momentary evidence of their short-lived journey in their wake. Sliding further down the glass, they dragged smoke residue along with them until their transparency was tainted with the smog of city life. It was strange how the simple act of watching them take their natural course had enabled me to relax the taut muscles in my back and shoulders and, with a bit of help from the exceedingly strong and bitter coffee, lessened the pain in my head.

Overnight, I had begun to ponder as to whet-her visiting my father was such a good idea or if it was even worth my time and effort. He had said some things about Wren that were unforgiveable. They riled me. He riled me. When I had left my lodgings that morning, I was still undecided, pulled by an unwarranted sense of loyalty to him, but the longer I sat in the coffee house mulling it over, the idea of the two of us in one room had me leaning more towards the conclusion that it would do more harm than good. I was fully aware he may disown me and relieve me of my duties as his heir, but, in all honesty, I knew it would be a blessed relief.

As I tipped my head back, draining the last dregs of the delectable beverage from my cup, I resolved to write to my father after Wren and I were married and settled, in the hope he would eventually come to his senses.

Casting that rather tedious task aside, I turned my thoughts to the other man I had to face and the blessing I would require from him.

The writing on the slip of parchment in my hand blurred as I stood on the step to the Davenport family home. The pain in my head was obviously getting to me more than I had thought, I mused, as I steadied myself against the cold stone of the wall and proceeded to knock on the door.

"Yes?" A man of about sixty stood rigidly in his black, starched suit. He peered down his nose with a sense of superiority as he eyed me curiously. "May I help?"

"I am here to speak with Mr Davenport, sir. It is about a Miss Davenport," I smiled, composing myself before the man as he scrutinised me from head to toe.

"Very well, sir," he sniffed. "Do come in. I will tell the master you are here, Mr ..."

"Darlington, sir. William Darlington," I offered politely, ignoring the nerves roiling in my stomach.

"Wait here."

As the butler marched off, I was relieved to have left my coat behind. The house seemed stiflingly hot; my skin, growing quite clammy as I began to perspire. I loosened my cravat just enough so that it was barely noticeable, if at all, the release of the fabric around my neck, offering me a morsel of relief. Flustered, I knew all too well this meeting had to be perfect, for the outcome of it mattered for Wren and I.

"Would you like to come through, sir?" the butler drawled, gesturing for me to follow him.

And, like a lamb to the slaughter, I did just that.

There was no mistaking the single similarity between Wren and her father, for she had the same soft blue eyes as he did. He was dressed in refined clothes, with a look of defeat etched into his features. His face brightened as I entered the room —undoubtedly from practice.

"Ah, you must be Mr Darlington." His lips pinched into a forced smile as he offered me his hand to shake. Honestly, I was not offended; I felt for him. The evidence of something weighing heavily on his mind was apparent, explaining his lack of enthusiasm.

Hoping it was some sort of guilt over the way Wren had been treated, I dismissed the nerves that had plagued me. My body cooled, and the pain in my head began to drift away.

"I am, sir. I hope you do not mind me intruding."

He gestured for me to sit. However, I was not

nearly as relaxed as I would have liked to have been and was quite unable to accept his kind offer.

"Not at all, young man. Thomas, the man who you met at the door, said you were here regarding my daughter; is that correct?" he prompted.

"Yes, sir, indeed it is."

"Splendid. Although..." The man looked thoughtful. "I cannot say I have seen you amongst the crowds of the season this year. Oh, nevermind, for it matters not." Mr Davenport waved his hand in front of his face, dismissing my lack of presence amongst the ton.

"You wouldn't have, sir." I coughed to clear my throat. "I have not been here in London all season. I have been-"

Before I could inform Mr Davenport of my whereabouts or indeed ask him what I had intended to, the door to the parlour burst open, and three women bustled through. I knew within seconds which one was Primrose because Wren had described her perfectly, so I assumed the only two remaining faces belonged to the last two names that Wren had made me aware of. I bristled at their presence yet hid my feelings towards them behind my schooled features.

"Ah, Lucella, dear, allow me to introduce you to Mr Darlington. We were just discussing an important matter with regards to our daughter."

"Is that so, Mr Darlington?" She smiled primly,

sashaying further towards me as though I were her prey. Her dark hair and pale skin deceived the eye, but the malicious soul I knew she possessed profoundly soured her beauty.

"It is, madam." I inhaled to soften the tension cascading in a burning, fiery liquid over my shoulders and down my back, my jaw clenching against the anger rising within me. I could not allow the protective beast I harboured to reveal himself, for fear of ruining it all.

"I don't recall seeing you at any of the balls we have attended," Mrs Davenport simpered.

The deluded woman batted her eyelids coquettishly, as though she were young and unmarried. Every move and expression were thoroughly distasteful, making me extremely uneasy in her presence as well as that of her husband and daughters.

"Therefore, I assume you are one of those who like to simply look from afar," she continued, tittering falsely. "Well, I am afraid if you are enquiring after Primrose, she is already spoken for." She smirked, her hips undulating with emphasis as she sashayed back to her daughters.

Good Lord, the woman was unashamedly brash and highly deluded. Her lips were thin, lines puckering at the edges from years of spiteful words at her eldest daughter, yet still she believed herself to be attractive. It was confounding. It may have won Mr Davenport's heart and loosened his purse strings, but I could see her for everything she pretended not to be.

"It is not Primrose, madam. Perhaps I should explain."

"Ah, then it must be Gladys. She is a fine young lady, aren't you, darling?" she crooned, turning to her younger, yet still as hideous, replica.

"Oh, Mama, you will have him change his mind if you do not let him speak. However, I must say you are a wonderful mystery, Mr Darlington, for I do not remember you at all, yet I am quite thrilled that you have sought me out." Wren's sister tittered just like her mother had, as though it had been practiced several times before. Her features sharpened as she pursed her lips into a puckered, simpering smile.

"I'm afraid you misunderstand me, madam, miss. It is neither Primrose nor Gladys whom I seek to be my wife. The daughter I am referring to-"

"I do not have any other daughter, Mr Darlington. You must have the wrong address for the lady you seek," Mrs Davenport spluttered. Her features paled to a stark white against the ink black of her hair as she struggled on the precipice of her most guarded secret. The fear in her eyes told me she knew all too well I was about to reveal my knowledge of the precious gem she had robbed the world of.

The extremities of her floundering made me wonder what exactly she would do if we had been anywhere outside of the Davenport family home where others would witness her for who she really was. The people in the room already knew very well there was another daughter, and yet she still acted abhorrently. 'She is a disgrace of a mother,' I snarled inwardly.

My need to protect Wren clawed at my insides. "You do, Mrs Davenport. You have three daughters."

Mr Davenport raised his hand as both Wren's poor excuse of a mother and just as poor of an excuse of a sister moved forward, their neck muscles taught with the tension of outrage, ready to raise their voices and object once more. Their bodies froze at the man's command, limbs trembling as their anger permeated the air.

"Yes, we do have three daughters, Mr Darlington. You are speaking of Wren, are you not?" His lips curled with obvious joy. No longer confined to the tedium of what he had expected, his eyes danced. My news seemed to have lifted a heavy burden from his shoulders.

"I am, indeed, sir. I have come here to ask your permission for her hand in marriage."

From the corner of my eye, I could see the little bounce Primrose gave as the news fractured the tension in her body. As I turned, a grin stretched across her face, one that met her eyes without hesitation and was filled with genuine warmth and excitement for her sister.

"You cannot marry that!" Mrs Davenport roared. The colour had returned to her cheeks and was deepening further as her beady, dark eyes stared at me in utter rage.

"Get them out of here at once," Mr Davenport bellowed towards the door. When neither movement nor answer came, he turned to his youngest daughter. "Primrose, darling, perhaps you could do the honour of taking your disgrace of a mother and sister from this room, so I may speak with Mr Darlington."

Mr Davenport's tall frame expanded as he pulled his shoulders back, appalled at his wife and daughter's behaviours. Gladys was scowling, her eyes boring into me as though disgusted that I should do the obvious thing and choose the most beautiful woman in the world over the miserable, snivelling wretch that she was.

"Of course, Papa." Primrose was still beaming, although slightly wary, as she coaxed her mother and sister from the room.

"Don't you dare give him permission. Do you hear me?" Mrs Davenport screamed as Primrose placed her hands at her back, refusing to let her turn to face us.

"You have done enough damage already, woman. Just get out!" Wren's father was fuming. His hands trembled with anger as he fell back into the chair.

"Please have a seat, Mr Darlington. I can only apologise for my wife and daughter. I'm afraid your visit has seen to it that I have finally snapped. I cannot, nor will I, allow their appalling behaviour to continue."

"Please do not apologise, sir. I am grateful you have agreed to speak with me."

"The gratitude is all mine, Mr Darlington. I am afraid I have let my Wren down quite a lot in her life, and with you just being here, seeking my permission to marry my firstborn, you have made me all too aware of just how weak of a man—of a father—I have been."

"Wren speaks kindly of you, Mr Davenport. She has never uttered a word otherwise," I offered, trying to ease the mood.

"That sounds very much like Wren. I am so pleased she has found a man who will love and appreciate her for the young woman I know her to be."

"Do you not need to know about what I can offer her, sir?" I asked, confused by the quick, albeit unsaid, acceptance of Wren and I.

"Do you love Wren, Mr Darlington?" he asked, his eyes locked on mine.

"Yes, sir, with all my heart. I have never met

anyone like her before. When I am with her, nothing else matters, for everything falls into place."

"I thought as much," he smiled thoughtfully. "Although, by the way you stood your ground in this room in front of all of us here, I didn't need to ask at all. You are a better man than I, Mr Darlington, and I give my blessing to you both."

Stunned and elated, I shook his hand. "Thank you so much, sir. Wren will be thrilled by the news. I shall take my leave."

"Just before you go, young man." Mr Davenport gestured to the seat, gently ordering me to sit back down again as he poured two glasses of whisky from the crystal-cut decanter. "Before you leave, I would like to know you a little better, so please, won't you have a drink with me?"

I lowered my body back into the seat, wondering whether he had had a change of heart. My expression must have told him as much, for he chuckled softly.

"Oh, don't panic, Mr Darlington; I have not changed my mind. On the contrary, I couldn't be happier for my daughter, but I would love to hear how you and my Wren came to cross paths."

"Yes, of course, sir, but before I forget," I began. I held Wren's letter towards him. "Wren has asked me to give this to you in person."

"Mr Darlington! Mr Darlington, please wait." Primrose ran towards me, her cheeks speckled with the pink of exhaustion as she caught her breath, yet she still managed to smile profusely.

"Miss Davenport?"

"I am so glad I have caught you. Please tell me Papa gave you and Wrenny his blessing." She clasped her hands in front of her chest as her breathing finally slowed to a normal rate.

"Indeed, he did, Miss Davenport. I am a very happy man."

"I am so glad. I am ashamed to say that life—well, Mama, actually—has been rather cruel to Wrenny. I only hope you will love her as she deserves to be loved."

"Have no fear of that, Miss Davenport. And may I just say, it hasn't been just your mother who has been cruel. You have all played your part in keeping her here." Although Primrose didn't deserve my anger, I couldn't hold my tongue as the words quickly spilled from my mouth.

Guiltily concerned by my forthright accusation, I thought Primrose would at least retaliate, yet she simply looked embarrassed. "Yes, Mr Darlington, I am ashamed to say that we, meaning my father and I, could have done more to have made things better for Wrenny," she smiled thoughtfully.

The dimming of her once-happy eyes ruthlessly pushed my conscience over the edge, rendering me suddenly awash with regret. "Forgive me, Miss Davenport; I have spoken out of turn, for Wren has always spoken so highly of you and your father. *Especially you*. I am just a little vexed at your mother and sister's behaviour today. I should not have taken it out on you, and for that, I apologise."

"There is no need to apologise, Mr Darlington. What you've said is nothing I have not thought to myself, and believe me, I have given a great many hours of my time to the stalwart regret of my inaction to help my sister. Why, only the other day I wrote to Wrenny, informing her that my fiancé and I will be visiting her in Somerset," she began, her fingers twisting the fabric of her gown with a palpable guilt lingering in the air between us. I felt terrible for my part in it.

"That sounds wonderful, Miss Davenport," I offered.

"Indeed, we will be travelling tomorrow. Of course, I would like her to meet my fiancé, but much more than that, I would like very much to apologise to her for my part in all of this. I know it will not make up for the past, but I hope it will be a start."

Primrose's shoulders lowered gently as the burgeoning apprehension of expressing everything she'd wanted to say fell away, leaving her lighter than she had been before. It revealed the sincerity of her words, convincing me she had spoken the truth.

"I know she will be glad of your visit," I smiled, encouragingly. "I suspect, with my being here, I have given her too much time to think, and, most likely, she will be fretting about my return. To think of her like that concerns me, so perhaps you could do me a favour, Miss Davenport?"

"Yes, of course, Mr Darlington. What is it you would like me to do?"

"Please, could you tell Wren that you have seen and spoken with me and assure her that I have every intention of returning to her soon?"

"Are you not leaving tomorrow, now that you have Papa's permission?" Wren's sister looked surprised.

"I am afraid not, Miss Davenport, for I have another matter or two to tend to. I will be a day or so behind you."

Primrose nodded. "Very well, I shall pass on your message. I am sure she will be very relieved to hear it."

"Thank you, Miss Davenport."

Chapter Twenty-Four

Wren

I had tried, emphatically, to keep my body and, in doing so, my mind busy, what with William being patently absent from my days, but they still seemed to drag terribly. The evenings were the worst, of course, for it was the time when everything slowed down to a dawdling, leisurely pace, releasing the awful silence from the void his absence had created. I only wished I could fill it again with his laughter and teasing, no matter how much he could make me blush. When my mind wandered, it wandered where it had no right to, filling my chest with angst and pain from fears that my mind insisted on playing out in graphic, theatrical scenarios inside my head.

"I 'ope you ain't worrying needlessly again, duck," Rose grumbled playfully. "He will be back soon, and all the 'urt you're causing yourself will have been all for bleeding nothing. I'm telling you that man worships the ground you walk upon."

My shoulders slumped, never quite relaxing as I

wished they would. "I know you are right, Rose, but my insecurities will not leave me alone. They steal my chances to hold on to all the assurances William gave me before he left. What I would do to have even a morsel of confidence." I sighed heavily. "It is a terrifying thing to have your mind cloyed with the cruel words of others. It denies you the opportunity to believe in what is patently obvious. Even as I speak this, you can hear that I know all you say is true, but there is no glue of confidence to merge what we speak of with the power of belief. There is only a void of a million nonsensical questions and assumptions that I cannot relinquish. I wish I could just have a little faith in the person I know I truly am, yet I find myself doubting her with such fervour." I placed my hand over my heart as I closed the book on my lap. "I despise feeling like this, Rose." I swallowed against the ache in my throat, chastising myself for the tears pricking at the backs of my eyes.

"I know, duck, or at least I think I do, but if you ever start doubting yourself, you just come and ask me, and I will put those thoughts to rest by telling you the truth. Now why don't you read to me for a bit 'fore bed. I've always loved the way you read those books. You always make 'em sound so much more real somehow."

"Alright then, Rose." I picked up my copy of Jane Eyre. I'd given up on Wuthering Heights, for

Heathcliff was always a little too dark in personality for my liking, which in turn disturbed my dreams in the most peculiar ways. Jayne Eyre was a favourite of mine, and since William had returned to London, it had been a great source of escapism, even if only for a little while.

As I turned the page and began to read, there was a polite knock on the front door of The Aviary. My heart soared, hoping William had returned. "I'll get it, Rose," I beamed as I swiftly stood, absent-mindedly dropping the book on the floor, and headed out into the hallway.

The rapping on the door sounded again. It was gentle and familiar, but I knew it wasn't William. Although disappointed at having to wait longer for him to return, there was no mistaking the knock that had sounded so often on my bedchamber door. As a child, Primrose had visited my bedchamber every day since she had been old enough to climb the stairs without the fear of falling, and as we reached our older years, the daily routine had continued, binding us together with a stronger bond than I had with any other in my family.

"Primrose!" I exclaimed happily as we both stood facing each other. "I am so glad you are here."

My sister stepped forward, instantly curling her arms around me, the strength of her embrace signifying how much she had missed me. I reciprocated with the same tenacity, confirming that her feelings were indeed as my own as I held her tight for a few more seconds, but there was something in the way she buried her head into my shoulder that had me concerned.

"Oh, Wrenny, I have missed you," she whispered. "Did you get my letter?"

"Yes, of course. Come in, come in."

Primrose was followed by a tall gentleman with hair as golden as her own. His eyes were a deep green like our mother's, but they were somehow softer and kinder. "Wren, this is James Devoe, my fiancé."

As the man turned his face further towards me, the air rushed in a cold stream through my slightly opened lips and down my airways, where I held on to it, bitterly concerned about the reaction he may have to my appearance. Yet, after a few seconds, my lungs relented their grasp, the air expelling into the room as he simply smiled and took my hand.

"It is a pleasure to finally meet you, Miss Davenport. Primrose talks of you often."

My eyes flitted to my sister as if for confirmation that this man before me did not recoil at the obvious differences in my physique.

"Isn't he adorable, Wrenny?" she beamed, gazing lovingly up at him.

"I believe it would be improper for me to agree to that when he is your fiancé, Prim, but yes, Mr Devoe appears to be a decent young man. It is a pleasure to meet you, Mr Devoe. I apologise for my initial silence, but I do not meet many people, and so I do not always know what to say." I was ashamed of the dishonesty of my excuse, but there never was a correct way to explain the predicament of my spine that would not draw attention to it.

Primrose released Mr Devoe and stepped towards me, clasping her cold fingers around my warmer ones and squeezing them gently. The look in her eyes assured me she knew all too well what I was thinking, yet her gaze offered me a spark of confidence that I needn't worry.

"Come through to the drawing room," I offered kindly, my hands still secure within my sister's. "Rose will be wondering where I have disappeared to. Please leave your bags there, and I will take them through in a moment."

"No need, Miss Davenport. If you would care to point me in the right direction when the time is right, I will carry them to the rooms," Mr Devoe offered with a contagious smile. "A young lady should not be made to carry a man's luggage, nor any luggage for that matter."

"Thank you, Mr Devoe. That is extremely kind of you, and, please call me Wren as we are to be family.”

“Rose, this is Mr Devoe,” I announced as we settled in the parlour.

“James, please,” he offered. “That goes for you too, Wren. I prefer to use my first name in good company.” The man’s smile was kind as he addressed Rose.

“Oh, you’ve done well with this one, Miss Primrose,” Rose crooned. “Shall I make us all a cup of tea?”

“That would be lovely. Thank you, Rose,” James replied, his eyes roving inquisitively over the décor of the room.

Rose pushed down on the arms of the chair in which she was sitting as she made to move towards the kitchen. “It’s okay, Rose; let me. You stay there,” I offered.

“Are you sure, duck? It don’t feel right, me just sitting ‘ere.”

“Absolutely sure.” In truth, tea was a perfect excuse for me to exit and regain some of my composure. It had seeped slowly from me in beads of perspiration as I had stood stoically in front of our new guests. My eyes had been fixed on James, whom I found myself watching with scrutiny, analysing every flicker in his eyes, every pinch of his lips, and every word he said, always nervously considering whether there were any hidden criticisms or mockery within them that I ought to have seen.

'What were you thinking, Wren?' I chastised myself. 'The man seems so kind, so why would he hide anything?'

The doubts of his sincerity plagued me, and I hated it.

"I will help you, Wren." Primrose stepped into the kitchen, startling me. The teapot lid slipped slightly from my grip, clattering against the teapot itself. My nervous state was apparently quite obvious, even to the most oblivious.

"Let me," Prim offered, prising the teapot from my fingers before I dropped it and smashed it upon the quaint stone floor.

"Thank you," I whispered.

"Wrenny, I came here because I wanted you to meet James, but I also came here because there are things, I feel I must say to you. They have been left too long unsaid, and it bothers me that I have allowed it to be like that."

My brows pinched at the centre, confused by what she could possibly mean.

"Sit down, please, Wrenny, while we are blessed with some privacy. James and Rose will be perfectly fine for a little while without us."

I did not expect an apology from Prim. From my point of view, she did not owe me one. If anyone owed me such a thing, it would most definitely be my mother and my other sister, even my father to an extent, but not my Prim. "Prim, you do not need to apologise. You and Rose have always put me at ease."

"I do, Wrenny. I could have said more when Mama and Gladys were cruel, but I have always been too afraid to speak up. Even when I have tried, I allowed Mama to silence me." My sister paled as she arranged the teacups on the tray. "I have been a terrible sister to you, and for that I am truly very sorry, Wrenny."

"Oh, Prim, you are a nincompoop," I laughed. "One would believe you have never met our mother."

Primrose chuckled as the light in her eyes began to glimmer amongst the needless glisten of unshed tears. "What do you mean? Of course, I have met our mother. The woman is infamous to us Davenports."

"Exactly. You did your best where I am concerned, and I couldn't have asked for more from you. You have nothing to chastise yourself for because there is nothing to forgive."

"Thank you, Wrenny," she sniffed daintily. "That means an awful lot to me, although I dare say I shall chastise myself rather frequently before I can ever rid myself of the guilt I carry."

"That is ridiculous, Prim, and quite frankly pointless. You have a lovely fiancé who adores you, so he and the wedding are those whom you should turn your mind to rather than something that is simply untrue."

"He is rather lovely, isn't he?" she grinned, her cheeks brightening into a delicate shade of pink.

I nodded, warmed from within to see the sparkle in her eyes as she spoke of him.

"He was the one who suggested I speak with you about how I have been feeling," Primrose added.

"He knows about me?" A leaden weight dropp-ed into my stomach.

He knew my existence had brought shame on my family because of the curve in my spine.

My insides burned with shame at the revelation, even though it was the truth, and one could not escape the past no matter in which direction they may decide to flee. There really was no right way of meeting new people for me when the matter of my persistent insecurities was involved. The raised shoulder was obvious when facing them, and so was the limp when I walked, so it neither mattered whether they met me for the first time without prior warning nor whether they were told beforehand, for it clearly made little difference. Either way, I still had the most desperate desire to vanish into thin air.

"I only told him because of how guilty I was

feeling, not because I thought he would be unkind to you." Primrose sighed. "Mama really has made you feel worthless, hasn't she?"

A tear snaked down from the corner of my eye. This was the first time I had let my sister take a glimpse at the damage our family had inflicted upon me.

"Oh, Wrenny. I wish you could see how beautiful you are. I believe Mama knows it too, but she cannot rid herself of the jealousy she feels towards you. You should have seen her face when Mr Darlington showed up."

"William? William visited our house in London?"

Primrose nodded, her lips pinched in a suppressed smile, deepening her beautiful dimples.

"Do you know why he was there, Prim? Oh, you must tell me," I pleaded. My tears had dried, only to be replaced with a tidal wave of nausea swirling in the pit of my stomach.

"I do. Would you like me to tell you?"

"Of course, Prim. Please don't tease."

The light glittered within my sister's eyes as she grinned, letting out the tiniest squeal of delight whilst squeezing my hands. "He was there to ask for Papa's permission to marry you."

My mouth was devoid of moisture as I waited, desperate to hear the outcome of that particular event, but she allowed me to simply stare at her while she moved back around the kitchen table to finish preparing the tea tray.

"Oh, Prim, you are being most cruel," I groaned. "Please tell me what Papa said to him."

"Well, I don't know exactly what he said to him, word for word, but what I can tell you is that you will need to buy a wedding gown very soon."

Elated at the news of Papa's permission to marry, as well as the message William had asked Primrose to relay to me, Rose, Prim, James, and I spent the rest of the evening in the drawing room, where the hours bled into the early morning, each one filled with chatter about the events of the season that I had missed.

I wholeheartedly approved of James, for he was attentive and kind towards my sister, and not once did he make me feel as though I was a monster. My sister had chosen well, I mused. And I was glad of it.

"Are you sure James will be comfortable remaining at The Aviary? I feel rather rude stealing you from him whilst we take a trip into the village," I asked Primrose as she sat close by my side in the curricle.

William had arranged for the vehicle to be returned to us, and I quietly thanked him for being so thoughtful, for now that I had been into the village once, I was keen to try again, but this time with Primrose. I cannot say I would have been as keen if it were just me, but with my sister at my side, I did not feel quite so vulnerable.

"Steal me? You make me sound like a basket of bread," she giggled. "I am sure James will be just fine. In fact, he thought it was a wonderful idea. Last time I spoke with him, he was positively brimming with happiness at the prospect of wandering the land so he can get a better view of the area for when we live here. So, fret not, my dear sister; you have definitely not stolen this basket of bread from anyone." Primrose softly chuckled with amusement as she nestled closer at my side.

"You are going to live at The Aviary?" I inquired nervously.

Perhaps it was selfish of me, but I found myself suddenly engulfed in fear. I could feel every detail of the plans William and I had made for our lives at The Aviary begin to crumble beneath my feet. If Primrose and James were going to live in the cottage, I did not know where William and I would live. The very thought that The Aviary would no longer be ours made my stomach flip.

"Oh, heavens, no, Wrenny. James would like to buy a plot of land nearby so we can build on it and I can be close to my favourite sister." Primrose squeezed my arm gently. "Besides, The Aviary belongs to you. Even if Papa offered it to me, which he did not, I might add, I would not accept it purely on those grounds."

I didn't know what to say. Perhaps I should have said thank you, but I was ashamed to have ever panicked. The guilt at having put my needs before my sister and the new life she had ahead of her felt terribly selfish. Instead, I lovingly patted her hand, hoping it would relay everything I was feeling.

"Talking of The Aviary," I began. "Did William or Papa mention anything about it to you? Anything about me being allowed to remain here?"

"It just so happens that Papa did mention it. After Mr Darlington left, I was a tad confused as to why he wouldn't return to you at once. He said that he had a few more matters to tend to. Well, you know what I am like, Wrenny, I was forced to embark on a little detective work. Nothing too drastic, but I did manage to squeeze some information from dear old Papa." Prim paused for effect as she pursed her lips playfully, waiting for me to beg for the rest of what she knew.

"Oh, you are awful, Prim. Please tell me. If you don't tell me soon, I shall be so nervous, and then this curricle will veer off track, and you and I shall be submerged in that terribly dirty ditch over there," I begged. If I hadn't been in the curricle, I believe I may have gotten down on my knees, for I was beyond desperate to know.

Prim grinned wickedly. "I'm sorry, I am being awful, aren't I? Long story short, Papa happened to mention he would be handing over the deeds to The Aviary to you both as a wedding gift."

Primrose wriggled on her seat, her teeth clenched in a smile, splitting her face as a bubble of excitement burst from her lips in a breathless squeal. "You and I will be neighbours. Isn't that wonderful, Wrenny? But you must act ever-so surprised when you are told the news officially, in case you weren't meant to know yet." Primrose pouted, her eyes filled with mischief.

"I will be the world's best actress, so you shall not be discovered for telling all, I promise, Prim," I chuckled. "And thank you for telling me. I cannot believe how much has changed in the last few months. It makes me positively giddy to the point of being thoroughly scared that all the walls of my dreams, slowly rising around me, will crash down with a single blow, specifically one referred to as our mother."

"Oh, Wrenny, you mustn't think like that. I've met your William, and, being the rather protective sister that I am, I felt it was my duty to question his intentions. I can assure you that that man loves you as a man should, and I have no doubt you will be Mrs Darlington very soon. And as for Mama, I believe Father will be having none of her nonsense from now on. Now less of this pessimistic attitude because we have wedding gowns to peruse and purchase."

Chapter Twenty-Five

Wren

The curricle wobbled, the movements jittering through our bodies as we travelled over the uneven roads, the horse happily pulling us further into the village. Primrose giggled at our battle to stay poised and rigid upon our seats, an act that was always expected of the young ladies we were.

"Can you imagine what Mama would say if she saw us like this?" She grinned, then cleared her throat. "'*Primrose, it is not considered ladylike to allow one's body to be thrown about like that. Sit up straight this instant before we are seen!*'" Primrose mocked, joyfully. As the vehicle hit the next rocky mound, she snorted, sending her into further fits of giggles.

"Ah, I see you have also inherited the Davenport snort." My cheek bones ached from smiling. I had never before heard her laugh the way she had been then, and it really was so lovely to have her there by my side.

"Guilty as charged, m'lord," she replied. The

words blew from her lips in an extended breath as she wiped away a tear of amusement. She placed her hands over her stomach, taking deep breaths as she tried to regain control with considerable success.

The countryside finally merged with rows of houses, fields and trees, replaced with bricks and mortar. Familiar stores rose at their edges in the distance, and I realised we were almost there.

William's absence seemed to peel back a protective layer, leaving me feeling rather exposed and vulnerable. Perhaps it was the finely dressed strangers, not hesitating to take a second look in my direction, who had been the ones to tear it away. Their supposed freedom to stare begged the question as to whether they believed I could not see their unkindness. My shoulder muscles burned in response as they locked me in a prison of self-loathing, the tension creeping over my body, inch by inch. "Perhaps we shouldn't have come here," I whispered close to my sister's ear. "People are staring."

"Oh, really? They must be wondering where such handsome young ladies have come from. Just smile and wave, dear sister." Without another word, Primrose raised her hand and waved at the lady glaring in our direction, only to be rebuffed as the lady tilted her head and looked down her nose at us. "Oh, dear, someone is in a rather fraught mood this morning," Primrose sneered. Her eyes darkened as she turned them on the woman, crimson creeping into her light pink cheeks. It was the first time, I believe, I had ever seen her truly angry.

Exasperated, I dragged my hand slowly down my face. The lady had made me feel embarrassed to be myself.

Why do people feel the need to lay their unwarranted and unrequired judgement upon others merely for the way they look?

"Perhaps Somerset is as bad as London, Prim," I choked out, mortified for my sister to have to deal with it as well. "I can't seem to escape people like Mama and Gladys. The last time I came here with William, I didn't notice anything like this. I'm so sorry, Primrose; I have only embarrassed you."

Primrose spun to face me. "That is quite enough of that, Wren Jennifer Davenport. That creature over there is undoubtedly an ignorant beast who, I have no doubt, was raised amongst the worst of the aristocratic society. You only have to look at the latest fashion she is wearing to see that. However, it is plain to see that there is no fabric or sense of style that could ever give her a morsel of decency because she is simply rude. You will never apologise for embarrassing me again, because being with you is never an embarrassment. Do you understand, Wrenny?"

Lost for words, I nodded.

"Good. Now keep that chin up. You have more beauty in your little finger than she does in her entire body, so I have every reason to believe the puckered stare she gave you has nothing to do with your beautiful extra curve but more to do with her lack of any. One could iron one's unmentionables on her body," she smirked. "Personally, I would be more inclined to use the facial area," she added in a whisper.

The lady's eyes narrowed at the secrecy of Primrose's additional comments. The frustration of not knowing what my sister had said appeared to tremble through her body, manifesting as a very visible spasm in her jaw.

My mouth fell open as heat rose, cupping the apples of my cheeks, at witnessing my sister's obvious displeasure with the woman. I didn't know where to look, so I simply stared at Primrose, silently begging for her to keep walking. I wanted to be as far away from the situation as was humanly possible.

As the woman's lips puckered with rage, my sister's eyes glimmered with smug satisfaction, revelling in the victory she had had over the stranger. "There. Much better," she huffed, curling her arm into the crook of mine. "I believe we came here to peruse and purchase, Wrenny, and peruse and purchase we shall. Come along."

Primrose huffed as she pulled me forward, outraged at the scowling lady and, I assumed, my insecurities. The scowling lady's eyes followed us as we walked past her. I tried to keep my head up to appear confident and unfazed, but the tension of the shame and awkwardness engulfing me provoked a throbbing ache in my spine and a searing heat in my shoulder. Both fervently burned beneath my flesh, making it considerably difficult to hide the pain from my face.

"Can we help you, Madam?" Primrose halted, making me teeter slightly. My steps quickly became an awkward shuffle on the tips of my toes as I tried to stop in time with her. I had been a fool to believe she had said all she had wanted to say, for it appeared there was most certainly more she had to get off her chest.

Primrose faced the acidic glare of the lady whose black, beady eyes were seemingly trying to bore into my flesh. "Your face seems to have gotten stuck in the most terrible expression," Primrose sniffed haughtily.

The woman's fierce eyes expanded into a horrified glare as she realised my sister was demanding as to why it was that she would not release me from her sights.

"I-I..." the lady stuttered, her face crimsoning as she struggled for words.

"Nothing to say?" Primrose inquired, scowling.

"No? Oh, it appears you are not quite as stupid as you look."

Primrose's words had left both the lady and I quite speechless. It seemed Prim harboured all the venom of our mother and sister, only releasing it as she fought to protect me.

Our feet made quick work of the pavement as Primrose dragged us into the nearest shop.

"There, that shut her up," Primrose beamed over the trembling of her body. She was livid. It was obvious by the way her eyes were no longer her usual soft blue but had frozen into an icy-cold hue.

Taking her gloved hand in mine, I hid the fact that I was lost for words, for I wasn't sure who her anger was meant for. Perhaps it was all for the scowling lady, or perhaps there was, as I suspected, a little reserved for me.

"I am so sorry you saw me like that, Wrenny, but most of all, I am sorry you have to deal with people like her. They're all nincompoops. Nasty, ignorant nincompoops."

I was relieved to hear her explain her anger with no mention of any blame for me, yet I could not help but feel partially responsible for her ever having to face that situation in the first place. I hugged Primrose tightly.

"That's enough of that, Wrenny. I know exactly what you are thinking, and I must inform you that you are utterly and absolutely incorrect. You are not to bear any blame for the actions of others. She is just another version of Mama, that is all."

"Thank you," I whispered. "But I don't like to see you get upset over me. Let them stare, Prim. I have to get used to it if I am to live my life, do I not?"

"Maybe, my dear sister, but that does not mean they do not drive me to utter despair, nor that, whilst you are in my company, I will not do all I can to protect you from those monsters. People are cruel, and they should be told as much." Primrose folded her arms, incensed at the memory of the ignorant lady.

"Mama would disagree with you, Prim. I do not want her to be unkind to you."

"Oh, Wrenny, surely you must see how much I despise Mama. Of course, I love her—as much as I believe you do, despite her despicable ways—but I cannot bear to be near her anymore. She is the very reason I encouraged James to consider moving here and, of course, because I wanted to be near my favourite sister." Primrose smiled, revealing the dimples I'd thought the altercation with the scowling lady had erased.

"Oh, Prim," I beamed, curling my arms around her again. "Let us just hope that Papa won't change his mind about The Aviary then."

"Of course he won't, Wrenny. I think William's visit struck a rather guilty nerve in Papa. The way he spoke after he left... Well, let's just say he feels he has not been the best father to you at all, and, quite frankly, Wrenny, I agree with him. None of us have been the best to you. I know I've said it before and you said not to, but I don't think I will ever stop feeling partially responsible for your years confined in that house, so I am bound to keep repeating my apology."

"You mustn't, Prim, but if you do feel the need, you must bear one thing in mind, and that is that if my life hadn't been the way it has been, then I would never have been here in Somerset, therefore I would never have met William. It has been the path I was meant to travel all along so that I may be here, standing with you outside the dressmakers about to be measured and fitted for our wedding gowns—*both of us.*

"Did you hear me, Prim? I said *Both. Of. Us,*" I repeated. "Something neither of us had ever even considered before. Everything is changing." A flutter of excitement wriggled through a crack in the solid wall of doubt I'd built and kept hidden within me. The small wings of the wonderful creature beat gently, fanning a golden liquid warmth that swirled pleasurably beneath my ribcage, making my breath stagger.

Amongst all the talk of our past and present, we found ourselves outside the dressmakers. The most prettiest shop in the entire village with all the wonderful fabric, dresses, reticules, and bonnets displayed, just so, in the window.

Prim's eyes widened at the sight. "I will try," she muttered, replying to the conversation we were having, yet never taking her eyes from the window. "But whilst we are here, Papa has told me that you must have a new wardrobe as well as a wedding gown."

"Papa said that? Truly?"

Primrose tore her eyes from the pastel blue gown that we both knew would look absolutely divine on her and nodded triumphantly. "Yes, he jolly well did, Wrenny," she beamed, shaking her reticule slightly so I could hear the jingle of coins within it. "There are notes too," she grinned mischievously.

"Oh," I breathed, unsure how to react.

"Oh, indeed. Now let us get you the best gowns one can purchase," she squealed excitedly, then quickly lowered her tone to a whisper, "and some new Wrenny-sized and perfectly perfect unmentionables."

Heat rose to my cheeks as Primrose giggled with glee at the secrecy between us.

"Ah, Signorina, you have returned, I see," Toni beamed from behind the rich mahogany counter. "But no Mr Darlington?"

"Not today, Toni, but I have brought my sister with me," I smiled. "Primrose, this is Toni, the best modiste in England. And, Toni, this is my sister Primrose."

Primrose bobbed in a subtle curtsey, mirroring Toni's. "It is indeed a pleasure to meet you, Toni, for we both have a very special request, and I have it on great authority that you are the very best."

Toni's eyes widened with intrigue. "Come, come, sit down, and we can talk more," she encouraged, gesturing to the soft seats at the back of the store front. "I am excited to hear your request."

"I am indeed very honoured to have been sought out to make wedding gowns for such lovely ladies," Toni managed to say even with the pins held fast between the pinch of her lips. Or at least, I hope that is what she said, because I replied believing that to be the case. Oh, how terribly embarrassing if it wasn't...

"I wouldn't want anyone else to do it, Toni. You have been extremely kind to me, and your work is exquisite," I replied, as she pinned the hem of the dress, she had insisted I try on.

The dress was a rich, deep claret, simple in design, yet extremely elegant. It felt almost fraudulent to wear such a glorious gown, but I could not deny how much I loved it.

"Oh, Toni, are you sure they will not want this dress?" I asked breathlessly. "It's simply divine."

"It was meant for you, Wren." She smiled

kindly at me through the reflection in the glass. "There are times when one makes a gown, and it simply speaks to me. Who am I to argue with it when it tells me who it was meant for?

"When people see you in this, they will come from far and wide to my little shop, wanting to be as gorgeous as Wren Davenport, so it will be all so very worth it, Signorina."

"I hope I don't let you down, Toni," I offered wistfully.

"Of course you won't. *Sei una bella donna.*"

"Italian always sounds so romantic; what did that mean?" I inquired.

"Sei una bella donna means you are a beautiful woman, Wren.

"There," she announced. "All done."

"Thank you for saying that, Toni." My voice was suddenly husky with emotion. It was all I could manage to convey to her, yet it felt meagre for the words she'd said and the kindness she had shown me. I suspect she would have thought me quite barmy if I had burst into tears, but luckily for both of us, I had managed to refrain from such a display.

"When they see you and your sister in my creations looking so spectacular, especially your wedding gowns, my little dressmakers will have to expand," Toni exclaimed with a beaming smile.

"Well, with Primrose, I am sure you shall see such formidable results, for she is a true beauty and shall be married in London, but for me," I began, clearing my throat. "The wedding will be just a small one here."

"What a shame the world will not witness both of you looking so glorious, Signorina," Toni remarked, her voice laced with consideration as though she had been trying to read my thoughts. "But alas, there will be some who will see, I am sure." Toni squeezed the top of my arm gently as she gazed at me, a glimmer of understanding twinkling in her eyes. "You will be what we Italians call *squisita*, or if you prefer, what you English call exquisite, Signorina. Don't ever doubt that."

"In your creation, how can I not look exquisite, Toni?" I chuckled, trying to buff off the intensely awkward atmosphere my insecurities had plunged me into once again.

"With or without the gown, you will still be the most beautiful bride, Signorina. You must not give others permission to affect you the way they so obviously do."

"I don't give them permission," I objected, not unkindly. Even as I heard my own voice, I was ashamed of myself for the pathetic lie.

"Yes, you do, Wrenny!" Primrose called from behind the curtain. "If you didn't, then you wouldn't worry so much about people like that horrid woman earlier."

"It is not as simple as to just ignore." I exhaled

as a knot formed in my stomach. I did not have the words to explain how the look someone gave me could imprint itself and remain in my brain like a daguerreotype poised on display on a mantelpiece. "When someone stares or says something with intentional malice, it is not as fleeting as to leave your memory in seconds," I continued. "One cannot simply forget and brush it under the carpet, despite very much wanting to. I feel like I am on the edge of a dangerously steep drop. Those people are poking and prodding me as I just teeter there, waiting to fall off, and then there are people like you wonderful ladies." I turned to face Toni and my sister now that she had finished redressing, and the curtain was drawn back to reveal her. "You are the ones who are pulling me back to safety on that horrid edge. Unfortunately, though, the simple truth of it all is that I need to be the one to help me to safety, but I need to find a way to hold onto the part of me that knows I am a good person."

"And beautiful too," Toni and Primrose added simultaneously.

"That is something I may learn to feel some day," I whispered, as my voice escaped in a rasp.

Emotions had caught me in a chokehold and were considerably difficult to swallow back down.

Toni grabbed my shoulders and turned me back to face the glass. "Look at her," she demanded gently. "Look at that lady in the glass. Do you know what I see?"

I shook my head.

"I see big blue eyes filled with kindness and the most gorgeous chestnut hair that twinkles in the light. I see sweet freckles speckled across your face, which are adorable, Signorina."

I smiled coyly as a hint of laughter burst from me.

"And that smile," Toni added. "*Mamma mia, Signorina*! If that doesn't light up a room better than any gas lamp, then I don't know what does. Have faith in yourself, Wren. Start to open your eyes and shut the hatred and jealousy from others out; maybe then you will see yourself as we do."

"Rose, Rose, are you home?" I called breathlessly as Primrose and I struggled through the door with the many boxes of new garments and rather pretty unmentionables. But as well as the new gowns and the promise of the most glamorous wedding gown to follow, I had pocketed Toni's and Wren's kind words deep within my heart and carried them home to The Aviary with me, determined to keep them for eternity.

"We've had the most glorious day," I beamed, determined to forget those who had treated me so abhorrently.

"Keep walking, Wrenny; I'm going to have arms

like one of those chimpanzees if we don't put these down soon. And, if you are not careful, I will even start making the same sounds," she chuckled.

"I'm going as fast as I can, Bossy boots," I laughed, colliding with the wall as I ambled in the wrong direction, my vision severely hindered behind the mountain of boxes in my arms.

"'Ere let me, duck." Suddenly, I found half of our purchases released from my arms and a cheerful Rose looking at me as she held them in hers. "I trust you 'ad a good day then?"

"Oh, yes, it was wonderful, Rose," Primrose trilled. "Wrenny is going to be the most beautiful blushing bride that the nineteenth century has ever seen. I cannot wait to see her in her gown on the day of her wedding."

"Me neither, duck. Ay, it ain't 'alf good to 'ave you 'ere as well, Primrose. To see Wren have company nearer her own age and spend time doing things like this... well, it's lovely to see," Rose called back as the three of us clattered through the hallway, taking the last few steps to my bedchamber, where we gratefully released the entire mountain of expensive goods onto my bed.

Primrose exhaled as she clenched and unclenched her fingers, her muscles cramping where they had been tightly moulded to the rigid boxes. "It is very good to be here. Mama was driving me to insanity." She rolled her eyes, then grinned. "And, of course, I simply had to see Wrenny. Is James here?" she added, poking her head out through the open door, hoping to see him.

"Yes, duck, he's just out the back, chopping some wood," Rose replied.

"Good heavens, Rose; you have domesticated him already. I shall have to go out and leave him here with you a few more times if you are this good at it. You will save me quite a bit of nagging, I suspect. Not that I would allow him to refer to it as such, for it is merely a succession of requests one expects a husband to adhere to," Primrose smirked, mischievously.

"I heard that, Primrose." James leaned against the door frame, his shirtsleeves tight over his broad muscles as his hair clung to the beads of perspiration, darkening the golden hue to a golden brown.

Seeing him standing there, my sister curling her arms around him as he leaned in to kiss her only made me pine for William all the more. They were two very different men; James was fair, and William was dark, one with dark green eyes and one with piercing blue. Both had broad shoulders with defined muscles, but William's physique did something thrilling to my insides where James' did not.

"Did you ladies have a good time?" he asked, pulling my sister closer towards him.

"Yes, thank you, James. Primrose is quite the protector," I added, glancing teasingly towards her curled against him.

"Oh, I know, Wren. She can be quite feisty when she wants to be." A teasing grin tugged at the corners of his mouth as he hid it in the kiss he placed upon the top of her head.

Primrose cheeks flushed a strawberry pink at the obvious intimate joke between them.

"Well, on that note," I smirked, "I insist Rose and I put all of this away while you two get properly settled in your bedchambers... individual bedchambers," I emphasised, turning my back to them as I tried to take up my role as the older sister.

As soon as they could no longer see my face, I secretly smiled, amused at the peculiarity of my gentle chastising words whilst also feeling the most wonderful warm elation at seeing my sister so happy and besotted with James, and James with her.

"Of course," Primrose agreed, coming to my side to collect her things. "Sorry," she whispered.

I nudged her playfully with my elbow, unable to hide my joy for her. "No need, little sister. I believe that you and I are not really that dissimilar," I winked.

She gasped at my confession, revealing those sweet little dimples once more.

Chapter Twenty-Six

William

"Father," I muttered sternly, the message in my tone emphasised further by the cold, detached, curt nod I bestowed upon him as he stood by the fireplace. He rocked back and forth on his heels, hands clasped behind his back, as the flames attempted to warm him.

Perhaps they were hoping to thaw his arrogant, frozen heart.

"Come back to beg for forgiveness, have you?" he snarled gleefully. He narrowed his eyes as his lips curled in wicked amusement.

Some things would never change, I thought, as I berated myself for even contemplating visiting him again. I should have kept to my decision to write once Wren and I were married instead. Yet, despite convincing myself I would never darken his doorstep again, there I was, a great, big looming shadow, staring at the man who was supposed to be my father.

"I have not, Father," I quipped. "For I do not believe your forgiveness is required." This was not going to be easy, I could tell. If my pride had not held me steadfast in my endeavour, I would have turned away from him and that house, there and then. The man was a waste of my time and breath.

"Deserved, you mean?" he sneered. The manner in which his eyes dragged up and down the length of my body, assessing me, was as though I was no more than the dirt on his shoes. As a son, it did indeed hurt, yet as a man, it infuriated me.

"No, that is not what I meant at all." I pinched the bridge of my nose as the tension rose within the room. I hadn't returned for an argument, I reminded myself. I simply wanted to know whether what he had said in Somerset had all been a matter of heated words, spilled quickly in a moment of anger, a tantrum, if you were, for we both knew I would not allow him to have his say in whom I should and shouldn't marry.

"Really? Not for the violence?" he taunted.

"Perhaps, for that, I can admit I was wrong," I conceded politely as I placed my hands back into the pockets of my breeches. "But you must also admit the part you had to play, Father."

"The part I had to play?" the earl snorted sardonically. "Please, William, enlighten your father, for I fear to be suffering a terrible bout of memory loss." The Earl swished the amber liquid within the tumbler in his hand, leaving viscous trails of alcohol dripping idly down the inside of the glass. His manner, deliberately feigning that of disinterest.

"You were extremely rude towards Wren," I seethed, keeping my voice calm, afraid to escalate the matter at hand. "She didn't do anything that warranted your unkindness." I ground my teeth together, the muscles bunching and stretching tautly around my jaw as I fought back my impatience with the blaggard.

"I very much doubt she understood a word I said," he mocked derisively as he peered into his glass to avoid looking at me. "Creatures like her never do. I am surprised she is allowed to live amongst good, respectable men and women."

My fists clenched as my short nails dug into my palms. "You really are a despicable man, aren't you?" I hissed. "I have always known you are a pompous arse, but never did I think that you would ever stoop so low as to be like those I despise."

My father stared at me with an expression of consideration, his eyes assessing me as though he wondered whether or not to add some other useless derogatory comment to the conversation.

"And, yes, Father," I continued, as he moved away from the fireplace and leaned over the back of the deep brown leather wingback chair. "It appears I am learning that I despise you too. Very much as it happens."

"Oh, boohoo," he ridiculed, curling his lips. "If you are trying to make me have pity on you and that harpy, then don't bother. I have said all that I needed to say, but I shall do you the honour of repeating it in perhaps much simpler terms, so you may understand this time," he sneered. "William, if you marry her, I will no longer have a son nor an heir."

"You think I actually care about all of that, don't you? Let me enlighten you, father, I do not give one fig about a pompous title, nor about your money," I roared. I was beyond the realms of livid. My anger had burst through my limits of patience, inflamed by the way in which he had referred to Wren as a harpy. How dare he? There was simply no sense in even trying to be civil with him. "Good grief, you are more delusional than I gave you credit for. You can keep your title and shove it where the sun doesn't shine!"

"I bet she told you to say that, didn't she?" he blustered. "Didn't she?"

Laughter rolled from my lips. I couldn't help myself, for the man was utterly ridiculous. "You are not worth the breath in my lungs, nor a minute more of my time. I bid you the day you deserve, Lord Darlington, and may we never cross paths again."

Before he could answer, I turned on my heel,

the roar of his temper following me to the front door.

"Is that a threat, boy?" he bellowed. "Is it?!"

Without a reply, I slammed the front door and walked onto the street and into the crowds.

My heart danced rapidly beneath my ribcage as my feet echoed the beat upon the cobbles beneath the soles of my shoes. I was surprised to feel gradually lighter the further I walked, as though I had left a tremendous weight at the door of my childhood home. My mind had swiftly grasped onto the memory of Wren's lips against mine and her soft curves as I held her in my arms. She was my home, I realised. No bricks and mortar would ever be sufficient without her, for my heart would always be wherever she was. The memory of Wren brought me to my senses, directing my feet towards the city centre, my last point of call and a rather spontaneous one, before I could return to her the following day.

The jewellery stores in the city were vast in comparison to the lone shop in the village, where I had previously purchased Wren's engagement ring. Despite the magnificence of it all, I found myself feeling rather clueless and far more indecisive than I had ever been. The walls were brightly lit, creating a glittering river that flowed over the finely cut gems, the smooth, polished gold, and the twinkling silver trinkets. The store was busy, albeit with no more than four or five customers, whereas I believe, in the village, the jeweller would have been lucky to have received such a number in a week, let alone a day. One would think the idea of such a quiet life in a village would seem rather boring, but to me, it was an extremely appealing prospect, one I very much looked forward to returning to. The city was restless and demanding, but in the countryside, it was a much slower-paced life with the captivatingly beautiful scenery that lifted one's spirit, but most of all, my heart was there, in the hands of the young lady I adored.

Everything seemed too grand and ostentatious as men and women bustled about, oohing and aahing at intricate pieces they found such obvious delight in. Indeed, there were many exquisite pieces, yet there appeared to be nothing that was on par with the elegance of Miss Davenport.

The wedding band I'd hoped to find had to be of a delicate design to suit her delicate hands. It had to have a certain something of which I was not entirely sure at that precise moment, yet I knew that, whatever it was, it had to be worthy of a rather prestigious position upon the hand of a lady who possessed the gentlest and kindest nature I had ever known.

Time ticked by, the noise sounding more and more like the impatient tap of a foot upon the floor. It was irritating, so much so that I was almost ready to concede to being a useless fiancé when I spied what I had sincerely hoped would be the one.

Three glittering topaz stones sat neatly in a row. All three were set deep within a sparkling silver metallic hue. The gems were of a generous size, yet neither overbearing nor flamboyant. Their crystal-clear blue glimmered much like the surface of an ocean, yet perhaps more likened to the summer sky, I wondered, what with the intricate flourish of silver leaves twirling in a vine to wrap around the wearer's finger. The silver foliage snaked over and around the ring, finally curling into three tiny leaf cups, a topaz mimicking a raindrop in each.

"Very good, sir. You have a fine eye for beauty." The jeweller stepped forward as he breathed in the scent of another sale.

I smiled. "It is for a very special young lady, sir. She deserves the very best, and, despite it being silver, there is no other band here that matches the elegance of this ring."

"I do not believe gold to be finer than silver, sir," the jeweller offered kindly. His honesty surprised me, for I was sure he would encourage me to buy another, rather more expensive, yet hideously gaudy piece.

"Yes, indeed," I replied, glad to not have been made to doubt my decision. "This one is perfect for the lady in question. I shall take it."

Most probably afraid I would dither and, or change my mind, the jeweller set to work, retrieving the ring from behind the glass cabinet and placing it onto the counter, where I examined it closely.

"Shall I put it in its box, sir?" the man asked.

"That would be most kind. Thank you."

The gentleman nodded quickly, a gentle smile creasing his face as he carefully plucked the ring from the display case and placed it into a leather box with a golden clasp. His hands worked with such diligence that one would have believed he was placing a sleeping child into their crib rather than a ring into its box.

"There you are, sir." His eyes glittered as he slid the small package towards me. "I wish you and the young lady a very happy marriage."

"How did you know?"

"One can always tell when a man is in love, sir. It is a wondrous sight. A gift to your heart and a gift to my eyes." The jeweller's eyes practically disappeared as his mouth widened into a broad and encouraging smile.

"Thank you, so much," I breathed, taken aback by his kind nature. It was astonishing, in a pleasing way, to know that some people out there were blessed with fathers like him rather than those like mine. I suspect that if he had been my father, he would have given me his blessing and full support, but it was neither hide nor hair, for nothing could change my parentage nor Wren's. We had each other, and that was all that mattered in the grand scheme of things.

After the last disastrous carriage ride from London to Somerset, I took the liberty of purchasing a carriage for Wren and I, the new Mr and Mrs Darlington-to-be. It was a most fortuitous purchase, I thought, because not only would it give my love and I the freedom to travel further, but it would also give me rather a convenient way out of London as soon as I was ready to leave. The length of the journey was perhaps a little disparaging, especially as I knew I would be in charge of the vehicle, but it was either that or take the risk of arriving in Somerset with some other bone broken at the hands of another. No, I had lost all faith in strangers of the carriage-driving variety, and I was not about to commit an act of recklessness that may ruin everything.

The emerald green silk shawl I purchased for Wren sat neatly on the top of a pile of gifts, sitting on the velvet-padded seats within the carriage. There were several boxes, each gift bought out of a sense of longing to be home with her in Somerset. To have known her less than a year, perhaps not even half a year, and to feel her absence like that of chasm within me, confirmed what I had always known and the reason why I had proposed to her. I was utterly in love with Wren. There was no other lady for me, only her. It was with that in mind, my feet carried me from the jewellery shop, eagerly towards and into even more shops to spend as I pleased.

There were books within the neatly stacked boxes, a purely selfish gift, so I could listen to her read as she delved deep into another's life until the excitement and wonder glimmered in her wide eyes. It was thrilling to watch her so captivated. There was also a pair of matching silk gloves for the emerald shawl, which would, no doubt, bring out the rustic hue of her chestnut hair and the delicate pink of her lips, not to mention the freckles scattered across her face like little stars. The last gift was not for me to claim to have bestowed upon her, yet the thought that I could be the one to hand it to her was just as magnificent. I could not wait to give her that particular one, most of all. It was to be the very first thing to place before her when I returned... Well, once I had said a very thorough hello first, of course, and then I knew I would give it to her.

I shook my head as though my sinful thoughts of Wren would disappear from my mind with such a simple action. She had filled my dreams every night, making the reality of the mornings rather dreadful, for when I would turn to face the other side of the bed, there was nothing but a cold sheet and untouched linen.

'Get yourself together, William,' I grumbled. The journey, although partially done, was not yet over, and I may as well have made myself as inebriated as that buffoon who had tipped the carriage, for the sinful images of Wren were consuming and a tad distracting, to say the least. Actually, they were far beyond distracting, especially when all I could think about was her blissfully naked against me with that ring firmly placed on her delicate finger.

Concentrate on marrying her first, William.

Tapping the extra special gift, secure in my top pocket, I set out on the last stretch of the journey, uttering a solemn vow to marry Wren as soon as was humanly possible because all the waiting was no good for a man when his lady heated his blood so splendidly as she heated mine.

Chapter Twenty-Seven

Wren

The warm shade of marigolds blossomed across the early morning sky, momentarily turning the countryside into a shimmering copper kingdom. Primrose and I had left the cottage early, endeavouring to collect an array of wildflowers for a simple yet elegant wedding posey for Rose. The land was a sea of green, awash with a myriad of fragrances and colours, teasing the eye with such splendour that, in the end, we simply allowed temptation to guide our hands. We diligently gathered cornflowers, daisies, buttercups, foxtails, and some other flowers I had no name for until we were more than satisfied with the generous display placed neatly at an angle in the wicker basket I was carrying. All that was left to do was to take them home and tie the ivory lace ribbon around them, the one I had reserved especially for the occasion.

"Do you think Rose will like them, Prim?" I asked, holding up the array of pretty flowers in front of us. I was indeed thrilled with our efforts, but I did not want to simply assume when others may disagree.

"I think they are beautiful, Wrenny. I don't think there would be a lady alive who would not love them," she beamed, tilting her face towards the sun.

The light caressed Primrose's hair, flecks of burnished gold flickering over the honey hues of her tresses as she basked in the beauty of the morning. Her chest rose and fell as she inhaled the cool, crisp air. How I wished I could have been as carefree as she seemed in that moment. Despite trying to keep myself busy, William remained resolute at the forefront of my thoughts. As much as it pains me to admit it, I was petrified—petrified that he had changed his mind, and I would never see him again. The words he had said, the promises he had made, and even the beautiful ring he had given to me as a reminder of his love were dwindling of their power to keep me strong as each day passed. Instead of the confidence I had once felt, in its place there was the most hideous nausea roiling in my stomach, intermittently rising upward into my chest, where it would clench my heart unkindly every time I dared to think of him.

"I do love it here, Wrenny," Prim breathed as she lowered her face and opened her eyes to look at me. She was wearing a soft pink satin gown with an ivory lace trim at the neckline and sleeves. The bodice cinched in at her waist, enhancing her womanly curves that, in the eyes of lecherous men, denied the truth of her innocence so clearly displayed in her dainty features. The delicate shade of the fabric was pretty against her golden curls as they continued to glisten in the glow of the morning sun, the light coaxing the hidden freckles towards the surface of her porcelain skin. "The views are divine, and I feel like I can breathe here." She laughed. "I know that sounds rather silly, but it is the only way I can explain how it makes me feel."

"It doesn't sound silly at all, Prim," I smiled assuringly, simultaneously wrapping my arm around her waist and placing my head on her shoulder. My navy-blue gown diminished against her in comparison, but I was too thrilled to have my youngest sister by my side to be fazed by the thought of merely blending into the background. In fact, I relished the idea of not having eyes on me at all; it made a wonderful change.

Primrose curled her fingers around mine as our hands met in front of us. "There is a freedom here that one cannot possess in London, Prim," I sighed. "And I don't mean because I was kept in the house all day either. Everything is brighter and somehow cleaner here."

"Yes, that's it, Wrenny. That's exactly it," she sighed dreamily.

Our new gowns swished about our legs as we made our way back to The Aviary. In hindsight, perhaps we should have thought to wear less expensive attire for collecting flowers, but the way my new gown made me feel overrode any sensible opinions I should probably have considered when deciding what to wear. Although Primrose looked as stunning as she always did, I was making the most of the new clothes Papa had bought me. It made my heart swell to think my father had thought of me so kindly, but as we were forced to wade through tall, dewy grass and amble over compacted soil, I wondered whether my desire to wear one of my new gowns was going to be the most hideous mistake I had made to date.

The soil was dry, but with the occasional need to hold onto the rough stone walls for balance, the art of prayer was all that stood between the fabric splaying across the filth-trodden earth and our sincere hope to avoid the disaster completely. Thankfully, despite their ancient appearance trying to fool us into believing they would crumble beneath our fingers, the walls proved to be rather sturdy.

"We are home, Rose," I called out as we stepped through the entrance to the cottage.

The air was palpable with a nervous yet excited

tension. Apprehension of the looming event the day had to offer lingered throughout the cottage.

"Just coming, duck," Rose called. There was a tremble in her voice as she sighed rather loudly, shortly followed by the tap of her feet on the floors as she made her way to the door of her bedchamber.

Skirts of a pearlescent grey gown appeared at the foot of the door, then eventually the rest of Rose followed. She closed her eyes as her chest heaved in a forced intake of breath, then exhaled, breathing out the obvious anxiety riddling her thoughts and body. For a lady so obviously nervous, she looked positively regal. She was the absolute personification of beauty as she turned towards us, her hair scooped in the perfect chignon, so soft it made one wish to reach out and touch it in awe. Her cheeks were flushed with the most wonderful champagne pink, complimenting her glittering grey eyes; the shades of her irises, emboldened by the elegant gown she wore.

Until only a few days prior, Rose had been adamant she would make do with one of her old and rather well-worn gowns for her wedding day, insisting it was a perfectly fine dress as it was her Sunday best. We had agreed, obviously, for we knew Rose's stubborn streak was far too staunch to commit to a discussion on the matter. To argue that she deserved to have something new for her special day would have been rather pointless, to say the least. However, after witnessing the glimmer of waning confidence in her eyes, Prim and I had come to the decision that there were other ways around the subject entirely. We had our own agenda; one we'd sneakily tucked away for our eyes and ears only. It was nothing too drastic, of course, for we simply borrowed one of her gowns and smuggled it out of the cottage, where it accompanied us on our rather convenient visit to the modiste. Thankfully, Toni was extremely confident that she could acquire all the necessary measurements from the older gown and, in doing so, would be able to make an elegant wedding gown, perfect for our Rose. And the talented modiste certainly did not disappoint.

"Oh, Rose," Primrose and I beamed in unison.

"Do I look daft?" Rose questioned.

"Absolutely not!" I replied. "You look divine."

"Charles is not going to know what to do with himself," Primrose teased kindly. "You look exquisite, Rose. Tell her, Wrenny."

"Yes, you really do," I encouraged. "Charles is a very lucky man."

"Go on with you," Rose grinned. "You'll have me blubbing in a minute. Ain't it unlucky to cry on your wedding day?"

"I have no idea, Rose," I smiled, a little choked with emotion. "But if you don't cry, I might."

Rose's eyes dimmed suddenly, the candle of confidence behind them flickering, threatening to snuff itself out completely.

"Whatever is the matter, Rose?" I soothed gently, placing my hand at her elbow and leading her towards the kitchen.

"Sit here, and I shall get you a cup of tea to steady your nerves," I offered as she lowered herself into a wooden chair.

Primrose had followed intuitively, setting abo-ut making a pot of tea, all the while seeing to the flowers I had almost forgotten about.

"Whatever is the matter, Rose? Primrose and I are quite concerned. Can you not see how my sister is so beside herself that she is actually making the tea all on her own?" I jested, hoping to ease the atmosphere, when suddenly, out of nowhere, a cloth hit the back of my head.

I turned quickly to see Primrose chuckling delightedly at a target well and truly hit. "I'll have you know I am quite a dab hand at tea making," she tittered.

"We will be the judge of that, won't we, Rose?" I teased, turning back to the woman in question. However, she was still rather lost in her thoughts and hadn't heard anything we had said.

"Do you think I'm too old to get married, duck?" she muttered quietly.

"Too old to get married?" I asked, slightly astounded, even though the question should not have been surprising at all, for she had broached the subject before. "How can one be too old to love, Rose? It is not possible. What say you, Prim?"

Primrose hurried towards the table, giving Rose a wide berth, careful not to spill any tea on her, which would surely have spoiled her beautiful wedding gown. The day would have been ruined before it had even started. "Surely, I do not have to put into words what utter nonsense that question is?" my sister chided gently. "Do you know there are people out there who spend their entire lives alone, Rose? How dreadful to imagine spending your life never thinking you are worthy enough of love from someone other than your family. It doesn't bear thinking about." Prim shuddered.

"But I've already been married once before, duck," Rose added solemnly.

"Then you are even luckier than most, Rose," Prim soothed kindly. "You only get one life, so don't waste it. Be thankful you have never been one of those poor people who are forced into marriage solely on the grounds of a business transaction between their families." Primrose shuddered again. "Now that would be a worry worthy of your time, but to marry a man whom you love and one who loves you in return is indeed a gift, Rose. Thank heavens you have found a man such as Charles, I have found James, and

Wrenny has found William. We three are very lucky indeed."

The mention of William tightened my stomach with a nervous ache. The days were dragging on, and I didn't know how much more of the burden of waiting, as well as my insecurities as to whether he would return, my fraying nerves could endure before I broke. Any inner strength I may once have possessed was slowly dwindling; doubts persistently wearing it away with jibes conjured by my own mind about my appearance. Images of him with another young lady taunted my imagination as he stared lovingly into her eyes and she into his. Of course, she was a young woman who was nothing like me, and those images hurt immensely. My brain was bludgeoning my self-worth with every syllable it uttered within my head. And, every day, I grew closer to convincing myself that he had indeed had a change of heart.

"Tell Rose I am right," Primrose demanded, desperately seeking support from me as she pulled my attention away from the discomfort twisting my insides into terrible knots.

"She is, Rose," I assured her. "She may be my youngest sister, but she is indeed very wise... sometimes."

Primrose narrowed her eyes at me playfully, aware of the backhanded compliment with which I had attempted to goad her. Rose smiled at the banter between Prim and I as I gently nudged my sister's arm, nearly knocking her off her seat.

"Well, someone had to have a brain in this family," Primrose retorted, giggling as she corrected her posture.

"What's all this?" James loomed in the kitchen doorway, his eyes sparkling with mischief as he locked them solely on Prim. "Was someone mentioning how they needed intelligence in the family, and that is why Primrose is so desperate to be my wife?

"Understandable, of course," he grinned, straightening the cuffs of his shirtsleeves. "For my intelligence is rather renowned." James pinched his lips together to stifle the unstoppable smirk, failing miraculously as the satisfaction of Primrose's reaction gripped his expression.

Her eyebrows were at least half an inch higher than normal, whilst the rest of her features attempted to feign disdain for the man she so clearly adored. Like her betrothed's effort at acting, she was disappointingly unsuccessful. "Oh, I believe your hearing is impeccable," she announced, her mouth twisting, returning the playful smile. "For we were discussing intelligence; however, it appears you may require a dictionary to understand what the word means." Her delicate nostrils flared as she pursed her lips.

James gasped at her words, clutching his chest

as though she had wounded him.

"For if we were discussing intelligence, dear," she continued, sauntering up to him. "We would obviously be discussing..."

James lowered his face to hers and captured her lips with his, denying her the chance to continue her cheeky and rather witty retort. "You were saying?" he asked, as he permitted her to come up for air.

"Nothing, darling," she blushed.

"That is what I thought. Now, I believe there is a young lady here who is getting married and, being one of intelligent mind," he grinned. "I believe it is time we made our way to the church, or we shall have two very unhappy vicars to contend with."

"Are you ready, Rose?" I inquired.

Rose inhaled deeply, the backs of her legs pushing the chair away from her as she stood. "Ready as I will ever be, duck," she replied, squeezing my outstretched hand.

"This will be the most splendid day, Rose, I promise. But, before you set foot outside, there is one more thing you will need," I reminded her as I picked up the flowers. "Your posey."

Prim had tied an elegant bow of ivory lace around the myriad of delicate wildflowers, arranging them so beautifully. They were truly breathtaking. It looked as though nature herself had arranged them.

"There," I smiled, placing them into her hands. "Flowers, just for you, Rose."

"They're beautiful, love. Thank you."

"Beautiful flowers for a beautiful lady," James remarked as he took her hand and looped it through the crook of his elbow.

"I guess that just leaves us then, Wrenny," Primrose chuckled, taking my hand and mirroring James. "Please let me escort you, Miss Davenport," Primrose jested, deepening her voice and squaring her shoulders playfully as she tightened the link created with our arms.

"Oh, why thank you, sir. You are too kind," I replied haughtily.

Slowly, arm in arm, we followed Rose and James to the awaiting carriage.

Chapter Twenty-Eight

William

As I stepped out into the cold, crisp air of the early hours, the morning had not yet broken, yet I was more than ready to begin the last leg of my journey. After freshening up and devouring a hot meal, I'd tried desperately to sleep in the lodgings I had paid heavily for, but alas, sleep never came, just a flurry of incessant thoughts and waves of anxiety-filled impatience, memories of Wren playing over in my mind, teasing me, knowing I could not simply reach out and touch her. The never-fading vividity of the scenes proved that efforts to drift off to sleep were indeed futile, and so I had little choice other than to relent. However, to lay there utterly useless, simply wasting valuable time, was certainly not on my agenda. If I couldn't sleep, then the least I could do was make the most of my waking hours, ones I could use to make tracks. The sooner I left, the sooner I would be reunited with Wren.

The inn was cloaked in the thin veil of the receding night sky as I left it far behind me. The fading darkness loomed over the carriage, its inky hue bleeding upon the roads. It created daunting, eerie shadows, cast far and wide over the scenery ahead in a watery shade of obsidian, whilst the light of the stars jittered nervously as the day threatened to hide them from the world.

The wind whipped about my face as I encouraged the horses to travel a little faster. Its rough claws, dragging through my hair as I scoffed at the irony of the effort, I had painstakingly made to smarten myself up before I'd set off. There were creases folded into my breeches; the heat of my body had pressed them into tight, closely aligned, and withstanding ridges deep in the fabric. I sighed rather loudly with exasperation. If the state of the fabric of those was anything to go by, and the sting of the cold upon my face, I knew I was a dishevelled mess of a man.

There was nothing I could do, I conceded, shrugging my shoulders, for The Aviary had risen into view just beyond the subtle rise of the bridge, and there was neither the time nor any practical method in which to remedy such a situation. However, in one last attempt to resemble that of a man with a little sanity, I grabbed the reins in my left hand, then raked my right hand through my hair. My only consolation was that Wren had already seen me in a much worse state once before. I dread to think about what I must have looked like the first day she laid eyes upon me. I was a mess, with blood dripping from my head down the side of my face, my body practically crumpled at Charles's side. Hurrying back to be with her, eager to hold her in my arms, I was positive I must have looked at least a little better than I did then.

Impatience constricted the muscles of my abdomen as the carriage bounded towards the cottage. The ache in my stomach intensified as another wave of apprehension fought against the rising enthusiasm I had at the thought of seeing Wren. My emotions were twisting with an unbearable strength as anxiety coiled fervently around my innards.

I inhaled and exhaled slowly, trying desperately to ease the discomfort and regain some composure against the rapid beat of my heart, afraid I would make an utter fool of myself in front of her. Holding Wren close to me again, to know she still loved this ridiculously uninteresting and apparently quite nervous man, was my only desire. My love for her was indeed most fragile, or perhaps it was me who was fragile. I was a man scared to make one wrong move or to say one wrong word, knowing she would have the power to bring my world crashing down around my ears. I wondered whether she even knew how much she had turned my life around, and, more than that, I wondered whether she knew I feared I couldn't live without her.

The crackle of grinding grit crunched beneath the slow-turning wheels of the carriage as the rhythm of the horse's hooves petered out. It was too quiet, too still. Thinking no more of it, I clambered down from the front of the carriage, pausing quickly, making one last attempt to remedy my ruffled appearance, then collected the mound of gifts I had returned with. My hands fumbled with the boxes and bags until I finally managed to balance them within my arms. Confident they were safe there, I headed towards the door, where I knocked and waited.

Disappointed that there was nobody home, I pushed the door open with my hip and went inside. The door creaked on its hinges as it revealed the hallway of The Aviary. Deep, comforting aromas greeted me amongst the homely hues of the décor, but the eerie silence, filling every inch of the cottage, did nothing to stave off the unsettling feeling I had. Ridiculous thoughts and fears were tumbling about in my brain, but there was one in particular that was quite prominent:

'What if Wren thought I was not coming back and has returned to London?'

Although it may sound quite far-fetched, I had been away a little longer than I had intended, and I had no idea whether Primrose had relayed my message. *How could I trust Wren's sister when I hardly knew anything about her other than my love's terrible past experiences, ones her sister had been embroiled in? Who was to say Primrose's spoken regret for her part in it all had been sincere?*

"Pull yourself together, man!" I grumbled to myself. "If Primrose didn't relay the message, then surely her father would tell Wren all we had discussed when she arrived back in London.

"One way or another, Wren will come to know I have not deserted her," I muttered, reassuring my pounding heart whilst it appeared to battle against the scrambled mess of worries and answers flitting about in my brain.

Panic suppressed, I searched The Aviary for signs of life. I checked the drawing room and kitchen, even peeking through the door of Wren's bedchamber. *Any sign of inhabitance would do*, I thought.

Everything was exactly as it had been when I had left for London, and then I noticed Jane Eyre laying open on my love's bed. The relief quickly expelled itself from my lungs in a loud and welcome sigh. She was still very much in Somerset.

There was no more chance than a cat in hell without claws that I was going to sit around and simply wait for her to return, for I had waited long enough to see Wren, and time had been rather unfriendly. It had stretched quite painfully. In fact, it had been far too excruciating for my liking. There was no way I would simply remain inactive.

A breeze rushed towards me, its subtle warmth ruffling my recently combed hair. It filtered underneath fabric, pushing open the freshly pressed suit jacket I had donned only a few minutes earlier, brazenly revealing the clean shirtsleeves and high-waisted breeches beneath. If I was going to find Wren, then I wanted her to see me at my best, not in the state of dress in which I had returned. My feet made quick work of the path to the rickety gate, and soon enough, I was well on my way towards the vicarage, where I hoped Charles would have some idea as to where Wren could be.

"Morning William!" Bernard slowed his cart to a halt as he pulled in beside me. "You off to the wedding?"

"Wedding?"

"Ain't you heard? The vicar is getting married to his Rose," the farmer beamed. "Just on me way to it now. Bit delayed 'cause I 'ad to fix the gate 'fore I left or the sheep'll get out. Maggie's already there, mind. None too 'appy about it, but it is what it is."

"That may explain where Wren is, then," I replied happily. "I don't suppose there is room on that cart for one more, is there? I know that sounds rather cheeky, but I have been away, and I am quite impatient to see her again."

"Say no more, lad. Jump on. There's plenty of room for the both of us!"

"Bernard, you are a Godsend, ol' boy." With haste, I climbed up beside the farmer, and we set off towards the church.

"Been anywhere nice, William?" Bernard asked as I sat back, holding on for dear life. The man was bang up to the elephant where driving was concerned, yet it did nothing to keep one's derriere firmly fixed upon the seat.

"Well, I wouldn't say nice, exactly," I ground out. "But I did return to London for a few days in order to resolve some rather important matters."

Bernard remained expectantly silent as he allowed me to continue.

"I intend to marry Wren and relocate to Somerset," I announced, thrilled to say it out loud.

"Ah, that's wonderful news, that is, William. We'll be neighbours, of sorts. I assume you'll be staying at The Aviary?"

"Yes, that is the plan." I patted the front of my jacket, the deeds of the cottage secure within the inside pocket, a physical reminder of the future my love and I had. "I am not normally an impatient man, Bernard, but I do hope to be a married man sooner rather than later. I have missed her terribly."

The farmer chuckled softly. "Ah, young love. I remember when me and my Maggie were like that. I mean, we still are now, I s'pose, but the stresses of my work keep me out all hours, and I'm normally knackered by the time I get 'ome."

"You know, if you are looking for an extra pair of hands on the farm, Bernard, I am seeking employment," I offered eagerly. Working on Bernard's farm certainly wasn't beneath me, far from it; I relished the prospect of the outdoors even though it was hard, physical labour, and was quite sure the income would be a blessing, one of immense proportions to Wren and I whilst we waited for my paintings to find their rightful places in the world.

"Would you really want to work on a farm, William? It's dirty work, not to mention 'ard on the ol' back at time," the farmer questioned. "And I don't s'pose it will be the money like you are used to in London, but it will be a decent enough wage."

"I assure you, Bernard, I am not afraid of hard work, and as for the money, I expect nothing more than what you would pay anyone else."

"Well, then, William, I believe you 'ave yourself a job," he beamed. "I would shake your 'and, but I think ol' Belinda—me mare, that is—might get ideas if I let go of the reins."

I laughed alongside the man. "Indeed. I think I have had enough of being thrown from vehicles, Bernard."

"Ah, yes, I remember. We certainly don't want no repeat of that now, do we?" he grinned.

"Today is a good day, Bernard. I can feel it." My chest swelled with elation.

"Well," he replied. "Let's get ourselves in there, and then it will be a better day for me. I 'ave a feelin' I might have a bit of making up to do with Maggie 'fore it gets better for me."

Bernard's face crinkled with mischief as he tugged gently on the reins and steered the cart to a stop outside the church.

Chapter Twenty-Nine
Wren

The morning dew drops glistened as they nestled in the grass and settled comfortably upon the vibrant green leaves of blossoming flowers, each flower feeding off the warmth and wondrous glow of the sun, its golden ethereal fingers tenderly caressing their petals, enticing the closed buds to fall open and bask in its glory. It was the perfect day for a wedding, I mused as I mimicked the flowers, turning my face towards the sun and allowing its warmth to caress me too. The hurt of William's absence was tearing the centre of my chest wide open, and I needed all and anything I could to soothe the ache beneath my ribcage as I pulled myself back from the precipice of tears, for they were threatening to spill over in an unwelcome waterfall. This was not my day, I reminded myself; it was Rose and Charles's, and I did not want to spoil it by allowing my fear to swallow me entirely.

Primrose gave my hand a reassuring squeeze.

Sometimes, I found myself wondering whether she could see into my mind, for she knew just what I was thinking without me speaking a word of it. I was glad to have her there by my side, for her presence seemed to soften the sharper edges of the longing that lingered within me for William.

"Come on," she whispered. "Let's go inside."

Silently, I followed her, drinking in the vibrant citrus yellow of the proud daffodils scattered in resplendent bouquets by the hand of Mother Nature, their roots deep within the soil in front of the low stone walls. Marigolds, more orange than yellow, rose up beside them. Their colours alone were enough to lift a little of the heaviness from my heart, and with a rather deep breath, we stepped out of the light and into the dimmed church.

"Oh, I should have brought a shawl with me, Wrenny," Primrose exclaimed quietly. "It is rather chilly in here, isn't it?"

Nodding in agreement, I could not help the shiver vibrating in my muscles. The church was indeed cold in temperature as well as in colour, with its stark white walls. The sudden plummet in temperature erased the spring season from the atmosphere, yet my eyes hungrily wandered towards the pews, searching for the merest fragment of colour in order to welcome it back.

"Thank heavens Charles has decorated," I

whispered, drinking in the revelation of the fat crimson roses, bursting through the monotony of lifeless shades. They were set in deep green leaves, densely bunched upon vines as they weaved over the edges of the pews. Some had been arranged in tall vases, their stems rising from the darkness to present their magnificent crowns of velvet petals for all to peruse with awe. There were several tall vases placed sporadically around the altar until it resembled a fully-fledged rose garden. Charles had made considerable effort with regards to the décor; the attention to detail, and particularly the choice of bloom, was exquisite. His love for Rose was indeed quite evident.

"Let's sit close, Wrenny, or I feel I may freeze without any warmth," Primrose jested as we took our places in the pews. "Oh, thank heavens," she breathed, fidgeting, as a thick band of sunlight streamed through the stained-glass windows to where we were sitting. "We are in the perfect spot."

Primrose was right, for the sunlight offered a much-needed warmth, rescuing us as it thawed the icy edge of the chill upon our skin. "Perhaps we won't need shawls after all," I smiled, my gaze shifting to the guests, eagerly waiting in their designated seats. There were several others just arriving, apologies being uttered as they squeezed past those who were already seated. An excited chatter of breathless whispers danced in subtle echoes, then gently faded into an attentive silence.

There were rows and rows of faces; most I did not recognise. Charles and Rose had certainly made many friends in the short time we had been residing in Somerset. The vicar had confessed it had grown considerably since he had first arrived, but never did I think it was that many. Both he and Rose had spoken with tremendous joy at the new faces and growth of the church community. Rose had absolutely blossomed over the months and seemed the happiest I had ever seen her, and as the organ played and she stepped forward, leaning on the arm of James, she revealed her newfound happiness to everyone who cared to observe.

A contagious joy danced across Rose's face as everybody twisted in their seats, turning inquisitively to catch sight of the blushing bride. And she was indeed blushing, but not because of the attention of all those around her; it was merely a natural response to the attention of one man she so obviously adored. Rose's eyes glittered with profound emotion as she gazed longingly at Charles. I wondered whether anything, or anyone else, existed to the marrying couple as their eyes locked. It was heavenly, as well as an honour, to witness someone so dear follow her heart down the aisle as the music guided Rose towards a proud, emotional, and joyfully beaming Charles, standing ever-so patiently at the altar. It was then that I knew if I was to return to London, Rose would be alright, and that meant a great deal to me.

Although I hadn't discussed it with Prim, I had made my mind up; I was to travel back to London the very next day. I couldn't put off the inevitable any longer, for William's absence was devouring me on the inside, and I was beside myself with worry in case something awful had happened to him. His father had made it exceedingly obvious that he was not a man to be messed with, and I would not leave William there alone with no one to help him. I was prepared to face the ton if I had to, even if I would have to come face-to-face with an unrelenting barrage of ignorance for my efforts. But then there was the other unthinkable alternative, one where I would have to face the rest of my life alone without him. I would rather have been placed on a stage and ogled by the entirety of the aristocracy than face that dismal future. Nevertheless, I did have to face the possibility that William had indeed changed his mind. And, if that really were to be the case, I would need to move on with my life. One thing I was most certain of, though, was that I could not, nor would I, spend my days cooped up in that house again. Primrose had said Papa had promised me The Aviary, and so, whilst I was forced to endure my extremely brief visit, I would stake my claim upon it, then hastily take my leave to return to Somerset. Of course, that meant I would have to face my mother, which I did not relish the thought of, but needless to say, it was quite necessary.

Oh, how much bravado I claimed to myself—a blatant lie as I shook at the very idea of it, blaming the cold when I was confronted as to why I was shaking. It is laughable, really, yet I knew I would do it. I had to.

The air around us seemed to shift slightly as we focused upon the ceremony in all its splendour. I simply assumed it was merely due to the palpable emotions bouncing off the walls as they radiated between the happy couple and amongst the multitude of onlookers, each one lost in a silent, awe-consumed gaze, yet the prickles on the back of my neck suggested there was something or someone else.

I dared not hope it was the first person who sprang to mind. If I allowed myself to believe for even a morsel of a second, I had the distinct feeling that I would be sorely disappointed.

"What are you doing, Wrenny?" Prim whispered, interrupting my thoughts.

I looked at her, confused by the question.

"You were shaking your head," she said, aware I did not realise I had been doing such a thing.

"Was I?"

My sister nodded.

"Oh, I was lost in thought. We best be quiet, though, or we will ruin Rose and Charles's wedding." I was hoping I could halt the expected influx of questions I would have had if we had been at the cottage without a care in the world.

"They're already married, Wrenny. Look," she smiled.

Rose and Charles were indeed married. The golden band gleamed around Rose's finger until it was hidden from view by well-wishers gathering around them to offer the newlyweds their heartfelt congratulations. "Oh," I gulped, consumed by guilt from getting thoroughly lost in my thoughts on Rose's special day.

"Rose didn't notice, Wrenny. Don't feel bad. To be honest, I don't think she or Charles would have noticed if a lion walked through here. They only had eyes for each other.

"What were you thinking about, though?" Prim inquired.

"Tomorrow," I blurted. The wedding ceremony had concluded, and there really was no perfect time to say what needed to be said. Although not ideal, I admit, it seemed like it was as good a time as any to tell my sister of my plans.

"Tomorrow? What about tomorrow?" she asked, eyes wide with concern.

“Yes, what about tomorrow?"

My breath hitched in my throat at the deep, gloriously masculine rumble at my back. It was accompanied by the intoxicating fragrance of sandalwood and starched linen, and I knew. I just knew... and yet, I could not bring myself to turn around.

The ache, which I had kept so safely guarded within the chamber of my chest, was screaming to be released. It seeped through the barrier via the fracture William’s voice had created. My throat ached in response as it seemed to close around the pain of my fears.

“Won’t you turn to face me, Little Bird?” William’s arm snaked around me, his large hand gathering my much smaller one as he laced his fingers through mine.

I didn’t dare speak, for fear of releasing the flood of emotion, I was barricading behind my lips. It had built up into a tremor that was vibrating freely through every inch of me.

“Wrenny, it’s okay,” Prim encouraged. Her delicate fingers stroked my arms as she motioned for me to turn to William. My body followed as the first tear slipped from the corner of my eye.

His piercing blue eyes locked with mine, the warmth and desire behind them darkening the ring around his irises as he brought his hand to my face. His thumb traced from the corner of my eye and down the side of my cheek as he wiped away the first sign of what I had been trying to hold in, but as he spoke, I knew there was nothing that could hold back my feelings for him. "Dear Lord, I missed you, Little Bird," he muttered, brushing his lips over my cheek. I shivered, silently revealing how much I had missed his touch, or perhaps it was how much I had feared I would never see him again. "I will never leave you again, Wren. I promise. You do believe me, don't you?"

Afraid my tears would become considerably less silent, I simply nodded my answer. The corners of my mouth had begun to lift as he smiled at me. There was a mischievous glint in his eyes, one that never failed to lighten the tension between us.

"Good," he grinned. That breathtakingly beautiful lopsided grin. "Because when we get home, I intend to show you just how much I've missed you."

"Mr Darlington!" Primrose chastised playfully. "That is my sister, you are propositioning. I hope you intend on making an honest woman of her?"

Being swept up in the emotion, I did not care who had heard the conversation between us, yet my body still insisted upon adhering to propriety as it annoyingly released the warmest, and probably pinkest, patches upon my cheeks.

"Do not fear, Miss Davenport; I have every

intention of doing just that. Now ladies, please, let me escort you back to the cottage."

William took my hand, slowly leading us out from between the rows of pews. The sensation of his skin against mine made me feel safe. Since he had left, I suppose I felt as though I had been in freefall, never knowing when and if I was to be saved, but there he was, the man I was truly in love with. I could touch him, see him, hear him, and yes, even smell him. He was my home.

Primrose shuffled up close beside me, discreetly nudging me with her dainty yet rather pointy elbow as she poked it into my side. Her eyes were dancing—the signature excited look I knew so well from her early morning visits in my bedchambers in London. "I told you so," she whispered. "I knew he would come back. Didn't I tell you?"

"Yes, you did, Prim," I happily conceded. "You know, I was on your side. I may have been a little pessimistic, but I secretly prayed you would get your chance to prove me so very wrong on this occasion."

"Well, in that case, it is only right that I get the biggest slice of wedding cake," Primrose chuckled. And as she pulled James to her side, we made our way out of the church to start the not-so-long walk back to The Aviary.

Chapter Thirty

William

To begin with, I did not understand why she would not turn to face me; however, it was the subtle tremor in her body and the rise and fall of her delicate shoulders in time with every breath that enlightened me. I had left her for too long. Her fragility resounded off her, so much so that I was scared to place my hands upon her, for fear she may break. Nevertheless, unless she could summon the courage to turn and reveal her vulnerability to me, I knew I would eventually have to touch her.

Slowly and very softly, I curled my arm around her waist. "Won't you turn to face me, Little Bird?"

Wren hesitated, her shoulders practically touching her ears. Fear was a mountain beneath her flesh. It was only when her sister gently guided her body towards me with words of reassurance did she turn.

Her soft blue eyes were wide, the rims tinged with a subtle pink as a tear rolled over her cheek.

"Dear Lord, I missed you, Little Bird," I whispered, cupping the side of her face in my hand, my thumb brushing away her tear. She leaned into my touch as our eyes met. Guilt nestled like a fist in my gut, the expression upon her face made my heart ache for her. "I will never leave you again, Wren. I promise. You do believe me, don't you?"

A smile tugged at the corners of her lips as she nodded. Although it was a faint, slowly blossoming smile, my heart swelled to see it spread across her face. *'My sweet, beautiful Little Bird,'* I smiled to myself.

"Good, because when we get home, I intend to show you just how much I've missed you," I grinned wickedly.

Wren dragged her teeth over her lower lip secretly as Primrose playfully berated me for lack of propriety, her mischievous glint most likely matching my own. Squeezing her hand, we made our way out of the church.

"Wrenny, would you mind awfully if James and I took a carriage?" Primrose inquired as she wrapped herself around her fiancé. The subtle, excited bounce of her ringlets exhibited the obvious exhilaration coursing through her veins. "It's simply because James wants to show me some land, he thinks will be perfect for our home. You don't mind, do you?" Primrose's eyes were dancing as she looked from Wren to me and then back to Wren. I had assumed her excitement was at the thought of spending time alone with James, yet as her lips curled into a devious smile, her subtlety about why she was bouncing left a lot to be desired.

"Of course not, Prim. We shall meet you back at The Aviary," Wren replied.

"Thank you, Wrenny. You two have fun," she winked, then quickly dragged James away.

Wren laced her slender fingers through mine and brought the back of my hand to her lips. "I missed you so much, William," she whispered, lifting my hand a little higher and placing her soft, velvety cheek against it. "I was so scared you wouldn't come back." Wren's voice was hoarse with emotion.

"Oh, Little Bird, if you only knew how much I need you," I offered, guiding her away from the crowd and beyond the view of others.

"Where are we going?" she giggled, her feet hurrying, attempting to keep up with my strides.

Suddenly, I stopped, swinging her around to face me as I pushed her with my body against a high stone wall. "I don't think I can walk back to The Aviary without doing this first," I breathed, leaning forward. Arms either side of her, palms flat against the wall, I moved closer until the soft curves of her breasts pressed against my heaving chest.

"William." Her voice was barely audible as my breath brushed her arced neck, her involuntary movement inviting me to taste her pale skin.

Lips to skin, she moaned, her arms drawing me closer as she grabbed my shoulders, sliding her hands to the back of my head as she combed her fingers through my hair. What we were doing was reckless, and this was not how I wanted it to be the first time I was to make love to her. She deserved better than this. "We mustn't, Little Bird," I groaned. "But please believe me when I say I very much want to."

Words froze on her tongue as I pressed my mouth hungrily upon her perfect lips. She sighed into my mouth, our breaths rapid with something far more than lust. "Come, before we do something, we mustn't," I growled breathlessly, disentangling our lips.

Wren's lips were swollen from our kisses, her eyes sparkling and a little dazed. How I had managed to control my need for her astounded me, but I couldn't allow my mind to wander in that direction, for I would soon find my body entangled with hers again and repeating the sinful act, most likely in some secluded spot on the way back to the cottage. Instead, I scooped her up into my arms, intent on carrying her home. She giggled. Her laughter was musical and precious. She was precious.

"William, I am perfectly capable of walking," she offered, her arms curled around my neck as she gazed up at me.

"I am very aware of that, Little Bird, yet if I do not make haste with you in my arms, I shall not be responsible for what this particular man is capable of when in the privacy of the countryside and in your company." I needed cold water to cool the heat soaring through my body and perhaps a looser pair of breeches. Good lord, the woman was an oblivious temptress.

"Alright there, ol' chap?" James smirked, smacking me on the back with more gusto than was perhaps necessary.

"I am now," I confessed discreetly. On another occasion, I may have tried to feign ignorance, but both he and Primrose had witnessed our return to The Aviary. Wren was looking gorgeously tousled with swollen lips and a dazed, soppy smile, and, well, I had a rather off-kilter gait to match my ruffled hair and heated face.

"Want to confess your sins, William?" James snickered mischievously.

"There are no sins to confess. I was perfectly respectable," I grumbled, accepting the large brandy he passed to me. His eyebrows were almost at his hairline in an unsaid accusation.

"Don't look at me like that, James. As much as I wanted to devour Wren, I was every bit the gentleman. Although I may have to bring the wedding forward," I smirked.

"What are you two talking about?" Primrose inquired. "Wren, these two look like they are conspiring," she added, tilting her head back towards Wren yet keeping her narrowed eyes fixed firmly on us.

Wren's eyes mirrored her sister's, yet there was jest in her narrowed gaze. "Sorry, Prim, I'm afraid William wouldn't do such a thing," she replied, amused as she wrapped one arm around the back of my waist and placed her free hand on my chest.

"Oh, that's nice, very nice indeed," James snorted, holding his chest as he feigned a terrible pain. "Where is the sentence that proclaims that I wouldn't do such a thing? I'll have you know that such insolence can fatally wound a man."

"Sorry, darling," Primrose began, batting her eyelids as she sauntered towards him. James's face softened, expectant of his betrothed's retraction of words. "But I know you better than that," she added, then hurried away, the trill of her laughter left in her wake.

As James willingly chased after Primrose like two naughty children, my eyes met Wren's. The sight of her made my heart flip, and my hands wander, cupping the curves of her perfect bottom as I pulled her closer. She squealed, biting that blasted bottom lip again until my blood burned hot with desire beneath my skin.

"Little Bird, I will tell you one thing I said," I growled, brushing my lips tenderly over hers.

"Oh, yes? What will you tell me?"

"Simply that I cannot wait much longer to marry you. I want you to be my wife as soon as we can arrange it all. Hell, I would marry you right this moment if I could," I confessed, nibbling the lobe of her ear. *What the hell was wrong with me? I had not long managed to cool down.*

"I can assure you, the feeling is entirely mutual," she sighed, pressing herself closer to me.

"Oh, heavens, Little Bird, I had almost forgotten. Your father wanted me to give you this." I exclaimed quietly.

With all the events of the day, the memory of the folded parchment within my pocket had slipped my mind, but as Wren had leaned against me, the deeds to the cottage pressed into my skin through the fabric as a reminder.

"It is official, The Aviary is now yours," I smiled, passing the deeds of The Aviary to her. "Your father insists you are to have it. His words were something along the lines of, 'It is the least I can do.'"

"It belongs to us, William. The cottage is part of our future, not just mine," she beamed, placing her hand over mine.

To hear her talk of our future was exhilarating, but before I permitted myself to bathe in the glory of our future, I had to tell her all that I had meant to earlier. "That's not entirely everything I need to get off my chest, either," I continued. "Because, despite being rejected several times, I might add, fortune seemed to have followed me, and I met another art dealer in London. He wasn't a local man. To be truthful, it was a meeting by pure chance, but he was extremely enthusiastic about my work, and I have agreed for him to take my art pieces farther than London, much farther."

Wren's eyes were wide and curious. "How much farther?"

"Paris!"

"Oh, William, that is marvellous! I am so proud of you."

My breath caught in my throat. Her words had rendered me speechless.

"What is it, William? Have I said something wrong?"

I shook my head. "Not at all." My voice was husky. "Nobody has ever said that to me."

Wren was the first person in my life who had ever told me that they were proud of me.

"Well, I suppose you will have to get used to it. Although..." she uttered nonchalantly. "We really can't have it going to your head, so perhaps I shall have to try to limit how many times I say it." Her petite nose wrinkled as a cheeky smile creased the corners of her eyes.

"Yes, well, there is that." I raised my left eyebrow, chiding her humorously. "But you may have to say it one more time today, for I do believe I shall be working for Bernard on the farm as well."

Wren gasped. "Well, how can I deny how proud I am of you when you have done so much so that we may be together?"

"Well, Little Bird, you have me there, for I don't believe it is possible. Perhaps you can offer me a reward?" I pinched my lips together and quickly raised my eyebrows, then dropped them again, urging her to ask me what my reward could be.

"And pray tell, William, what is this reward you seek?" she asked warily.

"Oh, I'm so glad you asked..."

Epilogue

Wren Jennifer Darlington

One week after William returned from London, my husband made good on his promise. Fired up and impatient to the last, he set about tying up the loose ends so we could marry sooner rather than waiting the duration of a month, as we had previously planned. The wonderfully foolish man believed it was his reward for all the work he had so diligently set his mind to, but truth be told, I was just as eager as he was, if not more, to begin our lives together.

Mrs Wren Jennifer Darlington. The name is smooth on my lips, and dances off my tongue in the sweetest music I have ever heard. I suppose some would argue that my title was Viscountess Darlington, but William and I had spoken about it at length, and, what with the way he had left matters with his father, he was reluctant to keep his title of Viscount, to say the least. He would never admit it, yet I knew the Earl had hurt him immensely. The pain in his eyes was evident to those who cared to look, and the title was another harsh elbow to the gut every time it was muttered. I could not, nor would I be responsible for that.

"What are you thinking about, Little Bird?" Elbow bent with his hand beneath his head, William lay on his side, carefully trailing the tip of his finger over the bare skin of my shoulder. Lovingly and rather brazenly, he traced the soft curve of my breast in a not-so-subtle attempt at making his way towards the fold of the linen sheet, which was all that covered me.

"I know what you are thinking about," I chided gently. "But we have to help Primrose and James today. We promised."

William groaned.

"I'm sorry, my darling, but I promise I will make it up to you later," I offered, leaning over to kiss him.

William's eyes darkened with a lustful look, which was, oh, so very familiar, even after two months of marriage.

"William!" I giggled. "We really must go."

What an utterly forceful woman I was, said no man or woman on earth, for I could not resist my husband.

It was strange to be so confident in his arms when I was laid literally bare. It wasn't always like that, for when we were first married, despite loving him as fervently as I do now, I had years and years of built-up insecurities. They were a barrier I had to break through, and all in just one night.

"Are you okay, Little Bird?" William had soothed. "You're trembling."

"This is all new," I'd whispered, my throat dry with apprehension.

"We don't have to do anything tonight if you are not ready, Wren."

My husband was ready to wait for me if I had said that was what I had wanted, but it wasn't what I wanted at all. I'd wished to be with him the way a wife should be with her husband, yet there was the overwhelmingly obvious fact that he had never seen me naked before.

"I do want to." My voice was hoarse as our eyes met. "It is simply that I am afraid you will not like what you see." My throat constricted with the pain of my past.

"Come here, Little Bird." William lowered me down onto the bed. "I love you. I love everything about you. You have nothing to fear from me."

A tear streamed from the corner of my eyes as I swallowed, my gaze never leaving his. With the tiny morsel of courage I could muster, I raised my hands and pulled him down towards me. "I love you too, William," I breathed against his lips. "I am ready."

That night, even as I fought against my desire to hide my back from William, he coaxed me out of the shadows, which I had spent my whole life being swallowed up by. As his hands and lips explored every inch of my body, and in the moment that we became one, my husband made me feel like the most beautiful woman to have walked the earth.

I needn't ever have felt the need to break through my insecurities alone, for with William, we brought them crumbling to the ground.

"What time do you call this, Mrs Darlington?" Primrose narrowed her eyes at me, a gaze full of playful chastisement.

"Are we late?" I asked innocently, as a blush crept up my neck.

Primrose folded her arms over her chest, raised her eyebrows, and tapped her foot on the floor. "Yes, Wrenny, you are."

"What's all this about?" William stood flush against the back of my body, his arms protectively curled around the front of me.

"I was just inquiring as to why you are late," she smiled.

"We thought we would take the opportunity for a little vigorous exercise before we came here," William teased. "Walking, of course. It is such a lovely day after all."

James slapped William on the back, his face ripe

with a knowing smile. “Nothing like a bit of exercise first thing in the morning, ol’ boy,” he winked.

“What would you like us to help you with?” I interrupted, afraid I would combust with the searing heat of awkward embarrassment.

“Come on, Wrenny, let us leave these men to their innuendos. *hmmph!*” Primrose grinned secretly as we headed down the hall, where I simply knew I would receive the most inappropriate interrogation of my life.

By mid-afternoon, the rather regal country manor Prim and James now owned looked absolutely splendid. If it hadn’t been for their fortunate find so close to The Aviary, well, as close as one could get, that is, then it may have been years before they would have had a home built for them. In the month they had married, Primrose had blossomed, which I expect was from many things. Of course, it may have been just one, but if I were to hazard a guess, I would have said it was all four: being in love, marriage, independence, and the first few months of being with child. My sister was positively radiant.

“Do you think it will be a success?” Primrose asked, dragging her teeth over her bottom lip.

“Of course it will, Prim,” I soothed. “I assume you have invited quite a few?”

"Yes," she nodded. "Probably more than I should. Even Papa," she added, her eyes meeting mine. "You don't mind, do you? I didn't extend the invitation to Mama or Gladys, and I know Papa hardly ever sees them now that he has found somewhere else to live. Do you know that he is thinking of moving closer to us? Won't that be wonderful?"

"Slow down, Prim. Everything is okay. It will be an amazing ball, and, truth be told, I am quite looking forward to seeing Papa." My poor sister was rambling with nerves.

"Oh, that is a relief. I have been so worried, Wrenny. I never want to upset you."

"You should have just asked me earlier, Primrose. I could have put your worries to rest sooner," I offered, wrapping my arms around her. "Tonight will be the talk of all of Somerset and beyond. For the right reasons, of course," I quickly added.

Primrose chuckled against my shoulder. "I love you, Wrenny."

"And I love you too, Prim," I smiled. "Now, I do believe we have a ball to prepare ourselves for."

Primrose and James's new home thrummed with exuberance as William and I were relieved of our coats by the couple's new butler.

"May I take your coats?" he drawled, a twist in his lips revealing his softer, more amiable side than that of his role.

"Thank you, sir," I replied, handing him my light cape. I was relieved not to have burdened him with anything heavier.

The butler's amber eyes twinkled beneath his bushy silver-white eyebrows as he placed my cape over the inside of his bent arm. "And you, sir? May I take your jacket?"

William offered him his most handsome smile. "Thank you, sir, but I think I shall keep it on for a bit longer."

"Very good, sir."

"There are so many people," I breathed. "Perhaps I should have worn something over my shoulders," I commented.

It was the first ball I had ever attended, and I hadn't a clue what I should wear, but with Toni's help and exquisite taste, I was standing beside my broad-shouldered, dashing husband, who was wearing rather tight, splendidly fitting breeches, I might add, in a dress that was fit for a princess, yet I wasn't sure, as stunning as it was, if it should really have been me who was wearing it. The battle of insecurities in William's presence may have been won, yet amongst society, the subject was still rather a sore one.

William kissed my ear. "You are the most beautiful woman in the room, Little Bird, so spread your wings proudly. You do not need a cape, for you are perfect as you are."

A pleasurable shiver rippled down my spine, and I thanked the heavens for the thick fabric of the bodice that stood between my suddenly wanton breasts and the eyes of strangers, not to mention Rose and my rather nosey sister. "Stop it, William," I grumbled playfully. "You'll have me drag you back to the carriage, and I shall miss my sister's first ball.

William grinned wickedly as he waggled his eyebrows, obviously not adverse to the idea at all.

"Patience, dear husband!" I quipped, failing miraculously at stifling what I thought was a rather wicked grin of my own. "Now, let us mingle amongst the guests."

William grabbed my hand and tugged slightly. "Do you think we will have to stay here until the very end?"

"Oh, heavens, no, my darling. An hour and a half should suffice. I shall be far too tired for anymore. Do you know, I believe I have a headache beginning, so maybe no more than an hour." I briefly pressed myself against him and batted my eyes innocently. "What say you, husband?"

"I say we begin the hour right now, Little Bird," he growled softly into my ear, then eagerly whisked me into the throng of guests.

The hour passed in a medley of introductions, happy chatter with wonderful new people, and a few contented moments in the arms of my father. Together, we unburdened our souls from the past, strengthened our bond, and planned a future as the family we were always meant to have been. Sadly, I knew my mother would not be a part of that, but truth be known, I am not sure if I could have forgiven her for all she had done to me. I had a new family, a mixture of old and new, blood and not, and I could not have been happier.

"How is your head, Little Bird?" William purred suggestively in my ear.

"It's rather strange you ask, darling, for I fear I have a rather nasty pain in it. Perhaps we should leave these lovely people to it? Would you mind, terribly?"

"Anything for you, my love," he crooned loudly.

William practically dragged me from the ball as though his breeches were on fire, the music and laughter fading behind us. Placing his hands on my hips, he hoisted me into the carriage.

"Let's go home, Little Bird. I believe someone needs to be reminded just how much I love her," William drawled as he leaned forward and kissed my hands.

"I am hoping that someone is me," I teased.

"You can count on it, Little Bird, for I intend to remind you tonight and every night for the rest of our lives."

William leaned forward, placing his forehead against mine. "Little Bird, teasing and blatant lust aside, I hope you know I mean every word."

"I do, William. I really do."

I was complete.

I was home.

I was free.

But most of all, I was loved.

The End

ALSO AVAILABLE

Printed in Great Britain
by Amazon

43843383R00212

One Face Two Minds

Living under Two Cultures

Kaushal K. Srivastava

ISBN-13: 978-1533279415
ISBN-10: 1533279411

First Published in 2016

For further information contact the author:
kkps44@yahoo.com

Available from
Amazon.com, Amazon.co.uk
and other online booksellers

We become not a melting pot but a beautiful mosaic. Different people, different beliefs, different yearnings, different hopes, different dreams.

Jimmy Carter

It is just like when you've got some coffee that's too black, which means it's too strong. What do you do? You integrate it with cream, you make it weak. But if you pour too much cream in it, you won't even know you ever had coffee. It used to be hot, it becomes cool. It used to be strong, it becomes weak. It used to wake you up, now it puts you to sleep.

Malcolm X

I have a multicultural background, so I tend to have an open mind about things, and I find other cultures interesting.

Viggo Mortensen

Contents

Preface

Immigration has changed the face of the Western world in recent decades. The ever-increasing movement of people between continents has brought different cultures face to face. People deeply rooted in a particular way of life have landed in other societies with different sets of social and cultural parameters - this is euphemistically called globalisation. In a sense, they are living under two cultures, eager to avail themselves of the opportunities of the West but hesitant to come out of their ingrained cultural shell. The dichotomy they face is the subject matter of the stories in this anthology. Though they are especially centred on the interaction between Indian and Western social values, I'm interested in the universal implications of two cultures meeting. The younger, mobile generation of the digital age may see its own image in these stories; this will also be a test for the success of this work.

It would be desirable to say a few words on my own background, which has a bearing on the framework of this book. As a physicist, I have worked in India, Australia, England, and the United States; and during this journey I have seen many societal changes from a close distance. Post-retirement from Bhagalpur University, India, I have reflected upon the emerging social and cultural themes and expressed them through my writings. The present work is an important link in that endeavour - my other publications are listed at the end of this book.

Prof Kaushal Kishore Srivastava
Melbourne, Australia
Email: kkps44@yahoo.com
June 2016

1. A Short Meeting

The scholarly teacher told Kavita "Select eight to ten students from the class for this month's debate keeping a good proportion of boys and girls." Kavita was a second-year student of the college and she had become acclimatised both academically and socially to the environment. She was agile, soft-spoken and studious, praised for her sharp mind in the class, and respected by teachers.

Kavita asked, "Sir, what will the topic of the debate be?"

The teacher replied in a grave tone, "The subject is confidential and will be announced ten minutes before the debate. That is, the debate will be extempore, and more importantly the names of speakers for and against the motion will be decided by flipping a coin."

Kavita had neither seen nor heard about this type of debate and hence felt astonished and excited. She thought this form of the debate was itself an attractive subject and started analysing its merits and challenges.

During lunchtime the college canteen was crowded and noisy; she sat at a corner table while her piercing eyes looked for someone. Soon Kavita waved Kamal towards her table and explained what the teacher had just said. He was well known in the class for his witty remarks and debating skills. In his opinion such a debate would cultivate original and balanced logic among the students and help with their development across a range of areas. Both of them consulted other students, discussed the logic of the proposed novel debate, exchanged ideas, and then finalised a panel of about a dozen willing participants.

The day had arrived. Those present were very enthusiastic as two teachers acting as judges took their respective seats on the podium. The topic for the debate was announced: "In the opinion of this house the present generation of Indian youths is rapidly coming under the influence of

Western education." The teams in favour of and against the motion were selected by flipping a coin, and the audience greeted them with a noisy thumping of their desks. Kavita was chosen to support the motion whereas Kamal had to oppose the motion. It was an annoyance that both of them had to speak against their natural inclinations. They regarded each other obliquely, imagined their mutual hesitation, and then became immersed in framing their arguments in the next ten minutes. Other participants turned seriously to collecting their points for and against the motion.

Kavita's father was a junior government officer and her mother was a teacher in a secondary school. Her brother, younger by three years, was enrolled in the same school. This family of modest means, while fulfilling its basic needs, was very alert to ensuring a good education for the children, in the hope of guaranteeing them a much better future. Kavita was not under undue family restrictions but was expected to remain within reasonable bounds, keeping in mind the prevailing social traditions and economic constraints. Despite living in a big city she stayed far away from modern fashion trends but was gifted with natural charm and beauty. She had read about Western education in books and listened to lectures by those who worked in the West after obtaining degrees there, but she found it difficult to reach a definite opinion about the ramifications of their education from this limited experience.

Kamal's father, on the other hand, was a high-ranking officer, who led a household supplied with modern amenities. He had spent some time abroad and their day-to-day living reflected elements of a Western lifestyle. Kamal had naturally been influenced by his father and harboured a strong desire to seek a Western education.

The debate started with cogent and logical arguments from Kavita: "In my surroundings, including college, my neighbourhood, and the markets, I see a wide network that is made of foreign culture, foreign fashion, English newspapers and magazines, et cetera. English is prominently used in parliamentary debates and it dominates television transmissions, news channels and educational institutions for higher studies. It reigns over the technological world, gives life to mobile phones, electronic gadgets and the knowledge industry, all of which have become an integral part of our lives. In fact, we are rapidly moving towards becoming 'global citizens' in all respects, and the meaning of the word 'foreign' has effectively changed. That is, whatever was 'foreign' years ago has become 'national' today, and that includes foreign education. It is not necessary to prove something that we see every day with open eyes, especially in the context of youths, who are the voracious consumers of these services. Therefore, I strongly support the motion of the house." The audience supported Kavita's contention by giving her a standing ovation.

From the opposite team Kamal took the lead. "Truth is not only that which is easily visible. If it were, the importance of culture, national pride, love, intimacy and long-cherished human values would have been short-lived, but it is not so. The great nations of the world proudly preserve their languages, traditions, cultural heritage and lifestyles like precious treasures, which cannot be seen by the eye but only felt. They have fought painful wars for generations in order to preserve those values and countless people have made sacrifices for them. The Indian youth is also conscientiously dedicated to those ideals; the so-called influence of Western education is temporary and a means of earning good fortune in this materialistic age. I oppose the motion of the house with full conviction." The audience became almost delirious and praised Kamal with prolonged clapping.

The debate was quite engaging and interesting and speakers from both sides put forward commendable arguments. Finally the panel of judges announced, "Both sides have secured equal scores and therefore the winning team must be decided by flipping a coin."

Within a moment Kamal stood up and proposed with humility, "The prize for winning the debate ought to be awarded to Kavita's team, which has given a sense of pride to the young women assembled here and inspired them to hold their heads high in society." Kamal's gesture was well appreciated by the audience, and Kavita thankfully acknowledged it with a tinge of smile, and her eyes became wet with sentiment. Perhaps it was the first moment of mutual attraction commonly perceived as love. Both described the details of this eventful debate to their families, that night. Their names were no longer unfamiliar to the other's family members.

Whenever Kamal and Kavita faced each other in class they did not fail to say a cordial hello and usually spent a few minutes discussing their studies. They encountered a demand from their friends: "We want a party to celebrate your joint victory at the debate."

"Why not?" said Kamal with exuberance. "I am ready – we can meet today in a city restaurant after the class."

A cautious voice prevailed. "I won't be able to come to the city in the evening hours," replied Kavita, and she did not change her mind despite requests from her girlfriends. Sensing their mood, she proposed, "We could meet tomorrow in the college canteen, sweets from my side, snacks from Kamal's." This indicated her respect for college life and also for middle class family constraints – a combination of modernity and tradition.

The activities in the canteen were subdued on the last day of the week, as many students had already left the campus. Kavita, Kamal, and about a dozen friends gathered around a larger corner table in the canteen. As decided, Kavita ordered the sweets, Kamal the snacks, and others contributed towards cold drinks. The afternoon was pleasant and the fragrance emanating from the garden flowers formed a natural welcome for the guests.

Kamal started the conversation. "Initially I felt despondent, for how could I criticise a foreign lifestyle from the podium while enjoying its comforts? But, I don't know, like a wave of fresh air I felt an inner strength that inspired me to defend our Indian values with a sense of pride."

Kavita intervened. "It was the first time I had strongly supported the growing influence of foreign culture, which has little relation to our day-to-day middle-class living."

Rajiv said, "It was easy for me to defend the role of foreign education as I am accustomed to using most modern comforts and services."

"This debate has taught me an important lesson – that considering the opposite point of view is an essential dimension of balanced thinking," Savita uttered, sipping a draught of cold drink.

"We should remain prepared to face adverse situations," supplemented Kavita, swallowing a piece of sweet.

In a pensive mood, Sanjiv broke his silence. "I don't know how dedicated expat Indians are towards our cultural traditions, but we should try to understand their points of view also."

"The present generation of youths finds its future in composite culture," Kamal continued, "and Kavita's description of moving towards global citizenship was very relevant and praiseworthy."

This manner of thoughtful conversation spawned many new ideas and fostered closer friendship within the group. Finally they decided to collectively thank the teacher in charge for his efforts and guidance. Kavita offered, "I can make a thank-you card, which we can all sign and present to our teacher." Everyone heartily agreed.

Many of her friends had gone ahead but Kavita was detained because her delicate dupatta, a flowing cloth from shoulder to knee, had become entangled in a sharp corner of the table. Kamal looked back, disentangled the threads and replaced the dupatta on her shoulders.

She blushed with discomfort, and followed Kamal hesitantly, her eyes fixed on the ground while their silence became burdensome. Kamal broke the monotony, "In this college very few girls use a dupatta. Most sport Western dresses. Today I appreciate the gracefulness of this Indian adornment."

Pleased, Kavita asked, "Does anyone use a dupatta in your house?"

"No, there is no young lady in our family." In the meantime, a rickshaw had appeared on the road and Kavita got ready for a ride.

Hesitant, Kamal asked, "Can I have your mobile phone number?"

It may have been the sprouting of the seed of love, but Kavita replied, "I don't have a mobile."

Kavita returned to college the next week with a beautifully crafted thank-you card later signed by all the students. She and Kamal presented it to the teacher, who loved the gesture. He asked them to submit a summary of the debate, along with a passport-sized photograph, for inclusion in the forthcoming magazine commemorating the college establishment day, which would be attended by the Education Minister and celebrated with much fanfare. It was a pleasant surprise and they were excited at the prospect; such a meeting might help them in career advancement. A two-year old photograph, taken at the time of her admission into the college, was still lying in Kavita's bag. She eagerly showed it to Kamal and asked if it would be acceptable. He did not approve; a new photo was needed. She explained the entire context to her mother, gaining permission for a visit to the city photo studio.

When Kamal learnt of this, he also decided to visit the photographer on the appointed day. As Kavita reached the studio she was surprised to see him coming out, and they acknowledged each other with a smile. She introduced her younger brother and went inside. Kamal had already impressed upon the photographer that he must shoot an attractive but dignified picture of Kavita. When she received the prints two days later, she couldn't resist smiling at her own images – she told herself she looked attractive.

On establishment day, a group of five girls, including Kavita, welcomed the Education Minister with a bouquet of flowers, the singing of the national anthem and lighting of the ceremonial lamp, which symbolised victory over darkness through the wisdom of knowledge. The media covered the events in the newspapers, with photographs, and Kavita had a prominent place in them. The days spent in college were memorable for her, and Kamal had gained a place in her thoughts. Over the next few days he collected her photographs from the college magazine and local newspapers and placed them on his study table. When his mother saw them, an unknown apprehension crept into her mind.

The examination season was fast approaching and many of the college activities were thinning out. More than a month had passed since the last function and that month remained uneventful for Kavita and Kamal except for casual meetings now and then. Finally the examinations were over and the college closed for the long vacation, extending over six weeks. Kamal ventured to ask, "The coming year will be our final year in the college and also academically demanding. Can we meet once or twice for a cup of coffee in the college canteen? Or the library?"

Kavita replied thoughtfully, "I doubt that I will have the time. And I don't have a mobile phone so I wouldn't be able to let you know." Smiling shyly, she added, "Time goes very fast, enjoy your vacation."

He remembered her smile every day for the next six weeks.

"Anything special during the holidays?" Kavita asked as she faced Kamal on the first day of the new college year.

"Nothing special, I was just thinking about our future career and job prospects."

"Our career? When did you become plural?"

Noticing her smile, Kamal confessed, "Yes, it was mainly about my own career but occasionally your picture also emerged, I don't know why. I should be more careful in choosing my words, with your analytical mind."

"I appreciate your openness. Would you like to have a cup of coffee? Do you remember your offer?"

"Yes, I do. Black or white? How much sugar?"

They ordered coffee and snacks while sitting in a corner of the canteen. "I forgot to ask how you spent your time," Kamal said. "Anything worth mentioning?"

"We attended the wedding of one of my cousin-sisters in a different town. It was entertaining but a bit burdensome for the family."

"Can I ask why?"

"Leave it for some other time." She did not want to talk about the financial burden imposed on the bride's family, not unusual despite modernity.

The smell of coffee was inviting. "Do you like coffee?" asked Kavita.

"Yes, I do but its flavour is more satisfying today." She sensed its poetic meaning but kept quiet. Kamal continued, "What are you planning to do after passing the final exams this year?"

"I have decided to take up a job in the field of information technology; my father's finances may not permit me to go for higher education immediately." Kamal was astonished at her frankness; most of his friends did not like to share family matters so openly despite their long association.

"And you?" she asked.

He self-consciously volunteered that he had opted for higher education in a large Indian city or even a foreign country.

As time passed, the two naturally became closer emotionally. When it was Kamal's birthday, he invited Kavita to his party, planned for the daytime so she could return home well before dark. The party was boisterous and full of youthful celebrations. A stain of curry on Kavita's dupatta was immediately and apologetically cleaned by Kamal, who also moved to rearrange her long black hair, which had fallen over her face. Her spontaneous blush at the sensual touch did not go unnoticed by his mother, who could see that there was love between the two.

The party continued much longer and the spell of darkness descended. Out of concern, Kavita's mother came looking for her in a rickshaw and, after being questioned by the guard, she was allowed inside. She was welcomed only half-heartedly. "There was no need for you to come by a rickshaw at this hour, Kavita would have gone back in my car," said Kamal's mother. Kavita felt guilty; she touched the lady's feet with respect, took leave of her friends, and accompanied her mother in the rickshaw. She heard: "The clash between rickshaw and motor car is normal, but their adjustment is very difficult." She said to herself, "This is a social mystery, not found in books."

The final exams were over within a few months and both Kavita and Kamal passed with high ranks. It was a moment of elation, and the beginning of a new phase of life. Kavita got a job offer in a local company and Kamal was admitted to an MBA program in a different city.

She received a message: "Can we relive our shared moments before I leave this city for a journey into the unknown world?"

She replied, "I was just thinking of the same, the place should be the college canteen, which has been a witness to our friendly bonds."

Soon they were again seated at the corner table of the college canteen where they had often met. Kamal opened his mind. "The sharp corner of the table is still eager to catch your dupatta; the scene is engraved in my memory."

She replied shyly, "You have snatched the words from my mouth, how can I forget? That's why I decided to come here."

"I had no idea you also felt so deeply the moments that have become a part of my journey," he said. "In this diary I have given life to those shared moments, thoughts, aspirations and my own imaginations. This is a gift from me, but there is one request – please open it only after I leave this city." His voice choked with emotions, he continued, "Can I ask for something in return?"

Kavita started sobbing. "Just say it, do not hesitate." Drops of tears were visible in her eyes.

"A picture of yours to keep."

She could not deny him. Both were driven emotionally and an eerie silence prevailed. Kamal took her hand. "The setting sun at the horizon looks cheerful, do you know why? Because it is eager to embrace the glorious morning."

"I will remember these words. They are a source of hope."

They left in silence, saddened but mentally entangled.

Kavita could not sleep for two nights; she was curious to open the diary. When time permitted she found the pages were written with great feeling, their memorable moments and togetherness preserved in touching words she had never anticipated. Lastly he had written, "The tender plant of my love could not blossom because it did not get nourishment from my family. I will feel greatly relieved and immensely happy when I hear you have a loving life partner, which will be easier when I have gone away." Sitting alone in her bed she started crying, her tears the only witness of the storm in her mind. There were no words of consolation around her, not even his phone number.

Time being a great healer, her emotional tension subsided, and she found solace in her office work. Her parents became anxious for their daughter's marriage. Given that Kavita was well educated, beautiful and in a good job, her father thought it would not be hard to find a good match for her. Her mother said, "Get a few prints of your recent photographs." When she reached the studio for prints she learnt that it was Kamal who had asked the photographer to shoot her pictures in a particular way. She couldn't help wondering whether this was also his way of expressing love.

For more than six months her father took her marriage proposal to many families, both well-known from earlier acquaintances and new ones. Without exception all of them were highly impressed with her qualities and wished her well, but at the same time expected a handsome dowry, which was beyond his reach. She was perturbed at her father's growing anxiety and his failing health. For the first time she saw the ugly face of a society which was devoid of values and enmeshed in false pretensions, where money commanded greater respect than personal qualities. She thought to herself, "Perhaps the parents of Kamal were bound in the same deceptive chain." Time was running fast: more than one year had passed, she had no information about Kamal, and she felt as if the atmosphere had become dreary and oppressive.

One day, by chance, she saw Kamal's mother from a distance in a shopping area; she jumped to her feet with excitement, and almost ran towards her with eagerness. "Hello, aunty, how are you? How is Kamal?"

She replied sardonically, "He is very busy with his studies, nothing to worry about," and moved on with a friend. Kavita guessed his mother had avoided her and was deeply hurt by the encounter. She wondered why human nature was so inscrutable.

Feeling despondent, she was trying to unravel social relationships when she received a proposal from her company that lit up her spirits. They wanted to assign her in the company's foreign office in Melbourne, Australia. Within two months she was in a new country with a very different set of social and cultural values.

Then events took a dramatic and unexpected turn.

As a prudent member of Generation Y, Kavita settled into her new job professionally but often wondered about her social identity, which was not uncommon among new migrants. One day I, the same teacher from her college, was travelling by train in Melbourne when Kavita entered the compartment. We noticed each other with surprise and she gladly took a seat in front of me. After initial hesitation she opened up. "The working days are busy and time-consuming but loneliness prevails at home especially during weekends. Life seems to have become machine-like, devoid of any enthusiasm despite all amenities. Socialisation hardly goes beyond 'hi' and 'hello'. The sad faces of my parents often appear in dreams ….."

I realised she must be emotionally perturbed, she had described so much about herself in one breath. I intervened with sympathy. "In this phase of life you need a friend, a partner, for companionship, who may lessen the painful shadow of isolation from your heart and mind. Try to understand the composite culture of this country, adopt something, leave something, come out of the rigid grip of the Indian culture, and this will give you a new light." I continued, "These days Kamal is also in this country and his phone number is with me." I offered my visiting card. "You may call me whenever you are in need." I got off at the next station.

When she got home Kavita opened a Facebook account and wrote, "The tender plant of first love is still alive and waiting to blossom, and the pages of the diary are my prized possession." She pasted the same well-taken photo of herself and transmitted it through the web. After a few hours Kamal's picture came alive on her phone with the message, "The scene of your dupatta entangled in the table's corner appears before my eyes even today, your photograph adorns my study table…" She read the entire message, her eyes became moist and she burst into sobs. After regaining her composure she phoned him with trembling fingers, feeling more panicky than excited.

She heard 'Hello,' from the other side and started sobbing aloud, while Kamal was frantically repeating 'Hello, hello,' his voice also choked with emotions. They could not speak but they sensed their affinity and their hearts felt a bond. It was one of those moments in human relationships when emotions are more powerful than explicit words.

The next day Kavita was present at the airport to receive Kamal with a bouquet of bright red roses. They remained in a prolonged embrace, their heartbeats told the story, and tears strengthened their resolve to surmount all social hurdles. While driving together Kamal broke the silence. "In this country personal relationships are not hostage to financial status, everyone has the liberty to live as they choose. Our love could not flourish in our own country but will blossom in this foreign land." She breathed a heavy sigh of relief.

Soon Kamal's parents approached Kavita's parents and proposed to solemnise their wedding at the earliest opportunity. Although initially reluctant, Kamal's parents had soon realized the depth of his love for Kavita and gave the union their blessing. In the presence of friends and relatives, the couple became life partners by taking an oath before the sacred fire. In a message to her teacher Kavita wrote, "A short meeting with you gave me new light and a gem-like partner. The spirit of Melbourne prevailed. We will come soon to seek your blessings."

There is light across the horizon. One only has to look with an open mind.

2. Facing an Unknown

Khut, khut, khut!

It sounded like a knock at the front door. Rajeev was busy working at his computer. Half past three in the afternoon, and he was alone. His wife Sheela had gone to pick up their small child from a nearby school and she was expected back any moment. He wondered, "Who is at the door? Sheela has the key and she does not like to disturb me." When he heard the knock again, he shouted, "just coming," and ran towards the door, adjusting his crumpled shirt and ignoring his untidy slippers.

A young Asian woman was standing at the door. Attractive, probably in her early thirties, she stood there silently. "What's the matter?" Rajeev asked in an indifferent tone.

She replied politely, "My name is Wendy Taei. While going this way I got attracted to the *om* painted in gold on the wooden board outside your house. Most probably you are an Indian and there is a tradition of welcoming guests in your culture."

He hesitated for a moment, thinking, "A woman who has said so much in a single breath should be well educated, even professional, and hence there must be some reason for knocking at the door without prior information," and then invited her in. Before she could step inside, his wife's car was appeared at the front gate and he felt a great relief. Rajeev introduced them. "This is my wife Sheela, and this is Wendy Taei, who has just arrived here."

"But you did not introduce yourself?" asked Wendy.

"I am Rajeev and I work for a technical company."

"Is there no surname?"

He felt defeated and uttered, "Saxena," realising that the young woman was sharp-witted and cleverly talkative.

Once inside, Rajeev went back to his study. Sheela escorted Wendy towards the kitchen and said, "I will prepare tea after giving some food to my child and in the meantime you can read some magazines."

"I would like to address you as 'sister' instead of using your name," Wendy replied.

"Fine, now tell me how do you speak such good Hindi? Where did you live in India?"

"Sister, I am not an Indian and neither are my parents. My father had a job in India and during those years I had a chance to study there in school for five to six years. This provided me with a golden opportunity to study Hindi and to understand Indian cultural traditions and their essence. In subsequent years I went there on a few occasions but have lost contact for the past fifteen years."

"Then which country do you belong to? By appearance you look like an Asian."

"In this modern age a person is identified less by his or her country and more by belief and profession, especially in my situation, where my own country abandoned me."

"I will not ask this question again – perhaps there is some painful memory behind it and I don't want to hurt your feelings."

Wendy kept quiet.

While serving tea, Sheela invited Rajeev to join them. Looking at Wendy, he said, "It appears you have already established a rapport with Sheela. She enjoys talking to people. Can I also know something about you?"

"I came here a few months ago and live with a lady-friend. I work in an aged-care facility for two days and at the asylum resource centre for a few hours per week. This gives me just enough to financially support myself. I would like to enrol in a computer course in order to qualify for an office job."

"Do you also have a family here?" enquired Rajeev quite casually.

Without answering, she stood up and got ready to leave. Sheela offered her a lift in her car, but she declined. "I already have a valid bus ticket which will be wasted. I shall consider your offer on some other day."

“You can call me for any help and we can try to meet again.” Sheela scribbled on a paper and gave it to her. “Keep my phone number.”

“Thank you for the tea. I will be happy to maintain this sister-like relationship.”

Rajeev and Sheela were surprised that Wendy did not divulge any information about her whereabouts or family but she wanted to foster a sister-like relationship within their family. They became a bit suspicious. *Perhaps things will surface at the next meeting,* they thought. It was obvious that Wendy was capable of living confidently and fearlessly – a praiseworthy attribute in women.

A week passed. Sheela wanted to talk to Wendy but she did not have her phone number. It was a pleasant day, and Rajeev and Sheela decided to go for a stroll on the beach. Melbourne's coast is very beautiful and extensive, and it becomes a favoured spot for people on hot sunny days. The sun was reaching the evening horizon, and the rays falling on the golden sheet of sand were inviting, and rather pleasing. Hundreds of people were sitting in groups on the lush green lawn, a short distance from the water, groups of children were playing here and there, and many were walking on the long concrete path near the coast line.

Rajeev and Sheela were among them, walking and watching the dance of the tide. From a distance Rajeev saw a lonely figure standing almost at the water, looking into the waves very intently, like a motionless statue. When he returned after half an hour he saw the same scene, and naturally became curious and told Sheela. Both of them fixed their attention on the figure from a safe distance so that no one could doubt on their motive. They spent another half an hour before the sun went down beyond the horizon, and then the figure started moving away. Though darkness had descended they felt that the figure resembled Wendy Taei and they decided to explore further. As they pursued the figure cautiously, but from a close distance, their suspicion gradually changed to belief. Both were astonished, but they did not consider it appropriate to confront Wendy at this time.

Several questions arose in their mind: "Was she waiting for someone? Why was she looking into the waters as if something was hidden there? Was she thinking something untoward about her life?" They became grave and alarmed, discussing the possibilities between themselves, but they could not come to a logical conclusion. They became quite doubtful about her identity, even her name. "Was Wendy Taei was a fake name? Where does she live? Why is she alone? Where has she come from?" The questions became more important.

After a few days Sheela saw Wendy by chance in a shopping centre and waved. Wendy responded by waving her hand too, but soon went outside through a nearby gate. When Sheela followed Wendy hastily said, "I have to go for some work, I will see you next time." At this indifference Sheela felt both indignation and surprise. Why was she shying away? She had sympathy for Wendy but she needed the time and means to communicate it. She decided to spy on her to find out the facts.

She visited three aged- care centres in her area and enquired about a nurse or helper named Wendy Taei. At one place she could locate her name but the manager declined to give any further information, at Wendy's written instruction. At Sheela's persistent requests, the manager mentioned that she had been working there for the last two months on a part-time basis but emphatically declined to give information about her working days or hours. Sheela returned home with a burden of sadness but she did not lose patience.

The next day, after dropping her child at school, she went early to the same aged-care centre and sat in the shadow of a tree, at a safe distance from the main gate. She wore a large hat to partially cover her face so that Wendy could not recognise her from afar. At around noon Wendy walked into the centre and Sheela became alert, but she got another surprise. Wendy talked to a woman at the reception counter and came out within ten minutes! An Asian man was waiting outside the gate; she left with him.

When Sheela, in a pensive mood, entered the centre she saw an old woman at the reception counter and decided to take another chance. She told the woman, "My grandmother is about eighty years old, she has problems walking, and we are going away for two weeks. I would like to get her admitted in this centre for that period. I have heard about a female helper of Asian origin who speaks Hindi and I would like to talk to her, because my grandmother also speaks Hindi and she will find it more relaxing in the company of that helper."

"That helper has just gone out. She will be on leave for two days. I think she has some mental worries that she does not want to share with anyone. She has not been able to overcome the complex legal hurdles for asylum seekers in this country. Today she was looking very disturbed; she needs the peace and sympathy of friends."

"Can I know her phone number or home address?"

"This information is available from the manager only and it is also a matter of personal privacy. I can't help you. If you leave your phone number, I will pass it on when she is back."

"I will come again, thanks for your time."

Sheela thought: *The lady divulged more than expected, does she understand what privacy is?*

Now she knew that Wendy was living as a refugee and probably someone from the government was probably keeping an eye on her activities. She did not known where Wendy lived before coming to Melbourne: was she in a detention centre or in a different city? Has she come alone or is there someone else with her? Many questions cropped up in her mind. Why did she leave her country despite being well educated and skilful in manners? What were her compulsions? How did she come to Australia, in a boat? Her womanly compassion was on display.

She discussed the whole situation with Rajeev and they decided to reach Wendy and extend all possible help. That was a logical and prudent step, considering Sheela's innate sympathy for a sisterly woman in distress. Rajeev analysed, "If Wendy is really under mental stress, any psychologist or well-wisher would advise her to spend time in a peaceful environment and that's possibly the reason she was standing at the seashore like a statue for long hours. It is quite possible we can find her there." Sheela agreed with this reasoning and she decided to spend a few evenings in disguise at the coast. She could always call Rajeev, if needed.

Sheela did not see Wendy for two days. She wondered whether this approach would succeed – after all, how long would she be loitering aimlessly at the seashore? It was Saturday, the third day of the search, which she decided would be the final day of her spying, and she asked Rajeev to come along. Now there were four eyes, and that Rajeev took his binoculars so that he could survey the extended seashore from a safe distance. Both arrived early in the afternoon as the weather was congenial. As time progressed, the crowd thickened and a large number of people could be seen playing in the waves and walking on the path. After a little while, Rajeev again saw the same scene - a statue-like figure intently looking into the water! He cautioned Sheela and they moved forward; now Wendy was clearly visible through his binoculars.

When Sheela put her hand on Wendy's shoulders from behind, she was so astonished she began to panic. She was grave, her wide eyes seemed focused on something and her mind seemed in a different world. Sheela said very casually, "It was Saturday, so we also came here for a walk and saw you looking into the waters very intently. What are you searching for in the ocean?"

"I am searching for my soul in the ocean."

Sheela was not ready for this type of unexpected answer; she could not believe her ears, and asked, "What did you say?"

"What you have heard: I am searching for my soul in waters."

Sheela persisted, "What do you mean? I have heard that

the soul resides in one's body; some sages consider it a part of the Supreme Being."

"This is imagined by philosophers who are away from the complexities of the real world. I believe that an individual's soul is integrated with his or her interactive community, cultural pursuits and wider human values."

"Even if I accept your logic, how can you find your soul in the sea?"

"Yes, it is a clash of opinions. The waves of infinite oceans touch many civilisations in their journey and they teach us a useful lesson. I honestly believe the waves pounding these shores must have touched my country and they contain the fragrance of my great culture, the identity of my community. When I pierce these waves, I see a glimpse of the same identity and culture. After all, what is soul? Who has seen the physical or material form of the soul?"

Sheela shot back, "If that is so, if you are so committed, why did you leave your country or your community? What were your compulsions? Without soul life becomes a burden, desire for life ends, so why have you landed into this unknown society of different cultural traditions? Can I know the name of your own country? I ask this question again under very unusual circumstances, though I had earlier promised not to ask about your ethnicity or country of origin."

"It makes no difference; my perspective would remain the same irrespective of my place of origin. Yes, why did I come here as a refugee, what were my compulsions? They are meaningful questions and I will answer them at an appropriate time." She started sobbing with a burst of emotions.

Sheela embraced her. "I am sorry that I have reopened your wounds."

Realising the gravity of the situation, Rajeev intervened, "Let us go for coffee."

Wendy followed silently.

While walking to a nearby restaurant, Sheela thought, *Wendy is educated, skilful and trained in two languages – she may have received higher education as well – and despite that she had to leave her country as a refugee. Her compulsions must have been enormously painful, even life-threatening, and it is not easy to assess her internal grief. I should try to know about her past but within her conditions, and in the meantime it is important to alleviate her mental agony."*

The restaurant looked full but they got a place in the corner, which was dimly lit and less noisy. Very little light fell on Wendy's face and she liked it. She surveyed the restaurant with her penetrating eyes, as if she had some apprehensions, and then took her seat without hesitation. Rajeev was standing in the queue for coffee and snacks; there were a few others in front of him. Sheela looked into Wendy's eyes and broke the heaviness of the air. "You call me sister, don't you? This gives me some authority to know about you and also a responsibility to help you, but this can be possible only with your cooperation – there is no pressure on you. I do not want to impinge upon your privacy."

"Sister, I also want to make use of your affectionate feelings with full understanding but I need some time," Wendy replied.

Rajeev placed the coffee tray on the central table and stretched his hand out to pour coffee into their cups. Wendy also stretched out her hand. "Please give me a chance."

"Why not," he replied.

"How much sugar for you?"

"One teaspoon."

"And for you, sister?"

"Sugar one teaspoon, but no milk."

"Why this? Any complaint against milk?"

"I take lactose-free milk; I am a bit allergic to common milk."

"I will be mindful in the future."

By the time they finished their coffee, darkness has already descended. Rajeev offered, "I will drop you at your house, you may come in our car."

Wendy was hesitant but agreed when Sheela insisted. "There is one request: you will drop me at a distance from my house." Sheela and Wendy occupied the back seat and indulged in small gossips, a sign of growing openness. Sheela volunteered, "It is Sunday tomorrow. I go for yoga and meditation at five o'clock in the afternoon and Rajeev remains at home with the child. It is said that a regular practice of meditation removes mental tension and enhances inner strength. The history of Indian yoga and meditation is very old; some of the ancient sages even compared them with the 'nectar of life'. I can pick you up if you decide to join, just give me a call."

"I have also heard about these practices but never experienced them," Wendy replied. "I will join you at the right time; there is no need to pick me up."

At five o'clock Wendy entered the hall and glanced over at the people already seated for the yoga and meditation session. She took her seat beside Sheela. There were some twenty-five people, men and women in almost equal proportion, and most of them had passed their youthful age. The atmosphere became serene as soon as the instructor entered the hall. For fifteen minutes they performed a few mild exercises, including breathing and posture-related ones, and thereafter they were asked to close their eyes and sit straight in a comfortable, attentive posture. A deep voice said, "Try to remove the memories of unhappy events from your mind. Remember ten actions that are beneficial to mankind, such as giving food to the hungry, helping the poor, assisting the disabled, and fix their image in your thoughts. Deviation of mind is natural, but try again and again. Try to prevent bad thoughts from entering into your conscious mind; it will take time to succeed but do not be disheartened."

After ten minutes they were asked to open their eyes. A short discourse on the importance of yoga followed. The instructor spoke again in a mild voice: "Try to concentrate your roaming mind on a central point – it could be the picture of a god or goddess, an imaginary source of light or even the image of an object. Whatever you choose should always remain as your mental focus; the mind will deviate but bring it back." A unique reign of silence and tranquillity prevailed, which Wendy had never experienced. This practice lasted for about fifteen minutes. When people started leaving, the instructor came forward and told Wendy, "Probably you have come for the first time, you look a bit uneasy and mentally entangled. The practice of meditation will give you inner peace and open new doors for a meaningful life."

She replied, "Yes sir."

Returning from the class, Wendy enquired, "Sister, when will you come again?"

"Why, what's the matter?"

"I would like to come again."

"Next Wednesday, at the same time. This class is held twice a week and I come regularly."

"This is the reason you are so kind and your company gives a satisfying feeling."

Four weeks passed. Wendy came regularly and also practised one day at her home. Sheela was impressed at the visible change in Wendy's behaviour and her response to situations. Wendy herself felt this change: she was working with greater efficiency and without unnecessary mental strain and her colleagues noticed this as well.

It was Sunday morning. When Wendy called Sheela, it was Rajeev who came to the phone. "Rajeev speaking."

"Good morning, Rajeev-ji. Wendy here, I want to talk to my sister."

"Today you sound very happy, what's happened?"

"First I will tell the sister, kindly call her?"

"Yes, she is here."

"Sister, good morning. My salary has gone up and I have been assigned a part-time job in the office as well. In celebration I want to give a party. In my house the space is very limited, so I want to bring some cooked food at lunchtime to share with you. Will you have any problem?"

"It would be our pleasure. I will wait for you, and please tell me if anything is needed."

The food Wendy prepared had a combination of Indian and Asian tasty dishes. In place of sweets, she had cooked a cake full of dried fruits and coated with a thick layer of chocolate, which was especially enjoyed by Rajeev and their son. When Sheela asked for its recipe, she said jokingly, "One day we can prepare it together - maybe Rajeev-ji will also learn." Smiles appeared on all faces; it was a sign of normalcy returning into Wendy's life. Rajeev had to go; he thanked her and disappeared.

The weather was pleasant; Sheela and Wendy went out into the garden with their coffees. Wendy initiated without prompting, "Sister, today I want to ease my mental burden. I had thought of doing it many times but could not muster enough courage. It is related to my past life and you were also keen to learn about it. It is your unbounded support which has given me this courage."

She continued, "I have a degree in higher education and was in a decent job in my country, my husband was a high-ranking government official and his family was well known in political circles. After a few years of marriage, a revolutionary organisation raised its voice against the regime and became powerful in a short time. In their opinion the centralised regime, with its machinery of self-serving bureaucrats, was responsible for extreme poverty, backwardness and rampant corruption prevalent in our society, and they called upon the masses to overthrow the regime through armed struggle. A section of the population took to the streets and the government also used its forces to ruthlessly crush the revolt. There was much bloodshed, but the fire did not extinguish.

"Looking at their heavy losses, the extremists changed their strategy. They believed that it was the educated class who ran the administration and so they decided to destroy it. In this strategy a large number of working intellectuals were kidnapped and killed. They spared the elders, who were not capable of actively opposing them. My husband also became a victim of this tactic; his body was found outside the city. I also started getting threats - one day I escaped their trap by sheer chance. Out of fear I left the city, moved to a relative in a remote village. But after two weeks the same threats started coming. The network of extremists had spread far and wide. Ultimately, I succeeded in leaving the country with the help of a European friend. After leading a hard life for two years in Eastern Europe, I could arrange my trip to Australia with whatever money I received from the sale of my ornaments and other valuables. After spending five months in a detention centre I was permitted to live in the community and so I am in Melbourne. This is my short story, the intermediate chapters are very long. Occasionally, I used to get mentally disturbed and in one of those moments I had knocked at your door."

She became silent for a few moments, as if gathering her thoughts. "When life was in danger, survival was the central purpose. For this life's journey a new purpose, a new commitment, a new philosophy are needed. Just to remain alive and enjoy the comforts is not enough. I have full faith in your guidance as you inspired me to experiment with yoga and meditation."

Sheela was moved. "Your one duty should be to help others, you have yourself experienced it. Wherever you are standing today has been possible only with the cooperation of many good Samaritans – it is quite possible that some of them have put their own lives in danger. So as far as the question of life's philosophy is concerned, it is a wide open subject. I am neither a scholar of religious matters nor an expert in philosophy, but I can tell you something on the basis of my experience and you are free to analyse it."

"I would definitely like to hear."

Sheela continued. "In Indian culture the sermon of Lord Krishna enunciated in the Bhagavadgita 'karamanye vadhikaraste, ma phaleshu kadachana', has a special significance. It means humans have a right to work only with no right for the fruits thereof, in other words the achievement of fruits arising from the efforts should be left to God's will. This provides a right balance between *karmwad*, the obligation for doing work, and *bhagyawad,* the belief in fate or fatalism. Those who depend on fate only can become lazy, whereas those who believe in efforts only can become arrogant, and both these conditions are harmful for humans. The sermon of Lord Krishna shows you the middle path. In cases of failure you can gain control over the grief by considering it partially fated and, similarly, in cases of success you are saved from the destructive grip of self-arrogance by considering the success as God's will."

She concluded, "If you have faith in God, you will also have to believe in His blissful intervention in your life, knowingly or unknowingly. I have faith in God, I don't know about you."

Wendy was listening very attentively. "It was probably God's intervention that I knocked on your door seeing the iconic symbol *om*. You have opened my eyes."

Rajeev returned from work; evening was approaching. Sheela offered, "Let me drop you at your home." Today Wendy looked satisfied and more matured internally; she did not object.

Wendy slept well through the night and had a strange dream in which she was dancing with a male friend, but his face was blurred. Surprised, she woke up. *What could be its meaning?* She wondered. W*as it a premonition of what was to come?* When she stood up before the mirror the next morning, a thin smile appeared on her face!

Two more weeks passed. Wendy attended yoga and meditation classes regularly, and the changes to her facial expression were easily discernible. Some of her colleagues enquired about it but she ignored them politely with a smile. Sheela phoned. "Let us go out for a cup of tea."

With an enigmatic smile on her lips, Wendy asked, "Is it possible to easily forget the memories associated with one's past life? Can those images be removed for all times through the practice of meditation?"

Perplexed at this serious question, she replied, "I have been living in this country for the past fifteen years but my weakness for India has not ended and it is not likely to end in the future either. My experience of the years spent there, the accumulated feeling of pleasure and pain, and many memorable moments are a part of my own history and they influence me even today. However, there is a difference in thinking that I would like to explain."

She continued, "We live in the present, and this gives energy to our life – it sustains it, rather. Try to live 'the present' in its entirety, digest its controlling power, dream for future amidst its shadow, and learn lessons from the past. If five years ago my leg was broken, then remembering its pain does not mean that I should break my leg again – rather, one should take care not to stumble again."

Wendy's eyes were wide with surprise at this logic and she uttered loudly, "In your logic there is a strong desire to live with dignity and I respect it. I will try to adopt it in my life."

Leaving the restaurant, Sheela said, "Rajeev has talked to a good institution for your computer training; you may come and discuss the details within the next few days."

"I will definitely come."

After the yoga class on the Sunday evening, Wendy came back to Sheela's house. Rajeev told her, "I have discussed a suitable computer course with the principal of the institute. See him to enrol in the course. The course is of three months' duration; its fee is about two thousand dollars, including books and other accessories. The semester will start after four weeks and at that time you will need a laptop computer, which usually costs five to six hundred dollars."

Dejected, she replied in a low voice, "Thanks for your time but presently I am not in a position to spend this much. I will see later on."

Sheela said politely, "Why so, I will help you."

Wendy protested, “I am already burdened in your debt; please do not show further mercy so that my self-pride is hurt. You have a family, lots of financial commitments, and therefore accepting any financial help from you is not reasonable.” She became sentimental, which Sheela could hear it in her voice.

Realising her emotions, Sheela proposed, “I am offering a loan, you can return it in due course.”

“Still, it will be a burden in my mind.”

“Fine, you can pay me some interest, I will accept that.”

They could not help laughing at this business-like approach. Sheela felt a sense of relief; tears of happiness could be seen in Wendy's eyes.

Rajeev was watching a Bollywood movie in the living room; Sheela invited Wendy to join them. There was a colourful and attractive wedding scene, full of the songs and dance sequences for which Bollywood is famous. Wendy enjoyed this entertaining movie and then joined the family for dinner. When leaving she whispered, “Sister, I will let you know how much of a loan I need from you, and we will go together for my admission at the institute.”

In bed she could hardly sleep, the scenes of her own wedding came alive. How happily was it celebrated with festoons and colours! Her married life was full of charm, but that was soon overtaken by tragedy. She was in pain, but there was no one to console her.

Wendy busied herself in computer class. There were ten people in the group - six male and four female - and their faces were representative of a multicultural society. After a month, they were familiar with each other. One Saturday the institute planned a group picnic and the teacher urged them to come in their national dress as far as possible. Wendy took a colourful dress, a *salwar kurta,* from her suitcase and gazed at it several times, her old memories woven in its embroideries. She hesitated initially but dressed up - it was the only dress in her possession. Her beauty blossomed in this dress, she remained glued to the mirror for some time, abruptly smiled at herself, and passed into a fairy world for a few moments.

The picnic site was located in a beautiful park full of trees and a velvety green lawn. They entertained themselves in various ways – telling funny stories, singing songs, playing games – and Wendy in her turn told a few jokes. After many years she spent some happy hours in a free surrounding and realised that this society could also provide energy for life. Suddenly a classmate appeared in front of her and asked, "Can I take your picture?"

"Why?"

"You look beautiful in that dress."

With a fraction of a smile she complied. "It's fine, but please give one print to me also." She thought, *shooting photos during picnics is a common thing – others have also fully used their cameras - then why hesitate?* Had she possessed a camera, she might have done the same." She remembered her own effervescent days in the college, when she had gone for picnics with friends on several occasions.

On Monday everyone was present in the class. They said hello to each other as if one day's picnic had made them close friends. At lunchtime Wendy would sit at a corner table in the canteen and read a magazine while eating. Today, as usual, she was completely occupied in a magazine; her eyes were fixed on the open pages.

"Can I sit here?"

When she raised her head she saw the same person who had snapped her picture in the picnic and replied unwittingly, "Yes, you can." He placed a photo on the table and remained silent. "The photo has come up very well, thanks," Wendy said.

"A beautiful face is needed for a good picture, your face is very photogenic," he replied. "I have retained one print as a souvenir. I hope you will not mind." There was burdensome silence at the table when he introduced himself. "My name is John Mori. Mori is the name of my village and also my surname, as per local tradition. I have come from Africa, my father is of

Indian origin and my mother a Kenyan. At home we could speak broken Hindi, sometimes laughable, but here the common language is English. In this city I am living alone as a paying guest."

Before Wendy could say anything he brought two cups of tea from the stall and offered her one. Perplexed, she uttered, "Thanks, it was hardly needed. I take tea very occasionally." She continued, a bit hesitantly, "I am Wendy Taei. I live with a lady friend and have a part-time office job. I can speak Hindi, and I find myself closer to Indian culture." Lunchtime was over, they left for class.

They continued meeting occasionally. As time passed they saw each other more often and their initial reservation subsided greatly. It was no wonder that they started feeling unexplained attraction towards each other. Humans, after all, are social animals and have a natural tendency towards comradeship, especially when facing isolation. For the past several years she had to face emotional turmoil and live in a restricted environment, now she had regained her freedom and she was enjoying it.

Time also played its role. Sheela had gone to India for three weeks, which gave her additional freedom. Now the semester was ending, hardly two weeks were left in final exams and the teacher had already announced the schedule. Exams were held, results came out: Wendy had secured first position in the class. The graduation function was to be held the next Friday and the top mark would also receive a medal. Sheela would return from India before then. Wendy phoned her. "Sister, please bring a pair of *salwar kurta,* which I want to wear for the graduation function next Friday. While watching the Bollywood movie at your house I saw many colourful, vibrant dresses and I would appreciate something like that."

Sheela said a bit teasingly, "What's the matter, have you found a Krishna?"

"No sister, why hide from you?" Wendy replied. "But I

have resolved to relive my life, it is possible that one day I will find a Krishna also."

The day of graduation, Sheela came as a guest. The chief of the institute presented certificates to all the students. They all congratulated each other and shook hands. When Wendy came to the podium to receive the medal for the highest achiever, she was profusely applauded in a prolonged clapping from the audience. Her face was beaming with self-confidence and shinning with happiness, and she was looking glamorous in the colourful dress. "Can I take a picture?" John asked. He captured Wendy's smile in his camera, moved closer, and whispered "Lots of congratulations."

"To you also."

He placed a small coloured box in her hand. "A little gift, in the memory of this occasion."

Sheela's sharp eyes saw a glow of happiness in his and thought if her guess was correct, this was a day of great happiness. At the end of the function Wendy introduced them. "Sister, this is John Mori, my friend. John, this is my sister, whose deep affection has inspired me to adopt a new life."

The next day Sheela gave Wendy a gift packet. "Congratulation on your success and my best wishes."

"What's inside?" Wendy asked.

"Open and see."

Wendy saw a beautiful wooden board engraved with *Om Shanti* – let there be peace – in metallic gold. There was a card, which read, "These words will bring happiness, peace, prosperity, and godly energy into your life. They contain the seeds of Indian culture, nurture them with your faith."

A voice prevailed: "There is life on the other side of the horizon also. One has to realise it."

3. Shadow of Dark Night

A menacing, moonless night; the power was off, impenetrable darkness everywhere.

It was past midnight when Reeta was suddenly awoken from a dreadful dream about her husband; drops of perspiration appeared on her forehead. Her husband, Henry Watson, was a military captain, presently posted at the invisible front of terrorism in a distant land. Fidgeting, she peeped into the adjoining room where her mother-in-law and sister-in-law were fast asleep. There was no one to share her restlessness, so she found solace in a glass of cold water. Sipping it, she softly patted the head of her two-year-old son, who was sleeping soundly in a nearby cot. She then lit a candle, and tuned the radio on softly. She listened to various twenty-four-hour news channels for a while but there was no news about a military skirmish anywhere. She prayed for the safety of Henry, recited *Gayatri Mantra,* the hymns from Hindu religious scriptures, and returned to bed, but did not sleep well for the rest of the night.

Reeta's parents were from India; they had come to Australia twenty-five years before, when she was a little girl. Now well-settled in Australia and running a successful family restaurant, they regularly visited India. To Reeta these visits provided the exhilarating experience of meeting her extended family and assimilating Indian culture and language.

She was feeling depressed in the morning, with a headache and swollen eyes. When her mother-in-law asked the reason, she started sobbing. Hearing her sobs, her brother-in-law, John, came running and asked the same question; he had never seen his sister-in-law in such a distressed state. After Reeta regained composure she said, "Last night I saw a fearful dream in which Henry was badly wounded in an encounter with the enemies. His gun had stopped working during a shower of bullets from the enemy side – that was the strangest part of it. I can't analyse the meaning of this dream." She also described how she listened to the radio news and remained upset for the whole night. They impressed upon her the need to remain calm and have courage. John said, "I will try to talk to my brother over the telephone today."

The Watson family lived in a small city without a high-ranking military office; it had only a public relations office, which lacked modern communication facilities. John introduced himself to the duty officer as Captain Watson's younger brother doing an engineering course and enquired about his brother. The duty officer said, "We do not know where Captain Henry Watson is posted right now, that is known only to the regional commanding officer of the country and this information is confidential. It's impossible to talk to Captain Watson. However, an important message can be sent to the chief officer stationed in the capital for further action. The chief officer may permit Captain Watson to talk to his wife by a special phone."

"What a situation!" John grumbled. "My brother is fighting against unknown enemies in a distant corner of the world, endangering his own life, but his restless and worried wife cannot even talk to her husband. This situation is simply painful, even inhumane. Is there no a way out?"

"I sympathise with your sentiments," the duty officer replied. "I am also a soldier, and I have also been through such agonising situations. But we have chosen this path voluntarily; we are aware of the possible calamities in our profession. Your emotions have little relevance. At best I can send the message of Captain Watson's wife to the headquarters as a gesture of goodwill. Please do tell me, what's her message or problem?"

"Last night my sister-in-law had a dreadful dream about Captain Watson and she is mentally upset. She will have the peace of mind after talking to her husband," John replied hesitantly.

"Any dream-related message or request is simply ridiculous," the officer retorted. "You are a student of science;

do you really believe in dreams?"

"You are probably right. However, if you do receive information about physical injury or casualty of soldiers, please remember the name of Captain Watson and let us know immediately."

John told Reeta about his conversation with the duty officer. She observed, "A clash between heart and mind is not unusual. On the basis of reasoning I may arrive at the same conclusion as the officer, and also you if my guess is correct. I will try to pacify myself and wait for any message from them."

There was no news on the television or radio regarding an armed clash or soldier casualties; for Reeta this was good news. On Sunday morning, after several days of mental tension and uneasiness, the family had gathered around the table for breakfast. It was a pleasant, sunny morning and the weather forecast was also congenial. John proposed a barbecue – he could invite his friend's older brother, a military commander who had returned from the frontier some time ago. They all agreed. Reeta looked at John with a question in her eyes. He simply blinked. They seemed on the same wavelength.

They were still at the breakfast table when an important announcement came through on the television. "Mother's Day falls on this coming Sunday and the Government has formulated a very special plan to allow mothers to send a message to their sons serving at different fronts. They are requested to send their written message in a sealed envelope to the nearest military office within the next two days. The soldier's name and the mother's phone number should be written on the envelope. Efforts are also in place to enable the soldiers to talk to their mother, and all necessary information will be given shortly." This news was like a life-sustaining boon for the entire family.

The message from Henry's mother reflected her innate affection for her son and Reeta's intimate love for her husband. "Keeping a balance between a family's bonds and national duty is the right ladder for success," she wrote, her hand trembling. "May God give you courage and long life! I start my day with

your memory, and Reeta finds you in her dreams every night. Your charming son is now familiar with your photograph and he is eager to play with you in person. We hope to embrace you soon, after you have fulfilled your responsibilities at the front."
John drove towards the military office with the envelope in his hand.

Reeta was happy at the barbecue; she hoped to talk to Henry within the week. John offered a drink to their guest, the military commander, and asked him to share some of his thoughts about the soldiers' life at the front. He had already briefed him about his brother Henry.

"I am keen to know about life in general and the challenges at the front." Reeta also aired her curiosity. "Where and in which country were you posted?" she continued in the same breath. "What type of enemies did you face?"

The restlessness in her voice was too obvious; it made the commander cautious. From the habits he'd picked up in the military, he became alert and decided not to say anything that might have an unintended effect on her mental state.

"Where and at which front I was posted is confidential, as per our service code, and I cannot violate it. Even my family members do not have that information. Your question about the nature of the enemy is equally complex. Fighting against terrorism is not like fighting a normal war; in this case it is hard to identify who is your enemy and who is your friend. It is almost impossible to work without the cooperation of local personnel but their faithfulness is never guaranteed. Those who were friends for months turn into enemies – a cover of nationalism seems to descend on them from nowhere. There could be a genuine reason or simply helplessness behind this change, which we are not fully aware of.

"Our life is always in danger but there is no dearth of valour, no laxity in performing duties," the commander continued. "Our world disappears if we're killed; on the other hand, the national honour one gets has no parallel in this lifetime. Death can overtake anyone in any accident, so soldiers are not afraid of death."

"What do you think about the family bond?"

"This is a very subjective question, it has no easy answer. How to maintain a balance between national duty and family obligation has always been a debatable point."

"Did you ever think of the delicate situation that may arise for wives and young children from fatal accidents?"

"The government has devised many ways for families who have lost dear ones during military actions to make an honourable living. In this country we are witness to that system and it strengthens our dedication."

"Its other side is equally relevant - the attitude of the family," interjected Reeta. "Do you get recess at the front? How do you spend time in recess?"

"One gets recess regularly, there are means of entertainment, and celebrations are also held on special occasions. However, one also has to face continuous gunfire for several hours and this requires alertness even during the recess because the enemy's intention remains unpredictable. This does create some short of mental pressure on all of us."

"Does it leave any long-term effect on the soldiers' personalities?" John asked innocently.

"I imagine it does, but it is difficult to say to what extent and it can be quite subjective too. That's why there is a provision to send them back to their home country after a fixed period. Of course, they can be called back to duty when needed."

"Any other relevant issues that might have come to your attention?"

"On one occasion I had suspicions about an undesirable sexual relationship – one may even call it sexual abuse or sexual harassment. Lately it has been discussed openly and the administration is also worried about its fallout, especially now that women are joining the army."

"It is a serious issue. What could be the reason for this

type of abuse?" asked Reeta in a melancholic tone.

"In my opinion, it results from the combined effect of mental tension and the natural urge of youthful times. Perhaps such relations happen under uncontrolled circumstances without prior intention, and thereafter both parties feel ashamed of their immoral behaviour. By that time it is already too late and guilt may affect their personality in an unpredictable manner. It is like a major accident caused by a careless lapse. In such cases, the goodwill of the family works like a powerful medicine."

"Can you overlook the cases of rape or sexual abuse among soldiers at the fronts?" Reeta seemed worried.

"Absolutely not. But I am not a psychologist who can analyse someone's mental state. One has to grasp the underlying situation before arriving at any conclusion."

"How can the wider society know about these sexual harassments if the soldiers keep their mouths shut?"

"I have no appropriate answer."

A ray of anxiety appeared on Reeta's face.

John served the second round of drinks as well as grilled lamb chops; at an adjoining table, a variety of breads and dips were laid out.

"The lamb chop is delicious, which spices did you use?" the guest asked enjoying the meal.

"Did your gun ever stop working halfway through an encounter with the enemy?" Reeta asked suddenly.

"That's an unusual question, why do you ask? Any specific reason?"

John had wanted to say something but he withdrew at her glance. The guest had sensed this and he weighed his reply very carefully.

"I have never experienced this, but occasionally we find that the enemy possesses highly sophisticated modern weapons, which are superior to ours. Symbolically, you may see it as the failure of our guns."

Reeta found a plausible way to decipher the meaning of

her dream.

"Let us have our tea, it is getting cold." She took a deep breath of relief.

It was the morning of Mother's Day. Captain Henry was expected to call his mother at around eight o'clock. Half an hour had passed and all eyes were focussed on the telephone. On such occasions even a short waiting time becomes biting, and time appears to have stopped. The small child was crying and so Reeta went to the kitchen to prepare milk. Within moments the telephone started ringing.

"Mother, it is Henry speaking. Happy Mother's Day and my best wishes. I received your message - my heart melted with emotions, but a sense of duty prevailed. Hope to see you soon. I am talking through a satellite phone and I've got a slot of three minutes only. Where is Reeta? Is that the voice of my son? Is he crying?"

"Yes, he is a naughty one - attracted to your voice! Reeta has gone to bring milk, I have asked her to come immediately."

The telephone got disconnected before Reeta could reach it. She started weeping in her heart. *It appears God has also become unkind.*

Two weeks passed and Reeta gradually returned to normal. She got her son admitted into a childcare centre and resumed her part-time job at the office. She was welcomed by her colleagues and re-established her identity through hard work. Within a month senior management was impressed by her skilful handling of her responsibilities.

"The nation's capital is holding a seminar for our industry and I have proposed to send you as one of the main participants."

When Reeta raised her eyes from the computer keyboard, she saw her chief officer standing by her side.

"How can my two-year-old child live without me?"

"The seminar is for two days only and it is scheduled for the next month. The departmental minister will deliver the opening address and you will get a chance to meet senior government officials. In my opinion you will be able to forcefully put some of our proposals before the audience."

"I will let you know of my decision."

"Thanks."

The next morning, when she stepped out of her home, she found a sealed envelope lying at the door but the sender's name was missing. It appeared that someone had very carefully placed the envelope at the right place so that she would be the first to find it when she left for the office in the morning. She picked up the envelope and put it in her bag. She opened it in her office, when she was alone. She curiously pulled out a plain white paper. It said:

"I am standing at attention, the commander is in front of me, the cap of honour lies over my head and your pictures are on my shoulders. I want to see the pictures, but the cap would fall down if I turn my head. The dilemma is affecting me mentally. I am waiting for the right direction."

Her face became red, her ears became warm. "Who wrote this message? And why?" she wondered.

The picture of Henry became suddenly alive in her mind.

"Is he psychologically sick? Is he growing insipid about life? One may deviate from the right path in such mental conditions." Her thoughts started wavering.

Her mind was also disturbed on that day. She went to the city library and borrowed a few books on human psychology. During her college days psychology was one of her main subjects.

Late in the night she received a phone call. "It was Henry's message in the envelope. I have returned from the front." The call was disconnected. On enquiry, she found the call had been made from a public booth. Reeta became highly suspicious and alarmed. *Was the caller a spy? Has Henry fallen into the trap of a spy-gang who is trying to blackmail him?"* With a cool mind she thought: T*he messenger could also be a faithful friend of Henry's and I should not hastily arrive at* *misguided conclusions. It is always advisable to wait for more developments.* The debate continued in her mind for a long time, until the power of slumber engulfed her.

Reeta was anxious: she thought someone was keeping an eye on her. The company she was working for was a supplier of goods for the army and some people knew that her husband was a captain. It was possible that someone also knew about Henry's current posting, but nothing could be said definitely. She questioned herself. Was there a hidden agenda in sending her for the seminar? Only time could tell. Her curiosity increased, and also her determination. She decided to be more vigilant and this prompted her to see every passer-by with a piercing eye. She spent her time in the office as if everything was normal. When she was preparing to leave, the chief officer appeared behind her. "What have you decided about the seminar? We'll need to prepare some things and you will also have to fully grasp the marketing policy of the company. You will get the necessary help from your colleagues."

"I am ready to go to the seminar," Reeta replied immediately.

Nothing unusual happened for the next two weeks. The final draft of the new commercial proposal was ready for presentation and she was due to leave for the seminar. Just two days before leaving she found another sealed envelope at the door, again when she was leaving for the office.

"Is a company's profit the only main concern or also the longer-term welfare of the soldiers? Why the lukewarm attitude towards their growing mental illness and psychological dilemmas? Who is accountable for that?" said the message.

This was enough for introspection, and Henry's face suddenly emerged before her eyes. She became convinced that someone from the company itself who was behind all of this. Most likely he or someone close was enduring the vagaries of a hard military life, but he was hiding and keeping silent for untold reasons.

Reeta was driving to the nation's capital, with John in the passenger seat. The car was going fast on the highway, the morning weather was pleasant and the natural beauty of the terrain was captivating. John, aware of the statistic that many drivers felt sleepy during long drives and caused major accidents, kept talking now and then. After two hours they stopped at a McDonald's for coffee. The undulating landscape, rarely visible in a metropolis, was astounding. The row of cars moving on the elevated serpentine road gave the appearance, from a distance, of a chain of shining pearls under sunlight.

While they were enjoying the view, with coffee in their hands, they suddenly saw that one of the cars suddenly fell down the hill and, after rolling over two or three times, crashed into a large tree. Those with binoculars could see it was a major accident. Within a short time the traffic police were on the radio: "In a major accident, two persons have been badly injured; one of them is in a critical condition. Drivers are advised to remain cautious and pay attention to radio announcements." After half an hour came another message: "One person has died, and the other one has been admitted to the nearest hospital."

How brittle is human life! Reeta reasoned. *The separation between life and death disappears within no time! There is a big difference between this death and the death of a soldier - one burdens society whereas the other brings pride to the nation - though both indicate the fragility of human life,* she thought.

In the afternoon the chief of the army had organised a function for retired soldiers. Reeta was also invited. The deep respect and honour shown to the soldiers by the different speakers enhanced her admiration for them. Some of the elderly, confined to wheelchairs, were highly praised for their valour and sacrifice and they got a standing ovation from the large audience. There was a long list of martyrs who were paid respectful homage by serving army officers and the public. This was a new experience for Reeta and she realised the true meaning of 'the cap of honour '. The prestige of this "ornament" is a soldier's invaluable possession. Why would he disrespect it?

The seminar started on time, and Reeta was greeted by many who had come from different government and other organisations. The main issues were the procurement of supplies for soldiers and the long-term projects for their welfare. Several participants spoke about ensuring the quality of supplies, timely delivery, donation into welfare funds, and special assistance to those fighting against terrorism, and put up specific proposals for consideration.

"Most of the items for soldiers should be manufactured within this country in order to ensure better quality and that properly trained skilled relatives of the soldiers be given priority in jobs in such ventures," said Reeta from the podium. "This will increase the willpower and commitment of our soldiers fighting in very difficult circumstances.

"I also propose that a special project be started to assess the mental and psychological condition of soldiers serving on the global fronts for long periods," she added emphatically before the attentive audience. "They often become victims of isolation, living away from their family and from their cultural setting, and this produces an invisible mental shift in their personality. The degradation in sexual behaviours and the increase in sexual offences are manifestations of such mental illness. These factors can affect them adversely and their family life can become burdensome. In my considered view no soldier should spend more than one year continuously at a distant front."

"Any call to manufacture within this country is against the free trade agreement and also against the accepted norms of the world trade," protested someone from the audience.

"Does free trade mean selling goods only? Does it not involve fighting terrorism and making sacrifices along with our soldiers?" Reeta quipped, leaving her glass of water on the table. "Why do those countries, whose goods flood our homes, fail to face terrorists where our soldiers are shedding their blood day and night?" she continued in a piercing voice.

A heavy silence prevailed in the auditorium after her deeply emotional but logical argument.

"Where is the supporting evidence for what you have said about the soldiers' mental state?"

"I knew such questions would arise," Reeta replied. "I have already said that mental problems may remain invisible in the beginning - their damaging effects emerge gradually. But by that time it may be too late to reverse the damage."

A voice came from the corner: "Does this mean that one should simply believe in what you say?"

"Let me give you an example. If you have a headache, it is only you who feels it – no test can prove it, though medical science has become highly advanced. I have studied some books on psychology, which say isolation damages mental stability and causes depression. Its financial burden on a civilised society can only be guessed at."

The thoughtful silence was broken when someone from the back row applauded her with clapping. More hands joined in and the sound became louder. She got a standing ovation. Within a day she had emerged on a national platform.

She was greeted by the chief officer the next day. "I watched the entire deliberation on television and I welcome your views. The confidence in your presentation was definitely appreciated."

"But my proposals may not earn extra profit for the company. During this trip my thoughts underwent a sudden change and I could not restrain them from influencing my lecture. I had no such prior intention."

"I also believe that institutions engaged in trade or business have some social responsibility; not everything can be seen from the prism of profit and loss only. But I did not have the courage to voice my opinion publicly. It was expected from a member of the younger generation whose perspective combines the imperatives of the present and a vision for the future. These are indicated in your approach."

The newspapers gave a good coverage of her views and published many responses. She explained her views elaborately at various forums in the following weeks. Almost three months had passed when she received a phone call from the local military office. "Captain Watson is being brought by plane tomorrow morning. You may be at the airport at ten o'clock." Before she could ask where the flight was coming from, the call got disconnected. *What is the meaning of "being brought"?* She wondered. *Is Henry sick or is he incapable of walking himself? Or is this the normal language of military administration?* It was difficult to find out; the whole family spent an uneasy night. She could not believe the administration could be so insensitive to human feelings!

Reeta and John arrived at the airport with a bouquet of flowers. Her heart beat increased when the flight's arrival was announced. John assured her that things would be normal. She started reciting *Hanuman Chalisa,* a book of Hindu hymns, in her mind; remembering God in calamitous times was an old tradition in Indian culture. Drops of perspiration could be seen on her face despite the cold weather. To conquer her distressing emotions was not easy – after all, they were part of the natural identity of womanhood!

She could see Henry coming down the aeroplane's stairs with the help of an assistant. There was a bandage on the lower part of one of his legs and so his movements were not controlled. After he reached the floor, he walked slowly to the waiting room without any help from the assistant. Reeta embraced him, and John presented him with the bouquet of flowers. After an emotional meeting they left the airport. "This is the medical file of Captain Watson; you may call me if needed. He will remain on leave for two months and then senior officers will decide about his posting," the assistant said.

"Thank you for your help," Reeta said courteously.

The first few days were taken up in meeting with relatives and friends. Henry did not find much trouble in adjusting to daily chores. Reeta took care to give him his medicine on time and did not ask unnecessary questions. On Sunday morning the family was at the breakfast table. Henry spoke with his eyes fixed at the table. "About two weeks ago a group of terrorists suddenly attacked our camp in the middle of the night. There were four of us – two were guarding the camp and the third man and I were asleep. At the loud sound of gunfire, we jumped from our slumber and challenged the invaders with automatics weapons. Because of the darkness the invaders could not target correctly, but they kept on firing in a random manner. We had night-vision goggles and so it was not so difficult to target them. Two of the invaders were killed, my colleague received a bullet in his stomach, and one bullet pierced my left leg. Had we got more powerful night-vision goggles, we might have been saved."

"Any other event worth describing?" Reeta asked, eating a piece of omelette.

"Yes, about a month ago a psychologist arrived at the camp without prior warning. He showed his authority slip, and was permitted to talk to soldiers in the course of his research work. He spent one day in the camp and talked to soldiers randomly on different topics, some of which seemed quite irrelevant."

"What do you mean by irrelevant topics? After all, he was a researcher."

"'Did you have any dreams last night?' the psychologist asked suddenly at the lunch table. What type of research it was, I was surprised. He did not talk to me directly otherwise I might have insulted him," Henry continued without pause, in a raised voice.

Was it the result of that seminar? Reeta thought, enquiring, "What happened next? Were there any results from the research?"

"One person was called back to headquarters after just a week – I don't know what he had said."

The time was passing quickly - three weeks had gone by

- and Henry had almost fully recovered from the wounds in his leg. He had returned from the front after fourteen months, which was not a very long time. Reeta expected that after three weeks he would have become quite normal in their interaction and in his family life, but she was not satisfied. She observed that Henry was very cautious in conversation: sometimes he forgot the context, sometimes he became serious and introverted. She found it most astonishing that he hesitated in speaking face to face, with direct eye contact. Whenever she wanted to say something looking straight into his eyes, he lowered his eyelids. In the bedroom also she felt a dearth of warmth. When these symptoms persisted she anticipated that Henry was probably under psychological stress but she did not want to ask any questions.

Reeta got a phone call from the local medical centre. "Captain Watson has an appointment tomorrow morning for the medical check-up. Kindly bring his medical file too." The next day Henry was examined by the doctor. He was found physically fit, his wounds needed no further treatment, and his movements had gone back to normal. Both Reeta and Henry came out of the doctor's chamber.

"Would you mind coming into my chamber for two minutes?" said the doctor, leaning towards Reeta. "I want to fix up a date for the next appointment."

Henry walked away. "In the mean time I'll grab coffee from that stall."

"This letter was sealed in an envelope; it has been written by a consultant in mental illness." The doctor handed the letter over to Reeta and said, "You can read it."

Reeta read the letter very carefully: "I spent one day in Captain Watson's camp and watched his habits closely. Though I did not ask him any direct questions, I imagine he has become introverted because of some mental issue. He might become violent if asked about his camp life. As time passes, he may himself succeed in overcoming his problems."

"I will take care," she said with a deep breath and thanked

the doctor for his sympathy.

Reeta made some changes in her daily routine. On weekends she would go to a park with Henry and their son, and would choose a game in which Henry had to participate; she would place the child on his shoulders in a crowded museum or zoo; she would take lunch in a park or restaurant; she would ask Henry to sing a song for the child, and so on. On some pretext she managed to take Henry for dinner two or three times in a week, she would engage him in political discussions, his favourite domain, but took care not to mention anything related to his military career.

On Saturday evening, the restaurant was full but Henry and Reeta found a corner table. Henry ordered a kebab and Scotch while Reeta looked at the menu and ordered the main course. They'd had a round of drink but the main course had not arrived yet. In the meantime a friend of Henry's waved from the other corner and joined them for a drink. By the time dinner was served Henry had already consumed enough liquor; his eyes were getting red. His friend left for his own table.

"Today you have consumed a lot of alcohol, which is not good for your health," warned Reeta.

"It happens only occasionally."

The food was tasty, they were both enjoying it.

"Your selection of dishes is impressive," he praised her. "We may come here again."

"But you have to restrain your liquor – people usually consume more liquor with good food."

"Once we had consumed much more liquor, at the camp. It was the birthday party of a friend," he said, gulping the last draught of Scotch. "A few friends from the nearby camp also joined us; one of them was a lady who had taken training with me."

"What happened then?" Reeta encouraged him to open up. "Did you enjoy the party with your friends?"

"Suddenly I told her, 'You look like my wife', and she

simply smiled. It was summertime, the inside of the thick tent had become uncomfortable, and so we all spread out on the outside lawn. I had my liquor glass in my hand and the lady had hers, we chatted for some time then … I don't remember what happened."

Reeta got ready to leave, suppressing her eagerness to know more. "Let's go home, it's getting late."

Back at home, while in deep slumber, Henry was intermittently saying something difficult to decipher. Reeta left him undisturbed and lay on the sofa in a corner of the bedroom. Henry got up late, by which time Reeta was waiting for him at the tea table. He looked well slept with no sign of tiredness, and said in a low voice, "I am sorry, last night I got intoxicated. You were inconvenienced, I do apologise."

"The tea is getting cold, I will bring sandwiches in a few minutes", Reeta responded, smiling as if he had done nothing wrong.

It was Sunday, Reeta had no pending office-work to engage her attention. Henry's leave period was ending that week and she wanted to discuss his next posting, but he said abruptly, "I want to go to a church."

Reeta was astonished and reasoned to herself, *I never saw him going to a church in the past four or five years, then why today? Is it connected to last night's event?* Henry's mother had heard him and she intervened, "I know William Truman, the pastor in the local church. I will introduce you to him." Henry agreed.

Henry and his mother went to the large prayer meeting at the church. Afterwards, Henry was introduced to William Truman, who invited him into his private office.

"I have heard that confession of criminal conduct or human fault before Jesus Christ brings pardon from the Lord and opens the door to restart a happy life," said Henry in a quivering voice. "I have come for that."

"The church is a very pious and religious shrine and,

here, I am the representative of Jesus Christ," assured the pastor. "You can tell me your story with a clear conscience and without any fear."

Henry described what he had already told Reeta the night before, at the restaurant, and became pensive.

"Is that all?" asked Mr Truman. "Leave the judgement to the Lord, you must tell everything without any prior sense of guilt or innocence."

"I was under the intoxication of hard liquor, the lady was possibly also in a similar state, and with a sudden urge we got involved in a sexual act. Later, I was deeply embarrassed and morally ashamed. I am constantly disturbed by this mental burden and consider myself guilty before my wife."

"You may not be guilty in the eyes of the law but you are from the moral angle. Your moral guilt does not diminish simply because both of you were under the influence of liquor. By confessing your guilt you have tried to purify your inner self and the Lord will give you peace of mind. You must promise that you will respect the cherished human and social values in the future."

"I do give my solemn word."

When Henry returned home, he looked calm. Reeta came forward and embraced him.

Reeta and Henry spent their evening at home as their son had a minor fever. She decided to cook his favourite dish, chicken biryani. Henry joined her and cooked a vegetable curry made of cheese and green peas, which he had learnt at the front. They had a family dinner, followed by ice cream and coffee. "The child has a fever so you should sleep in his room for proper care," advised her mother-in-law. Henry also retired early for the night. That night he analysed the past events that were bothering him, he saw them in a new light.

Reeta got ready for the office and said that she would try to come home a bit early. Henry assured her that he would stay at home and look after the child, who seemed better. It was about three o'clock in the afternoon - the child was sleeping, Henry was the only adult in the house, watching television at a low volume - when the door-bell rang. He was pleasantly surprised to see Reeta and offered, "I will prepare tea." She went into the bedroom to change her dress. Within a short time he brought tea to the table and waited for her. He called her but there was no answer, then he went to the bedroom. Reeta was standing before a big mirror and she watched him approaching behind her. Suddenly he took her within his strong arms; she surrendered and became rather intoxicated in his warm breath. Within half an hour the tea had become cold. Henry prepared fresh tea and brought it to the table.

"The tea is very sweet," said Reeta with a smile.

"I did not add sugar, so how come this sweetness?" Henry uttered with surprise.

"You will not understand. Today I have got my real Henry, is it not enough?"

A smile appeared on his face.

Happy days flew like birds. Henry received a letter from headquarters saying that he had to report to northern military command in three days. Reeta's personal problems were over but the mystery of the message she had received in the envelope still intrigued her. She wanted to resolve it but did not want to say anything directly to Henry. She thought up a plan. Before leaving for the office she opened that letter, placed it on the television table and partially covered it by a book. Henry was the only person at home and his attention would automatically fall on the letter when reaching for the TV remote. This is exactly what happened when he switched on the television to watch the national news. He read each word very carefully: "... cap of honour ... pictures on shoulders ... waiting for ..." He said to himself, "This literary language must be from a scholar. How has it landed here?"

Reeta was curious to know the outcome of her plan so she came home from the office much earlier. She impulsively looked at the television table but the letter was gone.

"I have taken leave for two days so that we can spend time together. How did you spend your day? Do you have plans for the evening?" She went into the kitchen to prepare coffee.

"I have found a piece of paper with a short message written in commendable literary language," Henry said. "I wonder how it got here and I have kept it safe so it does not get thrown in the bin."

"Can I see it?"

It was the same letter she had left on the television table.

"I often borrow books from the library, it is quite possible that this piece of paper was in one of those books." She hastily added, "The style of writing is really very commendable."

While sipping coffee her mind was actively debating the options. *Why didn't I think like Henry? Could I find that scholarly person? It is not essential to unlock every mystery, otherwise life would not be called mysterious,* she reasoned with herself.

More than two months had passed since Henry left for his new assignment. During this period he had phoned twice and would be coming for a week at Christmas. Reeta decided to celebrate the birthday of their son during those days, she was satisfied. "The shadow of dark night has ended." She smiled at the inscrutable ways of destiny.

There was a knock at her door. "Please come in."

Reeta heard the chief officer say, "I had submitted a proposal to the government that our company would like to manufacture some technically advanced equipment for the army. They have agreed in principle and called for the details. I have constituted an advisory committee for this and your name is included. Any objection?"

"I was rather waiting for this, thank you very much."

4. Life at the Crossroads

It was a glorious bright morning in Sydney after several days of gloomy autumn sky. The matured rosebuds in the garden seemed eager to blossom in the brilliance of the early sunshine. But the warmth of a cosy bed was too alluring for Mohan, who had partly covered himself with a fur blanket, though he was awake and listening to music from a bedside radio. He was interrupted.

"Morning is already here, sunlight is filtering through the windows, yet you don't want to leave the bed. It is only Saturday, which is our day to do things at our speed. Tea is ready, please get up and join me at the table. Dipak has to go for tennis; he is getting impatient and looking at the clock time and again," Savita said from the bedside.

"In a single breath you have taught the lesson of love, duty and complaint, and left nothing for my discretion. I greatly appreciate your methodical work style but sometimes it turns home into another office."

"You can argue later. First get up and have tea. If it gets cold, you will have to prepare it again."

Mohan pulled Savita towards him and planted a kiss on her cheeks, "Darling, I am coming soon," he said and ran into the toilet.

"We have to go to a party this evening and I have prepared a list for shopping. After dropping Dipak at the tennis court, you can go to the supermarket. By the time you return, I will have enough time to finish the pending office work and respond to important emails."

There is nothing superficial in this conversation or lovely teasing between them; rather, the banter throws light on their intimate relationship, based on conjugal love, mutual authority, and unbounded happiness. This is the mirror of their present, but the direction of the story is going to change. Before that one needs to peep into their past, which essentially constitutes the beginning of this interesting story.

Years ago Mohan and Savita gained admission to a management institute in Delhi. They came from different cities and took up residence in separate hostels near the institute. Both were from middle-class families; they appeared well dressed but simple in appearance. Mohan's father was in a government job, while Savita's family was in the field of business.

In the very first week, when the class was full of students, the teacher said, “Prepare a background paper on the socio-economic condition of your home state and an objective blueprint for its development. The document should not exceed ten pages and it should be submitted within the next two weeks.”

Mohan, who was sitting in the front row, said inquisitively, “Sir, in this age of globalisation most of the experts are making extensive plans for the development of nations and continents but you seem to confine us within our states - why so? Will it not dwarf our thinking process?”

From a bench in the back Savita argued, “We are all students of management and there is a saying that education starts from home. Hence, our respective states are the first laboratories for our training, and I admire this type of study. Through this process we can understand the social and economic issues related to our villages, cities and states, and then we can visualise their larger forms on the huge global screen.” As the meaning of her statement percolated through the class, the students gradually approved her vision by thumping their desks.

“A well-written book on the survey of social and economic conditions of people in different regions came out only a few months ago. It is available in the library and you can use it as a supplementary resource material,” the teacher suggested before leaving the class. Most most of the students followed him in silence; it was their first encounter.

The next day Savita went to the library to borrow that book.

"The last copy of that book has just been borrowed by a student," informed the librarian managing the front desk.

"When will the book be available?"

"Books are given for one week. One has to pay a penalty if the book is not returned on time and a warning can also be issued for excessive delay. I can reserve the book in your name and you will be contacted when it becomes available."

"Okay, if this is the only way." Savita placed her identity card before the librarian. She looked disappointed.

Mohan was standing not far from the desk and he had heard their conversation. Savita had just left the desk when he said, "I don't know your name but I saw you yesterday in the class and heard your logical arguments. I have just borrowed that book and listened to your conversation with the librarian. You can take the book right now and return it to me after two days. Alternatively, I will return the book in two days and then you can borrow it from the library."

"Thanks for your offer. I will borrow the book later; it is quite possible that another copy of the book will become available sooner. I have already given my name to the librarian." She spoke in an obviously harsh tone.

This is an old technique to establish contacts with girls; I should be careful of this boy, Savita reasoned with herself.

She visited the library for two consecutive days but could not find the book. On the third day, before leaving the institute, she was again walking up the steps to the library when she saw the same boy coming out. To her surprise that book was lying on the front desk, and Savita borrowed it easily. *Alas*, she felt, *I could have thanked him!*

For several days they hesitated coming face to face despite seeing each other. Mohan feared being insulted again without reason, while Savita felt embarrassed at starting a fresh conversation. The next week the institute had organised a get-together for new students, an important yearly event attended also by some seniors and teachers. The class consisted of twenty-five students, of which about one-third were girls. They were requested to come in the attractive garb of their own state as dress is an indicator of regional culture, and collectively they would reflect the map of unified India.

The day soon arrived. The party was draped in seven vibrant colours, it was full of the energy of the younger generation and the humming sound of open atmosphere. Savita's multi-coloured lahenga-blouse, a traditional dress for girls, was eye-catching and the black eyeliner added beauty to her fair complexion. Mohan in his artistic Rajasthani kurta-pyjama and embroidered cap looked like a Bollywood hero. Similar distinct outfits could be seen across the large hall. The participants were busy gossiping and exchanging greetings, the main purpose of the party.

When Mohan faced Savita, he said, “You look very beautiful in this dress; be like that always. Please excuse me for my impertinence.”

There was a mild smile on her lips. “You are also not less attractive in any respect.”

After a short while the organiser announced, “You have all spent almost two weeks on this campus. I would like to request that you describe an event or experience that has influenced you. You have one minute each.” There was a flutter among the students on this sudden announcement. The students were called alphabetically.

“I had heard that women's nature is complex, hard to decipher. I showed sympathy to an unknown classmate, but received the burden of loneliness in return,” Mohan said when his turn came.

“I had thought a book could offer insipid education only, but it gave me a lively message,” Savita said in a solemn voice.

Many other interesting anecdotes were heard and appreciated. Finally the organiser made another announcement, “Whatever you have said has been recorded and will be published in the next issue of the magazine. I hope it will be a unique gift of your student life." There was resounding approval from all sides.

Savita thought there might be a message for her in what Mohan had said, but she was not convinced. If her guess was correct, what was its intention? She picked up a pen, thought to write something, but restrained herself because it might mean losing control of her emotions. She decided to wait. There would be other occasions when she could talk to Mohan and fathom his intentions.

Mohan, on the other hand, reasoned with himself, *Savita's reference to a book was probably an indication of our first meeting, which still occupies a place in her heart, but it was not pure imagination.* What was certain was the emergence of an invisible line of attraction towards each other. Time would tell whether this line deepened or disappeared.

The next three weeks were burdensome because of monthly exam, project work, and other academic engagements. Mohan and Savita were also busy; they had no time to meet. Once the exam had ended, Savita was relieved of the tension. As she was coming out of the exam hall, she saw Mohan coming from the other side.

"Hello Mohan-ji, how are you? How was the exam?" she asked suddenly.

"This first exam was quite important - I had to maintain an excellent grade for my scholarship. Now I am satisfied. How are you? Haven't seen you for a while."

"We met about three weeks ago, does it sound a long time? Perhaps you were waiting for me? Let us take a cup of tea in the canteen - any doubts?"

"What, hesitation with you? Let us go."

They occupied a corner table and Savita ordered tea and snacks.

"Is scholarship so important to you?" She initiated the conversation.

"I come from a middle-class family, my father is in a government job, and my only younger sister is a college student.

I have been a recipient of a national scholarship since my college days and that helps me financially. It is important even today and moreover it inspires me for thorough studies." Mohan explained the context in a friendly manner.

"You say all of this in our first meeting – don't you feel any constraints?"

"I knew this matter would eventually come up, so why not now?"

"It appears you believe in astrology." A smile appeared on her face.

Tea was served.

"How much sugar in your tea?" Savita asked.

"Today one spoon only."

"What does that mean? Do you take more sugar on other days?"

"Today you are with me, a bit of sweetness will also come from your company."

"You appear poetic! What you have just said is entertaining as well as satirical," she responded in a teasing tone.

"Rajasthan is famous for a variety of salted snacks and now they have captured the global market. My uncle trades in these snacks and he has a flourishing business in London, and he has invited me several times to visit his place. I don't know when it becomes possible." Mohan continued gossiping while chewing a piece of cheese biscuit.

Sipping a draught of tea, Savita said, "I have heard that Jaipur and Udaipur are very beautiful cities - the old palaces of Rajput kings are worth seeing and some of them are even heritage-listed. I hope to see them one day – even foreign visitors like to visit those places."

"There you will get a glimpse of Indian history and culture. If possible, I can accompany whenever you decide to visit," Mohan said enthusiastically.

"I will think about it when the time comes," Savita replied with a deep breath.

She felt more at ease; her initial hesitation had almost disappeared. In a lighter vein, she ventured, “I imagine you are a palm reader also, please tell me what my hand's lines predict.”

Mohan replied with a smile, “To predict something I don't have to read the lines on your hand, the results are before my eyes. I still remember your forceful and logical argument given in the class, which is a testimony of your sharp mind and down-to-earth approach. You are beautiful – this can be seen by even a dumb mirror! Who can defeat a lady who possesses the two gifted weapons of beauty and wisdom?”

“Now I will also have to read literature,” she uttered joyously.

“It is getting late, let us go.”

She realised Mohan was mild-mannered, intelligent and witty.

Three months passed, and they met occasionally. Because of the burden of their studies they did not find much time to spend together, but they were alert to each other's presence. The semester was followed by four weeks' vacation and most of the students left for home. Mohan presented Savita with a bouquet of flowers when he came to see her off at the train platform, and said, “Four weeks is fairly long, I am also leaving tomorrow, for Jaipur. Can I know your telephone number?”

“We don't have a phone at home, it is in my father's office. If you have an important message, you can use a postcard.”

“That probably won't be necessary.”

In this intervening period two things happened - Savita learnt that the blueprint of her project was judged the best in the class, and Mohan learnt that he was selected for the scholarship. This meant stability and distinction in their careers. They might have congratulated each other but that was not possible just yet.

When they returned after the holidays, they were jubilant and their faces gave the impression of self-confidence. Seeing Savita at the institute, Mohan promptly said, “I have seen the noticeboard, congratulations on your success! Today I want to throw you a party. I have other good news that I will reveal at the party itself."

"If that is your preference, let it be so. We should go to a restaurant nearby in the early evening."

Once at the restaurant Savita said, "Before ordering food, I would like to know your good news. Then we can select from the menu accordingly."

"I have been chosen for the scholarship," informed Mohan with humility.

"This party will be ours," exclaimed Savita excitedly, as if it were her own achievement.

The meaning of "ours" in her statement depends on the thinker's frame of mind - whether it was casual or indicative of something else.

"We are classmates, friends, and we can afford to be more frank and share our views."

"Why not?" Savita agreed. A glow of happiness appeared on Mohan's face.

It was a day of happiness and self-analysis for both of them. Mohan knew that Savita was knowledgeable, hard-working and dedicated. She was also ambitious, which was quite natural for a member of the younger generation. The seed of attraction towards her was sprouting within him, but what could its destiny be? He was also ambitious and gifted with a sharp mind - could they coexist mutually? While pondering these matters later that night, he fell asleep. Similar thoughts were cropping up in Savita's mind. She was attracted to Mohan, but she didn't want to express it. She was afraid of its implications - what could the outcome be? She wanted to proceed on this path after being assured of their future careers - after all, she believed in life's reality. She left the future to fate and closed her eyes.

Next morning both got ready for class as if they had no burden of last night's mental debate. They immersed themselves in the academic program of the next semester; both aspired to defeat the others in this race. Now Mohan and Savita were in different specialised groups so they were not able to meet in the classroom very often; they met occasionally in the canteen. She had become more prominent and her circle of acquaintance had expanded. Mohan had only a few friends within his close circle, which included some girls. The time was passing quickly; three months had gone by. In a month the students were to be sent for practical training for four weeks in different industries and they were asked to give their preferences.

While taking tea in the canteen Mohan broached the topic, "Where would you like to go for the training? As you rank first in your group, you will get the city of your choice."

"You have the same status, where would you like to go?" Savita responded.

"Your choice will also be mine. I have heard that training is not as engaging as studies, time is not so scarce, and so we can meet more often."

"The suggestion sounds enticing. Have you ever thought our friendship may change its nature if we live close by?" she interjected.

"That depends upon you," Mohan quipped teasingly.

"You think more objectively. I am yet to decide what would be more appropriate from a career point of view. Tentatively, I have considered Ahmedabad as my choice. It is a big capital city, a regional centre of global trade, home of many multinational companies, and also my parents are not far from here," Savita argued cogently.

"Your thinking is logical and business-like. That will enhance the probability of getting a job in that city for both of us." Mohan gave his input.

"I had never thought of the job prospect! In that case my first preference will be for Ahmedabad itself, provided you agree," Savita felt reassured.

"The fact is that I had already decided in favour of Ahmedabad, but I was waiting for your choice. I also believe we should begin our jobs there." Mohan gave his seal of approval with a degree of confidence.

"And life's beginning?" Savita looked into his eyes.

"Only time will tell."

These words showed a sparkle of togetherness; they had matured.

The flow of time is never hindered; it has only one direction. It was the day of their graduation ceremony, which was to be followed by a tea party. This was also an occasion to say goodbye to friends. It transpired that half a dozen of them, including Mohan and Savita, had got jobs in Ahmedabad. One of them suddenly appeared before Savita and said, "My parents live in Ahmedabad - not far from the main city - and they would be happy to see you."

"Why? I don't understand. Many of us are going there, we can always form a social group," Savita replied innocently.

"You are still like an immature girl," said Mohan, who had heard the conversation. "The fellow has unhesitatingly said what I could not yet say. Not everything is said explicitly, some are felt by heart."

"I would be happy to meet your parents." Savita became sentimental.

"I have heartfelt respect for your emotions," whispered Mohan with courtesy.

The matter was taken up by their parents and in due course they entered into the solemn bond of marriage. A new chapter of their lives began.

As intended, both began their jobs in Ahmedabad. They were happy, had an enjoyable social circle, and their parents were satisfied. Their romantic life was full of intimate love and mutual respect. Savita proved to be a good house manager and she had Mohan's full support. They celebrated their first wedding anniversary in a five-star hotel; Savita looked like a queen of beauty and exuberance. She had never felt so elated; she was over the moon.

“On the next anniversary I want a gift that will be a symbol of our love and our image,” said Mohan, embracing her tightly.

“Are we ready for this? Life will change dramatically, we will have to make many sacrifices in lifestyle,” Savita replied, fully aware of his intentions.

“Our parents are active and in good health - we can definitely expect some help.”

“Not so soon, but I will think.”

They relaxed in each other's arms.

A few days before their third wedding anniversary Savita gave birth to a healthy boy, Dipak. She got full support from their parents in caring for the infant. He had just turned three when the family faced a sudden storm that created unexpected turmoil. The head office of the financial institution for which Savita was working was shifted to Mumbai and she was transferred there. As she held a senior position, she had considerable responsibilities and the chance of getting long leave was remote. Her elderly mother looked after the child at their house in Ahmedabad for a few months, but this had its own limitations. Ultimately Mohan decided to leave Dipak at his mother's house in Jaipur. This created a shadow of darkness for them: Mohan and Savita were engulfed by sadness, and the child was deprived of the natural affection of his parents - so crucial for the psychological stability of a small child. Mohan realised that he was damaging the future of his son, and it was unacceptable - after all, he had wanted this gift from Savita.

Both were acutely aware that the formative years of childhood often laid the foundations of a successful future, and so they tried their best to get new jobs in the one city, even at a financial loss, but they could not succeed in an era of global economic downturn. Dipak had grown: it was time for his schooling, which added an additional pressure. Once Mohan proposed that Savita leave her job, but she was not amenable. She argued that it would be hard to secure another job after a long break because of competition from new entrants in the job market. He knew there was a weight in her arguments: both partners needed to work for a comfortable lifestyle in a metropolis.

One day Mohan was at his desk when almost all the office staff had left. His eyes were fixed on the computer screen and he looked excessively tired. Just then his boss appeared. "What's the matter? These days you look a bit disturbed."

"Nothing like that, but life does not move in a straight path all the time," Mohan replied in a cryptic way.

"You can take me into your confidence like a friend - after all, we have worked together for several years."

Mohan was moved by his sympathy and he described his family situation. Within a week his boss invited Mohan for a cup of tea. "Our company has decided to open a branch office in Sydney, for which a capable and hard working person is required. To my mind, you could take that position and your wife would also find a suitable job there. I have seen Sydney - it is one of the most beautiful and liveable cities in the world. You can consult your wife and let me know. I am not doing you any favours; the company would have asked you in any event."

"I am grateful for your confidence in my ability," said Mohan with humility.

It took less than two months to complete the formalities. They landed in Sydney, from the past into the present. Savita also got a job of her choice. They started a new phase of their life and established themselves both financially and socially. Before they realised, Dipak was already six years old.

Mohan and Savita went to their friend's party. As it was a gathering of adults, they had arranged a babysitter for Dipak at home. This was in line with the local culture, which included many different elements, like providing separate bedrooms for small children, celebrating birthdays with friends of a similar age, working part-time in shops while studying in high school, and spending time with girlfriends or boyfriends. Consuming alcohol, dancing with friends and new faces, playing games, and engaging in other such activities were quite common at parties and they had become accustomed to them.

"Hello, Mohan, when did you arrive? Do you work here or are you visiting?" asked Menka, who suddenly turned to Mohan in the party. They had been classmates and knew each other. Menka was particularly known for her fashion.

"It's been eight years since I've seen you! I had heard that you were working in Mumbai but could not keep in touch. I am pleased to see you. My wife, Savita, is also at the party – she will be happy to see you," said Mohan with a friendly gesture.

"Yes, I remember she was a bright student and close to you. From Mumbai I went to London for two years, then shifted to Paris for a year, and finally I came to the Sydney office a few months ago," she responded happily.

"We have been in Sydney for the last two years; we both started in Ahmedabad."

"Let us have a drink, then we can talk at leisure," proposed Menka.

Mohan had already had two drinks, but he could not refuse when she prepared the glass. They sat at a corner table.

"Some white hairs are becoming visible - is it the burden of office-work or some other problem?" Maneka spoke in a tender voice.

"Your age seems to have stayed as it was, you are just like college days! Perhaps you have learnt some secrets in Paris?" Mohan complemented, a bit teasingly.

"Your eyes were hardly so penetrating in college days!" she quipped with a smile. They learnt that they were living in distant suburbs, but their offices were in the same area of the city. "You would need several hours for a home visit but we can meet occasionally for lunch." Menka gave her business card. Mohan scribbled his phone number on a piece of paper. By this time Savita had seen them and she waved from the other corner of the hall.

"Menka, you haven't changed a bit! I am happy to see you after so many years," Savita exclaimed in a welcoming voice.

They spent some more time gossiping while Savita was checking her watch time and again.

"Now we have to leave, there is a babysitter at home."

"We will meet again."

Mohan and Menka went to a restaurant for lunch. Unwittingly, Mohan picked a difficult topic. "You haven't married yet - do you ever intend to get married? Marriage is a sweet pillar of life, one should enjoy it at the proper time."

Feeling irritated, she questioned, "Do they, who do not marry, remain unsuccessful in life?"

Apologetically, Mohan replied, "I never said so. Success has its own touchstones and I just expressed my personal opinion. I got married soon after starting work, we have a six-year old son, and our life is going ahead on the right track. I do not intend to interfere in your personal domain."

She argued forcefully, "Your ideas are still conservative, I don't see any change. I grew up in Indian culture but could not fully comprehend it, today it is clearly visible. Its core principle is: get married, have children, remain confined in life's complexities, and consider it the key to success. You did not get a chance to see the world and experience the fruits of other cultures, you remained like a frog in a deep well."

She continued in the same breath, "Today's younger generation lives in a digital age, aspires to become global citizens, and considers the whole world as their own courtyard. There should be a commensurate change in their cultural perceptions otherwise life will be derailed. You are now in a foreign land - can you remain unaffected by the influence of its social and cultural traditions?"

Sensing her defiant mood, Mohan spoke in a conciliatory tone. "It appears you have deliberately avoided getting married. You are definitely a committed disciple of the younger generation, but don't you find this lonely life burdensome? A husband would have removed this isolation and filled your life with bouquets of happiness."

Menka laughed loudly. Mohan was surprised at what caused this laughter.

"Your general knowledge is far behind the times! Lunch-break is over, let us move. Leave something for the next meeting." She got up.

Returning home, his mind was reverberating with the echo of Menka's question, "Can you remain unaffected by the social and cultural traditions of this land?" He could not guess at what she was talking about. Was there something hidden in her remarks? He admitted she had seen the Western world more closely and experienced its merits and demerits; the next meeting might be more informative.

After dinner, Mohan and Savita were having coffee and watching the television; Dipak had already gone to bed. Suddenly, Mohan asked, "Tell me two important aspects of this country's culture – your perception is better in such matters."

"Why? What's the matter? We live here like guests, our own culture is the backbone of our life," Savita replied with a question in her eyes.

"We are no longer temporary guests, we are entering into the mainstream of this society. When something happens gradually, we hardly realise. Attending parties, consuming alcohol and dancing are its early manifestations. Who knows if we will do something else tomorrow?" There was concern in Mohan's voice.

Savita took a heavy breath and said, "Women's freedom and people's faith in willpower are the two visibly distinct features. Women are economically independent and free to make decisions about their lives, and so they are equal to men. Men and women freely choose their partners, enter into wedlock as per their choice, seek separation when exploited, establish relationships with others, and this is socially acceptable."

She continued, "This society is far ahead in facing arduous challenges and as a result this vast continent of immigrants has become a symbol of modern development. Just imagine, about two hundred and fifty years ago this country would have looked barren - neither manpower, nor resources! Immigrants from distant corners of the globe have made this country lively with their hard labour and commitment, and that speaks volumes about the work culture of this land."

"You are right, but is it possible to remain unaffected by this life style?" uttered Mohan thoughtfully.

Savita's mind was also wavering. Would she have to pass through this society's cultural turmoil? What would be its longer term effect on Mohan's behaviour? What could be expected from Dipak - after all, he was growing up in this society. She would have to safeguard her beliefs strongly. Tonight she did not feel that much warmth in Mohan's touch either; she was overtaken by slumber.

One week passed. Mohan had eagerly waited for a call from Menka but did not want to open his mind. When he phoned, he learnt that she was out of the city and left a message, "My general knowledge is waiting for you." He debated against himself. Was his attention towards Menka simply due to the novelty of her ideas or was it something else? What she said was like a gust of fresh air, an urge to see life through a different lens. He suddenly felt that his life had stopped, from an intellectual point of view, though materially it was going forward on a straight path. Logic, debate, competition - all had become dormant! Could Savita revive them? Did she have the required ability?

Perplexed at Mohan's passive mood at the dinner table, Savita broke the silence. "Next month Dipak will have school holidays for two weeks. Can we go to the coast for a few days? I would like to take a few lessons in surfing. If you come along, we can enjoy it together."

"The idea is superb, but can we learn surfing at this stage, when whiteness has begun to appear in my hair?" responded Mohan without much enthusiasm.

“Age is not a barrier to learning something new. What matters is commitment and willpower. Novelty is needed not only in ideas but in practice also,” asserted Savita. At the same time she became alert - a few white strands had also appeared on her head. Beauty was the most cherished ornament of a woman, the priceless jewel of attraction! Suddenly Menka's face appeared before her eyes.

It was lunchtime. Mohan answered the ringing phone, “Hello, who is it?”

“The one you were waiting for.”

“How are you? When did you return?”

“Will you ask everything on the phone?”

“Okay, we can meet today at lunch,” Mohan suggested.

“Today I am busy at lunchtime, what about dinner at six o'clock?” Menka proposed.

“Then I will be home late and Savita will start calling. Five o'clock should be fine, today coffee, dinner next time.”

“As you wish,” Menka agreed.

“I am sorry for being a bit late, there was traffic on the road,” Maneka said apologetically.

“Doesn't matter, I have reserved a table in advance.” Mohan received her at the entrance.

Coffee and snacks were served at the table. After their initial chat, Mohan said, “When will you update my general knowledge?”

If you are so eager, listen to my views: the day you first addressed Savita as your wife, do you remember? In modern society words like 'husband' and 'wife' have lost lustre, and have instead become insulting. Now 'partner', which is a symbol of equality and gender-neutral, is in vogue. More importantly, the partner of a male can be either a female or a male and this is also true for females. The two partners can be in de facto relationship - in other words the nomenclature 'partner' is above the traditional conservative bonds of marriage. Also, it is difficult to say what short of sexual relationship or orientation they have. This is the image of the modern Western culture which is obviously incompatible with the Indian tradition. I also face this contradiction in my own life."

"Do you have a partner? If yes, what could be the destiny of this relationship? Have you ever thought of its long term repercussions?" queried Mohan in a serious tone.

"I cannot answer these questions at present."

"I feel perplexed and disturbed after listening to you, as if the fort of my long-held faith has crumbled. I would like to have a drink, would you?" A thin layer of perspiration had appeared on Mohan's face.

Sipping on his liquor, Mohan elaborated. The word 'partner' is extensively used in business where the terms and conditions of relationship between 'partners' are explicitly written in black and white. However, I had never thought of its existence and implications in the context of personal and family life. Interactions between humans have infinite dimensions, including emotional ones, and they cannot be pre-determined or jotted down on a piece of paper. Today children can be conceived though artificial birth techniques or even through surrogacy, and so the sexual relationship is also losing its sanctity and being degraded. When I find you a victim of this cultural change, a shade of darkness prevails before my eyes and the future of social stability seems doomed."

Menka realised the gulf of difference in their perceptions towards life, though both belonged to the same generation with equal professional competence. She persisted, "A few days ago I attended a meeting of progressive women. I heard slogans like 'egalitarian marriage', 'equal marriage', 'fifty-fifty marriage', 'no sex in equals', and most of the speakers were young women. Though I could not fully comprehend the meaning behind these slogans, it was clear they wanted freedom from the bond of traditional marriage. Can I be blamed if I go with the modern trend?"

"It's time to leave," Mohan looked at his watch.

When Mohan described all of this to Savita, she said, “That's the reason you asked me about the way of life in this society and its influence on ours. Most probably Menka has become a victim of some mental illness, otherwise she would not have shown such contempt for the Indian culture. Which educated person can say life gets confined to 'get married, have children' in India? She had full freedom there, she has also seen the freedom of the Western world, and she was never under pressure to give birth to a child. Then why this short of perception?”

Alarmed, she continued, “She has to be shown the correct mirror of life to enable her to come out of the undesirable marsh. I believe you can help her, but be cautious so that you don't fall into it yourself.”

“I don't know what her intentions are. Did she deliberately encourage me to peep into her life or did it happen unwittingly during a forceful discussion? I don't want to spy on her, but will try to find out how she spends her life. Yes, you will have to come to the fore when needed,” Mohan took Savita into his confidence.

As planned, Mohan rented a small flat near the coast. Savita and Dipak were already in holiday mood. Because of school holidays the area was packed with tourists and the weather forecast was pleasant for the next few days. Sydney's famous golden Bondi beach was a big tourist attraction. Today it was crowded and a variety of scenes were visible: children were making sandcastles, men and women were enjoying sunbathing, boys and girls were playing football, and people were swimming in the turbulent waves. Savita was taking surfing lessons in the designated area, while Mohan and Dipak were playing in the rising waves. He saw how the coast constituted an integral part of the Australian way of life. They fully enjoyed the day and had a dinner of fish and chips, a favoured and distinctive dish of Australia.

On the second day they came early to the seashore. Savita started to practise while waiting for the trainer. Mohan prepared for sunbathing and Dipak found a playmate. After a while, when the sun became hot, Mohan went into the water. Savita seemed quite busy with her lessons. It was a clear day; the combination of blue sky and the blue ocean was captivating, the natural beauty was at its zenith, and Mohan was thrilled to capture the scene in his camera. Through the tiny lens he could see a womanly figure, which resembled Menka, but he was not sure. Clad in bathers, the figure was playing in the waves in the company of another youthful figure. Mohan considered getting closer but he stopped – Menka might be offended. He could not restrain his curiosity, he informed Savita, "I need to go to the toilet, and I am taking Dipak with me. We will return from the flat within half an hour."

Mohan grabbed his binoculars and returned within no time. Carrying binoculars at the beach was not allowed and so he surveyed the coast from a safe distance. Menka's image was distinctly visible, there was no room for ambiguity, and her companion resembled a white Australian or European. Mohan became certain that he would be able to recognise the fellow. A question flashed into his mind: *Is he Menka's partner or a casual boyfriend?* And then he self-reasoned: *They might be staying in a nearby flat or hotel and it might be worthwhile to keep an eye on them.*

When Savita heard the details, she exclaimed "Is Menka in some danger?" At the same moment a thought flashed through her mind: *Is Mohan taking undue interest? After all, why?* Becoming suspicious of the activities of a husband is the natural habit of a wife!

Savita concluded with a cool mind, "Menka is entangled in the complex web of the word 'partner' and its toxic grip has seized her. She considers it an essential element of modern culture and a pathway for progress in this global society. It is quite possible she has chosen this path consciously like many others of this generation, but why can't she accept it openly? When you asked, she refused to answer."

Mohan asserted, "In this country the number of unmarried partners is still relatively small and so this form of relationship cannot be regarded as an important pillar of the existing social structure. In fact any such insinuation is a false propaganda and even an insult to the well-accepted way of life. Also, it is important to note that those who live as unmarried partners never hesitate to openly accept their status."

A month passed but Mohan and Menka could meet only once for coffee. Today they met again over lunch in a relaxed mood. For the first time Mohan felt a seductive attraction in Menka's big blue eyes, a sensual warmth emanating from her sculpted youthful body. He felt a sensation in his veins, a faster heartbeat, which had not occurred in the past few years. He heard an unspoken warning and suddenly got ready to leave. He did not mention anything about what he had seen at the coast but decided to stealthily visit Menka's flat - he might see someone. He thought: *Monday is usually a busy day at the office; people don't take leave unless it's unavoidable, and Menka should be the same.* He made up his mind.

The next Monday morning he parked his car at a short distance from Menka's flat and looked around cautiously. After half an hour he saw a young, well-built man with Asian features coming out of Menka's flat and took his picture with his mobile phone. When the fellow drove away, Mohan followed him. The man entered a pharmacy in the suburbs. When he did not come out for about half an hour, Mohan went in and saw him dispensing medicines from the counter. Out of curiosity he phoned Menka's office and learnt that she was on leave. Mohan did not share any information with Savita, he would consider it later.

Mohan remained perplexed for several days. He eagerly awaited Menka's phone call - after all, who was that person? He was reluctant to ask Menka - it was a question of privacy. He was conscious that Menka might consider it a breach of her privacy, which was not only objectionable but most probably an offence also. It was wise to keep restraint in such matters! A few weeks had passed, during which time he saw Menka only once, in a shopping centre.

The events took a sudden turn. Savita left for India for a month to see her ailing father. It was the first time that Mohan lived alone in Sydney. He remained busy in the office during the daytime but the evening hours were monotonous and frustrating, and he also felt a bodily hunger in bed. Talking with Savita by phone gave him emotional support but that was not enough to satisfy the natural bodily urge. Amidst this, Menka called, "I am not well. I would appreciate your friendly support, I have no one else to unburden my mind to in these hours of isolation."

Mohan left his office a bit early and knocked at Menka's door. The man who opened the door was the same one Mohan had seen coming out of the flat about two months ago.

"Who is it?" Savita enquired.

"It is Mohan. I apologise for coming without prior notice."

"Why apologise? I am grateful that you came." She emerged from her bedroom. "You may go now, I will call you if needed," she told the other fellow.

"What would you like, tea or beer? You can take cold beer from the fridge."

"Right now tea will be fine. You are not well, let me prepare." He moved towards the kitchen.

"How sweet of you, Savita is really lucky."

"You still have mild fever, you need rest," said Mohan, touching her shoulders.

"It combines the heat of body and mind both." She took a deep breath.

"I don't follow you."

"Your innocence is alive even today," she murmured.

They faced each other while taking tea. It was Menka who initiated. "This man sells medicine in a local pharmacy and I got acquainted with him after a few visits. He lives in the opposite flat and often delivers medicine when I ask, and I pay him some tips in return. Today he came for the same purpose." She suddenly excused herself and went to the bathroom.

In the meantime Mohan casually strolled through the living room, saw a few packets of medicine placed on a corner table, and tried to read their names out of sheer curiosity. Some of the names seemed strange, as if they were written in a cryptic manner, and there was no mention of the dispensing pharmacy. "*Was there something suspicious?*" he thought.

"Which medicines are you taking?" enquired Mohan when Menka came back from the bathroom. "For simple cold, cough and fever one needs standard medications only. Can I see your prescription?" he persisted.

"No, I gave it to that guy."

"Then show me the boxes or vials he delivered."

"You have become demanding like a child! Okay, first finish the tea and I will see afterwards."

"Don't you sometimes feel scared at night living alone? How are your neighbours? Savita feels very uncomfortable when I go on tours, even for a few days."

Just then Menka's mobile phone started ringing. She immediately went into a room and closed the doors. In less than a minute she came out swiftly, pulled some packets from the drawer of the corner table, and went to the bathroom. Mohan twice heard the sound of the flush. When she came out, drops of perspiration were visible on her forehead.

"What's the matter? You look very disturbed? You've suddenly broken out in a sweat," said Mohan who also appeared anxious.

Before she could reply, there was a knock on the door. "May I come in?"

She knew who had come – only a minute before she had been warned on her mobile but she was still surprised at the quick action. As the door opened, the visitor surveyed the area with his penetrating eyes and then fixed his gaze at Menka. There was a silent question in his eyes.

"I live in this flat all by myself. Today I am sick and this gentleman is my friend who came here only a short while ago," volunteered Menka. She maintained her composure and looked normal before the visitor.
The visitor showed his identity card and said, "Madam, I am a police officer. Can we talk in private? It would be convenient if your friend went out for some time."

"Yes, why not?"

The officer said, "I want to ask some questions and I expect honest answers from you. I have reliable information that illicit drugs are sold in this area and a member of a gang has been seen entering your flat. Do you take drugs or give protection to the gang? I have asked these questions with full responsibility and I expect full cooperation from you."

"No, I don't take drugs and I have no contact with any such gang. I work in the trade department of a financial institution and some clients do come here to seek advice, but I have no interest in their personal life or personal business."

"Do you know this person or have you seen him?" asked the officer, showing a photograph.

"Maybe I have seen him somewhere but nothing beyond that."

"Can I conduct a search of your house?" The officer's gaze was not benevolent.

"No, you cannot do that. I will have to call my attorney. Have you got a search warrant from the magistrate?"

The officer thought for a moment and said, "If I have to come again, I will see. You are a woman without any companion and therefore I have to obey the rules to the letter."

Just before leaving he went to the bathroom, "I want to use your toilet." He looked around, saw the basin and the toilet, which was quite clean. Menka was saved from impending calamity.

Mohan remained on the lawn for about half an hour. The visitor had come in plain-clothes but his vehicle bore the insignia of local police. Mohan was astonished, but he preferred to keep quiet.

"Our tea has become cold, I will prepare it again."

"The visitor took a long time, was it anything special?" enquired Mohan.

"He was an officer of the local police. There are some law and order problems in this area and so he came to alert me because I am living all by myself."

Mohan anticipated that Menka was in some trouble, but she did not want to discuss it. He did not press; it might be embarrassing.

"It is already getting dark, I would like to go home. I had left the office earlier; which means some homework also."

"I can imagine you need Savita, but you'll spend the whole night there? Is it too late?" she said with a teasing smile.

"Savita has gone to spend some time with her father; these days I am alone. You can call me again if needed."

"Then what's the hurry? You can go after dinner, we could not find time earlier."

Menka got ready in very little time. She looked very pretty in an attractive semi-transparent dress; her youthfulness seemed to have blossomed again. Mohan looked at her with piercing eyes.

"What are you seeing so intently? Is this dress not appropriate?"

"It is cold outside, put a sweater on."

"It is okay inside, but I will get one if you say so." She guessed what was on his mind.

They went to a restaurant and occupied a corner table under dim light.

"Today you are my guest - try my choice. There should be some novelty," said Menka in a low voice.

"Why not? Coming with you is also a new experiment."

"I consider life as a laboratory. I do not hesitate to experiment with novelties both in ideas and actions," said Menka with confidence.

Within a few minutes a young waitress brought Scotch and soda to the table, "Can I mix your drink?"

"No, I will do that. Please bring some ice cubes and serve dinner in half an hour." Menka prepared two drinks. "Cheers! Let this evening be enjoyable."

In the very first sip Mohan realised the drink was much stronger than the average and asked, "Would you like to add more soda?"

"No, it is okay for tonight. Shouldn't there be something different?"

Mohan started the conversation. "My life is an open book. I have a wife, a son, a good job, and life is moving smoothly despite some occasional hurdles. You tell me something about yourself, we are meeting almost after eight years."

"I knew you would ask this question. That's the reason I am drinking Scotch - I would be able to face my past only after losing some senses!"

"Is there some deep mystery? How do you manage the responsibility of a high position when your mind is preoccupied?"

Menka filled her glass for the second time, while Mohan had not yet finished his first serve. He became alert trying to fathom the meaning of her words.

She replied, "The human mind is filled with complexities, and it is difficult to extricate truth from within especially when one's self-serving logical wisdom does not allow it. The influence of alcohol weakens the control of wisdom and then truth escapes from the mental prison."

"What you say is worth considering but one should exercise control. One should not cross the accepted boundary, and this applies to every sphere of life," reminded Mohan.

Swallowing a draught of Scotch, Menka uttered, "I don't know where to start - from the present or the past?" Mohan could see the red lines appearing in her eyes - the alcohol was having its intoxicating effect.

"One lives in the present; what is happening today is more important. History can always be read later, though it might also be important."

Excited, she raised her voice, "Okay, so be it. What I am going to say is like an explosion but it will simplify the future course. I do take prohibited drugs occasionally, especially when the burden of loneliness becomes unbearable. Today the police officer came to interrogate me about that. It was a rare luck that I had received due warning from my contact just in time and I was able to flush the contents down the toilet. I was saved but the police will keep an eye on me and a second mistake will definitely destroy my career. I am deeply perturbed and anxious, how can I face the world?" she lamented and became emotional.

They were silent eating dinner but there was a turmoil in their minds. Menka was vividly seeing her history, whereas Mohan was engrossed in judging the gravity of her situation. He broke the burden of silence: "If one stumbles in life, two things can happen - one breaks into pieces or stands up with new strength and determination. I am confident you will adopt the second option because you have the capability, the youthful energy, and my friendship. You must resolve to remain far away from drugs and I need that assurance right now."

"I will try to win your confidence, I will ..." She could not complete the sentence; her head tumbled. She was overtaken by alcohol.

"Are you all right? Should I call a doctor?" There was anxiety in Mohan's voice.

"My head suddenly reeled, but now I have my senses back. Please order cold coffee, I should be normal after that."

Half an hour later they were leaving the restaurant, but her steps were unstable and she grabbed Mohan for help. He gave full support - it was for the first time that he touched her so closely. Mohan was driving, Menka beside him. He kept on looking sideways; it was difficult to guess whether this was induced by anxiety or attraction. Menka's suburb was still several kilometres away and there was heavy traffic on the road.

"The moonlit night is very alluring, let us have a cup of tea." Mohan stopped his car at a roadside coffee house.

"Possibly your mind is with Savita. Alas, if only I were in her place!"

"Can I know something about your past? You have already talked about your present," said Mohan, offering tea.

"I already said it would be painful for me to face the past while mentally alert, so leave it for another evening."

"It's okay, I will reserve a place in the restaurant at your convenience."

"It is not necessary: next time we can meet at your house before Savita returns. This will give us the freedom of time and there will be no constraints on driving after drinks. Even if we get a bit drunk, there would be no one to watch." Menka favoured a relaxed atmosphere.

"It would not be wise for you to come to my place. A neighbour might see you and report to Savita."

"I didn't think to that extent." An inscrutable smile appeared on her face.

Menka walked up the stairs to her flat, but she could not remain steady. Mohan again supported her and she fell into his arms.

"Tonight's dream will be gratifying."

"How do you know what type of dream you will encounter?" asked Mohan.

"You are still immature! Try to understand a bit of poetic romance. I am still feeling a bit of dizziness, it will take time before the alcohol wears off. It is already late, you can stay here in my guest room," she implored.

"Not a bad idea, I will do that."

Menka went into her bedroom while Mohan switched on the television to watch a film. He was also feeling drowsy but he waited for the climax of the interesting film.

After sometime he heard, "I am feeling cold and a bit feverish as well. Could you take a blanket from the closet and throw it over my body? I appreciate your kindness."

"What short of kindness? I am watching television - I'm coming now!"

In the bright light of the bedroom Menka had become more transparent, she had not changed her dress. When Mohan was trying to cover her body with a blanket, their lips touched unwittingly and they felt a sensation. At that moment his mobile phone started ringing, and he jumped away quickly. It was Savita on the line: she wanted to stay another two weeks.

Mohan almost ran out of the room. He was fully alert, surprised and repentant. He pondered: *Why this weakness? The bodily fire had burnt the sanctity of wisdom for a few moments - how could this happen?* During this uneasy mental turbulence he was overtaken by slumber: perhaps the remaining intoxication of Scotch came to his aid! When Menka woke up after a few hours of sleep, she heard a noise coming from the guest room as its door was open. She entered and found Mohan talking in a dream, he was not intelligible but the words 'Savita, Savita' were clear. When she put her hand on his head, he loudly uttered, 'Savita, you have come' and grabbed Menka tightly within his arms. She did not protest, both became one in the darkness of night!

Mohan woke up late in the morning, his bodily tension had vanished. By that time Menka had become fresh, her face was glistening, and she was looking very beautiful in a red dress.

"Get ready soon, I am preparing tea."

"You look very happy, what's happened?"

"Are you not happy?" she retorted.

Without responding he went to the bathroom. After sometime both left for the office. Menka phoned twice but talked about business matters only, as if the events of the last night had not occurred, whereas Mohan remained preoccupied with them. He was not able to concentrate; his thoughts were wavering. Before leaving the office he called Menka, "I am perturbed at last night's events, I don't know how I will face Savita."

"Okay, tell me, how was last night's food at the restaurant?"

"Very tasty."

"Which items did you eat?" asked Menka with a sarcastic smile on her lips.

"What question is this? I don't remember. Relishing food's taste is the domain of the tongue – the mind does not need to store that information."

"You are right. Last night's event was caused by a sudden impulse, without premonition or pre-meditation, that quenched our bodily hunger which falls under the domain of the so-called 'material' world. Then why should mind, being the master of the intellectual world, necessarily preserve that information? That's why last night's event has no perceptible effect on me," she argued in her own way.

"It appears you have totally forsaken Indian values." Mohan seemed dejected.

"It is not like that, but there is a difference in my thinking. Listen to me carefully before coming to any conclusions."

She almost delivered a brief lecture: "According to Indian philosophy, the human 'soul' and 'body' exist separately and their needs are different. Though I am not an expert, I imagine the same is true, in a slightly different form, for the practical point of view. Accordingly, I put wisdom, self-realisation and knowledge in one category, whereas appetite for food, bodily hunger and material comforts come in the second category. Accomplishment in life comes only when the demands of both categories are fulfilled, but their paths are different. A hungry person will pounce upon food as a natural instinct; the control of wisdom gets slackened. Frankly speaking, we both were the victims of bodily hunger last night and there was nothing to restrain us, not even our wisdom, which was impaired by alcohol. One other thing: don't think that

I have developed love or intimacy or attraction towards you - that is Savita's sacred privilege only and I will never come in between."

"Were you a follower of the same principles in the past? For stability in life one needs a strong pillar, whether it be a person or an unshaken ideology. Okay, what should I say to Savita?" Mohan was quite bewildered by Menka's forceful arguments on a difficult topic.

"The ghost of Savita is still haunting you. It is hardly needed," she said laughingly. She put forward another perspective: "Whenever you worship a god, the priest tells you to concentrate on the target, to avoid external thoughts entering into your head, to restrain the agility of mind, and so on. This requires being immersed into the task or achieving oneness with that entity. Were we not in the same state when we became one for a while? Was Savita in our thoughts? She was neither at that time nor in the future! Do you understand?"

"I have to read a book on philosophy, and most probably on psychology also."

"Yes, you must read it before we meet again," she uttered with a sense of victory.

Spirited, she continued, "There is a difference between adoration and love. Have you ever realised this or thought about it? In the traditional culture of our country, which you always seem to admire, wives usually adore their husbands and consider them godlike. In this situation it is the soul-to-soul relationship which is dominant, but there is hardly any of the madness of love. Even if that madness exists, it remains alive during the initial years of marriage only and I don't have that experience. You ask yourself, and share your experience with me. It might help me resolve my issues."

Mohan intervened. "You consider the soul and body as separate entities, but I don't accept that. The soul has no existence without the body and, similarly, the body has no existence without the soul. They are like inseparable cause and effect; they complement each other. The wisdom of the soul governs the body, while wisdom can be earned through the actions of the body itself. I have read in myths that sages were able to leave their earthly bodies and roam in heavenly sky for long periods, and then return back to their earthly bodies. Perhaps you were referring to these ancient metaphysics, but I consider them simply speculative – they hardly have a scientific foundation." Menka offered him a glass of water as he seemed agitated and psychologically disturbed.

A week passed, they did not have time to meet. It was Saturday and the weather was pleasant. Menka phoned. "It is a beautiful day for going on a long drive. We can have lunch at the coast and practise a bit of swimming; I hope you have no other important engagement."

"Next week Savita is coming, so this week would be most appropriate. I shall reach you within an hour." Mohan seemed reconciled to what had happened.

After swimming for a while they rested on the golden sheet of sand and dried their bathers in the sunshine. Many others were also enjoying the warmth, sunbathing here and there. For the first time Mohan saw Menka's beautifully sculpted body up close and he could not hide the sensuous attraction in his eyes. Menka was on the same wavelength - she felt relaxed and a bit proud of her preserved charm.

"Would you have a cold beer? I also have some sandwiches," she offered.

"The beer is secondary to you. If I get intoxicated, the whole night will pass on the beach itself," he said relishing its dual meaning.

"Sometimes reality comes out more effectively when intoxicated," she quipped.

While sharing sandwiches and sipping cold beer, Menka opened a chapter from her past: "In very similar pleasant weather I was attracted towards a man on a European coast; he was working in my office. I had celebrated my twenty fourth birthday and gone to London about six months before. I always opposed orthodox constraints on women, believed in modern values and regarded men and women as equals, and I was known for these attributes. Soon I became friendly with a smart young man, which was quite natural. For two years we continued meeting, going to parties, spending holidays together, and quenching our bodily thirst. Thereafter the zeal of newness, or you can say the new-found enthusiasm, started dwindling; in other words, the spark of life seemed to be ending. I was not prepared for this; I got myself transferred to Paris."

"Was the fellow from our country? Was he familiar with your culture?"

"He was a European and his parents were also from a European background. I met them once at Christmas time."

"Then what was the reason for the separation?"

"Perhaps this repulsion was at the mental level; I don't see any specific reason." She became thoughtful for a few moments, as if she were travelling in her past. "I am fully aware that in Western countries one freely lives with a boyfriend or girlfriend, and they get married in due course or even opt out of the relationship. It is also a common practice to seek divorce and to remarry, and therefore having physical relationships is not a stigma. I am impressed by this legally accepted social practice and now it is also gaining ground in our country," she added.

"How was your experience in Paris? It is supposed to be more liberal."

She described it briefly. "In Paris I felt loneliness: passing the time was strenuous. My limited knowledge of French was also an impediment. During a seminar I came across an Indian youth who was a research officer in the university. His lecture on the comparative study of Indian and Western cultures was very objective and balanced. He said, 'Culture is not centred in thoughts only, it is also a mirror of our day-to-day life and therefore its form changes with economic and educational development'. This perspective is quite logical in light of the social changes seen during the past two decades and so the concept of a generation gap has emerged globally. As we live in the present, our way of life is immensely affected by these changes and it is not unexpected to be carried with the flow of time. If you look through this prism, my actions may seem more cogent. As a matter of courtesy, I invited him and his family for tea at my flat. I thought an academic discussion could also lessen the boredom of time.

"The next week he was standing before me, but he was alone. When I asked where his wife was, he replied that he was 'again unmarried'. When I queried about the youthful woman standing beside him at the seminar, he replied that she was his friend. I sensed a strange glow in his eyes. I was alone, and got a warning from my inner wisdom. At my request we went to a restaurant and spent more than two hours at dinner. We had an illuminating discourse on society and culture- related topics and especially at the emerging 'composite culture' in many parts of the world. After a long time I had finally got this opportunity and I was impressed by his scholarly depth. Before leaving, I asked what he meant by 'again unmarried'. He replied very casually, 'How do you describe getting free from the bondage of marriage?' This indication was enough for me." She took a deep breath and paused.

"Your story is interesting - what happened next? How far off is the conclusion?" asked Mohan eagerly.

She responded calmly, "This is not a story, these are some pages of my diary which I am opening for the first time. We continued meeting for more than three months, had stimulating debates on many issues, and on two occasions we became physically close, too. I thought his friendship would at least give me the much-needed intellectual satisfaction, but he had his girlfriend. That source of inspiration also ended when he left Paris."

She continued uninterrupted, "In this process I realised that intellectual engagements also have a magnetic attraction and I was overwhelmed. Now I can imagine why the words of great teachers, scholars, philosophers and religious leaders have magical influence. They provide food for accomplishment, as I argued earlier."

Convinced of the strength of her arguments, Mohan asked inquisitively, "Are they in contact with you? Do you talk to them?"

"The European was here about two months ago. He stayed with me, we went to beach to swim, but we had no physical contact. To engage in a sexual relationship without mutual consent is an offence in this country and he was fully aware of this. The man I met in Paris remains in touch through emails, we exchange our thoughts on many issues, and I am grateful for that. This short of friendship will probably continue."

She continued talking, "The loneliness of Paris was getting heavier and it took its toll. One day I saw a young man smoking a cigarette in a corner at the office and a strange smell overpowered me when I passed. When I asked, he said the cigarette included a medicine that lessened mental tension. I was tempted and took a packet from him. In reality the cigarette contained a prohibited drug - it had a hallucinatory effect, and seemed to induce temporary relaxation, and I got used to it, especially during weekends. Now I take very occasionally and I am trying to completely stop."

Mohan warned, "You keep intellectual, or so-called soul-related, necessities and bodily needs in two separate compartments, which I don't endorse. This belief is the cause of your downfall and it will get more painful with time. You have already faced its ugly consequences in the past and the present situation is staring at you. In order to find a balanced and fruitful direction in life you will have to change your outlook. I am not being judgemental, it is your life."

"You are probably right, but I need your support in this endeavour," she ventured.

It got dark as they returned home. There was considerable traffic on the road and Mohan looked exhausted after their long drive. He badly needed a cup of tea.

"You have become tired and your home is far away from here. It would be better if you stayed here tonight," said Menka. He agreed through his silence. Within a short time she brought tea to the table and changed into her nightdress.

"Are you going to bed so early? I had planned to go out for dinner."

"I am also tired, we can get food delivered. What would you like? Italian, Indian or Chinese? Spicy or normal?"

"Your choice is fine, as you like. A bit spicy would be quite tolerable."

She ordered by phone. "The delivery will take an hour, can we have a drink in the meantime?"

"Yes, why not?"

"I have decided the food menu, so you can pick the drink of your choice," she suggested.

Menka had a variety of drinks in her cupboard. Mohan opened a bottle of Scotch. She brought some salted snacks, they raised their glasses and said 'cheers'. The Miss World pageant was on the television - it was an exhibition of sensuous beauty and half-naked youthfulness!

Menka commented, "Until a few years ago such displays were controversial in India but now they have become common, which is an example of the changing social thinking. There are several other contexts that depict the ideological and economic empowerment of women. Can't we say it's a cultural shift? This undercurrent of cultural change is visible even in remote areas, it is not simply an urban affair."

Mohan opened his mind. "Why not? Culture is not an immovable monument or an absolute ideology, it gets affected by the way of life. Despite this, there are certain elements which have remained sacrosanct over the ages and they are the foundation of our culture. For example, faithful commitment between husband and wife is an important pillar of Indian culture, though in recent years the rate of divorce has increased. Similarly, the custom of friendship between unmarried boys and girls is almost non-existent, while it is prevalent in the Western world. What is needed is a balanced approach, which is a very subjective decision. How can one travel on two boats? One has to choose between."

"Do you mean choosing between the two worlds or remaining embedded to one way of life? If you mean that, I may not be ready to accept," she almost pounced.

"No, I don't think like that. Today we are members of a global society and it is the age of composite culture. The meaning is obvious, it is the synthesis of old and new values - it means renouncing some and assimilating some. What to give up and what to adopt depends upon your wisdom, it has no fixed criteria," Mohan explained his perspective.

He buttressed his arguments, "There are many Indians of our generation whose children are getting educated here - my son is one of them. In the future they will constitute the mainstream of this society and bear the influence of Western culture in a natural fashion. As parents our duty is to keep them abreast with Indian traditions through a variety of ways, like speaking Hindi at home, celebrating Indian festivals, telling stories from Indian mythology, spending holidays with relatives and friends in India, and so on. How much they absorb is a different matter, but we will have personal satisfaction."

Suddenly Menka changed the topic. "Are you happy with marriage? Has your attraction towards newness ended? Will Savita always remain committed to you? What happens if she changed her mind? These days, relationships are getting broken on flimsy grounds even in our country."

"I don't know about the future, but marriage does have an attraction and the word 'marriage' is respectful even in this society," Mohan asserted.

The whisky's effect had become visible in her eyes, she consumed an additional serve with food and her steps became unstable. When she leaned towards the bottle once again, Mohan prevented her. "No more, you are almost drunk and losing control over yourself."

"Today I want to forget my entire history, I am looking for a new path." She collapsed on Mohan's shoulders.

Mohan helped her reach the bedroom; soon she was fast asleep like a care-free person. Soon Mohan was also dreaming in the guest room.

The morning sun was shining with brilliance but Mohan was still in the bathroom. His mobile started ringing; Savita was on the line.

"I had called at the home number but it kept ringing, where are you?" There was some irritation in Savita's tone.

"Today I went to the gym a bit early and from here I shall be going to the office. I will be home by this evening, is there anything important?"

"You voice is wavering, is that due to alcohol? Do I hear a woman's voice also?"

"Your suspicion is unfounded. Now, you are returning in the next two days, so why this doubt?" Mohan pleaded.

It was the first time he had told a white lie so convincingly. His heartbeat increased and drops of perspiration appeared on the forehead.

That afternoon, Mohan was driving. Menka was in a pensive mood, almost lost in herself. Mohan broke the oppressive silence. "Savita is returning in the next two days. From now on it won't be possible to spend this much time with you, but you can always regard me as a friend."

"I will preserve your friendship like a priceless possession. There is no substitute for a faithful friend, especially in this foreign land." Her voice became choked. "Now I have given up drugs and I will also take control of my bodily hunger. Last night I was excited and most probably you were the same, but the self-control you showed was exemplary. It has opened my eyes. In a way, I have seen the control of wisdom and heard the voice of Indian culture. When you have that power, why can't I?" she said, winning over her emotions. Mohan kept quiet but he guessed the turmoil arising in her mind.

At a four-sided crossing, cars from all directions were standing still and Mohan joined the queue in his lane. The traffic light was off and they were all waiting for the green signal. In the meantime a police car with a loud siren approached the crossing, an officer got out and started giving directions. Gradually all left for their destinations.

Menka intuitively uttered in a loud voice, “I am also standing at the crossroads of my life and seeking a direction. The sound of the siren is like the rein of wisdom and you are like a police officer. This scene will remain in my memory.”

“I respect your imagination.”

5. Shared Journey

The night was dark, the train was going fast piercing the heavy silence in the air. The air-conditioned compartment was quiet. Occasionally the sound of *thuk thuk*, most likely when the train crossed ugly joints on its steel tracks, became audible from outside. The journey was long; the train would reach its destination before noon the next day if it continued its pace undisturbed. Rajeev, lying lazily on the upper berth, was trying to read a book but was unable to concentrate. He was not feeling sleepy either, so he changed his posture and managed to take a cup of tea from his thermos.

On the lower berth a young lady was trying to sleep but couldn't as she had already slept for a few hours. She was changing sides intermittently with a degree of uneasiness. On the opposite berth an elderly woman was snoring loudly, as if she was thoroughly tired from doing hard physical work at home.

Rajeev had already poured tea into his cup when he felt a sudden jerk of the running train and the cover of his thermos fell from his hand. The young lady almost jumped in her berth at the harsh sound of the falling piece and looked around with astonishment. Coming down from the upper berth, Rajeev said, "I am sorry that your sleep has been disturbed. The cover of the thermos slipped from my hand due to carelessness."

"It's okay. You can have tea sitting here," and she moved towards the window side.

Though the compartment was dimly lit Rajeev could see the lady had an attractive personality and her attire indicated that she came from a cultured family.

"Thank you. Can I pour some tea for you as well?" he asked politely.

"No, I don't like taking tea at night. And anyway, it is not desirable to take tea with a stranger," she replied somewhat hesitantly.

"I am not unknown; my name is Rajeev Shukla, which is written on my ticket. I work as a technical expert in a telecommunication company in the city of Bangalore. Can I know something about you?"

"You have described so much in a single breath and so as a matter of courtesy I also have to say something."

"There is no compulsion, it's at your sweet discretion. I never intended to put any pressure on you."

"It is not unusual to chat and pick up acquaintances during a long journey. It has happened to me on earlier occasions also."

"Do you often take long trips? I get tired during a long trip; loneliness becomes burdensome and boring. You caught this train in Delhi - do you live in Delhi?" Rajeev asked curtly.

"You have asked so many questions at the same time, I don't know where to start. First is that I am also going to Bangalore where I work for a multinational financial institution. To attend meetings I travel to Delhi headquarters every three months."

"These days consultations, and even major discussions, can be done through video conferencing unless there is something of a confidential nature," Rajeev argued.

"My parents live in Aligarh and I am able to see them when I'm in Delhi. Sometimes they come to Delhi if my program schedule is tight," she said.

Rajeev persisted. "Where were you educated? I have completed my entire studies in Delhi. After graduating from a public school I was admitted into an engineering college and was lucky to regularly get home-cooked food. I have been in my present job for more than a year. Even now, my mother readies a packet of food whenever I go on a long trip. She prepares very tasty ginger-based tea and that is what I have brought with me."

"If that is so, I may take some of that," she said in a nonchalant tone.

"As you like." He passed his thermos towards her.

"The tea is really very tasty. I completed my graduation from Aligarh Muslim University and then joined a management institute in Delhi for an MBA degree. While residing in a hostel I became accustomed to living more independently and, as a result, I have no particular fascination with food. I have been in this job for the past two years, a maid cooks for me, and occasionally I like to go to a restaurant for a change," she continued in a low voice so that the woman on the opposite berth would not be disturbed.

"And where does your husband work? If he is posted out of Bangalore, you may not see him very frequently. He should be with you."

"You are much ahead of yourself. I have heard that science students become more objective and do not fall prey to easy imagination, but you seem quite different. You are probably easily carried away by the emotional flow."

"Why? Did I say something wrong? If it has hurt you, I apologise."

"I am still unmarried, and I don't want any discussion on this topic."

"I am ashamed at my thought. I don't know how it came into my mind."

The train stopped at the next station, which was a big junction. Because of the noise from incoming passengers the woman sleeping on the opposite berth woke up and suddenly asked, "Are you people going on a honeymoon? You kept talking as if you did not get enough time at home."

They were not prepared for such a question and so Rajeev replied hastily, "We both work in the same company, we are friends, and so we did not notice the time while talking. Now you can sleep comfortably, I am going to my upper berth."

Rajeev tried to sleep but could not. Time and again the face of the young lady surfaced before his eyes. He was surprised, why this? Was it some strange attraction or a delusion? The young lady was also astonished: Why the similarity between Rajeev's conjecture and the woman's unexpected question? Was it just a chance or did it contain a mysterious message for the future?" Suddenly an old chapter of her life, which she had managed to bury with a great difficulty, came alive. This chapter contained a natural love story that could not blossom into reality, but still occupied space in her unconscious mind.

She trembled. Would she have to go through that agony once again? Tears appeared in her eyes; she covered her face.

When they got up in the morning the elderly woman was not there, the cabin was half empty. The young lady was in the toilet when someone from the pantry car arrived to take orders for breakfast. Rajeev ordered toast and an omelette for himself and thought about the young lady - *she might be vegetarian.* So besides another serve of toast and an omelette, he also ordered a vegetarian packet for her. She had washed her face but appeared tired. She sat near the window and looked at the passing fields.

"It appears you did not sleep well. I have ordered breakfast for you." Rajeev broke the silence.

"I had a mild headache and so could not sleep," she responded.

"I have medicine - please take it with tea. The breakfast should be here within half an hour."

"You are probably right."

She lay down after swallowing the tablet and Rajeev became immersed in the day's newspaper. At the same time he inquisitively looked at her face several times from behind the paper. Now he could see her charming face, which was partially covered with curly black hair and he felt an impulsive attraction. Unwittingly, he had just stretched his hand to arrange her hair when she changed sides. He came to his senses - touching her face could have created an ugly situation!

She heard, "The breakfast is here," and sat upright.

"I don't eat omelette, you can have it," she said politely.

"These days many girls have stopped eating eggs, fearing weight gain. Are you one of them?"

Before she could answer, Rajeev's mobile started ringing - the voice of a woman was easily audible - and he walked away towards the door while talking.

"Was that a phone call from your wife? I could have moved away and given you privacy."

"You have also committed the same mistake I did - a wrong guess. I have not been fortunate to find a wife as yet; that was a call from my secretary. I have an important meeting at three o'clock and she was reminding me," said Rajeev in a friendly tone.

A thin smile appeared on the young lady's face.

The train was due to reach Bangalore very soon and passengers started preparing their baggage. Arranging his scattered articles, Rajeev volunteered, "Do you need a porter to carry your suitcase and bag? The exit is at a distance from this platform. I have only one light bag and I can help you."

"Someone will be there at the platform to receive me and I do not need your help. Thanks for the offer," she said. The train entered the outskirts of Bangalore.

"We will soon be leaving but I do not know your name. I neither asked nor heard you mention it. Am I not worth it?" There was an emotional tinge to his voice.

The youthful lady pulled a card from her handbag and put it into his hand. Rajeev read 'Hamida Gulshan' written in bold letters, along with her office address.

"You can contact me on my office number or leave a message," she added.

"Do you need my number?"

"No, I will find out if needed."

The train touched the platform. Both said goodbye.

Rajeev remained busy for the next two days. He had wanted to call Hamida but restrained himself, thinking she would also be busy in the office. It was obvious that she was a Muslim, which was also corroborated by her education at Aligarh Muslim University. The name 'Rajeev Shukla' indicated that he belonged to a high Hindu caste. Rajeev had heard about the orthodox views of Muslim families, especially about social restrictions on women, but he had never seen it from a close distance. He was very impressed by Hamida's courteous behaviour and he developed a desire to peer into her life.

Rajeev phoned Hamida but she was busy in a meeting and the office was expected to close in an hour. He decided to leave his office in half an hour and go straight to Hamida's office complex. He parked his motorcycle under a tree not far from the main gate and waited. Within a short time she came out with a young guy and they waited for a taxi. Rajeev decided not to come face to face and simply waited without being seen. A taxi stopped and both of them stepped in. Rajeev followed the taxi by motorcycle. After a while the taxi stopped, Hamida went into a flat, and the taxi moved ahead with the young guy. The flat looked decent from outside and this area was also more expensive. Rajeev reasoned: *She must be in a well-paid job and it would not be appropriate to knock at her door without prior notice.* He dropped his intention of seeing her today."

When he called the next day at lunchtime, Hamida picked up the phone.

"How are you? I thought we could chat for a few minutes if you have time."

"Thanks, I've also been thinking that since yesterday and I was waiting for your call. Will you have time for coffee this evening?" she asked.

"As you like," Rajeev said in a pleasing voice.

Both of them went to a prominent restaurant at the appointed hour. Hamida had already booked a table in a corner away from the noisy section. They greeted each other with a friendly look.

It was Rajeev who initiated. "We met by chance on the train for a few hours, but your friendly conduct gave me a unique feeling and that has attracted me here. I want to preserve it." He continued in the same breath, "I also have another intention, but I need your permission before expressing myself."

"Yes, please go ahead. Frankness is always rewarding," she said without any hesitation.

"I believe you come from a Muslim family. Despite that, you are open-minded with modern attitudes, which is quite different from the general tradition. I would like to peek into your life and get inspiration from it. Believe me, I am not a spy - that has no place in my life. What I should know and what I shouldn't is entirely at your discretion."

"It appears you have been carried by emotions. There is nothing inspirational in my life except some ups and downs, which have greatly affected me both intellectually and socially. I am really surprised at your frankness. At our very first meeting you have declared your intention of looking into my life, especially the life of a young woman, which is simply extraordinary. It is indicative of your immense courage and sensitivity," she reasoned with confidence.

Rajeev succinctly put forward his views. "We are members of the younger generation, the so-called 'Generation Y'. We can weigh orthodox and traditional notions on the balance of logic, adopt the correct path, and convince our parents as well. To speak candidly with an open mind is our generation's special and commendable characteristic and so I spoke frankly about my intentions. Perhaps you have also absorbed this conceptual change, which has encouraged you to accept this uncommon lifestyle. Was it ever possible for a traditional youthful unmarried Muslim lady to live independently, far away from her parents?"

She replied wittingly, "It appears you have also studied psychology and gained the skill of reading someone's mind. I am impressed by your arguments and I would try to honour your intentions, but the time and speed will depend on me. Eating more than required at one time may cause indigestion!"

Both laughed. Coffee and snacks were served on the table.

"How much sugar in your coffee?" Hamida asked, looking into his eyes.

"One teaspoon, and the rest will come from your smile," quipped Rajeev.

"You are a poet also!"

"One effortlessly becomes a poet on such occasions."

A smile appeared on her lips. Hamida felt more at ease and relieved, she was convinced of the genuineness of Rajeev's intentions.

She opened the first window on her upbringing. "You are right, I do come from a Muslim family. At the same time there is a beautiful statue of Lord Krishna in our home and my parents offer prayers on His birthday as per the Hindu calendar. When I enquired about this custom, my father said that he had seen it from his childhood and he never understood its mystery. Most probably this tradition has been upheld for several generations."

Rajeev tried to be methodical. "It is uncommon, but not entirely unexpected or surprising. Hindus also offer prayers and gifts at the tombs of Muslim saints; some people even observe the fast during Ramadan. These are symbols of religious goodwill and common cultural heritage. Aligarh is close to the Mathura-Vrindavan region, which is intimately related to Lord Krishna's saga, and your ancestors might have acquired a statue of Krishna out of respect and belief in a composite culture. It is also possible that among your ancestors someone had married a Hindu girl and that created an interface of the two religious traditions. It is not our duty to solve this mystery."

"In Aligarh I became friendly with a classmate, Salim, who had a sharp mind. In debates we used to be on opposite teams and we often won prizes. Therefore, it was not unnatural to get acquainted and become friends. He came from a different city and lived in the college hostel. We often faced each other in the library or canteen and said hello, but refrained from staying together for long. Friendship between a boy and a girl is seen with suspicious eyes; ultimately we had to remain within this society." She opened the first chapter of her life with a tinge of sadness.

"What does Salim do? Where is he now? Do you have any current information about him? If he is intellectually sharp he must be in a good job. Do you ever talk to him? I remain in touch with my college friends on Facebook and try to meet them occasionally when it's convenient." He threw out a volley of questions and opinions instinctively.

A bit annoyed, she said tersely, "Again the same haste, the same excitement. You rapidly fire so many questions, as if I am the caretaker of Salim. I will tell you about another, more interesting chapter of my life but later on." On regaining composure, she continued, "I am sorry for my raised voice. In the meantime, would you tell me something about yourself and your family? You could have got a good job in Delhi, so why did you come to such a distant place? How do you spend the weekends? Don't you feel the burden of isolation?"

Rajeev responded, "My father is a retired government official, he owns a flat and gets a pension, which is just enough to sustain without fanfare. My mother is a housewife and she looks after the household. Occasionally I give some support. My older brother, Sanjeev Shukla, is an officer in a London Bank and last year he got married to a European girl. The wedding took place in London and all of us had participated."

He continued, "I started my job in Delhi and came to Bangalore on promotion. Also, living independently in the wider world is an integral part of modern life and I wanted to experience it. I have some interest in music, which fills my lonely hours; shopping and watching films on the weekends are also on my list. I have a flatmate for casual chats."

Hamida took her turn: "My father is in a government job and he will remain there for three more years before retirement. My younger brother, Rahim Gulshan, is a final-year student at college and he's interested in politics. He is the secretary of the student union and accomplished in giving speeches, like a matured person much older than him. I live alone in my flat, a part-time maid cooks for me and cleans the area. I love vocal music, especially Urdu *ghazals*, and take sitar lessons from a teacher each Saturday. Occasionally I have to finish office tasks on the weekends and time flies away fast."

She looked outside; the darkness had just descended.

"It is getting dark, let us go," she said leaving her chair.

"If you don't mind, you can take the back seat on my motorcycle."

"No, I will take a taxi. If you have a business card, you can give it to me."

"Thanks, we will meet again."

On Sunday morning, the weather was pleasant. Hamida phoned, "If you are free we can go for a picnic in the city park, which is regarded as very beautiful. I will bring some food and you can bring some drinks - this will keep our bags light. There is also a well-stocked restaurant in the park where we can spend some time. You can wait for me at the main gate."

"Yes, I will," agreed Rajeev enthusiastically.

Both arrived at the park, which seemed rather crowded, walked together to a distant corner and finally sat on the thick sheet of green grass under the shadow of a tree. Rajeev offered her a can of chilled Coke and Hamida opened a packet of potato chips.

Rajeev could not restrain himself. "I am eager to know the important elements of the second chapter of your life. I have been waiting since that day."

Hamida obliged. "After graduating from the college I succeeded in gaining admission to a management institute in Delhi and its hostel. On the very first day, during an introductory and welcome session for new students, I was both astonished and delighted to see Salim, and we greeted each other with a wave. As time passed, we became closer, often lunched together, and also went to theatres on a few occasions. One year passed like a flying bird and we landed in the final year of study.

"It was time to decide about future professional plans and, in this context, I was consulting Salim about various course options while sitting on the open lawn of the institute. Other groups of students were also scattered here and there, some were just lazing around in the warmth of the sun. Suddenly I saw my father approaching us, perhaps he had already seen us when we were busy in discussion." She spoke with a degree of consternation.

"Dumbfounded, I enquired nervously whether everything was all right and why he had come so suddenly. My father replied very casually, 'Everything is fine. I had to come here at short notice for urgent official work and I didn't have time to notify you in advance. The office-work did not take much time and so I thought to catch you in the institute. I will return by the evening train.'"

Rajeev sympathised. "I can imagine the awkward situation you had to face. It could have been equally embarrassing for Salim."

Hamida elaborated, "Salim was standing beside me and I introduced him to my father. He was pleased to know that Salim had also graduated from Aligarh; he enquired about his family and seemed satisfied. If he had any apprehension or suspense in his mind, his facial expression didn't divulge it. When Salim wanted to take his leave, he asked him to join us for tea. We moved towards the institute canteen. The half an hour spent in the canteen looked unending but it passed well.

"When I went home after a month, my father confronted me: 'What do you think about Salim? He looks physically smart and quite civilised in talks. It appears he comes from a respected family.' My response was, 'He is only a friend, and I've known him since my college days in Aligarh. He used to be my opponent in debates, he is gifted with a sharp mind, and he won prizes on several occasions. In Delhi we frequently meet for academic discussions, which is what we were doing on the lawn that day. I have no idea about his family and I have never tried to know.'

"He heard me patiently and then beseeched in an emotional tone, 'This society always looks suspiciously at the friendships between young boys and girls, especially in our community. It is very easy to spread salacious rumours; some people have a habit of berating others, which is a symptom of a perverted mind. Therefore, if you agree, I can gather some information about Salim's family and go ahead for your wedding. In the meantime you will have to observe caution and avoid unnecessary meetings.'

"'Before that I need Salim's permission - I don't know what he wants - the thought of a wedding never cropped up into our minds. I can inform you after consulting him. Please be assured that I will never do anything that could damage your prestige and honour,' I replied resolutely."

"What happened after that? It appears the climax is not far off," Rajeev became alert.

"Where is the question of climax? There is a natural flow to events, nothing is unexpected," Hamida countered.

"Despite that, it is important to know what happened next. It is obviously connected to your present condition," he persisted.

"If so, you will have to pay a fee. Let us have some food, I am feeling hungry." Hamida stood up and arranged her crumpled dress. She blossomed in her beautiful artistic attire.

"Can I imprison you in my mobile phone? Its beauty will also add up," Rajeev said, a little teasingly.

"Again the same poetic language! Next you will say the scent of my hair has been imprisoned! Yes, but only for you," she replied in the same vein.

"You are quite photogenic; I will send these photos to your email."

"Now, you tell me if someone has ever entered your life? Whether a friend, a classmate or a beloved?" Hamida seemed curious.

"Yes, as a classmate and competitor. Anushka used to be sometimes ahead of me and sometimes behind me on the merit list, but she always tried to be ahead, as if it was her only priority. I never felt a friendly bond, though she often appears on my Facebook. She is also an officer in a multinational company and lives on the other side of this metropolis. It is possible you will see her one day. In my opinion genuine friendship precedes a love affair." He was equally candid.

"I will think whether I should tell you more because that involves the story of two families. To say something about myself is my right, but saying something about others requires much consideration," Hamida said thoughtfully.

"I praise your wisdom, it shows your maturity. I would like to call it a source of inspiration. One thing more - your frankness is worth appreciation," Rajeev commended.

"Let us go, it is already late. We will meet again."

Two weeks passed. They talked a few times on the phone but could not find time to meet. Hamida was in office when Rajeev called. "Next month there are public holidays for four days, you will probably also have free time. I have read about the ancient Hampi civilisation and its glory, and its archaeological remains are on the world heritage list. It is easy to go there from Bangalore – it's an overnight train journey. Visiting for two or three days might be educational and you might like it. My company has a guesthouse there, if you agree I can try to book two rooms."

"It's a good idea, I will let you know after checking my arrangements. I have also read the history of Hampi and learnt that the pillars in some of the temples produce musical sounds when tapped with fingers. The excavation of several sites by the archaeological department has brought into light the remains of large ancient structures which are of great interest to historians and tourists."

"Then this trip would be of interest to you too. I will wait for your confirmation."

The day arrived. Roaming through the remains of Hampi they sat on a large stone block. There was a good crowd of tourists, many of whom were foreigners, holding expensive cameras.

Hamida seemed a bit grave and self-involved. Before Rajeev could ask why, she intuitively started, "Today I would like to tell you about the remaining parts of the second chapter of my life, which are like these ruins - buried into oblivion but with a spark. In fact it is these ruins which have inspired me – who knows, my story might also have a message, just like these ruins."

"I will remember this day and this backdrop," Rajeev agreed.

"But there is one condition, it will remain between the two of us only."

"You can rely on me."

She described patiently: "I returned to Delhi and my father's question weighed heavily on my mind. Two months passed but I could not muster the courage to talk to Salim on this pertinent issue. I didn't know how he would react and the veil of feminine shyness also burdened me. One day we were preparing a project report in the library, and there were many books and magazines scattered before us. Amidst this, Pranav approached and gave a wedding card to Salim. On the envelope was written 'Salim and Hamida', which simply infuriated me. Why our names together? Was it a nasty joke or did it have some meaning? Pranav was close to Salim, but we were simple acquaintances with the occasional hello. Salim was also perturbed and decided to take up this matter with Pranav."

She continued, "I could not be normal for several days, Salim was probably in a similar state, and for a week we hesitated to face each other. Finally I realised that I had to face the issue rather than avoid it. Salim thought similarly but he was worried about my reaction. One day we sat on the lawn and discussed the issue with an open mind.

"It was Salim who started. 'Seeing us together a lot, friends would quite naturally imagine that we loved each other and the logical conclusion would not be far away, that is, our wedding was underway. What they think is not important, what we think is important. Do we love each other but find it embarrassing to express it or is it totally a misconception? I have meditated over this matter during the last one week and my response is positive. I am waiting for yours.'

"'I also nurture the same feeling, but I had no courage to express myself. You have taken an enormous load from my mind. Now I can confidently face my father and you will also have to take your family into confidence,' I uttered in an emotionally choked voice. Salim kissed my hand and tears of happiness filled my eyes. It was one of those rare moments that come into a woman's life. I heard him say, 'We can complement each other and fill the void with love.' I was over the moon," she said with a deep breath.

Rajeev was listening carefully and he said, "During our brief association I have observed that your self-confidence is your guide in difficult times and it is an important dimension of you. I am simply bewildered at how your future path got derailed."

She added, "Time passed happily and after a few weeks Salim went home for a short break. After he returned I learnt that my father had visited his home but he didn't know what talks were held. I also thought it was the first formal meeting between the two guardians and nothing much could be expected. The final examination was approaching and that was a more important consideration.

"When I came home after finishing exams, my father explained the situation: 'Salim's father welcomed me with full courtesy and I brought up the proposal of your wedding with Salim. During our social introduction it came to light that we are Sunni Muslim whereas they are Shiah Muslim and therefore this wedding is not possible. He strongly believed that it would lead to their being ostracised by the community, which would be too oppressive to tolerate. He emphasised that the prestige and future of the larger family could not be sacrificed at the altar of one wedding. You have also seen how we faced the ugly consequences of the religious conflict between Sunni and Shiah communities, on several occasions, and so I agreed with him.

We, as guardians, decided to keep quiet until your examinations were over.'

"Both Salim and I got a mental shock but time gave its healing touch. Had we ever imagined this cruel destiny, we would have never travelled on this path." She could hardly speak.

Rajeev wiped the tears dropping from her eyes with his handkerchief and said, "It is as if you have come out from a burning fire which was extremely painful. This has enhanced your self-esteem and added glitter to your personality. I am blessed with your friendship. Let us go to the guesthouse, you need rest."

"I feel relieved. I had heard the burden of anxiety gets lighter when shared with others; today I can feel it. I don't know how Salim is."

Rajeev had many questions emerging in his mind, but he kept quiet.

That evening, at tea time, Hamida was quiet and in a pensive mood.

"Can I ask something?" Rajeev broke the boredom of the atmosphere.

"If it is connected to my story, don't ask. Please don't reopen old wounds."

"But my query is about that only."

"Okay, I don't want to disappoint you. But this will be the last question." She conceded.

Rajeev asked, "Do you still love Salim and want to live in his memory?"

It was like an explosion; she was dumbfounded. It took several minutes before she could regain her composure.

"My love or intimate attraction towards Salim is not alive and therefore the question of becoming his life partner does not arise. But I do have sympathy for him. Whatever happened was beyond his control and he cannot be blamed. He is the history of my life that cannot be obliterated. What is required is the right perception that can sustain the onslaughts of society. I don't know where he is today, what condition he is in, but if he needs my help I will try my best," she said with a cool mind.

Rajeev was moved. "Your thoughts are commendable, a source of pride for anyone. A profound message is hidden in your story." She felt comforted.

Rajeev delivered a brief lecture: "Orthodoxy based on caste and religion is still dividing our society while in terms of education, trade and culture we are moving towards global citizenship. The difference between 'national' and 'foreign' is evaporating and composite culture is taking roots among the younger generation. I feel its influence in my personality, I don't know about you. My older brother is married to a European girl - you could not imagine it a few years ago."

"I am equally progressive in thoughts, but it is the question of family bonds and social links which cannot be seen by the same lens. You are fortunate, more independent, and above many of the traditional restrictions. My situation is not similar to yours."

Rajeev nodded. It was time to say goodnight.

Rajeev went to the lawn and ordered the morning tea. When Hamida did not join, he knocked at her door.

"What's the matter? Didn't you get a good sleep? I have already ordered tea and sandwiches. We can chalk out today's program while taking breakfast." Rajeev seemed anxious about her well-being.

"I received a phone call from home late at night and afterwards I could not sleep properly," she said half-heartedly in a dejected voice while picking up a piece of sandwich.

"Is there anything in particular?"

"I will tell you later."

Today they were walking through the ancient temples of Hampi. They saw some of those well preserved artistic pillars that produced musical sounds. Hamida's musically trained ears could catch the difference in harmonics when she tapped at different parts of the pillar, and she was overwhelmed at its science. Perhaps in those days temples embraced dance and music besides being a place for religious rituals.

Standing in front of one of the pillars Hamida uttered, "When I play on the sitar the emerging notes appear incoherent, but their harmony becomes alive here."

An old man facing her responded in a fatherly voice, "Daughter, notes become melodious when they are dedicated to someone, as was the case with Meera. You need one partner, real or imaginary, to which you can dedicate your feelings."

Is there a seed of the future or god's will hidden in his statement? They wondered.

Does this indicate the beginning of the third chapter of my life? Hamida thought to herself.

"This man looks experienced," Rajeev said, looking at her inscrutable face.

Their friendship had taken firm roots in the past few months. It was Saturday evening and they were in a restaurant. Hamida received a call from her father. "I am coming to Bangalore with a friend in two days and you will know my purpose when I am there." The call got disconnected. Rajeev had heard the conversation and there was a question in his eyes.

"I did not tell you earlier, he has called several times. They are all worried about my marriage."

"What did you say? Their anxiety is genuine. The young girls of your age seldom remain unmarried, especially in your community."

"I have resisted until now; it appears they are under pressure. What should I do?"

"It is not proper to give advice in haste. First listen carefully, it is quite possible he has some suitable proposals. You can take time for your decision."

"The fact is that after the Salim episode I have decided not to marry, but I don't know his situation. It will be a breach of faith in him if he has taken a similar vow and not married as yet. His sacrifice will keep me restless for my entire life, then what's the purpose of such marriage?" Hamida opened her heart.

Rajeev reasoned, *Hamida is committed to a principle and there is depth in her vision. It is important to know the whereabouts of Salim.*

"Can I know Salim's last name?" Rajiv asked.

Hamida understood the relevance and said, "Akhtar."

Rajeev worked for a telecommunications company and he was an expert in digital technology. There were several names in the database but he located the right Salim Akhtar after matching his profile. He was in London working for a reputable media company. The next day Rajeev brought a proposal to Hamida: "Let us go to London for a week. My sister-in-law will be happy to receive us and we can meet Salim. Any objection in seeing Salim?"

"Thanks for your wise proposal, I have no objection." A glow appeared on her face.

Within a month they were received at London airport by Sanjeev Shukla, Rajeev's older brother, and his wife. After initial greetings Rajeev's sister-in-law invited, "There are two additional bedrooms in our house, you can stay comfortably without any formality."

"I have already booked a hotel for myself but we will definitely remain in touch. I was eager to see you," Hamida said, expressing her gratitude.

"Okay, I will drop you at the hotel, we are not far away from there."

The very next day Rajeev called Salim. "I am an officer in a telecommunications company in India and I would like to use the services of your reputable company for our global expansion."

Salim responded, "I would be happy to receive you tomorrow at three o'clock." Hamida heard their brief conversation.

Rajeev knocked at his door at the appointed hour. Salim was nonplussed to see Hamida along with the visitor: he kept on looking like a statue. “I am Rajeev Shukla, won't you invite us inside?”

Salim remained occupied, as if he had woken up from partial slumber, while Rajeev and Hamida sat opposite him at his table. It was Rajeev who broke the enigmatic silence. “Hamida also works in Bangalore, I met her by chance on a train. We often share our ideas like friends - it helps unburden our mind. I am a bit familiar with the history of your lives.”

“Can we first finish the official work? Then we can sit in a restaurant,” Salim became alert.

“If you can go through it, our next meeting would be more fruitful.” Rajeev placed a file before him.

“What you say is quite reasonable,” Salim agreed.

Just then Rajeev's mobile started ringing. He left the room. “Please excuse me.”

Now Salim and Hamida were face to face.

She saw a portrait on the table. “Your wife is very beautiful. Do you have kids also?”

Salim became sentimental; his eyes were wet. Regaining composure, he said, “She is my friend, Priya Jackson. I also needed a companion to unburden my heart. I have not been fortunate to find a wife. How could you think I would move on, leaving you in turmoil? I was eager to know your status, but did not dare to phone you and reopen our wounds. I have already resolved not to go ahead until I get an invitation to your wedding.”

“Such a huge sacrifice!” Hamida started sobbing.

When Rajeev entered, both were tearful. “Let us go downstairs for tea.”

They gradually settled after some table talk.

“Can I meet your friend?” Hamida asked, leaving.

“Why not? She also works in an office, I will call you after consulting her,” replied Salim.

Hamida reached her hotel; both were silent in the taxi. “I would appreciate it if you stayed for some time.” Rajeev followed her and they sat in a corner of the restaurant. He ordered for coffee. Hamida was pensive; she described almost word for word what had happened in Salim's office. With a penetrating look Rajeev said, "My respect for Salim has greatly increased, I bow before his sacrifice. Now I realise how foresighted you were, how truthful you were towards Salim. The ball is now in your court, you have to see the ground reality."

That night they were at Sanjeev's home for dinner: Rajeev and Hamida, Salim and Priya. The atmosphere was subdued but friendly, soothing music in the background.

Priya held Hamida's hand and said, "Salim told me about you a few months ago and I am pleased to see you. All expectations seldom bear fruit in life, hurricanes come and life changes its course, one has to seek a new direction. I came across Salim when he was sitting in a park in a dejected mood, and my sympathy turned into friendship. He is very emotional and honest, from his conscience, his personality has influenced me. You may like to know that my father is from Germany and my mother is of Indian origin, and they happened to meet in this country."

"What you say looks like a divine message for me and this meeting will remain memorable. Taking care of Salim is your duty, what I could not do has become a part of your destiny. You are like my younger sister, please do not deprive me of this honour," responded Hamida with humility.

They returned from London. Hamida had been to a foreign country for the first time, she got a glimpse of the Western culture. She realised that life could not be imprisoned within the precincts of rigid ideas, and the younger generation was capable of accepting new paradigms with an open mind. If this is the trend of the future, could she be a part of this flow? She answered to herself, *Why not?* She was thoughtful when she left the office, she saw Rajeev coming towards her.

"Can we have dinner in a restaurant?"

"Yes, of course," agreed Rajeev.

At the table Rajeev started the conversation. "Have you thought about Salim's resolution? The rudder of his life also lies in your hands, you should make a decision."

"I fully understand this. I have spent many nights in a disturbed state, it appears as if I am committing a crime. Amidst this mental turmoil I received a call from my father two days ago. His health is deteriorating because of anxiety, and now he says that I have full right to choose my partner," Hamida described her situation painfully.

"Then why this delay? He has already sent some proposals," Rajeev reminded.

"My choice is before my eyes but not on my lips, I don't want to fail for the second time," she suddenly spoke with a degree of nervousness.

She bowed her head; she did not want to face Rajeev.

"What did you say? Say it once more."

Hamida repeated verbatim what she had just said and added, "I didn't say that in any excitement or without considering its full implications. I was pondering over it for the past several days, I don't want to live a dual life anymore."

"I am sitting in front of you - did you mean me?" Rajeev seemed perplexed.

"You are wise, is it necessary to say so explicitly? Haven't you heard of the woman's natural veil of shyness in such matters?"

Rajeev kissed her hands; it was the first time that he touched her. She felt the sensation and started sobbing.

"I will not allow your faith to be broken. I had the same feeling but was afraid of your religious convictions. Today I have found a priceless jewel, we will jointly face society."

In the following weeks the two families made all the preparations for their wedding. Rajiv and Hamida decided to get married in a court in Delhi. Invitations were sent to relatives, friends and well-wishers. The auspicious day soon arrived, and Rajeev and Hamida signed the marriage register and hugged each other. Their parents blessed the couple and shook hands with grace. Salim and Priya were there and they also took their oath to become partners.

The whole campus resounded with clapping. A voice came from somewhere: “There is light across the horizon; one has to perceive it.”

Rahim Gulshan came forward, thanked the guests and said, “During debates I have passionately lectured on composite culture, several times, but today I have seen it with my eyes and my resolution has doubled. This will enlighten our future path.”

6. Two Images in the Mirror

It appeared that someone was calling from behind me, but I could not find a familiar face when I looked around. I moved on but stopped as the same voice interrupted again. Within minutes a young man, well built with attractive features, appeared and said, "I am Rakesh, your old school friend from the village."

My mind struggled to identify his blurred image, which seemed to float in an ocean of memory packed densely in layers. I had left my village at the age of fifteen about two decades ago and never had a chance to return. Away from the village I remained busy in my studies at a city college and then shifted abroad. Today, many years later, I was standing in the same city, whose familiar soil still gave off the pleasant smell of yesteryear. The city had changed in many respects, but the old streets, iconic cultural pillars, and faces working in the college still enlivened my memory.

"I am Dinesh. After so many years I did not recognise you immediately and I am sorry for that. I greatly value your sharp mind and the keen sense of friendship."

"Is it not commendable that you remembered me after living in a foreign land for so many years?" complimented Rakesh.

"Let us sit somewhere and talk comfortably." Dinesh went into a nearby restaurant. He was apprehensive about whether Rakesh was his genuine friend and it wasn't prudent to share personal details with someone of doubtful acquaintance. He still remembered some of his school friends, the special features of some teachers, and the important events of those days. After placing an order for coffee he asked, "Where are our school friends? Are some of our teachers still teaching?" Rakesh updated him about three or four friends and said that two of them were working in local offices and he met them occasionally. Then he enquired, "Do you remember the day when we took shelter in Savita's home returning from school, because of the heavy rain?"

Dinesh remembered the scene like a film. Savita was their classmate but on that day she had not gone to school due to bad weather. Seeing thoroughly wet in the rain, she helped them dry their clothes and served cooked snacks and hot tea. Her father had also behaved very politely and offered help in negotiating the muddy roads. In those years there was no telephone, no mobile. The next day Dinesh wrote 'thank you' on a piece of paper and slipped it on Savita's bench in the class and she responded with a smile. After that he did not forget to say hello, out of courtesy, whenever he was face to face with her.

Rakesh blurted hastily, "You must be living very comfortably in the United States. I have heard that every facility is available there - the latest medical facility can be accessed, there is no topsy-turvy in daily life, people are judged on their merits despite some reservations, men and women have equal rights and can think independently, and so on."

Dinesh shared his experience. "Yes, but other aspects are also worth considering. Life seems to have lost some of its meaning due to separation from relatives and friends, the influence of foreign culture, a perceived loss of identity, a growing distance from festive occasions, and an overwhelming desire for reliving the past in native surroundings. One feels as if life has been divided into two parts and achieving a proper balance between them is a complex problem."

Rakesh felt as if Dinesh was not happy and so changed the topic. "How is your wife, and how are the kids?"

"Sushma took up a part-time job only a few weeks ago. We have a two-year-old daughter and a helper to look after her. Engaging someone is very expensive and so both of us have to work to maintain even an average standard of living. My parents came over once or twice but they often felt bored, and quite possibly their interactions with Sushma were also not cordial. Now I don't want to put extra burden on them," Dinesh explained. He continued, "Tell me something about yourself."

“After leaving school,” Rakesh started, “I got admitted into a nearby college, often took part in debates as per my interest, once received a prize and represented my college at a state level, and soon came into the limelight after winning the election of the student union. After graduating with high marks I secured a government job in the same town and my life appeared to have found a smooth track.

“I had completed just one year in my job when I got married, under pressure from my parents and other relatives. My wife came from a middle-class family, and she was beautiful but educated up to school level only. She could not go to college after marriage but she was good-natured and dedicated to the housework. Her sense of service and caring attitude soon won my family's appreciation. They also brought happiness to me and time passed smoothly.”

Rakesh continued, “We had just celebrated our first anniversary when the events took a dramatic turn. The state assembly election was coming up in a few months and the political parties became active. The heavyweight leader of the ruling party from our constituency was up for re-election and to win he needed youthful workers. Someone probably told him about my debating capacity, my ability to successfully address a large audience, my record of winning the student union election in a convincing manner, and advised him to invite me for the election work. One day I received a call from the leader and within a few days I was standing before him.

“Taking an active part in politics while remaining in government service is against the law, but the experienced leader assured me that I would be granted appropriate leave and would also be duly compensated for the work. I accepted his offer, moved into his constituency for more than a month, organised several corner meetings in villages, explained the right of voting and its consequences, and talked about the political manifesto of the party, especially for the common man, who was deprived in many respects. This also brought me closer to the people of the area.

"After the election the leader became an important minister and his influence multiplied many-fold. Sometimes he used to remember me, particularly when he had plans to come to my village. After a few months my school celebrated its establishment day and the honourable minister was the designated chief guest for the occasion. I was also invited to the function. All the official activities were conducted in a very cordial and peaceful manner, to the satisfaction of the honourable minister, and the function was coming to an end. At that moment someone from the crowd stood up and reminded the minister of the commitments he made at the election time."

Dinesh intervened, "This is often the case. Political leaders make many commitments knowing fully that they will remain unfulfilled and the innocent public gets cheated very easily. This is also seen in Western democracy, the leaders undertake policy decisions for which they have no mandate."

Rakesh picked up the thread, "The minister had promised to bring suitable proposals before the government within three months for the massive development of the village and its adjoining areas, but even after six months there was no mention of it. Several others also raised their voices and quite a few started shouting slogans against the minister. Taking advantage of the situation, some of them, possibly opponents, tried to malign his personal life as well.

"Judging the mood of the people, which might have disturbed peace, the police force advised the minister to leave under protection, and he seemed helpless. Within moments he saw me and, sensing his intentions, I went to the podium. I spoke in an assertive voice, 'The honourable minister is our guest, and giving him full respect is consistent with our culture. In a democracy the execution of any policy follows a slow process and this is especially evident in this country – a five-year project remains incomplete even after ten years and there is hardly any restraint on the escalation of cost. For the development of this village we must support the honourable minister and refrain from raising slogans against him. I am confident that he will bring the expected gift of happiness when he visits next time.' My assertion had the desired effect on the audience and the honourable minister also appeared satisfied.

"Within the next few days a man faced me with the message, 'the honourable minister would like to see you.' The minister was stationed in the capital city, one needs to prepare to go there. The messenger understood my hesitation. 'Please let me know your itinerary a few days in advance, all arrangements will be made.'

"Soon I entered the minister's grand official residence after undergoing a thorough security check. The extensive green lawn bedecked with colourful flowers, uniformed attendants, shinning motor cars, and an aura of grandeur, gave the impression of a mini king's palace. I asked myself, '*Do we elect a king in this great democracy? Then why the false pretence of being the people's servant?*' Soon I found myself standing in front of the honourable minister, dressed in white, and I bowed down and paid my respects, and was seated face to face. A uniformed attendant placed a variety of items on the adjoining table and I heard, 'We will take breakfast together.'

"'How is your work going? Are you satisfied with a government job in a small city? Does it provide scope for promotion as per your ability and talents? Are you financially self-supporting or do you get some help from your parents even now?'

"I felt a bit uneasy at the volley of questions from the minister, whom I had not even seen at such close proximity. It was difficult to immediately understand his motives but I replied with patience, 'Satisfaction is like a mirage in life's journey: it never comes into one's fold. I hardly know my destiny; the flow of life's stream is invisible and not always straight. However, living with my parents does give a kind of the emotional satisfaction that cannot be measured in terms of money.'

"He smiled and nodded, 'I appreciate your philosophical answer, but one has to assess the reality on the ground. Your ability will be stunted in your present government job, you have only five to ten years to achieve your high potential – beyond that, people often get sucked into the complexity of family problems. Hence you may have to transcend a small city's outlook, look at the bigger horizon, and search for new challenging avenues.'

“'For that I need higher education, possibly in a Western country, which was my initial desire but that seems impossible in my present situation,' was my truthful response.

“'To earn money, to aspire to wealth and prosperity, to establish identity in higher circles and to ensure a comfortable living for your family are not wrong but the conspicuous pillars of success for the new generation. Yes, the methods of their achievement can be different. As you have said, the path of higher education is one of them and many people have chosen it but it is not suitable for you at this juncture.'

“The minister continued, 'Politics provides another path but for that you will have to comprehend the mutual relationship between politics and administration. You may have to see their interplay, tricks, merits and demerits from a closer perspective. I can give you a chance by appointing you my personal assistant.' Looking at my white, bewildered face, he explained, 'You will get a good salary and live in a section of my residence, you would be there for discussions with higher officials and advise me, you may have to write my speeches for certain occasions, and so on. In my opinion you can perform these tasks efficiently, given your sharp mind and intelligence.'

“Impressed by his grip on life's vision, I opened up, 'What will happen to my government job? Will I be able to give my full attention while living away from my family?'

“'You will get leave from government service, you may go home for three to four days in each month, and you can expect greater help in special situations,'” he said.

“I became a little interested in the proposal after hearing all of this and asked for two weeks to decide. The honourable minister smiled, nodded, offered me a bundle of currency notes from his pocket, and said, 'This will cover the expenses you have already incurred, and something for your new clothes and associated necessities.' Despite my protestations, I could not resist. I also thought of returning the money in case his proposal was not acceptable. Within two weeks I began my new assignment. That initiated the second phase of my life."

Dinesh tried to continue the discourse inquisitively but Rakesh's mobile phone started ringing, and there was a message from the minister's office. Rakesh stood up, "We will meet again tomorrow."

The next morning Rakesh called, "Today I shall be going to my home village; the minister has a program there. You can come with me, we will chat on the way, and you can refresh old memories and have a feel of the country life." Dinesh agreed enthusiastically and soon they were both in a government vehicle. Dinesh felt as if he was watching an old but attractive movie and he was part of the legend. Intermittently, Rakesh explained some of the visible changes in the country side and informed him that Savita was working as a schoolteacher in a model village, which was not far off from their destination.

"Can we see her?"

"Why not?" Rakesh phoned her, "Wait for an unexpected gift of friendship." Rakesh sensed his keen eagerness and mentioned briefly, "Savita got married to a military officer only a few months after leaving high school and spent almost three years with him at the military headquarters in the city. Then her husband was transferred to a frontier area, where he had to confront militant infiltrators and terrorists quite often. After two years, during intense activity he was killed. He was honoured posthumously for his bravery, the family was duly compensated, and Savita was appointed a schoolteacher as per her qualifications. She lives within the school campus with her only son, gets support from her extended family, and I also try to encourage her now and then. She seems to have settled in this environment but I always feel sorry for her."

Within a few hours they were at her place. Dinesh and Savita looked at each other like motionless statues and tears fell down their cheeks: this emotional burst was more powerful than words of sympathy. Dinesh paid his respects to the photograph of her departed husband and wiped tears from Savita's moist eyes; this was a moment of genuine human feeling. He broke the painful silence. "Making a compromise with a cruel fate seems more plausible in the company of relatives and friends, but in Western countries the burden of isolation is much heavier than the financial one and so looking for a new partner has become an accepted practice."

Changing the topic, Rakesh said, "Within the next few months the state government will give Savita the *Baal Shiksha Ratna* award for children's education and she may get a chance to visit the United States. She has worked hard and done commendable work in popularising primary education among village-based children for several years."

"I will wait for you in the United States," said Dinesh enthusiastically.

"Though you have returned here after many years, I feel the same sense of closeness, as if nothing has changed," Savita expressed. She brought tea and snacks to the table.

"Tea and snacks are very tasty – like aeons ago," brought a brief smile to her face.

Leaving, Dinesh uttered, "Can I have your phone number?"

Savita could not deny. "If you have time before returning abroad, I will wait for you." She became sentimental.

Both Dinesh and Rakesh left for the destination.

On the way Dinesh asked, "Would you tell me something about the second phase of your life?"

"While working with the minister I became familiar with many high officials. Some of them became rather intimate, and I was drawn into the lucrative business of transfer and posting, seeing the exchange of loaves and fishes in political circles, observing the growing influence of greed and selfishness, and the neglect of the masses. Once I also witnessed, with acute embarrassment, the unethical play of wine and women in the minister's personal life. After that he became wary and suspicious of me."

Rakesh continued uninterrupted, "Just two months ago, he had to give a speech on the problem of farmers in his constituency but he could not go. I received a message on my mobile to keep the audience under control. After consultation with other advisers, I went to the platform to deliver the speech, which I'd written earlier, on behalf of the minister. During the speech I suddenly felt new energy, unbounded agility, the idealism of the student life, and my speech became inspiring, objective and full of youthful sparks. The audience gave me a prolonged applause, many of them proclaimed me their 'youth leader', and I was myself surprised at the scene. Whatever happened was sudden, without premeditation.

"I had said, 'It is farmers who overwhelmingly cast votes, give sacrifices, but most of the material benefits go to a handful of people including politicians and industrialists. Politics lacks transparency and this is damaging the image of democracy.' The minister got full reports from newspapers and other close advisers. When we met after two days, he looked reserved and thanked me very casually. A realisation dawned on me: perhaps he considered me his political competitor. Today I seriously think about whether I should work for him when suspicion has entered our relationship, but I am not sure whether it's a fact or just my imagination. Maybe, I should watch his actions more closely before arriving at any conclusion."

After listening carefully, Dinesh said, "The honourable minister must respect your merit and ideals. It is a travesty that merit is not properly rewarded here, whereas ability and logical thinking are accepted as strong pillars of the Western society."

Suddenly, Rakesh uttered, "Could there be an opportune opening for me in a foreign country?"

"Do you really want to go abroad and face an uncertain future? Here you are economically well off, connected with high society, blessed with a happy family - what else do you need for a successful life?"

Rakesh became pedagogical. "Financial well-being and social recognition are desirable up to a certain level, but they cannot be the sole determinant of our modern life, especially when they are politically grounded. After losing an election the minister will be deprived of his own power and lustre, and then who will care for me? In this country political leadership has become a lifelong profession and all leaders want to remain glued to the seat of power until their last days - as if they have some inherent enmity with youths of independent viewpoints. Under excessive social pressure they often choose close family members as their political heirs. In Western democracies one hardly finds a top leader who has given shelter to dynastic aspirations."

Excitedly, he unburdened his mind. "My desire to lead life based on my own abilities and hard work has not died as yet, and I want to give it a fair chance, for which a foreign environment would be more suitable. I would be thankful if you could help me in realising my dream."

This became a serious discourse. Much time had already passed. Rakesh pressed his foot on the accelerator and got home before darkness gripped the village. He introduced Dinesh to his wife, Ragini, who provided homely hospitality to their new guest. They spent some time together and got to know each other very quickly. Rakesh left early in the morning to oversee the arrangements for the ministerial programme, saying, "Dinesh, I will come back in the afternoon and take you with me."

At the breakfast table Dinesh and Ragini were finishing their tea.

Dinesh asked with concern, "How do you spend your time? Rakesh seems very busy and often lives away from you; this must be causing undue hardship."

Choosing her words carefully, she said, "One does not get everything in life, one has to make adjustments to the circumstances, but one cannot compromise with mutual love and faithfulness to each other," she replied candidly.

"Your commitment to Indian culture and tradition is commendable. If you have to move to a foreign country, will you like living in a set-up with such different values?"

She was logical. "My two friends live in the United States and I have heard about their life style, but making any judgement simply on that basis is neither prudent nor desirable. There might be differences in individual perspectives."

"This means your thinking is not restricted or confined within a predetermined mind-set."

"Today the world is getting closer, the influence of global culture is visible everywhere, and therefore one needs to have an open mind."

They touched many other topics, and Dinesh was impressed by Ragini's personality.

"Excuse me, I have some work in the kitchen."

In the meantime Rakesh called. "I am coming."

The next election was a year away and so the proposed event was quite important for the local leader-cum-minister. He was to lay the foundation stone of an electricity power plant, which was expected to give industry a boost. The leader was accorded a warm welcome by the enthusiastic crowd, and his speech was heard with rapt attention and praised by thunderous applause. The function was coming to an end when someone from the crowd asked in a loud voice, "Is this stone-foundation-laying ceremony just a ruse to deceive the people keeping in mind the forthcoming election or a genuine event? Can the honourable minister give his assurance that the actual work will start within the next two months?"

The minister was not prepared for this question. The government had not yet released the grants for executing the project and therefore giving a positive assurance to people in public could prove a big headache, but at the same time not giving a convincing answer might become a vehicle for losing the election. The leader appeared helpless; he looked towards Rakesh, and solicited his help through a familiar cryptic signal.

Realising the minister's dilemma, Rakesh came forward. "In a democracy the government has a joint responsibility; one minister is not accountable for any policy decision. A big project brings benefits to all, whether they subscribe to the ruling party or to the opposition. When rain comes, it covers the lands of all farmers – the rain-god Indra does not ask whether a farmer is his devotee or not. So the entire public should support the minister and put pressure on the government in a concerted manner for the execution of this important project."

The audience conceded his logical arguments and a voice was heard, "You really deserve to be our leader." The meeting ended, all went home, but a deep suspicion entered the minister's mind; he became envious of Rakesh's political sagacity.

Sensing the minister's inscrutable mood, Dinesh volunteered, "Rakesh is talented, the darling of the youths, you should feel proud of his achievements."

Later, Rakesh explained everything to Ragini and added that he might not remain with the minister for long and would feel badly stunted if he returned to his old job. She felt a shock at the prospect of an uncertain future, but expressed her faith in her husband's abilities and hard work. Rakesh returned to his job with the minister two days later, full of determination.

In the meantime the minister recalled and analysed the past events intuitively and finally decided to remove Rakesh from the public eye, the only question was how? He faced a chain of thoughts: *Rakesh might feel insulted if removed in haste; he would certainly not return to his old government job; if he entered active politics my own victory at the election might be doomed; if he exposed my black deeds out of vengeance the party could turn against me.* Given his talents and respectability, it was prudent to be patient and cautious. Also, morality demanded that Rakesh be given another respectable position so that he could hold his head high before the public as an honourable politician of the area. The minister's political foresight came to life; he waited for the right occasion.

Dinesh soon had to return home. "Can we ask Savita and Ragini to come over here? I would like to see them once more."

"Why not?" agreed Rakesh.

The minister had to go on tour. Rakesh politely asked if he could use the facilities of the house for two days, and explained the reasons. The minister agreed happily and instructed his staff to ensure that the guests were not inconvenienced. Rakesh fixed up the program for the coming Saturday.

On the day of the gathering the weather was pleasant, spring was youthful with lots of brightly coloured flowers, the warmth from the sun was soothing, and all of them were sitting on the velvety green lawn in the minister's compound. After the initial exchange of greetings Rakesh brought a tray of snacks and sweets, Ragini prepared tea, and they served themselves in a friendly atmosphere with plenty of conversation.

Dinesh asked Savita, "Have you ever thought of living in a foreign country?"

She expressed her views. "I have no objection to working or living in a foreign land, it is a personal decision. Thousands of people move between continents and make important contributions to global progress according to their ability. In this digital age the exchange of scientific discoveries, technological know-how, management techniques, intellectual property, and trade-related skills take place quite rapidly and, in my opinion, the old question of brain drain has lost much of its relevance. So far as I am concerned, I am deeply attached to this land, which is soaked with my husband's sacred blood, I see his soul's image every day in its surroundings, and therefore I am committed to spend the rest of my life in this country. Yes, I would definitely like to visit foreign lands as a tourist and learn from their cultures." One could easily see that her eyes had become moist with tears.

Dinesh apologised, “I am sorry that I have reopened your internal wounds.”

Rakesh intervened, “I agree with Savita's feelings and her determination, to a considerable extent, but given a chance I would like to go abroad and assess the dimensions of my own abilities and their limits. It transpires that my perceived talent has become blunted and I feel a bit suffocated.”

As the occasion was becoming emotionally charged, Dinesh proposed watching a humorous Bollywood movie and they moved inside. The comedy was quite entertaining, full of vibrant colours and dance, and it lightened the insipid atmosphere. The time passed quickly; Ragini proved an excellent host and served a variety of tasty foods, much to the liking of their foreign guest. Night prevailed, and rest was needed after a long day. Dinesh offered to Savita, “You may come with me, we have a spare room and my father would be happy to see you.”

The next morning, Savita, looking fresh and cheerful, was waiting for Dinesh at the tea table while his father was glued to the newspaper. Sipping tea, Dinesh whispered, “I shall wait for the day when I get a chance to welcome you in the United States.”

“To mark this meeting I have brought a small gift, I hope you like it,” and she spread a piece of costly silk on which a poem was beautifully embroidered in bright colours. The abstract of the poem was, “You came like a tempest, brought the gift of cherished memories, it is the reward of our meeting, convey my affection to your wife and children, this is our cultural tradition.”

Dinesh was overwhelmed by the depth of the friendly feeling and cultural insight latent in the poem. He suddenly kissed Savita's hand. “This gift will always remind me of my existence, in which you have an unforgettable place.” Rakesh had called and so they left.

Ragini welcomed them and asked Savita teasingly, “How was the night?”

Savita retorted, "You too?" and embraced her for several minutes, as if their hearts were talking!

Eating breakfast, Ragini said, "Dinesh-ji, a small gift for memory's sake," and spread a painting on a thick cotton fabric. It was an exquisite painting in which Rakesh and Dinesh were sitting together and she was offering a cup of tea. When she explained that the combination of four deep colours symbolised their deep-rooted friendship, her abstract critical reasoning was profusely appreciated. Rakesh was astonished at the artistic talent of his wife; he hardly had time to see her works due to his busy schedules.

Dinesh thanked Ragini. "This painting will decorate my table as a symbol of our friendship." Then he showed Savita's gift, which was equally praised for its literary composition ingrained with intimate feeling and its friendly message.

Dinesh pleaded, "Can I capture these memorable moments in my camera? Sushma is not here but she will be a part of our team, in spirit, through these pictures." He shot a number of pictures including a few romantic ones at his promptings. All the photos looked full of life in the advanced digital camera. The sun was going down on the horizon, and Savita and Ragini got ready to leave for home. Dinesh became sentimental. "Everything happened as if destined by fate – finding Rakesh by chance was a godly boon." Tears were visible in all eyes; the car picked up speed.

Minister Sahib remained in a dilemma for several days. In the mirror of time he saw two images of Rakesh – one of a hard-working talented youth and the second one of an emerging political rival. It was difficult to decide which one was genuine, but his political wisdom cautioned him to remove any perceived danger at the very beginning. Soon he arrived at a final decision. He planned to get Rakesh deputed to the New York consulate as a junior political adviser. This would enhance his prestige in the constituency and also allow the minister the option of using Rakesh in the future; he smiled and went for a drink.

Minister Sahib was still not at his headquarters. Rakesh invited Dinesh for dinner and they discussed many topics of common interest. Rakesh showed considerable eagerness about the American way of life and learnt that Ragini might have a much better prospect of flourishing in the arts field, given her imaginative skills. Dinesh had some perplexing thoughts about Savita; he wanted to share them with Rakesh but he refrained. Rakesh had also guessed a little but he did not press ahead – it was a complex matter.

A few days later, Dinesh had to catch his flight. "I am waiting for my flight at the airport. I had thought to talk with you face to face but could not muster the courage. I want to unload my mental burden with you; please don't misunderstand me. Your faithfulness towards your departed husband, innate feeling for the national pride, commitment to social traditions, as seen in your daily life, are commendable and worth my deep respect. However, a whole life cannot be sacrificed because of one painful event in the past; in other words it must not be allowed to overshadow your entire future. Time is a great healer, it provides a soothing bandage for the deepest wounds – one has to accept the power of time in all its ramifications. The increasing isolation in future years will make your life hollow and by that time it might be too late. You need a life partner, but that requires the consent of both mind and heart." Dinesh posted this letter to Savita's address.

Savita also received an album, sent by Dinesh, containing photographs of the days spent together while he was there. A photograph of his wife, Sushma, signed by her, was also in the album. Savita became enchanted by her own beauty and its natural attraction; she could not resist smiling to herself for a few moments. Perhaps the improved digital technology had played a part but that was beyond her comprehension. She realised that though Sushma was not so attractive, her face and eyes displayed an aura of happiness and the same was true for Ragini. Savita wondered: *Was it a gift from their life partner?* Her thoughts were broken by Ragini's playful phone call. "Keep the album hidden from people's teasing eyes." Savita guessed its hidden meaning. Ragini was unaware of Dinesh's letter.

Time was passing fast. Savita would peek into the album impulsively but did not know why. She heard her colleagues say, "Savita has changed a bit," and the mystery seemed to surround her. After a month something unexpected happened, which badly shook her day-to-day life. She received a letter.

"I am a civilised, well educated, and mature person. I have seen the statue of the goddess Saraswati – the symbol of learning, music, and unblemished thoughts – dressed in spotless white. I see that lively image in your personality. I have heard the lyric of love also emanates from the strings of Veena, the musical instrument worn by Saraswati. Can it happen? I will wait. I know a bit about your life's journey, I am a traveller on the same path, I am tired, and I need rest. Kindly pardon me for my intrusion, I could not control my sentiments. On the day of Sarswati's worship I will come to offer a bouquet of red roses at her statue."

To ignore the events of the past two months was not easy. Dinesh's letter, the silent message of the album, today's letter! Were they connected like rings of a chain or simply a game of fate? Savita developed a sense of fear and, for the first time, she felt a need for a close friend who could show the right path. She thought of Dinesh but felt a surge of helplessness; she could not sleep properly, her mind was restless, competing with reflections. After several days she regained full composure and analysed the whole scenario objectively. She phoned Ragini, who came the next day, prepared to spend the night with Savita. They embraced each other. "You are like my sister." She started sobbing.

"Not like a sister, I *am* your sister. I will never allow your confidence to be shattered," comforted Ragini.

After preliminary chats Savita handed over both the letters to Ragini. She read the letters very carefully so that she could digest the genuineness of purpose and the dignity of the written words. She said, "In very few sentences Dinesh has opened his heart. I had felt similarly, on several occasions, but did not dare to face you." She continued, "A feeling of emotional pain is hidden in the second letter. It appears the person has passed through a bad time; he is stranded in the middle of the life's stream and honestly hoping to cross it. Before taking any steps it is important to know this person fully, and you will also have to decide whether you are willing to accept him as your partner if he turns out to be the right person. This decision will need the consent of both your heart and mind."

Savita emphasised, "I am not ready to give any such assurance. In any decision my family's consent is essential – perhaps they will take time in preparing themselves mentally and socially." It was late at night, and both said goodnight. The next morning their lazy eyes clearly indicated that they did not have a sound sleep. The school was closed that day, so there was enough time to ponder and plan ahead.

At the breakfast table Savita initiated. "Sister, I have thought of a plan. On the day of goddess Saraswati's worship you will stay here. I have a good camera and from a safe distance you can take snaps of people offering roses at the statue. This person will definitely look around curiously searching for me and be easily identified. On that day I will stay inside my house; it is quite possible that he will try to write another letter. We can identify him through photographs, then we can decide what to do next. Until then, I would like it to remain secret."

"You have the ability to become a good spy," interjected Ragini.

"Time teaches everything. It is your responsibility to find a good excuse for coming to my place on that day. If something important happens, I will call you." Savita felt relieved.

After two days Rakesh came home unexpectedly. Hours went by, but Ragini did not divulge that she had gone to Savita's house, which he knew from other sources. He asked, "Is Savita in some trouble?"

“No, her son was a bit indisposed and so I went there for one night as a matter of courtesy.”

Rakesh felt suspicious but kept quiet.

At the earliest opportunity Ragini phoned Savita, explained everything and advised her to remain cautious so that their plot was not unravelled. Later in the evening Rakesh also called. “I have heard that your son is indisposed, if any help is needed don't hesitate to inform me.”

“Yes, I will and thanks.”

She had almost fallen into slumber when her mobile started ringing. “Who is calling at this late hour in the night?”

She recognised Dinesh's voice. “I have learnt that your son is sick, how is he now?”

She smiled. “Ragini has cleverly created this circuit to support her excuse.” She had become an integral part of this triangular relationship; the future was unknown but right now she felt satisfied.

The next week Rakesh was in the office when a call came from the Ministry of Foreign Affairs. Rakesh passed the handset into the minister's hand and went out of the office after getting the signal - that had happened many times in the past, especially when the topic was confidential. Despite being outside the office, he heard a faint, unclear message: “You can give the green signal to Rakesh, it might take a month or two before the entire process gets completed.”

He was surprised. “What relationship have I got with the foreign ministry?” He had realised that the minister's behaviour had turned very cordial for the past several days; thinking otherwise was perhaps wrong.

Coming out of the office, the minister said, “The world trade fair is going to be held in the nation's capital in two weeks and I am invited to be there; you will also come with me. We will fix up the program tomorrow – it might easily take four to five days. That will be the time of goddess Saraswati's worship in this city and there should not be much workload.”

Ragini was pleased when she learnt about it: now she could visit Savita without any anxiety. She thanked her good stars for this unexpected favour.

The fateful day arrived. Ragini had already reached Savita's by the previous evening, as planned. Savita was a bit nervous, but she felt relaxed in her company. The next morning Ragini proceeded to the venue where goddess Saraswati's statue was installed and took a camera in her bag. Soon people started filing up in a line to offer flowers and garlands at the statue, and she looked at each face with full attention. She also took some photographs intermittently, common on such occasions, so that no one could doubt her photographic interest. Within no time a man with an attractive appearance, clutching a bouquet of red roses, joined the line and kept looking around as if he was searching for someone. The line was long; she had plenty of time. She easily took several snaps of him, both from a distance and at close range, when he was in the line and when he was alone offering flowers at the statue. That was enough. She saw that even after having his turn, he remained, roaming the big enclosure for about half an hour. He accepted a handful of sweets offered by the priest and then came out with a sad face. She was one hundred percent convinced that he was the person they'd expected.

As Ragini was preparing to leave she heard the school principal, “Alok Babu, when did you come? You might have informed me.”

“So this person is Alok Babu.” She was enthralled. “I also got his name.” The principal moved towards the school building, walking along with him. She realised this man was also respected in the eyes of the school administration! She was excited, as if she had suddenly found a valuable treasure. She went, almost running with happiness, to tell Savita the entire story. Savita's face remained inscrutable. She uttered, “What next?”

“We will think together,” exclaimed Ragini, rejoicing at her initial success.

"I will send you some prints of the photos very soon," offered Savita.

"I can recognise him anywhere, there is no immediate need for the photographs for me but we may have to show a few to Rakesh. I imagine that Alok could also be in some of the photographs kept in the principal's office – look when you have time. If my guess is correct, you may get more information from some of your colleagues also." Ragini offered some relevant clues.

"Sister, it appears you have also learnt the machinations of the political office."

"I am leaving now, call me if something important happens."

A call came from Rakesh. "It will be three to four days before I can leave. The world trade fair presents a very engaging and attractive view of the world, and I got a lot of interesting information about the United States. Despite my hesitation, minister sahib has bought a warm jacket for me and I have purchased a beautiful sweater for you. Any news there?"

"Nothing, simply waiting for you." Ragini did not want to face any scrutiny.

After two days some political workers approached Ragini. "Madam, the inauguration of an exhibition is scheduled this afternoon. Rakesh-ji was expected to be there but he is out of town; your presence would be greatly appreciated." She was aware of Rakesh's popularity in political circles and she had participated in such programs on several occasions in the past. She agreed.

When she arrived, she was seated respectfully in the front row along with other important guests. One worker introduced her to the guest sitting next to her. "This is Alok Saxena, an industrialist of this area and a valuable patron of our cultural activities." Then, looking towards him, "This is Ragini-ji, wife of Rakesh Sharma who is the special assistant of our minister and praised for his sharp intellect."

Both greeted each other with folded hands. He said, "I have already met Rakesh-ji once in the minister's office; it is a pleasure to see you."

"I am also pleased."

Not long after, he broke the silence. "Rakesh-ji must be very busy; how do you spend your time?"

"I look after the family and do some painting in the spare hours."

"Do you also sell paintings?"

"No, I do it for my personal pleasure."

Ragini was a bit nervous after unexpectedly facing Alok Saxena in this situation, but she kept her cool and decided to take full advantage of the occasion. She enquired, "Is your wife busy somewhere else today?"

A line of sadness appeared on his face. "I am alone, we could live together for a short time only. Possibly it was god's will." She felt a freezing wind! Overcoming the burden of silence, he offered himself, sensing her curiosity. "My wife was killed in a motor accident two years ago; imagining it makes me restless even today." In the meantime the programme had started and the manager asked him to come to the podium.

Alok opened the exhibition by lighting the ceremonial lamp and addressed the audience in Hindi, saying, "This type of exhibition inspires our rural and regional artists to develop their talents, educates us culturally, shows a glimpse of affinity between humans and environment, and rightly entertains the budding children. Such events should be made a crucial part of school education. Personally, I support it and will continue to offer my help in the future. I wish you all an enjoyable time." The audience welcomed his views with prolonged clapping.

Ragini took a stroll inside the exhibition, chatted with artists, gave toys to children on behalf of the management, and then went outside. While she was waiting for a taxi Alok caught sight of her. "Please accompany me, I will drop you at your house." She could not deny the very polite offer despite her initial hesitation.

On the road she opened up. “Your speech was brief but full of meaningful ideas and inspiration. Despite your English-oriented education, you spoke eloquently in Hindi and this is exemplary for the younger generation.”

“I look forward to having you and Rakesh over for evening tea.”

“Thanks for your company.” Ragini reached her home.

Savita listened patiently to what Ragini said about her encounter with Alok and then asked, “Is it one hundred percent certain that he was the only person to offer roses at the statue of goddess Saraswati? I hardly see straight proof of that.” Savita's argument was logical but it was also a sign of her changing mind, now she had started taking interest in Alok.

“Let me find out a convincing way,” replied Ragini.

A few days later the school principal came looking for her. “Savita, I have to go for an important meeting in the afternoon. You should stay in my office and answer telephone calls or take messages if needed.” She was waiting for an opportunity when she could closely look at the group photographs hanging on the walls of his office. She found Alok prominently seated beside the principal in two of those photographs and she concluded that he was well connected with this institution. After half an hour, while she was engrossed, the telephone rang loudly and she jumped to respond.

“Can I talk to principal sahib?”

“Sir, he has gone out for a meeting. Is there any message?”

“My name is Alok Saxena, kindly tell him to call me at his convenience. And yes, what is your name please?”

Before she could reply, principal sahib entered the office and took the phone. “It's the principal speaking, what's the matter? In my absence Savita was looking after the office-work.”

From the other side: “It is Alok, kindly convey my thanks to her. I would like to see you in half an hour, I hope it is convenient to you.”

Savita was standing close by; she had heard the conversation clearly. The principal looked towards her. "Today you may be a bit delayed in the office."

"Yes sir, please don't worry, I can manage." She phoned her maid and gave some instructions.

As scheduled, the principal welcomed Alok and introduced him to Savita. They politely exchanged greetings, looking grave but dignified. Savita said, "Please conduct your official business, and I will arrange for tea in the meantime."

Alok intervened. "There is nothing confidential; rather your presence will help our judgement." He spread the map of the proposed cultural hall on the table.

When he methodically explained the facilities that would go along with the building, Savita exclaimed, "This will be excellent for the cultural development of the students." She brought tea.

"You are an expert in preparing tea," commented Alok while sipping from the glossy cup.

"Thanks."

Time slipped away very fast; it was getting dark. Alok proposed, "If you don't mind, I can drop you at your house. It's getting dark and you may not find a lift easily at this odd hour." Principal Sahib advised her similarly and she silently followed Alok. When Savita went to occupy the back seat of his car, he politely requested that she sit in the front seat and kept the front door opened. Savita initially hesitated, looked around, and finally complied.

Alok broke the silence. "I have heard that you are a living symbol of learning, music and pious thoughts, and I have realised this today."

"Who told you so?"

"It is not necessary to answer all questions, some are just understood."

Savita thought to herself, '*These are the same words written in that letter.*' Her heart beat suddenly increased, and she started looking out of the window.

“I am impressed that you can use literary language despite being educated in a foreign country,” she managed to say.

“I have interest in literature; it is easy to find a life partner in literature.”

“So you need a life partner?”

“No, only a friend for the present.”

“It appears you are influenced by Western culture.”

Savita reached home. Alighting from the car she urged, “Please have a cup of tea.” A ray of a smile appeared on his face; he took the bouquet of flowers from the car's boot, and followed her in silence. The room was small but artistically decorated. On the central table was a framed picture of her four-year-old son.

He said gently, “I did not consider it appropriate to offer you this bouquet in the office, I hope you like it.” She could see how similar it was to the ones in Ragini's photos. Now she was becoming convinced of Alok's true identity.

Savita went into the kitchen to prepare tea and snacks. In the meantime Alok was drawn to a half-opened envelope lying on the table, containing some photos, the same photos snapped by Ragini. He was astonished to find his own face in two or three prints. Savita just entered the room and grasped the situation.

She said, “On the day of goddess Saraswati's worship, the girls of my class took many snaps and you are visible in some of them. It appears that your faith in gods and goddesses has not diminished.”

“I didn't know that you are also expert in spying,” Alok uttered looking at her face.

She kept quiet.

“You didn't say anything?”

“It is not necessary to answer all questions,” quipped Savita.

He could not restrain his laughter at this ready-made answer, and a smile erupted on her face. While eating snacks he observed, "When tea is so tasty, how fulfilling the meal will be?"

"You will have to wait for the right occasion."

Later, she walked him to his car. "Thank you for coming."

"We will meet again."

Savita had a long chat with Ragini that night. Ragini concluded, "You have changed in one day. Congratulations for this unique day!"

The following week was a time of introspection for Savita. The school was closed for holidays, Alok was away from the city, and she had quiet days ahead. She looked into the mirror of her life, into the pages of the revered books, and reflected upon her own social experience. She kept pondering for several nights on the right step and ultimately found a source of light in the words of Alok himself: presently he wants only a friend! She reasoned: *In Western cultures life usually starts through mutual friendship, which assumes some other form in the future. Alok's desire is based on realism rather than sentiments; his skilful manners and sense of propriety cannot be questioned either.* In spite of this reasoning she wanted Ragini's opinion before taking any steps. When she phoned, she learnt that Rakesh was coming home the next day. She warned Ragini not to divulge anything to Rakesh beyond discussing what had happened at the exhibition, and advised her to elicit some additional information based on that. Ragini assured her that her lips would remain under control.

After a few days Ragini invited Savita out on the eve of a women's festival so that Rakesh would not suspect anything about their meeting. "You have a far-sighted, practical mind," commented Savita and accepted her invitation. They shared their stories.

Ragini said, "Alok is a civilised and thoughtful person in Rakesh's eyes. After the sudden death of his wife, he has become rather fatalist. Some proposals for his marriage have been received – it is rumoured that a relative of the minister is also being considered, but possibly Alok has some special preference."

"Sister, I respect your vision; it gives me inner strength," Savita uttered faithfully.

"I have no reason to doubt what Rakesh has perceived," Ragini asserted.

In the coming week Savita was to receive the *Baal Shiksha Ratna* prize from the minister in the state's capital. The minister told Rakesh, "This event is important for me also as a way to influence the public. You should invite some prominent people from my constituency; I will take care of their living arrangements."

On being told of the minister's wishes, Ragini asked, "Can Alok-ji also participate?"

Rakesh informed Savita. "You can invite one or two personal guests for the prize ceremony, this is minister sahib's direction."

Savita urged her school principal for his kind presence at the award function but he declined because of other engagements. Getting over her hesitation, she phoned. "Can I talk to Alok Babu?"

"Of course." The secretary handed over the phone to Alok.

"How did you remember, I was waiting every day."

"I did not know that. Can we talk for a few minutes, if you have time?"

"Let me call you in half an hour." She had called him today for the first time, and drops of perspiration were visible on her forehead from uneasiness. She drank a glass of water. Soon she felt composed and possibly more assured after getting over her initial hesitation. She was pacing up and down in the room, her ears were alert, and she was looking at the clock time and again. She felt as if time had stopped, and wondered whether it was a sign of sprouting tender love.

She jumped with excitement at the ring of the phone; she could not comprehend its mystery. Identifying his voice, she spoke impulsively, “Are you going to be here in the coming week? I have heard that you are quite often on official tours.”

“Your wishes must be fulfilled, official work has no business with that.”

She talked briefly about the prize ceremony. “You are welcome at the function if you are not too busy.” She stopped before saying that she wanted to see him there, but Alok sensed that inherent feeling of hesitation in a woman.

He offered, “I shall be leaving my office a bit early today. If you are free we can have coffee at a city restaurant – I can pick you up in half an hour.”

Savita also had to do some shopping in the city, so she agreed and told him to meet her at a certain place in the market.

They occupied a table in the restaurant and Alok ordered coffee and light snacks. They were more comfortable in each other's company after their initial hesitation was gone. “I want to invite you to the prize ceremony; your presence will make the occasion more enjoyable.” She spoke in a low voice. Her eyes looked down while he was gazing at her image in the shinning plate and trying to read her facial expression. “You are trying to look inside through my reflection – very clever.”

“I was just being imaginative, a natural instinct.”

They could not help smiling. Sipping his coffee he said, “I have already received an invitation from Ragini-ji, I was waiting for yours. I will definitely come.” Suddenly Savita felt the unexplained impulse to explain her family-like relationship with Rakesh and Ragini. Encouraged, Alok shared with her many of his life's events and experiences. Both felt relieved and emotionally bonded.

“I would like to leave now; I have to buy a dress for the function.”

“Can I assist you in your selection?”

“Why not?” A smile crept onto her lips.

Savita saw many medium-priced options but Alok's choice was very different. She said, “In my class I remind the girls especially to know their limits because ultimately they will have to balance their family budgets in the future. How can I ignore my own limit?"

"Now I understand why you have received this prize," commented Alok.

Alok dropped Savita at the gate of her house.

The prize ceremony was more than a week away. While Savita was planning her schedule, she felt an urge to talk to Alok. She had punched in his phone number but immediately restrained herself - he was probably feeling the same urge.

Then it was only two days left. "How are you going to the city and where will you stay?" Alok seemed anxious.

"Ragini and I have decided to travel by public bus on the day of the function and we will stay together," replied Savita.

"Both of you can join me if you haven't already purchased tickets. I shall be travelling by car – it is only a two-hour drive, and I have already booked a room for myself in a city hotel."

"I will let you know in the evening after consulting Ragini, though I believe she should not have any objections." She could not hide her willingness, which became obvious to the other party.

She called Ragini. "Sister, is there anything wrong about Alok's proposal?"

"If you are willing, it is acceptable to me."

"I will inform you tomorrow after deciding the timing, or you can talk to Alok yourself and confirm." Savita's eagerness was obvious.

"No, it is not necessary." Ragini smiled, sensing the excitement in her mind.

Alok came to pick them up. Ragini threw herself on the back seat and asked Savita to occupy the front seat by the driver's side. "You can keep an eye on Alok-ji so that he doesn't feel sleepy while driving." It was difficult to ignore this logic; they were on the road.

Savita started the chat. "Who else is here in your home?"

Alok replied, "My parents and one younger sister, who has the reins of the company in partnership with me. My father comes to the office occasionally when there is a special meeting or some high-ranking government official is visiting. My sister is unmarried and she will be leaving for higher education in a Western country very shortly. There are two full-time servants who skilfully manage day-to-day domestic works and I am usually free from such responsibilities."

"It would have been nice had your sister also come along – does she know about us?"

"Yes, she knows everything. She will soon meet you; right now she was a bit busy."

"We will eagerly await for that moment." Savita felt an unseen friendly bond.

Alok pulled a packet of chocolate from his bag, "Please finish it; otherwise it will melt in the hot weather."

"I have brought spiced tea in a thermos and salted biscuits."

"I have brought samosas and coriander chutney."

"I love it," rejoiced Alok.

They sat down in a beautiful park, rested for a while, and shared snacks with mutual appreciation. Two birds were playing at a distance: they were putting something into each other's mouth with their narrow beaks – it was a means of displaying their friendship.

"Let us reach my hotel first and we can call Rakesh-ji from there."

They were sitting in the hotel's beautiful garden. Alok ordered coffee and called Rakesh. "We are waiting for you," he said, handing over the phone to Ragini. Rakesh joined them soon at the coffee table and Alok said politely, "You should continue, I will be back from the rest room soon."

Rakesh was totally unaware of the growing friendship between Savita and Alok. He was astonished when he heard the entire story, and then Savita urged in an emotionally choked voice, "I need your blessings."

He exclaimed, "This is the first time that two women have independently made such a big decision, which has traditionally remained the domain of men – I am proud of both of you." Alok had just returned. "Alok-ji, congratulations on your novel friendship! Please consider me a well-wisher in this journey."

"Thanks for having faith in me."

The prize ceremony was due to begin at six o'clock that evening, which was several hours away. *This is an appropriate occasion to give a gift,* it occurred to Alok, and he left for the market. He reasoned: *Given her principles, Savita would not like a costly gift, she might even refuse to accept it.* Considering the delicacy of the situation he purchased a medium-priced attractive wristwatch and a bouquet of roses. The prize ceremony was well attended and impressive, and several people from different fields were honoured. As expected, speeches were delivered, photographs were taken by reporters, and a brief tea party followed. The minister seemed happy and instructed Rakesh, "Prepare a brief report of the ceremony for the newspapers. Besides Savita and the other prize recipients, I should also get a share of the honour in the eyes of the electorate. Also, you are my guest at tonight's dinner and don't forget to bring Alok."

Alok congratulated Savita. "A small gift from me."

"The wristwatch is very beautiful, thanks."

"If you don't mind, can I put it on your wrist?"

She kept quiet.

While putting the watch on her wrist, he touched her for the first time. Her heartbeat increased, her eyes looked at the floor.

The next morning, the event covered the front page of the morning newspaper: Savita looked gorgeous; she got a new identity, a new life! Smiling, Ragini told Savita, "Rakesh wants me to stay here for a few days, you can return home with Alok."

Savita sensed the purpose behind her proposal and kept quiet. They were on the same wavelength.

"Give me a call after you get there." Ragini said goodbye.

The car picked up its cruising speed.

It was Savita who began. "Your attraction towards me has become obvious, but what are your intentions? Now I have also started thinking seriously. In our culture friendship between a man and a woman is looked at with suspicion, and how long can we ignore society?"

"We cannot do something just because society pressures us to do so, though we respect the traditional views to a certain extent. Today the world is getting closer, a global perspective is taking root, and a composite culture is wielding its influence on our life. Is it not proper to allow these new considerations time to reign? Also, before we reach a conclusion, it is very important that I know your decision – I have arrived at mine."

"What do you mean by 'I have arrived at mine'?"

"Ask my heart," replied Alok.

She got the message. "Let us stop somewhere for coffee."

Alok ordered coffee and snacks. Rearranging her scattered hair, Savita confided, "Now the time has come for us both to appear before my father."

"You should initiate that step; I may flounder," Alok said.

He had already put one teaspoon of sugar into his coffee and was taking another serve when she barred his hand.

"Who gives you this right?" Alok seemed to protest.

"Your heart! Excess sugar is harmful for your health."

Both smiled, love had taken deep roots.

"Today I feel very relieved," uttered Savita.

Before going to bed Savita explained everything to Ragini. It was agreed that she should take her father into her confidence without much delay.

Before the week ended, Savita got a phone call from Alok. "My sister's birth day is in a fortnight and my mother has invited you especially to this occasion. I have already invited Rakesh and Ragini."

"I feel very nervous, can you see me before that?"

“My parents are of an open mind, my happiness is their only aim, and they want to see their would-be daughter-in-law. There is no cause for nervousness, Rakesh and Ragini will also be there with you.”

“Prior to taking this step I would like to tell my father.” She was still feeling shaky.

“Sure, if necessary I am ready to accompany you.”

“Thanks for your assurance.”

Savita had dinner with her father, while her four-year-old son played. The little fellow said in broken English, “Nana-ji, I want to go to the hills like my friends but Mummy says it is not safe to go alone. Why can't you come with us?”

Savita intervened, “Nana-ji is not feeling well; he would find it painful to negotiate the hills.”

“Then ask that uncle who was with you a few days ago. He gave me a packet of chocolate.”

Sensing a question in her father's eyes she intervened again. “Alok-ji is an industrialist of this area and he takes a keen interest in the development of our school. I was introduced to him by the school principal during an official meeting and after that we have met a few times. Despite being educated abroad he has a great respect for the Indian culture. He was also invited to the prize ceremony - Ragini and I went with him, and Rakesh is also familiar with him.”

“Daughter, I would like to meet him sometime.”

“Yes, Father.” Her dilemma ended unexpectedly.

On a Sunday evening her father welcomed Alok. “My daughter is your great admirer, I am pleased to meet you.”

“You are also like my father; your blessing is a boon for me.” Alok opened his heart in a brief sentence, which was enough for the elderly man.

The little fellow came running, “Uncle, my chocolate?” Excited, he ran away with his toy and chocolate.

As a good mannered hostess, Savita said politely, “Please come to the dining table, tea is getting cold.”

“Savita has told me about your personal tragedy, I deeply sympathise with you, and I believe in destiny. She has also passed through this fated agony.”

Alok responded with conviction, “Life's flow is deviated by hindrance, but does not stop. Now I have decided to accept a new stream, after some introspection.”

Looking into her father's eyes she said rather emotionally, “The flow of time and the role of destiny are very powerful. We all have to believe in them; logic has no end.”

Alok broke the seriousness. “The snacks are very tasty, I could eat them every day.”

“Eating fried snacks every day is not good for your health.” They laughed at the sharp comment.

The table talk continued. “What have you thought about Savita?” asked the anxious father.

“My thoughts are crystal clear: I need a life partner but I believe in some basic standards. The other party has an equal right to evaluate me, and that can be achieved only through the medium of friendship. I extended my hand of friendship towards Savita-ji only after knowing enough about her, and she has proved genuine. If she thinks similarly about me, we can move forward. Otherwise, we can remain good friends within the bounds of our culture,” Alok explained his position.

The elderly father became sentimental. “She is capable of making decisions both from the heart and mind. I would be proud of any decision she makes.”

Savita started sobbing, her head on her father's shoulders. Her decision was not far away.

The next week Ragini suddenly dropped in Savita's house. The minister sahib had found enough time to chat with her while she was there for a few days. He had enquired about some personal matters, including her opinion of living in a foreign country, their financial position, care of their parents; at the same time he had asked her not to say anything to Rakesh. She was surprised at his very courteous behaviour. She could not logically analyse the motives of the minister – a fearful suspicion had gripped her mind – and she wanted to review the situation fully with Savita.

In the meantime Savita had had a dream in which an unknown face said, "You remove the portrait of your departed husband from the bedroom and place it outside on the table meant for religious services. Gods are worshipped from a distance, they don't live together with humans." This strange dream had stirred her mind once more and she also wanted Ragini's company.

Sadness was writ large on Ragini's face. Savita was in a similar state of mind, and their meeting provided the much-desired emotional support. Ragini described uninterrupted the details of her meeting with the minister. With a degree of alarm she added, "Perhaps a sudden turn is likely in Rakesh's career – the minister's unusually warm treatment was unexpected and out of character in my opinion. There is an old saying, 'a lamp becomes brighter before extinguishing'. In politics every relation is weighed on the balance of profit and loss, and I get a premonition of the same."

"Has Rakesh said something?" queried Savita.

"Some time ago he confided that the minister's demeanour had become indifferent and he might have to leave." But the situation looked very different, at least on the surface.

"Sister, your alarming thoughts most probably have no basis. We will see when the time comes."

"Maybe, you are right."

Afterwards, Savita described her strange dream and sought to resolve its mystery.

"I don't believe in dreams – even so, its only relevance is to prepare you for a new life."

She conceded, "Your analysis seems logical."

It was just after midday, and they decided to go shopping. Both were enjoying tea in a restaurant when Ragini said, "Today it is a holiday. Will Alok-ji have spare time?"

"Ask him."

After sometime Alok joined them, “I am happy to see you both – another round of coffee and snacks?”

“How do you spend your time on holidays?” Savita seemed curious.

“In reading books, in imaginative worlds, and occasionally on golf courses.”

Suddenly principal sahib appeared from nowhere, exclaimed, “Alok Babu, when did you come here?” and took a seat at the table.

Savita introduced them. “Ragini is my close friend – rather my elder sister in all matters.”

Principal Sahib explained, “I came here to purchase a piece of furniture. I liked the piece but the wood has become hollow from the inside because of termites and there is no remedy.” Before anyone could intervene, he continued, “Loneliness, similarly, makes one's life hollow, and when the realisation comes it is already too late for any remedy. As age advances, the depth of this hollowness deepens.”

Alok and Savita looked at each other obliquely; both were grave. Rising from his seat, he said, “Alok Babu, a cultural event is going to be held in the school in two days, and you are invited. It is Savita who will manage the stage.”

Principal Sahib was gone but he had left an air of heavy silence.

Ragini's voice broke that heaviness. “It was just chance that principal sahib appeared before us. Whatever he said was not pre-planned or preconceived but life's philosophy was concealed in his statement.”

Alok yielded, “I have come to the same conclusion; his words have a powerful message.”

Bewildered, Savita questioned, “Does it have any connection to my strange dream?”

Alok raised his eyes. “Which dream?”

But Ragini closed the topic. “Possibly.”

Savita suggested, “It is a fine day, why don't we spend some time in the nearby park?”

Driving his car Alok enquired, "Savita, will you also present an item, a song or music, at the cultural event?"

"I haven't decided yet, but will you get time to go?"

"I will try – it will give me an excuse to see you once more." A smile came to her lips, which could not remain hidden from Ragini's sharp eyes.

She said, "When the tide of love comes, it does not subside easily and surfing under its waves gives absolute pleasure."

Savita was surprised at the depth of her observation, "How do you know?"

"Whether love is for the lover or the husband, for god or art, the feeling is the same. Sometimes I forget everything around me when deeply involved in painting, which is also a blissful state."

"You are becoming a philosopher," Savita observed with affection.

The cultural event was due to start very shortly, and most of the guests had already arrived. Principal Sahib escorted Alok Saxena towards one of the front seats, reserved for dignitaries. The school children presented an entertaining program of songs, music, and short plays for about two hours. Afterwards, Savita requested the guests to come onto the stage and present an item of their choice, which was enthusiastically supported by the audience. The guests responded positively, many of them came forward and presented poems, jokes and couplets. Alok in his turn sang a melodious Bollywood song. Lastly, Savita played her sitar, which kept the audience captivated and spellbound. Clad in a white sari, with black hair flowing past her shoulders and holding a sitar in her hands, she looked like a replica of goddess Saraswati. Alok felt as if his imagination had come alive and he remained lost in the dreamland. When she finished, she was greeted with prolonged clapping. In the meantime someone from the audience proposed that Alok sing a song to the tune of her sitar and this was so vociferously supported by the audience that they could not deny them. Their joint performance was enchanting and mutually inspirational. Savita arrived at her decision.

Alok's sister's birthday was approaching. Savita was convinced that his mother would certainly make a proposal at this occasion. She phoned Ragini. "If both of you come with me, that would be a great psychological help." She agreed.

Savita wanted to talk to her father once more before going to the party. She told her father, "Alok has invited me to his home for his younger sister's birthday party. It is quite possible that a question about our relationship will arise. I need your advice and fatherly guidance."

"I have already said that I would be proud of any decision you make and I reiterate that. A few days ago I learnt from principal sahib that your joint performance with Alok was indeed pleasing and emotional." This signal was enough for her.

On the day of the birthday party, Rakesh and Ragini arrived at Savita's house in the afternoon. Ragini teased Savita, "The lightening of beauty will fall somewhere today."

"You are always ahead in making jokes."

Rakesh left to do some work, asking them to be ready on time for the evening party. Ragini and Savita displayed their gifts – Ragini had made an attractive painting and Savita had knitted a multi-coloured cardigan. She had also purchased a woollen shawl for Alok's mother. Ragini praised her understanding: "It shows your sensitivity and maturity." The time passed in small talk and soon they had to get ready. Ragini stepped forward. "I will choose your dress." She selected one sari–blouse set, which was a bit glamorous but dignified: the mixture of colours was eye-catching but sober. Savita agreed to wear the selected outfit after some initial reservation. Ragini arranged her hair in a modern style and did her make-up. Standing before the mirror, Savita was struck by her own charming beauty. Ragini whispered in her ears, "Keep away from naughty eyes!"

Rakesh exclaimed, “How come, this new Savita!”

As soon as their car arrived at the gate, Alok came forward and welcomed them. He introduced them to his family members and close guests; his sister, Kamini, very lovingly embraced Savita and praised her as if the party was to celebrate her.

“Kamini-ji, your sweet behaviour has propelled me into a lovely world, thank you very much,” Savita said with humility.

“Then no 'thank you' and no formality – simply call me Kamini.” They were immediately on friendly terms.

Alok came along. “My mother is waiting for you, please meet her.”

Savita touched her feet respectfully, and the elderly lady embraced her with great affection.

“There is too much noise on this side, let us go to the other side,” said the elderly lady. She walked Savita around the big house and lamented, “This house is full of pictures but they are lifeless, voiceless, filled with gloomy messages, and I see the same scene in Alok's life. He is eagerly waiting for you in order to take another chance in life.” Her steps became unstable. “I am tired, let us sit and have a cup of tea.”

She went into the kitchen and looked for the kettle, but Savita moved ahead of her. “This is the duty of the daughter-in-law.” She helped her sit comfortably in a chair. It was not difficult to understand the meaning of this symbolic statement; Alok's mother sensed much relief.

“I have brought a small gift for you,” proffered Savita.

“This gift is most valuable to me, I will treasure it safely.” Tears of happiness filled her eyes, Savita could see.

In the meantime Alok announced, “It is time to cut the birthday cake, everyone's waiting for you.”

Ragini came to the kitchen to collect them.

The ritual of the cake-cutting was over, people wished Kamini a happy birthday and sang the occasional song. Putting a piece of cake into Savita's mouth, Kamini said, “The next function in this house will be from your side, and don't forget to invite me!"

"Have confidence in God, your desire will be fulfilled." Savita came forward and served a piece of cake to all the guests; she was already proving a homely host. Alok invited all the guests for dinner.

When most of the guests were gone, Kamini asked Savita to assist her in opening the gifts. Alok interjected, "Who will decide whose gift is to be opened first?"

"It is my birthday, I will decide." She put on the cardigan and observed, "I can't believe you are also skilled in handicrafts, besides being an expert in musical performance. I must take this lovely gift with me abroad." She decided to hang Ragini's painting in her office.

Alok uttered, "It appears I have become secondary and the second chapter of my life has begun from today."

Ragini saw the glow of a smile appearing on Savita's face; she nodded happily. It was getting late, and they prepared to leave.

"I will be back after saying goodbye to Alok's mother." Savita walked away.

The elderly lady became sentimental. "I will come soon to meet your father. I have kept a small gift in your bag, please keep its honour."

"Yes, Mother," she also became emotional at her touching words.

Rakesh and Ragini spent the night at Savita's house. Ragini said, "Can I congratulate you today for finding a new life partner? The rituals will take their course."

"Today I am ready to accept."

They embraced each other. "Our mission has borne fruit."

Ragini added, "I would like to see my uncle before returning home."

"I was going to propose that too – all of us, including Rakesh, will be there."

The next morning at the breakfast table Rakesh also congratulated Savita. Soon Savita's father joined them.

Ragini spoke first, "Kindly bless my younger sister for entering into a new life. Alok is a very civilised, capable and conscientious person – his mother will see you very shortly."

He embraced Savita and exclaimed happily, "I have already brought sweets!"

Savita took a small box from her bag, "Alok's mother gave this gift last night, but I did not have the courage to open it by myself. I was afraid of whether I would be able to honour it or not."

A beautifully packed gold chain emerged from the box and Ragini put it on Savita's neck. The elderly father exclaimed once again, "This indeed is its right place!"

"Respect for Indian culture is alive in your thinking."

The excitement and din had subsided, and Alok had also gone away for a few days. Savita was in a pensive mood. What will the response of her four-year-old son, Keshav, be? *Will he accept Alok as a part of his life, will he adjust with the extended family and, more importantly, will he approve of my decision in later years when he is grown up?* These were vexing questions with no definite answer. She felt perplexed and decided to see Alok's mother.

"Yes, your worries are genuine, I had foreseen them. You mother is not alive, so I will try to take that role. When you're at school you can drop Keshav at my place for some time, I will give him full affection. A small child is always hungry for affection, I am sure Kamini and Alok will follow my lead. This should lessen your anxieties."

Savita felt assured. Within a week Keshav was attached to the new set-up. Whenever Savita came to pick him up, she had to promise to bring him back again the next day. When Alok returned from the tour after a week he was rather overwhelmed and said, "Keep this routine, it is refreshing."

Savita replied, "As you wish."

Alok's father phoned Savita's father. "We need your blessing in welcoming Savita as my daughter-in-law – it will bring fortune to both the families."

"I was also thinking that – you are most welcome," replied Savita's father.

They fixed an auspicious day for the initial ceremony, according to tradition.

The next day Alok called. "I was often busy and out for the past several days, can we spend some time together?"

"I was waiting for that." Savita seemed exalted.

Driving together, Alok intimated, "My parents want to offer you some ornaments and dresses, as per family tradition. You can purchase those items of your choice from a reputed shop in the main city and Kamini might come along to assist you. We can drive there within two hours."

"I will have to honour their wishes."

They went to a restaurant for coffee.

Alok said earnestly, "I have wanted to tell you something for a long time but it is getting hard to wait any longer. Do I have your permission?"

"Go ahead, say without hesitation." Savita looked equally solemn.

Alok took Savita's hand into his own, looked into her eyes, and whispered in a low voice, "I love you."

Savita responded with equal eagerness, "I was waiting for these three words. I love you too."

"These three words are not less powerful than rituals or ceremonial hymns; it is our obligation to honour them." These words echoed in their minds for several minutes.

Jubilant, Alok said, "Had we been in a foreign country, we could have celebrated this moment with champagne, but it is only coffee here."

They raised their coffee glasses. "Cheers!"

On the appointed day the relatives and friends of both families gathered in a hall; Rakesh, Ragini and principal sahib were among the notable guests. A priest blew his conch at the auspicious moment, Alok and Savita exchanged their engagement rings and promised to be life partners, and well-wishers showered them with flowers. They decided that the wedding would take place at the local court after one month. The occasion turned into a mini-celebration with plenty of food and drink. People came forward and wished them a happy beginning. Principal Sahib added, "Time is like a huge mirror which preserves many images of our life, some blurred, some sharp; one needs to see the right image each morning." He continued, "If you ever see two images, always try to look into the present because we live in it. The past is like a dream, and the future is like imagination." Alok and Savita were thoughtful; these words had deep meaning for a 'life in action'.

Savita had returned to her bedroom to rest after a hectic day. The memory of Dinesh was knocking at her mind – it was his letter that had ignited the flame of desire for a new life that was being fulfilled. She earnestly wanted to thank him and personally invite him to the wedding. She could hardly sleep – she had been tossing and turning and was feeling uncomfortable.

She almost jumped when her mobile phone rang. Who could be at this odd hour – perhaps Dinesh?"

The voice was crisp. "Hello, Savita, are you listening? Is it too late?"

She said, "I had heard that a call from the inner heart travels a long distance, and today it has come true. I was remembering, and feeling restless to talk to you, and my feelings have travelled. I wonder whether this is telepathy!" Then she described briefly the events of the past few months and invited him for the wedding.

She opened her heart. "When Alok was placing the engagement ring on my finger, it seemed your shadow was present there to bless me! I wish it will come true."

Dinesh was equally candid. "I know it is very late in the night but out of some unknown attraction I felt an urge to call you. It is a matter of great happiness and satisfaction that you have got a loving partner, my sincere congratulations! I would love to come for your wedding but the possibility looks remote because of very busy schedules. Cheer up and good night."

Now Savita was feeling much better; her happiness had doubled.

The initial formalities had ended very happily. Alok and Savita started planning for their new life, which was quite natural. Amidst that, Ragini called, "Rakesh has been appointed a junior political adviser in the New York consulate and minister sahib has asked him to take up the new assignment within two weeks. Rakesh is also pleased but I am getting a bit anxious. He will travel alone and I will join him after a few months. This appointment seems to have come with the minister's knowledge, and that was possibly the reason that he asked so many questions and tried to assess my position."

Before Savita could respond, she added, "The next election is due within six months and at this juncture minister sahib needs a capable, experienced and locally known adviser. On that basis Rakesh is more influential, so why send him abroad? I suspect some mystery in this decision."

Savita argued, "One must face any situation as an optimist. Until now Rakesh has proved his ability and sharpness of mind on every occasion and I am sure he will do so in the future. If he is satisfied, you should not worry."

"Perhaps you are right."

On Sunday, Savita got up late. Alok was on the phone. "Have you seen today's newspaper?"

"No, I haven't. What's the matter?"

"First you read it then I will call. There is a news item concerning Rakesh on the third page."

She read the entire section carefully and tried to guess its immediate implications. The coverage included the news of his foreign assignment as well as some related political gossip. According to this coverage the youth wing of the party resented the minister and it was exerting pressure to make Rakesh their leader. It also mentioned that the general public was impressed by Rakesh's independent and objective views on many issues, that some powerful leaders had met him secretly, and because of these developments the minister had conspired to send him abroad. On the fourth page there was another brief report: Rakesh had no prior indication of this appointment, the minister had possibly concluded the deal without taking him into his confidence, and this had given rise to many rumours in political circles.

Savita called back, “I don't see anything unusual in this news – it's simple and plain.”

“I also think so, but Rakesh should remain cautious. Reporters will keep an eye on his every move and will not refrain from imputing any motive. In politics spicy rumours spread very quickly, there is no time left to differentiate between right and wrong.”

“I will certainly warn Ragini on your behalf.” Savita took it as a routine matter.

Alok continued talking. “There is an old proverb, 'no smoke without fire' and so rumours also have an attraction. Possibly, minister sahib considers Rakesh his political rival and Rakesh might have momentarily entertained the idea of becoming the youth leader of this area. It is hard to know the truth. But during the past three years whatever minister sahib has done to enable Rakesh to emerge as an important figure of this area is well known, and in return he must expect complete faith and confidence. It is possible that he has become suspicious of Rakesh's loyalty. By giving a high position in New York he has given Rakesh a unique chance to reach greater heights and at the same time added prestige to this area. Rakesh has to tread a long path and it demands the display of personal commitment and honesty. In my profession genuine commitment has great value and in my opinion politics is also a form of it. The first law of politics is 'trample your competitor, even if imaginary' and minister sahib is an established player of this game! He has just looked for a respectable solution.”

Savita was listening intently, and exclaimed, "Did you also receive a degree in politics?"

"I manage a business, it does not prosper without politics," Alok concluded.

Savita called Rakesh in the evening and made him aware of Alok's views.

Two days later there was another item concerning Rakesh on the fourth page of the newspaper:

> Despite several attempts the reporters could not contact the minister. Rakesh Sharma has said, "I have worked for minister sahib with my best ability and confidence, and I have great regard for him. Presently I have no interest in active politics but who knows the future – all rumours to the contrary are baseless. During the last two days many people have congratulated me and I am grateful to all of them. While living in New York my mind and heart will always remain with them."

Reading this report Alok thought: *Rakesh's statement has put a full stop to those rumours, but he has kept his option open for the future. This is a very familiar first move in politics, but I don't know how minister sahib will react to it! For him the coming election is more important.*

Time passed very quickly, and minister sahib himself was at the airport to see Rakesh off. He said authoritatively, "You will be a representative of this country in a foreign land, discharge your duties by remaining above personal views and ambitions." He assured Ragini that Rakesh would have no hardship there and she would be joining him within the next few months. He further advised her to keep in touch in case any help was needed. Ragini expressed sincere thanks for his magnanimity and felt relieved of her initial suspicions.

Rakesh looked at Savita. "I am leaving Ragini under your care, I am fortunate." Finally he turned to Alok. "You are now a part of this triangular bond, keep its honour. I am sorry that I won't be a witness to your wedding but Ragini will take my place – she is my image."

"We will save our wedding cake and see you in New York. Bon voyage!" Soon the plane disappeared out of sight.

Dinesh and Sushma were present at New York airport to receive Rakesh, and someone from the Indian consulate was also there. While waiting for the flight they came across each other. Rakesh passed through the immigration and exchanged greetings with all of them. It was Friday evening, and the consulate would be closed for the weekend. So Dinesh proposed that Rakesh spend two days with them and then he would drop him at the consulate office on Monday. The representative from the consulate had no objection but reminded Rakesh that he had an appointment with the senior political adviser at eleven o'clock. Dinesh went for coffee at a nearby stall.

Sushma turned to Rakesh. "I have heard a lot about you from Dinesh. In fact his visit became very enjoyable after meeting you and I have seen some pictures also. When is your wife expected to come over here? I have heard Savita-ji's wedding is also approaching soon."

Rakesh was gracious. "I am obliged that you have maintained such a close relationship even while living so far away. It may take a few months before Ragini arrives here and in the meantime I should be able to find a suitable flat with your help." Dinesh came with coffee and some savouries, and they proceeded towards the car. Their first meeting left a good impression.

The evening darkness engulfed the sky, and the unending arc of lights along the roads and the display of the multi-coloured brightness of New York City were eye-catching. Rakesh was astonished at the rows and rows of illuminated skyscrapers, at their anticipated wealth and the overall splendour of the city's heart. He reasoned that it was probably this city that led to the idea of heaven on earth! Dinesh broke his chain of thoughts. "The weather forecast is favourable and it should be nice to get around and become acquainted with the city." It was getting late so they had dinner in a restaurant.

It was time for rest after a long flight, Rakesh liked the guest room, which was simple but well arranged. Bidding goodnight, Sushma said, "You may call Ragini otherwise both sides will remain restless. It is the weekend so you can sleep in." The next two days went by unnoticed in conversation and enjoying the city life. By this time Sushma had entered the close circle of friendship and the veil of formality had almost vanished. On Monday Rakesh got to the consulate office in time.

His first day in the office was interesting and meaningful. The senior political adviser, his boss, in a sense, gazed at him mysteriously while welcoming him with a handshake and introduced him to other persons in his chamber. He said, "Looking at your qualifications and experience this appointment seems extraordinary, maybe the minister saw some unusual skills that are not apparent. I have heard that you are clever in delivering extempore and effective speeches at opportune moments and this is the first requirement of politics. However, in this country there are fewer lectures and a much more objective assessment of subject matters and policy issues, for which higher education and analytically decisive minds are needed. Let us see how successful you are in this environment. When a minister or a high official comes here, it is our responsibility to advise them on how to interact with the media and occasionally we also have to prepare their official statements. You can see me any time and other officials will help you in getting settled here or for miscellaneous works."

It became clear to Rakesh that he had to pass a difficult test and also uphold the dignity of the minister, who was obviously instrumental in securing his appointment. He said politely, "Politics and administration are complementary in our country and I will try to uphold their dignity." A ray of a smile appeared on the senior adviser's face.

Now that only two weeks were left until their wedding, Alok was finalising the list of guests and he advised Savita to have a look. The list already had Rakesh, Ragini, principal sahib and some colleagues from her school, and a few more were included at her suggestion. There were many names unfamiliar to Savita but seeing the name of minister sahib she queried, "Is he closely connected to your family?"

"Yes, Father has known him since long before he was close to being a minister. There exists a natural relationship between business and politics; there are several other names connected with politics but they are not necessarily in electoral politics."

Savita became inquisitive. "I have heard that heavy donations are collected by political parties from industrialists and entrepreneurs, and in return they are bestowed with many benefits or tax subsidies which become the medium of the common man's exploitation. Do you also give such monetary gifts to political parties?"

Alok analysed coherently, "Giving donations to political parties and taking benefits in return are two different subjects; they cannot be seen with the same lens. In several democracies of the world political parties are legally permitted to accept donations from individuals and the corporate world, especially at election time, and they have to furnish an account of their expenses. In return it is like a tradition to give some benefits but within an acceptable limit. The violation of such limits is harmful - it can become a tool of social exploitation which may generate social instability."

"You have started giving a lecture in political science; that is enough. Let's go out for coffee."

While they were having coffee Savita suddenly asked, "Did you have prior knowledge of Rakesh's new appointment?"

Alok was not prepared for such a question but he could not remain silent. He said, "A political leader does not see with two eyes only, nor does he listen with two ears only. Minister Sahib has access to high echelons, he is himself a skilful player in politics, so you can imagine how many images of an event are formed in his mind. His close advisers, sycophants, internal opponents, are also his eyes and ears. Perhaps, Rakesh has become a victim of split images, I don't know how. I see minister sahib only occasionally - I don't live with him - and he cannot be questioned either. Sometime ago he consulted me, he was a bit angry, and he could have harmed Rakesh, but he was also aware of your close friendship with Ragini. The appointment in New York consulate was considered the best way out."

Savita was overwhelmed. "You have already burdened me with obligation, how can I repay you?"

"What obligation between partners? This matter will remain between the two of us."

Savita divulged, "Your extra interest in the first newspaper report rang alarm bells and raised many questions in my mind. I am proud of you." She kissed his hand.

The highly awaited day had arrived. Alok and Savita got married in the court of law surrounded by a large number of well-wishers. Ragini signed as a witness on behalf of Savita, and Kamini did the same on behalf of Alok. They came out of the court as husband and wife, took blessings from elders, and accepted greetings from friends. There was a reception party in the evening, which was attended by guests and dignitaries. Minister Sahib could not come himself but he had sent a large bouquet of flowers and a congratulatory card with the message, "I have no daughter-in-law but I see that image in Savita. I hope she accepts it." Savita became emotional.

On behalf of the guests, principal sahib spoke. "We are extremely happy to see Alok and Savita as husband and wife. Their wedding sends a new message to society – toady women are capable of making honourable decisions about their lives. Some people may consider it the manifestation of Western influence, but this is indeed the preferable form of the modern composite culture." The hall resounded with clapping.

On the other side of the globe Rakesh was a bit upset because he missed Savita's wedding and he was not getting focused at his ill-defined job; in a sense he was facing minor turmoil within himself. The senior adviser called a meeting and said, "The foreign minister will be in New York within the next few weeks for a discussion on matters related to India's import of uranium. This is not a new subject; those who are opposed and those who are in favour are entrenched in their views despite numerous meetings and dialogues over the past several years. In order to win the debate, a new perspective is required."

There was a burdensome silence in the room when Rakesh asked, "What is expected of us?"

"There are three of you in this meeting, I expect each of you to prepare a brief preliminary document for discussion. The records of the past debates and dialogues can be obtained from my secretary for reference, but no photocopying please." Rakesh thought this was his examination as well.

After several days of churning ideas, Rakesh wrote, "India's import of uranium has been facing several questions for decades. The main question is whether India will use the imported uranium for producing nuclear weapons or for power generation and other peaceful applications only. On this point there is a clash of opinions both inside and outside India, which in fact is the right of a pluralistic democracy. But its conclusion should be drawn in the light of the age-old Indian tradition and philosophy."

He elaborated his arguments. "The journey of human civilisation from ancient times to the modern space age is ingrained in the hearts and minds of the Indian populace. The essence of spiritualism has travelled from east to west, the spirit of 'the world as family' is alive even today. They make up our heritage, our identity and our ladder for progress in the future."

In the end he concluded, "One should have binding faith in the world's largest democracy, whose foundations are based on truth and non-violence. The history is witness to the fact that India has never imposed war on any other country and it is bound by the same resolution even today. Giving uranium to India can bring development to a huge population; it will not increase the probability of spreading nuclear arms on the subcontinent. This is the voice of the Indian soul, the innate faith of the Indian masses."

Rakesh was reading an interesting article in the newspaper; its title was "People's faith in politics". It mentioned, "In a democracy the changing views of the masses and the administration do not match all the time. The views of the public at large have water-like mobility, whereas the administration seems rigid and unresponsive. After all, elections cannot be held on each issue!"

The telephone rang: there was a meeting in the senior adviser's office.

By the time Rakesh entered the office, two other people were already seated. At the direction of the senior adviser each of them read their notes and explained their view points. Then the senior adviser observed, "The notes prepared by Rakesh Sharma has newness, but can one win today's political debate on the basis of idealism, history, democracy, and cultural heritage?"

Rakesh argued, "The notes of the other two colleagues harp on the same familiar points, like the so-called international reservation on political grounds, the possibility of a regional war, the danger of the pilfering of nuclear materials, the lack of proper security due to terrorism, and they forcefully defend our position on these critical issues. However, these arguments are already well documented – this time they are simply dressed in different language. Though these points are very important, their repetition may not give any additional advantage."

"I will consider these notes carefully and communicate my observations to the foreign minister," observed the senior adviser.

Rakesh intervened, "Under the prevailing official procedures in our country the opinion of a junior officer hardly reaches the ministerial level, it is the prerogative of senior officers. A junior officer hardly knows whether his advice had any value or not. But this country is different, its official culture is different – here no voice can be suppressed and at the same time personal accountability is effectively enforced. I greatly appreciate this work culture and hence I expect you to forward all the notes with your own comments to the foreign ministry for a final decision from their experts." The senior adviser was a bit surprised at his fearless tone.

Alok and Savita were busy getting adjusted to their new life. She spent days redecorating the house to ensure a lively touch, finding ways to raise her son in a changed situation, opening gifts, dispatching thank-you cards to friends and relatives, and other small things. She wrote to Dinesh, "You suddenly appeared before me as a source of inspiration and my world has changed. I hope your ideals will guide me in the future also." To Rakesh, she wrote, "Your dedication, humility and sense of purpose always impressed me and I hope to learn much more in the future also." Several weeks had passed, and she hardly had time to talk to Ragini leisurely.

After completing his first major assignment in the consulate, Rakesh felt more confident and started taking a greater interest in political events. Reading socio-political columns in American newspapers became one of his main engagements. During midday recess he would go to a nearby restaurant and read newspapers while eating lunch in a corner. One day a young man approached and asked, "Can I have my lunch at your table?"

"Why not? I would be happy." The man was smartly dressed in a blue suit. Rakesh extended a welcoming hand with questions in his eyes.

Shaking hands, he said, "I am Richard Hamilton and I work as an independent newspaper reporter. At lunchtime I often see you reading newspapers very attentively, and I could not resist my curiosity in talking to you. I am sorry for the interruption."

"I am Rakesh Sharma, I work for the Indian consulate. The United States is like the centre of the global activities and the newspapers help me understand some of their ramifications. After a busy schedule I hardly find time to watch television at home."

"Did you find any interesting articles in today's newspaper?"

Rakesh became mentally alert. Could this be investigative journalism – so common in this country? He answered casually, "Yes, there is one interesting article on the opinion page illustrating the arguments that support the export of uranium to India and those that oppose. You might have heard that Indians take a keen interest in politics - they can discuss politics for hours for sheer entertainment without minding whether they have sufficient food at the table. I also have the same infection."

Richard was not far behind. "I have also heard that when Indian parliaments are in session the sale of cinema tickets goes down – people find free entertainment more engaging."

"You are a powerful satirist, you should try Bollywood!" retorted Rakesh.

Both laughed loudly; they found a natural bond of friendship. They also had a glimpse of each other's sharp intelligence.

Sipping coffee, Richard summed up, "Rightly or wrongly, the Americans have much less confidence in the political wisdom and commitment of Indian leaders, who seem hungry for life-long positions of power that give them access to all privileges and comforts. The persistent agitation of the masses against corruption and the criminalisation of politics has also attracted world attention and, occasionally, behind the screen, there is a talk about emerging instability in this largest democracy. Therefore one group opposes the export of uranium to India and it has prominently come to the surface in today's article. At the same time the other side strongly believes an assessment of India should be made on the basis of its glorious history, its successful democracy and the peace-loving nature of its masses. This group has openly advocated that the export of uranium to India be permitted for the economic development of its huge population."

Rakesh had also read the article and he was happy that his own arguments were consistent with the supporting views expressed, but he kept a low profile. He had to maintain confidentiality otherwise his job would be endangered. So he simply said, "I am not an expert in this field and it does not fall within my direct responsibility to comment on such matters. I hope the senior officials will take note of this article and perhaps forward it to the foreign ministry."

"I also hope so," Richard nodded.

Leaving the table they said, "We will meet again."

Rakesh wanted to refute the contrary points of view in this article but the question was how to publish it? Perhaps Richard could help.

He collected his arguments in the shape of a brief comment. "Attempts to frame new imaginary grounds in order to deny uranium to India are fallacious and totally unwanted. In my opinion mass agitations are a sign of a matured democracy through which purification of politics and society can be achieved. In the past also similar agitations took place and they strengthened the foundation of democracy though enhanced political awareness. In fact this awareness has preserved the unity and integrity of a huge country despite poverty and lack of material resources. In the United States such mass agitations have played an important role in ending discrimination between whites and non-whites; in Britain they were instrumental in alleviating the economic and social status of labourers."

The next day Rakesh confided in Richard and opened his mind.

"I will try to publish it under a fictitious name," assured Richard.

Alok and Savita had been married for two months, had settled into new life and were happy. They had just had lunch when minister sahib called and after formal pleasantries invited them for dinner. Alok became perplexed. "Why such haste this time?" On several occasions in the past he informed them two or three days in advance. Minister Sahib's wife usually lived in the village; she considered the huge ministerial mansion a fashionable prison and she could hardly stay in it for more than a few days in one stretch. These days she was at the mansion. Savita and Alok touched her feet reverentially and she embraced them affectionately. Minister Sahib and Alok went to the garden with their drinks and Savita busied herself by showing her wedding album to his wife.

Minister Sahib said in a low voice, "Today someone from the foreign ministry phoned that Rakesh had passed the examination and swiftly cut the connection – it appeared like confidential information. I immediately called back on the same number but there was no one there. Was he preparing for an exam? It is quite possible that he was preparing for admission into higher education, but in that case why disconnect so hurriedly? It was not a confidential matter. I am not able to understand the purpose and meaning of this phone call."

Alok also seemed nonplussed. "I don't know anything; maybe Ragini can shed some light. I have also studied in the United States and I don't think Rakesh could have passed any important exam within three months, especially with the burden of his official duties at the consulate." They walked in silence, as if a debate was going on in their minds.

After a while Alok broke the silence. "Most likely the word examination has a symbolic meaning, and it might be related to current activities of the consular office. Rakesh is blessed with sharp intelligence and he is hard working too. It is quite possible he has shown his unusual calibre there too."

"I will try to find out from my level, but in the meantime it will remain confidential."

"That would be appropriate. If I come to know something, I will notify you."

At the other end, the senior adviser invited Rakesh into his office, closed the door and showed him the fax received from the New Delhi foreign office, which said, "On careful analysis of the notes prepared by the consular staff and the opinions expressed in American newspapers, it was decided that Rakesh Sharma be entrusted with the task of preparing the final draft. For the convenience of the foreign minister a list of probable questions, their answers, and necessary enclosures be also prepared. This office would like to receive all materials within a week." Rakesh heard "You have passed the examination" and a brief smile appeared on his face.

For several days minister sahib could not find a reliable answer to his suspicions, and neither could Alok. Ragini was to leave for New York in two weeks. Minister Sahib himself called Rakesh. "Do you need something from here?" Under the pretext of this formality he enquired, "Are you preparing for some exam? Can I help in any manner?"

Rakesh's sharp mind became alert and he said politely, "I have no such intention."

Ragini arrived in New York. She received plenty of support from Dinesh and Sushma in arranging her house and she profusely thanked them. This deepened their bond of friendship and by this time Richard had also become well acquainted with them. One day she hosted a dinner for all of them. Richard had already heard about Ragini's paintings and he expressed his eagerness to see them. He observed, "A natural and powerful image of Indian family life can be visualised in these paintings and their exhibition would be interesting. If you agree, I can arrange that." Richard's proposal was appreciated by all.

The space was made available by a local school and its hall was given a festive look. Ten paintings were selected and Ragini prepared a brief contextual description for each one. Through Richard's contacts a notice for the exhibition appeared in the community newspapers of the area and the chief of the local council agreed to inaugurate the show. Rakesh invited some colleagues and Dinesh brought two people from his media advertising company. It was the first exhibition of paintings by an Indian housewife and this created a curiosity among local women. People came in good numbers, some speeches were given, local journalists interviewed Ragini, and on the whole the function was quite successful. All the paintings were sold out and Ragini got some fresh orders. In her brief speech Ragini said, "I am overwhelmed at the love and goodwill shown by the local residents and I am greatly indebted to them. I would like to donate fifty percent of the proceeds received from the sale of these paintings to this school and I hope the honourable principal will kindly accept it. I sincerely thank all the organisers for their enthusiastic support." There was a loud applause from the audience. The next day a full account of the exhibition, along with photographs, appeared in local newspapers. Ragini became famous overnight – she had never imagined that.

Time was passing quickly, and Ragini became busy in her work. After almost a month, Richard and Rakesh had lunch in their favourite restaurant. Because of the coming Easter holidays their workload was limited. Richard initiated: "I have seen several of your writings published in newspapers under fictitious names and people have shown interest in them. You have ability and dedication to become a successful journalist and then your domain will extend to the whole world. What you need is self-confidence and resolution."

"It is not possible while remaining in the government job – I cannot use my real name under the code of conduct. Also, leaving my job is a big decision; one needs economic resources for day-to-day expenses and survival," said Rakesh in a depressing tone.

"From the remuneration of your writings you may be able to survive."

"I will consider it."

At the dinner table Rakesh apprised Ragini of the discussion he had with Richard and sought her advice. She said, "Within a short time the meaning of my life has changed – I have seen a glimpse of my hidden talents. Through my paintings

I can make people aware of the salient features of the Indian lifestyle and its culture, which is also a part of a service to the nation. Before coming to this country I was just a housewife and there was no scope for my talents to flourish – even you were unaware of them. I very much agree with Richard's insight and assessment, and in the near future I should be able to partially support ourselves financially. Today the distinction between national and foreign is vanishing rapidly in the field of education, profession and cultural outlooks. In essence, we are rapidly moving towards becoming global citizens and the whole world has become one stage for action. You have merit and you can be a part of that platform."

Rakesh had never seen her being so forceful and logical. He argued, "There is strength in your logic, but I have a responsibility towards my country. Just now the foreign ministry has expressed confidence in me, appreciated my ability, and maybe they have greater expectations of me. At this critical juncture, resigning from the consulate is not justified and I can be charged with neglecting vital national interest. You should carefully consider both sides of the coin."

She shot back, "You are unnecessarily becoming sentimental and agitated – I haven't asked you to resign right now. Every job is a contract, not a lifelong bargain. Are people not changing jobs in our own country? Is it not a growing trend in professional services? Even the government sector is not immune to this. Moreover, your assignment at the consulate is neither permanent nor does it have a fixed tenure; it is a political appointment and it can be terminated any time. I still suspect there is a political reason behind all this and what's the guarantee that minister sahib will retain his position after the election? Even if he survives, will you continue getting his support? If you return to India, will you be happy in your previous government job? Will you silently tolerate the cynical comments of colleagues and the pressure of senior officers?"

Rakesh was listening to her attorney-like arguments in silence, and was dumbfounded. He concluded, "In a very short time your thinking has changed – it has logical insight and the influence of Western education. I will reconsider the matter."

"You can also discuss this issue with Dinesh."

"Yes, I will."

After a few days Dinesh shared his experience. "An occasion does not wait for anyone – one has to identify it and grab it at the opportune moment. If there are compulsions to remain within one's own country, and there are prospects of achieving the desired goals as well, then any lust or hunger for adopting a different way of life in a foreign land should be renounced. For example, Alok is working there despite being educated in the United States because he has a successful business, progressive future, and contacts in high political circles, which are essential in the Indian context. On the other side, Savita is very deeply and emotionally attached to the land for which her husband became a martyr. I did not have such compulsions and so I landed in this country. I am satisfied that whatever I have achieved here was unthinkable in my own country. My talents and aspirations would have been blunted there in the so-called 'rat race' of hierarchy. Whatever I have done in my field has also benefited business and industry in my own country, and this is the emerging global pathway. Ragini has rightly observed that the distinction between national and foreign is rapidly vanishing. The final decision lies in your hands, but caution is needed."

Rakesh agreed with him as a matter of principle and asked, "What short of caution?"

"You should be assured of getting a job offer for two years from any institution so that your visa gets revalidated. For this, you can talk to Richard."

Rakesh and Ragini thought over the matter again and concluded that it was more prudent to work in the United States for two to three years and then decide about the future course. Within a few days Richard arranged a meeting between Rakesh and the head of a big print media company. The meeting was fruitful and he had to make a final decision within two months.

Having coffee in a restaurant Rakesh said, "The foreign minister will be coming in two weeks. This information has already appeared in newspapers but details of his official engagements have not been announced yet and I don't know what my role would be, if any. I would only be able to make a decision after that."

Richard suggested, "There is no hurry but excessive delay is not helpful either. In this digital age the sale of newspapers is declining, dark clouds are hovering over print media and even their stability could be endangered. It is thoughtful and objective columns like yours which keep readers interested and a publisher would want to take advantage. In the meantime I would advise you to prepare one article on the foreign policy of South-East Asian countries for publication when your foreign minister is here."

Perplexed, Rakesh uttered, "Under my name?"

"No, under a fictitious name, as usual."

"I hope this is the final move on the chessboard!"

"I think so," agreed Richard.

Minister Sahib was alone in his mansion, watching the evening news on television. A private channel broke the news. "The foreign minister will be going to the United States of America within a week; the details of his official engagements are confidential but according to reliable sources a junior adviser has prepared the draft of probable questions and answers for the convenience of the minister." After listening to this announcement, he became delirious, as if his eyes of wisdom had suddenly opened and he shouted, "This junior adviser is none other than Rakesh." At this conclusion he was less pleased than angered. "How did he dare conceal this matter from me? He got that position because of me, it is a sheer breach of obligation!" He phoned Alok but he was not available.

The next morning Alok came and analysed the situation, "If Rakesh had really prepared the draft, he must have been under strict orders to maintain total confidentiality. Any breach would have been sufficient for his removal from the service and that would have exposed him to other disciplinary actions as well."

Minister Sahib's rage subsided to some extent but his inner bitterness did not die. A seed of anxiety crept into Alok's mind.

Savita called Ragini and made her aware of the news on the Indian television. She congratulated Rakesh and also advised him to remain cautious because success usually brings more opponents and jealousy. Ragini was surprised, "Why this congratulations? Rakesh has not told me anything about his promotion or achievement, you must be confused. In fact the exhibition of my paintings went unexpectedly well and many people have congratulated me, but that has nothing to do with Rakesh."

Ragini became perturbed, with a ring of suspicions, and she wondered if there was some conspiracy against Rakesh. When Rakesh got this information he became alarmed. "Could it be the work of the senior adviser?" But he feigned ignorance. Ragini did not pursue the matter.

The next day the foreign minister would be arriving and so the ministry had constituted a team of three advisers to assist him in official discussions. Rakesh was missing from the team; he was astonished because it was he who had prepared the final draft on the expected subject. On seeing Rakesh face to face, the senior adviser approached. "I am myself surprised. Your removal the last minute must have occurred due to some political intervention – even I was not taken into confidence."

Rakesh realised that Savita's innocent message was an indication of future events. He was sad but not without determination.

It was the third day of the foreign minister's trip; his performance at the press conference in Washington was satisfactory. Feeling relieved, he expressed his desire to talk to the person who had prepared the final draft and the questionnaire. The senior adviser replied, "He is in New York."

“Why? He should have been within the advisory team.”

“His name was recommended but the external ministry did not include him.”

The foreign minister did not pursue the matter any further. Before going to bed that night he called his personal assistant. “Find out who played a role in removing the name of Rakesh Sharma from the advisory team.” Next morning he got the answer. He was nonplussed to know that it was the same state minister who only a few months ago was instrumental in getting Rakesh Sharma appointed at the consulate. Puzzled, he said to himself, “The matter will be investigated after I go back.”

It was a day of recess for the foreign minister, and he got up late in the morning. At the tea table his attention was drawn to a short, but prominently located article on South-East Asia in the local newspaper. “In these countries most of the talented officers with sharp, critical minds are unable to perform independently without political support; even the operation of the foreign policy is not immune to this culture. The so-called clash between India and Bharat has now shifted from an economic to a political level and its consequences are unknown. The political storm of Naxalism and Maoism, loaded with economic considerations, brought unseen upheavals during the sixties and seventies, and possibly a modified form of the same may emerge in coming years. The growth of foreign influence is also not unexpected. Hence the preservation of foresighted meritocracy is very important.” The foreign minister speculated, *‘Was it personally directed towards him?’* and ordered one of the consulate officers to find out the whereabouts of the author. The officer contacted the newspaper's editor, who responded, “To divulge the identity of a reporter is against the ethical code of the newspaper. If you want to send a written comment on the article, it can be published.” The foreign minister decided to see Rakesh Sharma in the afternoon.

When Rakesh entered the foreign minister's room, he found himself alone, which was very unusual for his junior position. After initial greetings the foreign minister said, "I am seeing you for the first time, thanks for the draft you prepared. Your perspective gives new grounds and appears meaningful in the current scenario. Now tell me something about your life, especially about the ups and downs in your service career." Rakesh described the main points of his career, including his debating skills, government job, and working relationship with minister sahib. He said nothing about his dealings at the consulate office.

"Are you satisfied with the working pattern at the consulate?"

"Yes, sir, I have worked with the best of my ability and I have received full cooperation."

"Do you also write for newspapers?"

"No, sir, this is against our service code," he said with a bit of uneasiness.

The secretary entered through the side door. "Sir, it is time to leave for the official dinner."

Rakesh thanked God at the sudden end of his interview with the foreign minister, though perspiration had already appeared on his forehead. The articles published under a fictitious name reflected many of his views, despite being substantially modified by Richard. In a sense he was technically right that he did not write for newspapers, but in politics perception is often more important than the ground reality. He might have faced trouble had the interview continued a bit longer, and he realised that the needle of suspicion had turned towards him.

Late in the evening he told Ragini about this interview and apologised for keeping her in the dark regarding his recent endeavours with the newspapers. She had no knowledge about his writing under fictitious names but she always suspected something when she found him working on the computer for long hours. She analysed the situation thoughtfully. "Whatever you have done was the basic urge of your talents; a sharp mind cannot be restrained within the bounds of routine works, and there is no need for you to apologise. However, I must say that you cannot remain under the cloak of a fictitious identity any longer – truth always prevails. The long and powerful hands of the consulate can locate you and then you will appear to be an offender – action can even be taken against you."

Rakesh was alarmed at facing the truth. "I see the reality of the future in your statements." He embraced Ragini.

The foreign minister had returned. For two weeks there was peace, things proceeded in a normal manner. Savita called Ragini, "Alok wants to talk to Rakesh."

"Rakesh is not at home, is there something special? I will tell him to return the call."

When Rakesh found out, he thought: *Alok has not called me during these months – most of the information came through Savita. There must be something unusual.* He became suspicious.

The telephone rang. "Hello, Alok speaking."

"It is Rakesh. You called me, was there something special?"

"I want to give you information, and also a proposal. Minister Sahib has not been able to secure a nomination for the next election, the party has decided to make me the candidate and I have accepted it. If you would become my political assistant, I would be happy. I assure you I will fulfil all of your genuine demands."

Puzzled, he digested the news slowly. He said, "I need time to consider your proposal, any reason for denying a ticket to minister sahib?"

"I don't know the details, but it is rumoured to be connected with the foreign minister's recent visit to New York."

When Ragini heard this news she said, "Politics is not an easy territory for everyone, it is in your own interest to keep away from it. By remaining independent you may be able to serve your country more effectively, especially in the United States, where it is important to bring the Indian perspective to light on global and bilateral issues. Whatever you have done in a fictitious manner can be done with greater confidence and authority under your real identity."

"Tomorrow I will see the media chief and communicate my acceptance. On receiving the appointment letter I will notify the consulate office of my intention to resign – according to my contract I have to give them four weeks' advance notice."

Ragini continued, "In a way Alok's proposal has created an unexpected complication. Doing business with a friend is harmful for both people – especially when both are professionally ambitious. A clash of opinions is inevitable in politics, which might even take Savita away from us, and I cannot tolerate that."

"You are right," Rakesh consented.

Within one week all formalities were completed and Rakesh informed the consulate office.

He left a message for Richard. "On being inspired by your assessment and goodwill, I am starting a new life today. I cherish your friendship, and many thanks!" Today Rakesh felt as if he had no mental burden, he would be free to take his potential to new heights.

He called Alok, made him aware of the developments, and added, "I don't want to sacrifice friendship at the altar of politics. Savita's faith is most sacred to Ragini. I have decided to work in the interest of our country while remaining here, and I will be extremely happy if I can help you in any manner."

Alok was overwhelmed. "The path you have chosen is consistent with your ability and wisdom, and I am your partner in this endeavour. We can work together in a complementary manner, our destination is the same."

A voice intervened on the phone, "It is Dinesh. Both of you are the well-educated ambitious youth of the new generation; you can become global citizens without being the prisoners of preconceived notions, and you can bring fresh light into the country. Both of you have adopted a new way of life and I am a close witness to that. I will try to be an umpire in the future also."

Alok became sentimental. “Savita has accepted you as the source of inspiration; I am not far behind. Thank you for the goodwill.”

A voice reverberated: “Stars of hope shine beyond the horizon. One has to look for them.”

7. Journey into Nowhere

"I can see your future in your palms," said the astrologer-cum-palmist.

Manish was travelling with his elderly parents in an air-conditioned train to visit Haridwar-Rishikesh, one of the most sacred religious places for Hindus in India. The holy Ganges, originating from the snow-laden high peaks of the Himalayas known as Gangotri, descends into plains in Haridwar, where millions of pilgrims take a dip in its ice-cold water to purify themselves. Manish was a technocrat who had worked in London for the past several years with little faith in the purifying power of this mythological river, worshipped both by believers and non-believers. He was accompanying his parents, who wanted to take a dip in the holy Ganges at Haridwar.

Manish was engrossed in a book and the person in the opposite berth was looking intently at him. The expensive Omega watch and Montblanc pen were enough to indicate that he came from an upper economic strata. He felt uncomfortable when he was being scrutinised directly by this man's piercing eyes.

Once their eyes met and then Manish said, "Would you like to have a look at this book? Its title seems to have attracted you."

He replied, "I am only a fortune teller. I read palms and foreheads, but not thick books in English. Yes, the title of the book, *Clash of Religions,* is interesting and it must be entertaining for the younger generation, who hardly believe in ancient traditions."

Manish queried, "Why do you call it entertaining? That reduces the importance of all religions – entertainment is something for temporary pleasure only."

The astrologer responded, "It is highly subjective. I made a general observation as I perceive it these days. I apologise if your feelings are hurt. By the way, I am Swami Anand and I live in a Rishikesh ashram, not far from Haridwar. Can I know about you?"

"I am Manish. I work in London and I am taking my parents to Haridwar where they intend to take a dip in the holy Ganges. Then, we would like to spend a few days in the serene Himalayan atmosphere of Rishikesh as well."

He could see that Swami's special dress and *teeka* were different from the normal attire. He had heard and also read in books about such people roaming in religious places. Some of them could be dubious, and mainly interested in exploiting foreigners, whereas some could be quite knowledgeable without any lust for money. It required caution.

Suddenly, the astrologer said, "I can read your palms, your past and future."

Manish felt he was in a dilemma. His mind did not permit him to succumb to such superstitions, with no scientific foundation, but his heart asked him to give it a try – after all, he was travelling for a religious ritual, which is also a part of the same superstition! He did not want to say a straight no, which might be unkind to the Swami if he belonged to the rare knowledgeable tribe.

Sensing his son's hesitation, Manish's father intervened. "A clash between wisdom and belief, logic and faith, is not uncommon and it has no ready-made answer. A large part of religious traditions in all religions is based on faith, even God's existence. But one thing is clear - scientific perspective is hardly three to four hundred years old whereas religious perceptions have lived and shaped humans through centuries. People like us are at the interface of the two ages and we can hardly jettison one!"

He continued, "Even in this digitally advanced age, many highly educated and well-settled Indians from abroad come to complete the funeral rites of their parents or grandparents according to Vedic rituals, or to disperse their ashes into the Ganges. Do they really believe in the next life or the heavenly abode for the dead? Do they believe that offerings made at rituals will reach the dead in the next life? We are going to Haridwar out of faith, not to prove or disprove anything which is unseen."

Manish interjected, "Faith is unseen and imageless; it is an individual's mental state. But what the Swami is talking about is giving meaning to visible lines or biological features on our palms. It is like deciphering a genetic encryption, which is the domain of science, if it ever becomes possible."

The astrologer argued, "Science says that our bodily development is genetically programmed, like a computer run by software. What might be the visual indications or icons of that programming? The lines in our palms fulfil that job - they indicate our lifespan, mental faculties, general health, family life, emotional conditions, and so on. It is true the art of reading those features is difficult; it requires a deep study of many manuscripts in Sanskrit and self-reasoning. Those who have achieved any proficiency are blessed because they keep our heritage alive."

He continued, "There are several billion people on this planet but their hand prints are unique. Each one moves on a different trajectory of life, which is true even if the material and environmental conditions are identical. In a modern sense, one can say they are programmed to live differently."

Manish said, "There are astrologers or soothsayers who divide people into the twelve zodiacs and pronounce verdicts on their future course – how funny! By this token more than one hundred million people of India fall within the same zodiac and so they should lead a very similar life – can one imagine a more ridiculous proposition? How different is palmistry?"

His father shared his experience. "Let me tell you a story of the time when I was working as the sub editor of a prominent weekly magazine. The magazine had a permanent column of horoscopes. Once the columnist, a well-known astrologer of the city, had gone on leave for four weeks and I was asked to find a substitute. Despite my efforts I could not find one and so I myself prepared the column. I simply retrieved some old columns, reshuffled them, changed their wordings, and that served the purpose. Nobody complained."

Infuriated, the swami complained, "These are cheap statements to blame the whole community. I have talked on such matters at international conferences in Europe and America, and people have listened to me. I find that many prominent newspapers and magazines in the Western scientific world also publish horoscopes. If they are so absurd, why do they invest their intellectual and monetary resources on such topics?

"Astrology has been widely misused for monetary gains. Equating it with astronomy, which is a proven mathematical science, has taken its toll. Rather than calling it a science, it should be treated as a faith-based discipline. The palmistry is a bit different, it regards each person separately as the lines in their palms are different. I accept that more research is needed to understand the depth of this ancient knowledge," he added, concealing his rage.

"I did not mean to hurt your pride, I simply recounted a story. Your experience shows the other side of the story which is equally engaging," said Manish's father apologetically. "If you permit, I would like to add that most of the forecasts are of a general nature, often cloaked in ambiguity. They invariably include a random combination of elements, including the prospect of monetary gain, tension in the family, a visit by friends, concern for health, hurdles in service, hearty meals, chance of accidents, scope for promotion, and so on. One or more of these things do happen in day-to-day life – they hardly wait for a forecast by an astrologer. Based on their zodiac sign people are also advised to wear a precious stone, like sapphire, topaz or pearl – it catches the wealthy by their collar!"

Manish mediated. "If something has not been proved that does not mean it does not exist. A vast majority of our scientific knowledge has taken root in recent decades, a period much smaller than human civilisation. The laws of nature are still being discovered, the mystery of the universe is being unveiled, the origin of life is under the microscope, and the way the mind works is being probed. It is not inconceivable to get a better understanding of so-called destiny, which includes insight into the future."

He elaborated, "The belief in astrology or palmistry relates to the state of mind, its weakness and strength. Notions like 'brain mapping', 'brain implant', 'downloading the brain's memory' seemed science fiction not long ago, but they are now areas of active research that will show how the mind behaves. In the future they may shed some light on para-psychological visions, crystal-ball gazing, mind reading, premonition, power of prophecy, and so on. "

The swami seemed pacified but Manish did not show his palm. He would soon get out at the next station for a discussion at a meditation camp. He gave his business card to Manish and said in a low voice, "I can foresee you may encounter an unexpected problem - be careful. I will be in Rishikesh in two days." He disembarked, but left a seed of suspicion in Manish's mind.

The trio reached Haridwar, which rests on the foothills of the Himalayas and abounds in natural beauty. They took a dip in the cold, transparent and turbulent waters of the Ganges with the help of volunteers. In the evening they were present at the famous *har ki paudi,* the steps at Lord Shiva's abode, in order to observe the *aarti,* the devotional prayer with fire bowls. According to mythology, Lord Shiva and Lord Vishnu had visited this place and so it has unique religious importance. They were overwhelmed at the devotion of the priests and some other participants in the *aarti.* To their utter surprise they saw a few Europeans chanting and dancing, as if they had forgotten their physical identity and merged with the spirit of the goddess Ganges.

When they came out, Manish introduced himself to two of them. In return they happily introduced themselves as John and Helen – they were touring some of the ancient religious sites. Soon they became friendly and Manish invited them for a cup of coffee.

Manish initiated the conversation. "What brings you here? Do you really believe in these religious rituals? They might be simply a means of earning money by exploiting people's sentiments!"

John was dogmatic. "These rituals are the religious and spiritual heritage of India, these rituals have been happening for centuries before the Western world was on the global scene – the United States and Australia were almost desolate. They survive on our belief in the continuity of civilisation and we are hardly justified in questioning their relevance. Since faith is a subjective issue, one has freedom to think otherwise."

"It appeared you were deeply and emotionally immersed in the *aarti* - how come? Did you experience something extrasensory or supremely enjoyable?" asked Manish seriously.

Helen intervened. "We are devoted to a spiritual guru who has enlightened us about mysticism and some spiritual practices in Indian traditions. Devotional chanting is also like meditation, which is an exercise for the mind in self-realisation. Meditation is a process to tune the mind, to focus mental energy coherently, and can also be achieved through the repeated chanting of hymns. When you become immersed in something, losing your identity, it does give a blissful feeling - it's a matter of experience. A sculptor puts soul into a lifeless stone or a painter puts life into a mixture of colours only through a meditative process."

She added, "We have plenty of material amenities but a lot of mental stress. The meaning of life seems lost in the jargon of conflicting opinions. In search of blissful peace, Western society finds Indian spiritual traditions very attractive."

"Many of the so-called spiritual gurus have set up their ashrams in prominent Western cities and they have huge followers, so why flock to India?" Manish asked inquisitively.

John interrupted. "We are here to smell the true fragrance of an ancient culture. This is similar to seeing the Egyptian pyramids, though their descriptions are widely available in books and videos. This is also the essence of tourism, whatever your field of interest. In the same monument or temple historians see the social and political shadows of the time, whereas religious leaders see the seeds of a spiritual halo."

Thoughtfully, Manish's father observed, "Our younger generation is losing interest in the spiritual heritage of Hinduism, whereas the West is rediscovering and embracing its relevance. Believers like you are the best ambassadors of the Indian ethos."

Manish suddenly asked, "Do you believe in astrology or palmistry?"

John replied, "I have never experimented with them and so I cannot express my opinion. If I come across a knowledgeable person, I am not averse to getting some insight. By the way, why have you asked this question? Have you encountered some unexpected upheavals in your life?"

"Why upheavals? Can't one have curiosity about these practices?"

"There are people who actively practise tarot or other fortune-telling techniques even in Western societies – you might have seen one in London! I believe people are attracted to them when under mental stress, but I have no idea how reliable they are. They seem to exist in people's unconscious minds."

Manish realised the two Europeans were genuinely undecided, or in a fluid state, on this matter and that deepened his dilemma. The swami's words were still reverberating in his mind.

It was the third day of their visit. They joined an organised trip to the upper reaches of the mountains and enjoyed the company of many tourists. At night Manish's father developed some breathing problem and he had to be admitted to a local clinic. The doctor said, "Many elderly visitors coming from the plains develop this complication because of the cold and the sudden change of weather, but it settles within two to three days. However, it does create a problem for those with asthmatic tendencies."

Manish recalled that his father did not show such a symptoms, except for occasional coughing on the train. He wondered, was it related to Swami's prediction? Or was it a sheer chance? He took the doctor into his confidence and explained what the swami had said on the train. The doctor explained with a degree of confidence, "We don't believe in astrology, palmistry or fate. We are committed to our duty to patients. If we bring in destiny, our commitment will be diluted. This is how science has progressed, but it has failed to control our thought process, which has the deep imprints of evolution."

Smiling, he added, "Maybe, the swami saw your father coughing on the train and he guessed about his health in a general manner. These swamis are clever and understand human psychology. They often target seniors who are on religious trips."

"Can we call it a clash between science and society?" asked Manish.

"The clash you are referring to has myriad dimensions and they are unfathomable. What you have encountered could be a tiny part of it – it is more like a clash between proven science and fictional science." The doctor stated his viewpoints in a convincing manner.

Manish agreed. "It's like a journey into nowhere!"

He returned home with his parents but his mind was still preoccupied. "After all, why has this myth of astrology continued for centuries in many civilisations - though in different forms?" A few days later he was at his friend's wedding party, where he met a conservatively dressed mature man. They introduced themselves and sat in a corner with their drinks.

"I am Manish, a technocrat working in London."

"I am Ritesh, an academic in the field of psychology and philosophy. After spending several years in the West, and some time in Egypt, I am presently attached to a yoga and meditation institute not far from here."

Someone intervened. "Fact and fiction sitting together! What a sight!"

"What do you mean?" interjected Manish.

Ritesh smiled, "Well said - fact and fiction are the integral parts of our personality. They influence our thinking process all the time."

"What brings you to meditation?" queried Manish.

"I have read about some unrealised dimensions of the mind. If they are unlocked even partially, one may have a glimpse into those aspects that remain unexplained. For example, nobody knows what the true nature of consciousness is, how it appears or disappears. Meditation is like training the mind and I would like to give it a try, though it is hard to practise."

Suddenly, Manish asked, "Does astrology or palmistry exist in the same domain?"

Ritesh explained, "I am not sure, but astrology has a powerful psychological influence on human behaviour. It gives you solace if you fail in your efforts, and it diminishes your arrogance when you succeed. In other words, both success and failure can be thought to be partly fated – though fate has no verifiable existence. I believe astrology was a remarkable discovery of social science to make people humble and content, a necessary ingredient for social cohesion."

"You have opened a new horizon!"

8. Circle of Mystery

Mid-winter evening, sound of rain drops, shiver in cold wind, loneliness on roads!

Amidst the nature's oppressive sadness Rita was sitting alone in front of a fireplace - the darkness of loneliness was getting deeper. Who should she wait for was a futile question. She got divorced only last month and she was reluctant to accept this reality in her daily life. How could she? The mutual faithfulness of several years, the sweet memories of life's journey, the soothing comforts of a family life and the emotional bond with the past had their strong grip; she needed time to come out of that world. Her heart was weeping, but there was no one to console! Time is the only eternal, invisible, and powerful medicine which always gives a healing touch over deep wounds at its own speed.

Depressed, in a pensive mood she closed her eyes. She could hear nothing except her own heart beats. She travelled into her past and many vivid images appeared on her mental screen. She felt her life was like a movie juxtaposed with scenes of different flavours including youthful ventures, romance, pain and introspection - all of which are the natural pillars of a family life.

She saw a glimpse of those adventurous days when she had arrived in Melbourne about twelve years ago for technical education at a reputed University. She had come alone from a foreign country; she shared accommodation with a family friend who gave sisterly support. Soon she intermingled with the new surrounding and its multicultural ethos. The splendour of Melbourne, its vast golden coast and its extensive greenery enchanted her; she embraced them with an open heart. On the study front she spent her first year mostly with computers, books and lecture notes, and she passed the final exam with distinction. She became prominent and her circle of friendship, which included both boys and girls, rapidly expanded in the second year. She became more outspoken and engaged in her class. Her friends threw a glittering party on her twenty-first birthday and gave expensive gifts. On the insistence of friends, she tasted alcohol for the first time and started stumbling after consuming a full glass. A classmate, John Dickson, had come forward and helped her - a scene that still remained alive in her subconscious mind.

In a congenial atmosphere of the teaching institution the next two years passed rapidly, as if a flying bird got new wings. During that period she once went for a week-long camp with friends, away from the city into the woods and the bountiful lap of nature. It was a unique experience for her. For the first time she had seen, from a close distance, free mixing among youths that also included alcohol and sex. By this time she fully understood the difference between friend and boyfriend, and she strongly remained on the path of friendship. Soon after graduation she landed into a job with a multinational company and thereafter started living independently. Within the next few months, she met a smart young guy, Henry Gibson, who was working for a financial institution in the same office complex. They often met at lunchtime, debated, exchanged ideas, and became friends. Their friendship continued for two years and they got acquainted with each other's habits and orientations; and they were happy.

One day Reeta said, "Now time has come to change the face of our friendship."

"I could not understand," Henry said while sipping tea.

"Now we should get married; my mother has the same opinion. She is coming here next month and that will be a good occasion for our wedding." Reeta put forward her concrete proposal.

Smilingly, Henry replied, "Marriage is just a social formality - like a showpiece on the bench top. We are living happily as partners without the unnecessary constraints imposed by marriage. Our Prime Minister is also a traveller on the same path, then why can't we?"

Reeta said in a serious tone, "I need my own child who gets his father's surname."

This much indication was enough for Henry. They got married within a month; they signed a social contract. She clearly remembered these events which shaped her initial years in Melbourne.

Her eyes were still closed, she was mentally engrossed. Before she could enter into the next chapter of her past life, the telephone rang. She responded hurriedly, "Hello, it is Reeta here."

An anxious voice came from the other side. "Mummy, I am Sweeti. Tomorrow is the time for our meeting, do you remember? Please come on time, Sohan is also looking for you."

"How can I forget? I was counting days. I have already purchased chocolates for both of you; tell me if you need something else." Reeta was overwhelmed with emotions, her voice got choked, and she started sobbing. Tears fell from her eyes. Sweeti was five-year old but was more mature for her age. She felt her mother's helplessness and urged her to keep patience. Sohan was only three-year old; he thought Mummy had gone out for work!

Fate had not favoured Reeta; the situation crippled her. While granting divorce the court had entrusted the custody of their two children, Sweeti and Sohan, to their father who was financially sound to fulfil their needs. Reeta was holding a part-time job only that was hardly enough to shoulder the expected financial responsibility. Perhaps, the court also considered the fact that Henry's mother lived in the same locality and she had assured to look after her grandchildren. Sensing Reeta's discomfort and pain, the court permitted her to approach it again in future when her financial situation became favourable. Though she was technically qualified and had received high emoluments in early years of her job, she had decided to take up a flexible part-time job so that she could provide the much needed motherly care to small children. She had her husband's consent in that decision. But after divorce, she had to leave the family house and she moved into a small rented apartment.

At the appointed time Reeta was there to meet her children. Sohan came running and hugged her. Sweeti started crying, "Mummy, please take me from here. I don't feel comfortable and my classmates often tease me. The parents-teachers meeting is coming next week, will you come? Even for a short time - just for me!"

Reeta argued with herself: *Was it possible to re-join the broken bonds? Perhaps, but it would be difficult to remove the knots. She would try, just for the sake of the children. Emotion prevailed over dilemma.*

Tonight Reeta was perturbed, she could not sleep. She became thoughtful, several questions erupted in her mind. "Why was her faithful relationship with Henry eclipsed? How could the dark shadow of divorce engulf their happy life? Was she at fault or was it destined?" Her thoughts wandered into the past. Patiently, she recollected the sequence of some relevant events:

Sweeti's birth was celebrated with fanfare and Henry was quite happy. His mother visited them quite often and bestowed her affection on the little grandchild. But a few months after Sohan's birth, she had sensed an unexpected change in Henry's attitude and dealings. He spoke much less, came very late from the office, seemed grave and self-centred. She had tried to find out the reason but Henry silenced her by saying that these were the misgivings of her mind. During those days she had received a phone call from a bank's official, "Henry has not paid his credit card bills for the past two months; an excessive delay in payment can soil his credit history." She was astonished as Henry was very punctual in such matters and by nature he hated any form of loan. She remembered that on several occasions, when he was on a tour, he had instructed her to clear all accounts on time. Naturally, she had imagined whether Henry was under a financial strain. When she raised this subject over dinner table, he had tersely replied, "Keep away from financial matters when you are not in a job." These insulting words started reverberating in her ears! Sobbing, she fell asleep with the help of a sleeping pill.

The next morning she continued thinking of the chain of the past happenings. She grabbed the morning newspaper when having coffee. On the very first page she had read a prominent article on the emerging global financial crisis which could lead to the closure of some large banks apart from the bankruptcy of smaller financial institutions. Individuals were also warned of their deteriorating financial prospects. She had taken a heavy breath: *Was her suspicion right? Was Henry really under financial duress?* Under the circumstances she had decided to go for a job; this was needed for the economic stability of the family and the welfare of her children. She had spent the next few weeks searching for a job in her technical field and had succeeded in securing a part-time position as per her choice. Henry had gladly approved it.

It is this part-time job she has been holding for the past two years. During this period the company had offered her a full-time position more than once but she refused because the children needed her time. This job was just enough to support herself after divorce but she had to improve her financial status for assuming the children's custody. She was more determined now than ever.

The date for the parents-teachers meeting was approaching. Reeta was in a deep dilemma - should she call Henry? The emotional satisfaction of Sweeti was uppermost in her mind. She waited anxiously for Henry's call, perhaps he might be on the same wavelength, but was disappointed. Ultimately, on the night before the meeting, she phoned Henry, "It is Reeta speaking. Can we talk for two minutes?"

"Yes, why not? We have separated but we are not enemies. We can always honour the decorum of friendship." Henry replied in a cordial tone.

Reeta felt a sense of relief and explained how depressed Sweeti would be if both of them were not present at the meeting. Hesitatingly, Henry said, "I will reach on time, but it would be better if we refrain from talking to each other. You will chat with the teacher and answer her queries without any objection from my side. I will say something only when unavoidable, and at that time you shall not intervene."

"This process is respectable for both of us," Reeta agreed.

"Good night."

At the appointed time Sweeti's class teacher welcomed Henry and Reeta in her office. After talking about Sweet's educational progress, the teacher said, "It appears Sweeti is under some psychological pressure, she looks self-centred contrary to her age, and she lacks the aura of natural happiness on her face. She badly needs love and affection from both of you." As they were coming out of the office, the teacher reminded, "Both of you seem very reserved; perhaps this has affected Sweeti's behaviour."

Henry, who has been listening silently until now, suddenly lost his cool temper. "To give advice about the child is your duty, but to make any comment on our behaviour is not desirable." The teacher blushed, her white face became reddish with anger. Reeta was dumbfounded, but she kept quiet; she had promised not to intervene. Both walked towards their cars.

While driving home, Reeta kept on pondering: *Was Henry's behaviour gentlemanly? Was it an indication of his mental anxiety? Is he under some psychological stress?* Soon a picture emerged before her eyes - the image of what had happened about a year ago. One evening, they were having dinner when Henry behaved very unexpectedly. He threw his plate saying the food was very salty and shouted angrily "you are not a good wife" and went away without having dinner. His rude manners were so threatening that she had become fearful of him anticipating physical violence. After that event she became gripped with a fear complex, she hesitated being alone with him, and that also ended their physical relationship. Once she had thought of complaining to police, but restrained herself because of unnecessary complications and the perceived loss of prestige in social circles. She remembered many other small disputes which had nurtured discontent and suspicion between them. Her chain of thoughts was broken when someone honked his car from behind.

Reeta was trying to make her new life normal and worth living. She assumed greater responsibility, stayed longer in the office, and her earnings rose substantially. Now she could also take her children for shopping occasionally. The eternal wheel of time never stops; almost six months passed and Sohan's birthday arrived. She received a call from Henry, “Sohan's birthday falls on the next Saturday and I have arranged a small party at my home. Kids will be happy if you are there. If you want to do something as per your liking, I have no objection. This is an important day for all of us, especially for Sohan.”

“It is an occasion of happiness and I will definitely come. If you agree, I would like to come one day earlier for decorating the venue in the presence of your mother.”

“As you wish,” Henry said in a friendly voice.

That day arrived. Henry had invited small kids from the neighbourhood besides those from the Sohan's kindergarten. Some ladies also came along with their kids. The party went very well, kids made noises, sang songs, played games and enjoyed good food. Henry requested Reeta to help Sohan cut the birthday cake; and he took many snaps. Reeta proved a good hostess and looked after all the guests. The party had ended hours ago, darkness had fallen, but Sohan was still glued to Reeta. Sensing the mood of the kids, Henry told Reeta, “You can sleep with the kids tonight, they will enjoy the warmth of motherly affection.”

"No, I will not stay. One night's affection might weaken them, I don't want to leave them in an emotional whirlpool. They should be resilient and practical." Reeta went home.

Tonight, Reeta was again perplexed; several questions cropped up in her mind. She debated with herself: *The proposal for divorce came from Henry's side, and she simply consented half-heartedly. She expected that Henry would look cheerful after divorce and someone would enter into his life, but there was a strange gloomy shadow on his face and he seemed working like a machine without any internal enthusiasm. Why so? Is it not mysterious? Maybe, the curtain gets lifted in near future!* She fell asleep, but these questions haunted her in dreams also.

In a natural course, Reeta became busy in work and her colleagues were impressed. She felt a new zeal and time passed fast in this congenial atmosphere. During past three-four months, she had no chance to see Henry but she kept on meeting the children regularly. She considered the idea of keeping the children with her for one week during the forthcoming school holidays. She phoned Henry, "I would be happy if Sweeti and Sohan can live with me for one week during the coming school holidays. Do I have to take the court's permission?"

"It is not needed. Your proposal is acceptable to me. In fact your right on children is as sacrosanct as mine. The economic condition keeps on changing, but the bond of relationship is everlasting. If you need any help, please don't hesitate to call me." Reeta was pleasantly surprised at the respectful tone of Henry.

"Thank you very much."

The weather was pleasurable, the warmth coming from the sun was soothing. Reeta was playing ball with her children in a park close to a lake. There were other kids playing around and many people were just enjoying the beautiful sunshine of the spring season. Reeta was tired after sometime and she lied down on the velvety green lawn for the much needed rest. Within twinkling of an eye, Sweeti and Sohan ran to catch their ball which had just fallen into the lake's water. Reeta ran nervously towards them but before she could reach the lake's bank someone quickly grabbed the ball and gave it to Sohan. When she saw the man, she got frozen with surprise - she kept looking like a statue. It was that guy who broke the silence, "Are you Reeta? My classmate of yesteryears? My name is John Dickson; possibly you might be remembering!"

"Yes, John, I am indeed Reeta, your classmate. How did you come here? It is a pleasant surprise. I still remember the day you had supported me when I was getting unstable under the influence of alcohol. Today, you have saved me again from stumbling. Anything could have happened, had you not promptly saved the kids from entering into water! I don't know how I can repay your debt."

"Don't be silly and too emotional. I could have done that for any child."

"Let us sit somewhere and talk leisurely," said Reeta.

They sat on a bench under the shadow of a large tree. It was John who started the conversation. "I joined a British Medical College after passing out from Melbourne University. After graduation I practised medicine in a public hospital for several years and I was fortunate to find a lovely girlfriend there itself. We got married and we have a two-year old child. We came to this most liveable city one year ago; you can meet my wife - she is also in this park. The attraction of the lake drew me to this side of the park and luckily we met here."

Reeta told her story in brief that included matters related to her divorce.

"Any specific reason for the divorce?" John asked sympathetically.

"I also want to unravel this mystery, perhaps its key lies with Henry." Reeta became sentimental and her voice choked.

"Consider me a friend if I can help in any manner. This is my business card." John advised her to face it as a challenge which is not insurmountable.

One week's time was well spent: Reeta, Sweeti and Sohan rediscovered their inseparable bond. They enjoyed every minute of their stay in a small apartment which had forced them to sleep together and hear each other's heart beats. Reeta thoroughly enjoyed the company of her children; she seemed to have regained her lost smile and her exuberance.

The school holidays had ended, and children would be going back to their classes just after one day. Henry knocked at the door, he was there to collect Sweeti and Sohan. It was cold and windy outside, rain drops were also falling intermittently.

Opening the door, Reeta said, "It is very cold outside. Please come in and have a cup of tea. This will also give some extra time to children for packing up their stuff."

"Thanks, but no. I won't like to bother you unnecessarily. A dry tree does not give fruits."

"What do you mean? I didn't understand. It is you who had told that we could live like friends, then why this fuss? Can't friendship and tea go together?"

"Perhaps, you are right." A tinge of pain was hidden in Henry's hesitant voice.

They were sitting face to face across the tea table. Reeta served tea and said, "Can I ask you something? The condition is that you tell the truth."

Henry replied confidently, "You can ask but I may or may not answer. Be assured that I will be truthful in my response."

Encouraged, Reeta continued, "You must be remembering that it was you who had asked for divorce and therefore you should be cheerful after our separation. However, I see a gloomy shadow on your face. I had felt the same at the time of Sohan's birthday, nothing has changed. Why so? It looks mysterious, it puzzles my mind."

"I cannot answer your question or satisfy your curiosity. You will know everything at the right time. At this moment I can simply assure you that no other woman ever came into my life." Henry spoke emphatically.

Relieved, Reeta said courteously, "I greatly respect your frankness. I am eagerly waiting for the right time."

For several days Henry remained mentally occupied: he was seriously looking for the ways to unburden his mind by opening the window of mystery to Reeta. He knew she was also perturbed because it was this mystery which had brought a tempest in her life, and which also engulfed the innocent kids. However, he could not muster courage to face Reeta and explain the turn of events. Ultimately, he decided to write her a letter.

It was a Friday afternoon. Reeta had just returned from the office when she received a registered letter from Henry. Her heartbeat jumped, as if a bomb had exploded on her face. She took a glass of water, sat on the sofa, and opened the sealed envelope with trembling fingers. The letter read:

"Dear Reeta,

After several days of introspection I am writing this letter which answers many of your questions, clarifies my position, and lifts the veil of secrecy on events leading to our divorce. Lately, I have realised that it is your right, not my merciful dispensation, to know the facts which are intimately connected to your life and to the well-being of our children; and hence this letter. I don't know how this letter affects you, but it will certainly lighten my mind's burden; and thus it also serves my self-interest. I hope it reduces the wrinkles of anxiety on my face!

A few months after Sohan's birth, I went for the annual medical check-up. Shortly thereafter, the doctor called me and said that I was HIV-positive, but he wanted further confirmation. He drew a plan for my blood test after every three months, and advised me to practice safe sex and to reduce its frequency in the meantime. My world shattered and I became introvert - you might have noticed this change in my behaviour.

I kept on questioning myself, "How did I get infected with this virus?" I never had sexual relationship with anyone else except you. I remember that I had visited South Asia for office-related tasks prior to Sohan's birth. During that trip I fell sick and remained in a local hospital for a couple of days. The doctors suspected that I had malaria and they administered two or three injections. It is quite possible that the HIV-virus entered my body through those infected needles. Perhaps, it was so destined!

I was quite fond of your enchanting beauty and your youthful attraction, and I immensely enjoyed sex with you. Suddenly, it became a time of torturous trial for me. I was at my wit's end: how could I restrain myself from sex while living with you? Decidedly, it would have damaged our relationship - you might have thought that someone else had come into my life. Any such contention would have destroyed our family life.

After second medical test, the doctor confirmed his earlier observation. Then I became concerned, depressed, and I started thinking about its consequences. I had heard that HIV-infection shortens life and therefore it was essential that you became financially self-sufficient. The phone call by a bank official was a planned move in this regard and finally it paid off. I knew that people with technical qualifications were in high demand and you were one of them.

Almost six months passed, but my attraction for you never diminished - abstaining from sex was a nightmare. Then, with a very heart, I decided to secure divorce - your safety was very important for the kids. In order to prepare a valid ground for securing divorce, I deliberately planted bitterness and cruelty in our relationship. In that very context, once I threw away my dinner plate and misbehaved with you quite indignantly. I had thought that after being mentally hurt you would ask for divorce but you showed unexpected restraint. However, after that occurrence we were practically separated with no physical relationship. I considered it a big success. After one year of separation it became easy for me to ask for divorce and you gave your consent.

Now, the time has come that you get a new partner. You will be an invaluable asset, a source of inspiration, in anybody's life! This is the natural consummation of womanhood and you should gladly accept it. I will continue to be your friend and this will give me immense satisfaction.

Your friend: Henry Gibson."

A wave of sympathy flooded Reeta's heart, she started sobbing with an emotional burst. Her respect for Henry doubled, he had struggled with himself for her safety. In order to defeat this infection, Henry needed not only medicine but internal willpower and family's support as well. She decided to help him, to be his shadow henceforth. She prayed God to give her that conviction! She read the letter again and again until she fully digested its explicit words, implicit meanings, and the underlying spirit.

The next day, she phoned Henry. "I want to see you. At the time of wedding we had taken oath to be equal partners both in pleasure and pain, did you forget that? Then, why did you keep me away from your painful struggle?"

"There is a big disconnection between theory and practice. If both go together, life will move on a straight path, but it is not so. That's why the incidence of domestic violence, as well as divorce, is rapidly increasing." Henry said in a subdued tone.

"I don't want to argue with you - you are an expert in winning debates. I just want to see you and ask for something." Reeta insisted.

"What's that you like to ask for? You can take whatever you want; my life has been reduced to a burden." Henry bemoaned.

"Firstly, you make a promise to give me whatever I demand." Reeta was serious.

"If you insist, let it be so. I won't disappoint you."

Reeta urged politely, "I want to be your shadow; I want to feel your pain and pleasure. It does not necessarily include sexual relationship. We can live like friends - this is what you had said. This will make our life's journey fulfilling."

Henry was overwhelmed with emotions. Regaining composure, he said, "I had read about the Indian culture in books, today I am seeing its greatness. I feel a sense of relief."

Delighted, Reeta proposed, "This evening we will dine together in a restaurant."

"As you wish."

Reeta got a table reserved and she reached the restaurant a bit earlier. She welcomed Henry at the door and kissed his hand. With a surprise, Henry uttered, "Didn't you get fearful of my infection?"

"I know the HIV-virus does not spread through contact or eating together. Rather, meeting with people enhances the patient's psychological confidence and that works like a supplementary medicine," Reeta replied with affinity. They had a sumptuous meal made more enjoyable through their small gossips. They decided to go together for the doctor's next appointment.

Within a week, they were in the doctor's clinic. Looking into the fresh test results, he told Henry, "The virus has stopped multiplying, rather its damaging influence has diminished. You will have to take the prescribed medicine for the whole life. Until now there is no medicine which can eliminate the virus but its ill effects can be controlled to a large extent. It is always advisable to lead a disciplined life."

"Is this the latest medicine? Or are there some alternative treatments?" Reeta interjected.

"I have prescribed the best medicine. Some other formulations are under trial but they are not available in the market. Many reputed labs are conducting research for eliminating the HIV-virus and one should be optimistic."

Henry saw a ray of light: *perhaps he had crossed the dark tunnel of despair!*

On way home from the clinic, Reeta casually mentioned, "Can we take advice from Dr Dickson? He has worked for several years in a major British hospital; he may give some new suggestions."

Henry had already heard about Dr John Dickson. He said, "Our society is gripped with many ill-founded rumours and ugly misconceptions about HIV and AIDS. Extreme measures, like social boycott of infected persons, are also not uncommon. I don't want that my condition be known to people around me; even my mother does not know about it. Though Dr Gibson is an experienced physician, he may hesitate to offer any professional advice without seeing my medical history. Then, why to put him into a difficult situation?"

"Your reasoning is always irrefutable."

Time ran fast; more than six months passed without realisation. Henry and Reeta routinely spent some time together - in parks, restaurants and theatres. A thin line of smile also appeared now and then on Henry's lips - that was a sign of his impulse to recapture the vibrant images of the past. In one of those thoughtful moments, he uttered, "I want to relive my blessed past years; I don't know what is hidden in the future's womb." Reeta heard, but she kept quiet.

One day Reeta was in a pharmacy when Dr John Dickson suddenly appeared from behind. Before she could hide the packet in her bag, John's expert eyes had read the medicine's name. He said, "Let's sit somewhere and have a cup of coffee; we are meeting after several months." Reeta could not refuse. They talked about many things but she said nothing about the medicine. Prudently, John did not ask either - it could have infringed her privacy. But he was quick to analyse the situation: *Reeta is young, healthy and agile - she has not changed much from the university days. Then why this medicine? She never mentioned about any close relative who was sick. Then, is it for Henry? Is he infected with HIV-virus? Is it the reason for their divorce?*

Reeta stood up, "Let us leave, I am getting late."

One year had passed since their divorce. Both were again present in the doctor's clinic. Seeing the test results, the doctor said, "Your infection has subsided to a considerable extent, the medicine has proved very effective. There is no cause of worry, but you must continue the medicine. Now you can lead a normal life."

Henry asked eagerly, "What's the meaning of leading a normal life? I have completely abstained from sexual contacts for more than two years and eaten mostly vegetarian food. Is this the right course? If this is the definition of a normal life, it is hardly worth living!" He seemed agitated.

Raising his eyebrows, the doctor said with sympathy, "I had not asked you to completely abstain from sex. I had asked you to practice safe sex and to reduce its frequency, and the same advice remains valid even today. It is always beneficial to take healthy foods."

"Thank you, doctor!"

A new glow appeared in Henry's eyes. Reeta sensed it.

Tonight, Henry called Reeta, "Please excuse me for calling so late in the night, but I could not restrain myself. With your permission, I would like to say something."

"What's the matter? If you feel so restless, there is hardly a need for my permission. If you remain restless, how can I sleep?" Reeta said in a sleepy voice and then became alert.

Henry spoke excitedly, "You have been living like my shadow quite faithfully and I am deeply indebted. My shadow is a part of me, then why this separation? I want to keep my shadow close to my heart and mind." He opened his mind in a few words.

Reeta became sentimental. "I was waiting for this. We have already lost some years of our life, time has come to recapture those years." She burst with tears of happiness.

"Tomorrow, I will come to wipe out your tears."

"I will welcome you with flowers." She kissed the phone.

The next morning, Henry was standing before Reeta with a bouquet of red roses. While taking tea, they decided to remarry by taking a solemn oath before the court's magistrate.

They needed two-three weeks of time to accomplish their mission.

After a few days, Reeta came to invite John; and Henry accompanied her. "We have decided to remarry; we will take oath on Friday. We have invited a few close friends only and you are one of them." Reeta appeared content and graceful.

"I will definitely come. Thanks for the invitation." He hugged Reeta.

That day arrived soon. Henry and Reeta became husband and wife.

"I got back the elixir of life," Reeta uttered embracing Henry. Her emotional intelligence came on the surface.

"Same for me," Henry replied kissing Reeta. There was a prolonged clap around them.

John came forward. "A small gift from me." He placed a coloured packet in Reeta's hand.

When Reeta opened the gift packet, she found a box of condoms. She exclaimed, "What will I do with this!"

"Keep it in your hand bag." It was Henry's voice.

Just at that time there was a knock at their door. "Sir, the taxi is ready."

Surprised, Reeta asked, "Are we going somewhere?"

"Yes, on our honeymoon!"

Acknowledgement

Writing a piece of acknowledgement is not uncommon for authors. However, I feel bemused where to start from: I haven't been a professional author or poet – I remained an academic in physics for many long years. Post-retirement, I took up writing some poems and stories in Hindi as a hobby which developed into a passion. My books of poetry and short stories in Hindi were appreciated by many; and twice my poems were awarded at international competitions organised by the International Hindi Secretariat, Mauritius. I became a bit courageous and took up writing in English as well. I self-published two poetry books in English, which caught the attention many readers for their variety and multicultural theme. Then, my short story was published in 'Melbourne Subjective: An anthology of contemporary Melbourne writing (2014)' and it gave me the much-needed confidence. Recently, my poem has appeared in 'VerbalART: A Global Journal Devoted to POETS AND POETRY (2015)' and some are in the pipeline. I would like to thank these publications which gave me a sense of personal satisfaction.

I greatly appreciate the encouragement given by my daughter, Dr Ranjana Srivastava, who is a well-established author and opinion writer in prestigious newspapers and magazines. She has been a constant source of strength. My son, Rajesh Kumar, and daughter-in-law, Dr Taru Sinha, have always given their moral support. Finally, I would be failing in my duty if I don't express my gratitude to my wife, Urmila Srivastava, without whose support and patience this work would not have gone through.

Kaushal K. Srivastava

No culture can live if it attempts to be exclusive.

Mahatma Gandhi

Keep your language. Love its sounds, its modulation, its rhythm. But try to march together with men of different languages, remote from your own, who wish like you for a more just and human world.

Helder Camara

Globalization is a form of artificial intelligence.

Erol Ozan

Other books by the author

In English:

1. Beyond Blue Oceans: One World One People (2013)
   Anthology of poems.
2. Reflections: Poetry of Composite Culture (2014)
   Anthology of poems.

Available as Paperback and Kindle eBook from Amazon.com, Amazon.co.uk, and Amazon.in

In Hindi:

1. कविता दर्पण (Kavita Darpan)
   Poetry (Hardcover), Vani Prakashan (2013), New Delhi.
2. क्षितिज के पार (Kshitij Ke Par): नयी दिशा नयी सोच
   Short stories, fiction; Paperback 2013.
3. कविता कलश (Kavita Kalash): सांस्कृतिक संगम का दर्पण
   Poetry. Paperback 2014.
4. बोलती कहानियाँ (Bolti Kahaniyan): वैश्वीकरण की झलक
   Short stories, fiction; Paperback 2015

Title 1 available from a bookseller or the publisher's website. Titles 2, 3, and 4 available from Amazon.com, Amazon.co.uk, and Amazon.in

Made in the USA
Columbia, SC
20 December 2017